Silent Auction

Terri McGee

To Laurie....for everything....

Chapter One

"Hey, sweet thang, ya' busy?"

The voice that called to me from behind was full of back-country twang. *God, not another redneck,* I thought to myself as I straightened my back, flipped my long red hair off my shoulders, and turned around with the best painted-on smile I could muster. "Nope, what can I do for you?"

"Well....whatcha sellin'?" If his voice were a fluid, it would fill more than just a few beer bottles. Eyes heavy and half closed, he shot me what I am sure he thought was a sultry look as he tried to give me the once-over. From where I stood, I could already smell the liquor on him and I had the sudden urge to ask him if he chose to bathe in it rather than drink it like other civilized people.

No, you need the money. Take a deep breath and get it over with!

The effort it took to see past the disgust I was quickly building concerning the clientele that frequented Lucky's Girls was getting harder each night. What got me through was my daughter, Brighton. No one else was paying my bills...not even her dead-beat father, who I must say has more money than God yet refuses to even acknowledge that he was married...let alone, fathered a child.

"Table dance for 10 bucks; VIP room for 20. Aside from that, you're on your own, honey." Trying to sound as interested as I could in hopes of getting him to open up his wallet, I smiled and walked my five-inch-slut-walkers over to his table and sat on the edge of the empty seat across from him.

"Well, let's see here, you're pretty cute, ya' know. Maybe I got somethin' for ya'."

Yeah, I'll bet, I thought but kept my mouth closed. Glancing over to the stage, I watched as Ginger twirled around the silver pole that ran from the floor to ceiling, center stage. Catching my glance, she smiled at me, eyes wide as she acknowledged the possibility that I might just make some money on this slow, rainy night. While Friday nights are usually big payoffs for girls like us, the rain usually keeps the customers tucked away at home. And my big payoffs were nothing like some of the other girls; there was only so much I allowed myself to do for money and, well, compared to some of my coworkers, I made next to nothing. While I had some regulars, I did nothing to lessen myself as a human being—or a woman, for that matter—by doing anything beyond the call of duty as a dancer and this often cut into the tips I made compared to most of the other girls in the business.

"How 'bout the VIP treatment, Red?"

Confused for a second, I realized he was referring to my long red hair. Seeming pleased with himself at granting me a nickname, he raised his eyebrows and gave me a look that made me want to puke all over his dirty cowboy boots. While I wanted to ask if he was sure he could make it to the VIP lounge, I said nothing, just gave him a smile and stood to escort him up the ramp that led to paradise.

When it comes to strip joints, Lucky's was one that lead the upper end of the business; mainly due to them offering lunch in the afternoon and the owner being a bit more picky when it came to the hiring—and firing—of girls who called the place home. Lucky Serifino spared no expense when it came to running a respectable topless bar. Two large round staging areas made up the main floor with the bar sectioned in between them. Small, circular tables with leather seats were strategically placed between the bar and the two stages and made up the areas around the D.J. booth, which sat centered along one wall, and all spaces in between. Mirrors were everywhere, hanging from the top of each wall and reaching just below the midpoint—thus allowing for Lucky and his crew of managers to see everything going on in the joint from the back of the house to the front doors.

Black lighting allowed for costumes to glow, hid bodily discrepancies any of the staff had, illuminated the coloring in the wall-to-wall carpeting, and offered a more intimate feel to the place. The VIP section was one of two areas that were reachable by a steep ramp cornered near the front doors of the building; the other offered three pool tables and additional seating; which were also viewable due to the continuation of the mirrored effect in each section.

Staff on hand at Lucky's was attended to with as much enthusiasm as the overall image that he worked endlessly to portray. New hires underwent an extensive application process, had to agree to drug testing on the fly if Lucky deemed necessary, and were expected to uphold the law in all areas. No one was allowed to drink with a customer, unless fully clothed and off-the-clock and the reporting of anything illegal going on was expected by all personnel. The D.J.'s fell under the same scrutiny, as did the bar staff, the cook, and all members of the managing team. Lucky never hesitated to have either employee or guest escorted out and ensured the quality of the place at all costs. After all, if one of us got into trouble, especially with the law, it was Lucky who risked trouble with the liquor review board, city permits, and the legal system. It wasn't something he fooled around with.

Despite all this—I *truly* hated my job. At times, I even hated myself.

And nights like this one even proved that point all the more.

Heading past the D.J. booth with my drunken, nearly slobbering customer, I glanced up at Mick who was running the show tonight. Giving me a peace sign as he caught my eye, I nodded at him, acknowledging his message that I was due on stage in two songs; which meant the girl who was just introduced to the stage was on her first song and once her second one ended, I was up. General rule here at Lucky's...girls dance two songs—first one you keep your top on, second one you take it off. Bottoms and heels on at all times and if a girls' costume include more than that; say a belt or a jacket, she took them off at her discretion.

The VIP room was empty; which I hated especially when escorting someone who has had a bit too much of the sauce. Many came to believe that if the room was empty, they can try to gain access to areas of the body that are off limits. And I always seem to find more than one of those determined customers during the course of a shift. While some of the girls around here welcomed it, hell, even encouraged it if they thought they would get more money out of their customer, I refused. I don't care how badly I needed the money, in seven years I have yet to degrade myself any further than what most of society believed I was already doing and no wad of cash was going to change that.

My customer sank into one of the lounge chairs that graced the rear of the room; which really looked like a horseshoe with one entrance in and out of it. The leather-bound chairs just fell short of qualifying for the title of "love seat" but were overstuffed and comfortable. The point here is to get the guy as comfy as possible so that he would pay for more dances just to be able to continue to sit in luxury. And sometimes it worked and sometimes it didn't; dependent highly on how much the guy has had to drink so far and how much money was left in his pocket.

"You want me to start with this song or wait 'til the next?" In all honesty, I was ready to begin; song's already started, so it's a shorter dance for the same pay. Nodding heavily at me, I quickly prayed that he wouldn't pass out before handing over my fee.

As I began, I tried to focus on the 80's metal song that was currently being played and ignore the fact that I was about to get topless for this moron; who was now sinking further down into the seat probably hoping that I would turn and sit on him. Fat chance of that happening.

"What 'bout the bottoms, Red?"

"Huh?" Trying to ignore him without him knowing, the last few seconds of my dance was spent eyeballing the mirrored walls surrounding me; watching what was going on in the rest of the bar often helped me forget what I was really doing. Looking down at him, I nearly gagged at the come-on-and-get-closer grin he was giving me. "Sorry, what??"

"Y're bottoms...show me some..."

Shaking my head at him, I answered but never stopped moving. If you stop, a lot of guys will argue that they didn't get a full dance and try to get out of paying the full twenty dollar fee that it cost to use this section. "Sorry bud, bottoms stay on", I replied.

"I'll give ya' another twenty." *Yeah, like that'll work.*

Shaking my head again at him, I sighed and figured if I turned my back to him, maybe he would quit talking. Looking up towards the ceiling, I shook my long red hair, feeling it gently cover the middle of my bare back. Then, bending at the waist a bit, I ran both hands along my thighs hoping this would refocus his attention. I can touch myself pretty much anywhere I wanted—with some exceptions, of course—but he couldn't lay a hand on me. For the most part this act worked. Tonight however, it didn't.

Watching him from the mirror directly across from me, I saw him move before it fully registered in my mind. Sitting up quickly, it was like he had the whole act planned ahead of time and before I could react, he reached out and grabbed me by my hips and pulled me down into a sitting position directly over his now-grinding lap.

"Hey!" was all I could muster, which was barely audible over the blaring song that was nearing its end. His hands felt sweaty and cold and the force of his grab caught me off balance. With nowhere to go but down, I felt my ankle twist in my heel before I found myself being dry humped. His worn-out jeans felt hard and coarse on my nearly-bare backside and his hands groped forward quickly, trying to cover my breasts which were only protected by the thin layer of latex around the nipples.

In an instant I knew that if I didn't act, I was going to be in trouble. Bending my arm, I quickly placed my right hand over my left, made a tight fist, and drove my elbow into his side. Not expecting a fight, the guy winced backward as the force of my charge found home in his soft side and automatically let me out of his grasp. At that second, I pushed my body forward, only to find myself on all fours on the floor in front of him.

"Ha! Now that's better!" He gasped at the sight of me, and rubbing his side a bit, leaned forward more in his chair to reach me but once I hit the floor, I kept moving.

"Matt!!" I yelled, hoping the doorman was in hearing range, despite the music. My ankle screaming at me, my only option was to crawl to the chair to the side of me to try to stand. Looking for movement behind me using the mirror, I eyed the doorman as he suddenly glanced around the corner of the wall from his seated position at the front door, eyes wide and body ready to move at a moment's notice. Holding my stare for a second, he dashed from his position and moved quickly, not stopping until he had run the length of the ramp into the VIP room. "What the hell??"

"Get this ass outta here!" I yelled. Giving me a questionable look, Matt turned his dark brown eyes towards my customer and took a step forward. One of the things I love about working with Matt, he acts quickly, doesn't question a situation such as this, and is proud to be thought of as our protector.

"Hey, man, she tripped...she tripped, and...and landed on me! I was just trying to help her stand up!" As his words slurred their way out of his greasy mouth, Matt didn't respond, other than to grab the guy by the arm and yank him to a standing position. At six foot something, Matt was built. A former body builder, he had worked the gyms around town for most of his life before coming into the job he had now; which he swore he loved. Who else would pay him to stand around and watch girls take their clothes off? Along with the possibilities to kick the shit out of a lowlife customer such as the one I was dealing with now, what other dream job could a guy come up with?

"Get the hell out of here! You're done, man!" Keeping a hold on the guy's collar, Matt started the march down ramp and headed toward the front door.

"Wait!!" Leaning over the protective bar that ran along the short opening of the room, I yelled for Matt to stop. "He owes me!! Twenty!" I may not have been able to finish dancing for the creep, but I was damn sure going to get paid for it.

Matt stopped his escort by pulling back on the guy's shirt collar, nearly choking him. "Pay up, man." Anger replacing the lustful looks I had gotten from the guy just seconds ago, he glared at me, then tried the same with Matt, but sensing he was going to lose this battle, he reached into his front pocket and pulled out a crushed twenty dollar bill. Stuffing it into Matt's strong hand, he muttered something and tried to shake off the grip my protector had on him.

"Yeah, try it, man. You have no idea who you're dealing with." Matt replied with steam and pushed my offender towards the door. "Don't even bother trying to get back in. You're done."

And with that, the guy was gone. Taking a deep breath, I sank into one of the VIP chairs, pulled my bikini top back on and tied it before taking off my heel to try to get a better look at my ankle, which was now throbbing to no end. Matt, after returning to the inside of the bar, watched me for a second before heading off towards the D.J. Seconds later, the song that was playing ended and it dawned on me that I was due up on stage.

Shit, I thought, no way I was going to be able to walk down the ramp, let alone dance my set. Feeling it start to swell, I knew the only thing I could do at that point was take off my other heel and try to get over to the booth to talk to Mick. It's a good thing we were dead tonight. Missing a set was really frowned upon, especially on nights when there was a shortage of girls or customers; Lucky enforced the rule of every girl on the floor dancing her set, no matter what, if nothing else to keep the customers interested in buying another round. The more variety of flesh on the floor, the more likely a guy would be to stick around and spend their money.

"All right, all right, guys!! Give it up for Savannah!!" Despite the pathetic response from the four or five guys that served as tonight's customers, Mick was trying to keep them interested. "Now, up next, we got the one—the only—Sherrie!!"

Knowing it was my name, Amanda, that Mick was supposed to be introducing, I stood as carefully as I could only to see Sherrie's slender frame take the back stage. Searching to try to get Mick's attention, I found Matt instead, heading in my direction.

"Hey, hon, you're done for the night." Sensing my argument, he continued before I could open my mouth. "You need to get off that ankle, go have Frank take a look at it. No need in trying to finish the night and makin' it worse."

Sighing, I replied, "Thanks, Matt, you're my hero."

"I know, babe, remember that some night when you need other services!" Protector or not, Matt was still a man and despite all of our razzing back and forth over the years, he knew I considered him more like an older brother than potential lover, but it never stopped the teasing or the sexual innuendoes. And while I have to admit, Matt was sexy as all hell with his strong arms, wavy brown hair, and dark eyes, the last thing I needed on my plate was any form of a relationship. Brighton was all I needed to focus on.

"You need help getting' to the back?" Kidding aside, Matt gave me a serious look.

"Naw...I'm alright. Just hurts." Starting down the ramp, I suddenly stopped, remembering my twenty bucks. "Hey, Matt? That guy pay you??"

"Oh, yeah. Although you may want to try washing it before pocketing it. By the looks of that guy, you never know where that twenty's been!"

"Yeah, well, it all spends the same." Taking the twenty from him, I added it to the small wad tips and palmed them. "Thanks again. See you tomorrow night."

"I'll be here!"

Making my way slowly to the back of the bar, I ignored the glances from the other girls, who were now looking like death had warmed over due to the lack of customers in the place. After what felt like an eternity, I made it to the back door that led to the liquor storage room, bathrooms, dressing room, and the manager's office. Frank, the manager, saw me coming and raised his eyebrows at me. "What happened?"

Giving him a rundown of my injury, he had me sit in the office while he took a look at my ankle. "That guy gone?" He asked while gently turning my foot over in his hands.

"Yeah, Matt took care of him."

"Good." Sighing, he let go of my foot. "Looks alright, but it will probably be sore for a while. You should ice it when you get home. Call me if you want to take tomorrow night off."

"No, I'll be alright. Just need outta these damn heels and I'll be fine." Limping, I left his office and headed towards the dressing room, where a new batch of girls would be getting dolled up for a night that was sure to be disappointing...unless of course, something miraculous happens and the club became overrun with guys with full wallets and no common sense.

Shifts come in six hour intervals. As the bar is open for lunch every day and remains open until two in the morning, there is a lengthy rotation in the girls that work here. Typically, if you work the day shift, you stay on the day shift and the same goes for the girls who work the hours in between and the night shift. On any given shift there is usually anywhere from seven to ten girls, however the number grows as the night comes into full swing. On weekends, the numbers more than double as this is when the bar sees the most customers. I work nights, the eight-to-closing shift, in order to spend as much time with Brighton as I can before leaving for work.

The dressing room was housed just off of the manager's office—around the next corner to be exact. Expanding the width of the building, it offered bad lighting, worn-out carpet, and a single shower that no girl in her right mind would use due to the lack of interest from anyone when it came to cleaning and disinfecting. Lockers that were reminiscent of the high school years were stacked in two-by-two rows, the middle of them offering a slight sense of privacy for anyone too shy to change in front of anyone else. A solid-looking white-tiled counter ran along the front wall of the room and was graced with large square mirrors that ran from the top of the counter and stopped just inches of the ceiling due to the Hollywood-styled lights that ran along the length of the mirrors, separating the two.

With no doors cutting off the dressing room from the rest of the back of the house, women, managers, and other staff were free to enter and exit through the opening that was as large as your normal door frame; minus the door. If you were naked, anyone walking past would be privy to an eyeful and it didn't take long for any newbie to get accustomed to quick glances from passersby. Of course, the only people allowed in this part of the bar were staff and assuming everyone hired on had underwent Lucky's scrupulous background check, drug screening, and character examination, we all assumed we were being safely gawked at.

I entered the dressing room and tried my best to ignore the obtrusive smell of dusty make-up, sweat, and dirty socks. Two girls, both working religiously to hide away any ill favored wrinkles or age lines on their faces, glanced my way as I limped past the counter to the lockers.

"What happened to you, babe?" The one who called herself Amber asked; now eyeballing me byway of the mirror she was peering into. "Rough night?"

"Took a tumble coz some ass couldn't keep his hands to himself."

Turning in her seat, the other girl, Sarah, asked with a bit more enthusiasm than I expected, "He still here??"

Frowning at her, I simply shook my head at her and rounded the first row of lockers to disengage my own, get dressed, and get the hell out of here. Some girls around here, like me, can't stand the gropers while others...well, let's just say, the more they allow the gropers to cop a feel, the more money they tend to bring in. Sarah was one of those girls.

Pulling out my gym bag, I quickly dressed, slowing only when I had to put any pressure on my swollen ankle. When I was done, I shoved my outfit, heels, and make-up into the overstuffed bag and took one last look inside my locker to ensure it was empty. No matter how long you work in one place, in this line of business, you never left anything in a locker. Even keeping a lock on the thing won't keep thieving hands out for good. Too many stolen outfits and shoes, latex, make-up, and even money taught me that sad fact early on in my career.

Saying nothing as I eased my way back around the lockers and past Amber and Sarah, I slipped out of the dressing room and started to head back out towards the bar, only to have a sudden change of heart and turn towards the back door that led out directly to the parking lot. Because no one manned this part of the bar and the parking lot was dimly lit, no one was supposed to leave out this way, especially at night. But tonight I just didn't care. I was sore, tired, and fed up. Dead set on getting home, my thoughts were consumed with washing the crap off of my face, showering off the bar smell, and being there to put my daughter to bed.

If only I were so lucky.

Chapter Two

The parking lot was deathly quiet and dark. Before I could change my mind about leaving the bar from this side unprotected, the heavy metal door slammed shut behind me. As the automatic locks set into place once the door is closed, there is no other way back into the place except to walk around the building to the front and this thought raced through my mind as I stood there in the dark and tried to scan the parking lot for any psychos that may be lurking for an easy prey.

Practically empty, the only vehicles aside from mine included a beat-up Chevy pickup that looked like it had seen better days, a couple of dark colored sedans, and a van that looked light in color and I knew that each of these had to belong to customers due to the fact that night staff typically parked in the front of the building. Blanketed with a solid layer of dirt and gravel, this part of the parking area was not what you would consider as 'paved'. Consumed with potholes, it had no real order when it came to the distinguishing of parking spaces. Every once in a while, years really, Lucky would cough up the money to have the lot refurbished and even pay to have the markings of the spaces repainted. Despite his care in this area however, the lines never lasted, the filled potholes returned with a vengeance, and the only idiots that would actually use the lot were typically drunk when they pulled in.

Well, the drunks and myself...to speak truthfully. For seven years, I have parked back here, never thinking twice about it really. At least I never think twice about it until nights like this, when it was so dark that seeing my hand in front of my face was called into question and the lot itself was as dead as a graveyard.

As the sole streetlight that was located near the back of the lot was out, the only light granted between me and my dark blue Saturn came from the half-moon positioned high above me in the night sky. Looking up, I saw no stars, just darkened areas of space, indicating heavy storm clouds in the making. The smell of wet dirt invaded my nose and the air felt heavy and damp. Knowing that the rain could start up at again in any minute, I tossed my gym bag over my shoulder and began the walk towards my car which was located alone and to the right of the lot. Passing the caged grilling area that served as the cook's station during the lunching hour, a loud clanging stopped me in my tracks. Heart beating quickly, I turned to my right and, forgetting about my sore ankle, suppressed a curse when it screamed at me. Scanning the chain link fence that marked off the lot, I saw no one and tried to attribute the sound to a loose metal piece of fence that was shuddering softly in the breeze.

Gaining control of my breathing again, my hand instinctively covered my heart and I stood still for a moment with my eyes closed. After a few seconds of hearing nothing else, I opened them and limped as quickly as my ankle would allow. Reaching my car, I realized that my keys were still in my purse, which I had stuffed into my bag before leaving the dressing room. "Shit," I muttered to myself as I flung the bag on the ground and knelt to unzip it and find them.

Sifting through the bag in the dark was like trying to find a needle in a haystack and I cursed myself again as my fingers found everything, save my keys. Peering into the bag was no help as this side of my car was engulfed in darkness and as I tossed aside my costumes, a pair of thigh-high gold colored boots, my blood-red heels, and my make-up bag, I began to consider the possibility that I had left my small, black handbag in my locker.

Shaking my head at myself, I knew that couldn't be as I distinctively remembered looking into empty space before closing the locker door for the night. It *has* to be here! Finally, after shoving aside the contents of my bag to the left side of it, my fingers found purchase...the small handbag tucked into the right side and covered by the soft material that made up one of my outfits. Looking up at the sky again, I mouthed a 'thank you' to the man upstairs and zipped the gym bag closed after fishing out my car keys and returning the purse to its place.

Suddenly, the back end of my car lit up with bright light and I crouched beside the driver's side door yet again, this time instinct telling me to do so for some odd reason. Leaning back slightly, I recognized the circular shaped forms of light as the headlights of a vehicle; one that was entering the rear parking lot from the front of the building. Figuring it was another bar customer; I looked down at my bag and started to reposition the strap on my shoulder when I was suddenly aware that the back of my car was in the dark again.

Realizing quickly that the driver had turned off the headlights, I questioned the act as I stood up straight again and unlocked my car. Opening the door just enough to toss in my gym bag and get myself settled into the driver's seat, I slammed it shut and locked it, glancing over my left shoulder as I did. The car that had just entered pulled towards the back of the lot, headlamps still in the off position, and crawled into the last parking space along the fence, crunching bits of gravel and broken bits of tar as it coasted past. Even though it had to be about a hundred yards away from where I was parked, I couldn't shake the feeling that my safety zone had just been violated beyond end as I continued to stare at it and the driver's choice of parking spaces.

Weird, I thought, considering the fact that no one usually parked back here and the driver's act of turning off the headlights would make any obstructions in the lot impossible to see. I tried to give it no more attention as I put the key in the ignition but curiosity was getting the best of me. Why would someone park way back there when there are plenty of spaces closer to the building? It's not like the spaces up front are full—the bar was practically empty when I left and I doubt it has filled up in the last twenty minutes or so.

Shrugging at myself, I gave my head a shake in order to clear it and started to turn the key but automatically stopped upon hearing voices coming from the direction of the now parked car. Despite the closed windows, I could tell the voices were male and that they sounded angry in tone. Peering slowly over my left shoulder I noticed one figure standing on the driver's side of the car while another opened the passenger door to step out. Neither was clearly visible due to the lack of light and yet instinct kicked in as goose bumps ran along my arms despite my denim jacket. It was time to leave.

"Just get her outta the damn car!"

Despite the fact that I was positioned in my car with the windows rolled up, the man I presumed to be the driver shouted his demand home loud enough for me to hear. Not knowing if it was the tone of his voice, the fact that I was alone in my car in the dark, or that I was just paranoid enough to be scared, I suddenly knew that being seen would put me in danger. Slowly, I pulled the key out of the ignition and eyed the contents of the front seat with only a slight movement of my head; already considering alternative positions that would conceal my body until the men and their vehicle were gone.

My gym bag, tossed carelessly on the passenger seat posed my main problem. Moving as slowly as possible, I lifted it up by grabbing the side closest to me and shoved it enough so that it slid off the seat and onto the floorboard. The cup holders that were located between my seat and the passengers were empty. That's good, I thought, trying to calm my now racing heart. Steeling a glance over my left shoulder again, I instantly held my breath as the driver's view was directed in my location. Not sure if he could see me or not; the windows of my car were blanketed in a dark tint; I froze and closed my eyes.

"...still alive!!"

I don't know about anyone else, but I didn't need to hear the missing pieces to that exclamation to have my eyes fly open again. Looking over to their car caused me to gasp and I quickly threw a shaky hand over my mouth. The passenger had left the confines of the car at this point and having opened the trunk to the vehicle was now standing at the rear of the vehicle with the driver on his left side. Squinting against the night I tried to make out any definitive features of either man but could not. I also didn't dare move. I was stuck, in this position, until they either finished up whatever it was they were doing and left the scene or I passed out completely from fear.

Jerking suddenly, the driver pulled something out of the area of his waist and pointed it at whatever was in the trunk. A quick succession of bright white light immediately followed by a flash of orange made me jump in my seat and I cried out behind my now damp hand. Realizing that I was crying only made me feel worse as I came to understand what was happening only a few yards from my hiding spot. Whatever was in the trunk was being plummeted with bullets. As I could only see the shots being fired off because of the flashing hot light that marketed each pull of the trigger but could hear nothing, I knew the gun was housed with some kind of silencer device. Also, I had no knowledge of weaponry, aside from what I'd seen in the movies, I could only imagine what other details the gun may hold.

Ohmygod, ohmygod, ohmygod....my thoughts were scrambling at a thousand words per second. I couldn't move, couldn't breathe. As the tears continued down my face and covered my hand that was tightened over my mouth, I sat there unable to tear myself away from watching what was happening.

The passenger leaned into the trunk a bit and, with his right hand, shook something. I couldn't see inside the trunk—didn't want to—but I knew in my heart of hearts that it had to be a person. Now, a dead person. They wouldn't have taken the time or spent the bullets to make sure the spare tire was dead. Nope. Whoever it was in the trunk, *was* a person, and I suddenly prayed that I wouldn't be the next victim stuffed into their trunk.

Muffled sounds carried their way down the parking lot and I could no longer clearly understand anything that was being discussed between the two men but I continued to watch as they looked back and forth at each other and the still opened trunk, as if debating what to do now. The moment when the passenger glanced over his shoulder in my direction however, made me wince as if I had been slapped and I knew I had few options at that point.

I had to hide. Had to move. Had to do something more than just sit here. Aside from knowing what I had just witnessed was not the killing of a tire or other inanimate object that would be lying around in a trunk, I knew that if I was to be found out, I was would be next. Shifting in my seat as quickly as I could, I lifted both legs over to the passenger seat so that I could lay down, thereby lowering my head and body below the driver's side window.

In this position, I finally took a deep breath and began to pray. I am not normally a religious person, but at that point I would have believed that the gods of Babylon still existed and would have paid much homage if they were to ensure my safety. Thinking of Brighton, I shuddered, and then cursed myself as the edges of the cup holders in between the seats cut unforgivingly into my side. Shifting slightly to ease the pressure, I never heard the gravel being stomped on roughly around my car...didn't realize that I, the watcher, was now being watched.

Chapter Three

Once upon a time, I wanted to teach, dreamed of working with special needs children in order to guide them through the steps of learning everything under the sun. But the cost of doing so was always too high. Every couple of years, I would research the time, money, and effort it would have taken to complete a college degree in order to see this one dream come true and year after year, it was too much to ask of myself. I couldn't see going into so much debt with student loans and other costs including the time spent away from my daughter in order to accomplish this simple goal.

Hearing a steady *tap-tap-tap* on my driver's side window made me reevaluate the choices I have made in my life in a matter of seconds. I would give anything—*anything*, mind you—to be that teacher, office clerk, hell, even a fast food restaurant employee because of the simple fact that if I were, I wouldn't be here.

The tapping on my window continued and I dared to look up only to find myself staring at the front of a gun as it was gently rapped against the glass. Inhaling sharply, I knew my hiding place had been found and that I had nowhere to go.

Suddenly, and without so much as a warning, the gun was turned and the butt of it slammed into the window and instinct took over. My left arm covered my head as shards of glass coated the upper half of my body and I tried to protect my face and my eyes, which were squeezed shut with such force that a headache was threatening to surface. Hearing a deafening sound, it took my mind a second or two to realize that the earth-shattering noise was coming from me. I was screaming. Then, as suddenly as the violation of my hiding space had occurred, the inside of my Saturn was gifted with the smell of rain, sweat, and a cold breeze and I knew that the door had been unlocked and yanked open. Still, I couldn't move, at least not until I was forced to.

A large, heavy hand grabbed the back of my glass-covered hair and pulled unforgivingly. Still screaming, I tried to fight, now kicking my feet against the passenger side door, not fully registering the pain that was now shooting up my leg from my swollen ankle. Trying to fight back, the yanking of my hair quickly became too much to handle. What felt like hours, I was pulled out of the confines of my car in a matter of seconds, kicking and screaming the entire time and believing with all hope that someone would hear me.

"Shut the *fuck* up!!"

Not knowing which one had me, the driver or the passenger of the other car, I was pulled completely out of my hiding spot. My knees met the cold hard pavement at the same time my head was violently pulled backwards so that I was facing the ever-darkening night sky. The harsh smell of alcohol filled my senses and was mixed with something strong and pungent and sweaty. As the eyes of my attacker glared coldly into mine, my screams were cut off immediately and I searched his face for anything of value that could be later used as an identifier if I survived this and the law caught up with him. His eyes were dark, seemingly black, but in those swift seconds I couldn't decide if it was the darkness around us that made them look this way or if that was their actual color. A deep off-colored scar ran along one cheekbone, maybe an inch from his left eye and looked as though it hadn't been there too long because it was several shades lighter than the tan colored skin that covered the rest of his face. Thin lips curved into a smile as he silently registered what I was doing.

"Thinking you're gonna live through this, huh?" He sneered at me and the second he opened his mouth, I had to force off a gag reflex. His breath reminded me of wet garbage and as I tried to move my face away from his, he jerked back on my head again. "Nope...you're not going anywhere."

From the side, I heard the trampled steps of his partner as he came around the back end of my car and it was then that I wondered how long the both of them had been peering into my windows before deciding to drag me out. Unable to gain a full view of the guy, I listened instead; wanting to know if either had an accent, a lisp, broken speech patterns...something that I could add to the knowledge already building in my mind. I don't know if I have watched too many of those detective shows on TV....*NCIS, Law and Order, CSI*...but I knew that I had to have something on these two...even if I ended up only able to use such information after they've killed me and I returned to haunt the shit outta them until the end of time.

"C'mon, before someone else shows up!"

The other guy spoke in hushed tones but his urgency was still distinguishable and somehow I just knew that this had to be the passenger of the car that I had previously witnessed opening the trunk of their car. This must make the guy who held the death grip on the back of my head, and who would kill me just by breathing on me again, the driver. Not just the driver, the *shooter*, I reminded myself. And from what I could tell so far, the dominant one.

Yes, I have watched way too many of those TV shows.

With a hard pull, the shooter kept his tight grip on my hair and as he started to make his way back to their car, I either had to move with him or end up being dragged across the parking lot. My legs, shaking yet stiff with fear, complied at first, but really wanted to take over and run in the opposite direction. With both hands I grabbed at the arm of my attacker and tried to get him to let go but to no avail. Stopping suddenly, He held onto my hair and, with his free hand grabbed me by my jaw.

"You wanna play rough??" Glaring into my wide eyes, he smiled and gave me a nod. "We can play rough, sweetheart. I can make the last moments of your life a living hell, if you'd like."

Already there!!

I wanted to scream at him, but couldn't because the grip he held kept my mouth closed shut. As the tears began to once again fall freely from my eyes, he nodded again, seeming to take this as a sign of my weakness and submission. Turning away from me, he continued to lead me to the back of the parking lot, never once letting up on the back of my head.

No, no, no...not the trunk!! Not the trunk!!!

I just knew that I was going to end up there, with whatever was already lying dead in it, and I somehow managed to choke back a couple of sobs. As my mind continued reeling at what the next few moments of my life were going to be, any thoughts of continuing to fight were pushed aside. I was running out of energy. Giving up, as my mother would have said, accepting my fate.

The trunk of their car was still open, and as I was drug closer to it, the smell of blood and death met me head on. From the corner of the make-shift grave, I could see thin strands of light colored hair strung out from the inside of the trunk, draped softly over the edge of it. Blood had mixed in with the hair and looked as those it had been dipped in red paint in various places. A shift in the breeze caused the strands to lift gently, and not knowing how I could *see* this in such detail, I suddenly became angrier than I have ever been in my life.

I was not going to be a victim.

The realization of this hit me harder than my anger and in response to my newly found determination; I forced my body to come to a dead stop. Unknowing of my decision, the shooter, who still held my hair with a tight fist, was pulled backward along with my head. Turning to face me, he smiled, hatred building quickly in his eyes. "What—*now* you ready to put up a fight?"

"C'mon, Da—"

A sharp glare from the shooter cut off his partner as I immediately picked up on what the guy was about to say and held on to this new evidence for dear life.

Dan? Daniel?? Dave??? One of these may fit...

The look on my face giving me away, the shooter sneered and grabbed an even tighter hold of my hair, causing me to wince before I could stop myself. The tears were gone now, and I was trying hard not to play the helpless girl who was going to beg for my life. No, a plan was forming around the vibrant pain in my head and I was not going to give up as easily as he may believe or expect.

"And what do you think knowing my *name* is going to do for you, huh?? Think it's gonna get you outta this? Hate to tell ya, sweetheart, but all it will do is guarantee that you ain't gonna make it out of this alive! Not when you have seen our faces and now, because of *dipshit* over there, may come to figure out one of our names. Nope—you're a goner!!"

The joy in his voice sent chills up my spine and I realized that he was actually enjoying himself. That scared me more than anything else and as he gave my hair another hard yank to force me to move again, I caught a glance at his partner. Jaw set in anger, I thought for a moment that he was going to defend himself against the reference the shooter had given him but thought better of it when no argument left his pursed lips.

"Let's go, Hellcat!" He pulled even harder and my legs could no longer hold their stance against him. The back of my head felt like it was on fire and the pain from his grasp cursed down the back of my neck.

"Close the trunk!!" Yelling at the silent man behind me, the shooter dragged me closer to the back end of their car. For a second the other man didn't move, confusion building in his eyes. Then, as if a silent message were shared between the two, he looked at me and offered a half smile before walking around me to the trunk. Slamming the lid shut, I managed to briefly look down only to see the bloodied strands of hair get caught between the mouth of the trunk and the lid, forever sealing them in between. The movement of it all caused them to stir once again and lift gently in the air and at that very moment I believed that I knew, wholeheartedly, what it felt like to go insane.

The sight of it nauseated me quickly and I lurched forward as my stomach threatened to empty its contents all over the shooters boots—which I hadn't noticed until then. Black in color, the tips of them came to a point at the front and was covered with a silvery piece of metal. The length of them told me he had big feet, at least three to four inches larger than mine, which measured at eight and a half the last time I checked.

"Shit, she's gonna puke!" Mr. Silent finally spoke in a higher tone and I caught a bit of an accent in his voice. "Get her away from the car!"

They've got a dead body in the trunk and he's worried about the *car*???

"Nope. I'm gonna have some fun!" The shooter pulled me up to a standing position and without a second thought flipped me around so that my back was facing him. Pushing me down by my shoulders, he finally had to let go of the back of my head and for a split second, I sighed with relief, that is, until the middle of my back was offered a violent push. The side of my face met the cold metal of the hood and I didn't need to hear him say, *"Hold her down!"* to know what was going to happen next.

Oh, shitshitshitshitshit...

My mind was screaming at me and I knew that this was my moment. The only one I was going to get. Squeezing my eyes shut, I took a deep breath and the minute I felt *'dipshit's'* hands on my shoulder's in order to hold me down, I reacted with as much venom I could muster. Clenching my teeth, I stiffened my upper body muscles and raised myself up off of the closed trunk. In an effort to build on my strength before it was seeped out of every pore in my body, I dug my heels down on the crumbled tar under my feet and felt myself start to skid. Along with my head and my back, my ankle seared in pain but somehow, I managed to push it all aside, believing that I just may be able to save my own life.

The two behind me must have never thought that I would actually put up a fight and I heard both of them issue curses at me as I continued to push my body backwards by using the top of the trunk as a balance of power underneath my opened palms. Continuing to push until I was at least a foot away from the trunk of the car, I didn't care if I ended up falling on top of them.

Feeling the grip the one had on my head release fully, I whipped myself around; planning on kneeing whichever one was closest to me. I found pay dirt, in the driver, and drove my knee between his legs with all of my strength. The passenger, shocked, reeled backward, eyes wide with surprise while his mentor immediately bent and the waist and howled in pain. Seizing the moment, I dove around the two of them, now screaming my head off and took off running towards the front of the lot, already knowing that if I tried to make it back to my car, I wouldn't.

Suddenly, my eyes were violated with white light, coming from the opening of the lot, and while at first I was blinded by the glare, I knew that salvation had arrived. Running straight at the vehicle, from what my now dotted vision could tell was a truck; I started waving my arms, screaming at the driver to stop. Then, without warning, something hit me from behind...the pain registering before I could tell exactly what it was and I found myself pushed forward with such force that I had difficulty comprehending it at first.

The hard ground met the side of my face with a sickening thud. The sleeves of my jacket were pushed up towards my elbows as my arms bent automatically to brace my fall and bits of gravel and broken pieces of hardened tar drove into the palms of my hands and exposed wrists. My stomach, flattened against the ground beneath me, heaved uncontrollably and I knew that if the vomiting began now, it wouldn't stop.

Closing my eyes against the ill begotten image of myself that would just not go away, I felt my lashes brush against the roughness of the road that now served as a pillow. I slowly questioned the sudden feeling of something wet and sticky running across my back and down my sides as blackness danced behind my eyes. And at the point when I could no longer feel a thing, either in or around my body, that blackness continued to creep, until it took over and I was left with...well...nothing.

Chapter Four

The 911 operator was connected through to Central Dispatch while trying to calm the obviously distraught caller—*man...it's gotta* be a man—within five minutes of taking the call. The man, or so she thinks (unless of course she is aging way faster than her four grown children believe her to be and this is wreaking havoc on her hearing) sounded desperate, out of breathe, and, quite possibly, a little drunk. Either way, he swears that what he has witnessed has nothing to do with him...but someone, and he means *someone*, has got to get out to the parking lot of Lucky's Girls and quickly!

Central Dispatch answers the call almost immediately and relays to her that an ambulance and a police cruiser are en route to the scene and, adding a reminder to keep the caller on the phone, requests additional information. This process is mainly meant to prepare the guys who are coming to save the day to do so by not only prepping for the call concerning the injured—whether they are male or female, have been shot, drowned, attacked, are dead or alive—but so that they can also prep themselves for safety, accordingly.

Despite these procedures, and the instructions already well-known to the veteran 911 worker, she hears an audible click from her headset and knows immediately that she has lost her caller. Frustrated she clicks off, then, after reviewing the caller's phone number as it is recorded electronically once the connection was made, she clicks back on to call him back, but to no avail—the caller isn't answering. Waving her hand in the air, she catches the eye of her supervisor as he rounds the rows made up of her fellow 911 coworkers. The room, reminiscent of a warehouse, is stocked full of desks, computer systems, and warm bodies and does not quiet down as he reaches her. Instead it seems to grow louder as calls continue to come in, one right after another, on this rainy Friday night.

"I got this caller—no name, age, or description—came in about ten minutes ago. Says some girl is bleeding all over the parking lot of Lucky's Girls." Sighing briefly at her supervisor as his raised eyebrows tells her that he knows the place, she continues, "Caller thought the victim may have been shot, but he hung up. Before I could even get any real information from him, he was gone. I have nothing but the location for Dispatch." Then considering for a moment, she adds, "I'm not even sure it was a male who called it in, sounded...I don't know...high pitched or something."

"You try him back?"

Feeling the frustrations of a yet another long night, she sighs again, rubs her temples and assures him, "Yes, I tried to get him back. But the guy isn't answering. I'm not sure what is going on, but I need to log this with the original information from the call."

"Ok", he replies simply and slightly shrugs his shoulders. Despite the protocol of notifying the supervisor on hand if, and when, something like this occurs, her supervisor only nods once more before returning to his never-ending roaming between the desks. His lack of additional comment or instruction is close to infuriating.

"Idiot." Muttering under her breath, she ignores the desire to throw something heavy-duty at his retreading back—like her stapler that can staple twenty-five sheets of paper together with a simple push of her hand—and instead pulls up the information she has listed concerning the caller on her computer screen, at the same time she clicks back to Central Dispatch using her headset.

"Dispatch."

"Yes, this is Sofia Valdez, operator number 542891. Additional information pertaining to call number 0527129452 is available." The sequence of numbers, representing the month, day, year, and time of day (ending in number 1 representing a.m. and number 2 for p.m.) ensures that the conversation is on track and disallows for any confusion as to who, what, where, or when the call and request for services came in. Giving the woman with dispatch a moment to pull up the record on her side, Sofia paused briefly before continuing. "Unknown caller relayed the scene of a possible gunshot victim at the Lucky's Girls Club located at 1533 West Hillside Park. Caller disconnected the call prior to any other information was obtained, however, it is believed that the caller was male."

"Okay, Operator 542891, will dispatch the information to services approaching the scene. Thank you." And with that the call ended, leaving Sofia with a feeling that her job was not performed to peak standards, but before she could dwell on that thought, her line began ringing as soon as she clicked off with dispatch. Oh yes, another historical Friday night was already in the making...

On the other end of the spectrum, the dispatcher immediately connected with one of the emergency technicians riding along to the scene. Giving him the information that she had just obtained from the 911 operator, including the fact that there are no real details about the caller, the victim, or even the scene. Requesting that they take care—which she does now out of habit due to the sixteen years of services she has put in with this position thus far—she signs off the call, ensures that the record created in her computer system is complete, and leans back in her desk chair until the next call from 911 comes in.

Three blocks from West Hillside Park, Mark Franklin updates his partner, Mitchel Campton, with the details from their contact with dispatch. Not knowing what to expect, he unbuckles his seat belt and leaves the passenger side of the ambulance to gather both tech bags and ensure once again that they are each packed with gauze, antiseptic, gloves, and all the other tools they may need in dealing with a gunshot victim. Glancing around at the additional equipment available in the back of the large van, he nods to himself, assured that they are ready for just about anything as the van veers slightly to the left in order to avoid crashing into the backend of a car in the right lane ahead of them.

"*Jesus*, can't these people hear our sirens??" Mitchel exclaims as he maneuvers past the now slowing vehicle and repositions their ride back into the right lane as he speeds the van back up to fifty-five miles per hour. Hillside Park is usually never this busy...expect of course when a blaring emergency vehicle is trying to get across it. "Some people..." he adds, but doesn't finish as he approaches another intersection.

Lifting his masculine body back into the passenger's seat, Mark agrees with him. "Yeah, you know, unless you're there to save them, some people just don't seem to care."

Luckily, the intersection was empty on all sides, and Mitchel drove smoothly through it. "ETA, two minutes", he said automatically. Calling out the estimated time of arrival prepared not only the attending medic on the team, but the driver as well, even if only mentally in most cases. Having their heads on straight, thoughts in order, and focus right on the mark was essential in any emergency case and calling out the time often helped both medics prepare for their arrival procedures once they reach the scene.

Making a right into the parking lot of Lucky's Girls, Mark noted the growing crowd both in the front of the building and to the side of it, signifying that their victim may not be inside the club itself. Victims draw bystanders like rotting meat draws maggots, especially *bloodied* victims. And in either case, the outcome is often more than just a little bothersome, rather it's more disgusting if you asked him.

Girls dressed in thongs, bra tops, cut off shorts, and heels of every color met the emergency vehicle as Mitchel slowed it down to a crawl once he entered the lot, turning off the screaming sirens at the same time. The sight of the spectators indicated that none of them had bothered to cover up before venturing outside to witness the event and Mitchel automatically shook his head at them. Nothing against this type of profession, but neither medic needed the distraction at a moment like this. Mixed in with the entertainment were a few men, customers he assumed, and they all had the same look...wide eyes enhanced with a little bit of horror and excitement...again, *disgusting*.

Seeing the look in his partner's eyes, Mitchel reminded him of duties, while Mark simply nodded in response. Kid has probably never been this close to a topless bar, he figured, and couldn't help but smile a bit. Fifteen years his senior, and almost twenty years more experienced on the job, Mitchel has seen his fair share of bystanders, and victims, who were missing more than just one piece of clothing. While in the beginning, it can be a huge distraction; just a few times out in the field can help a guy move past the skin and focus on the whole point of being there. *Saving lives.*

Heading towards the back of the parking lot, Mitchel stopped the emergency van as someone just ahead of them began waving his arms, as if he were trying to land an airplane. His eyes wide, the guy was dressed in jeans and t-shirt, both of which were covered in what looked to be like blood. Assuming this was the guy who had called in to 911, Mitchel looked over at Mark and instructed, "Grab both bags and assess the victim, I have a feeling that we are going to need both bags on this one. I'm gonna try to get information from this guy."

"Sure." Mark replied simply, the excitement of it all warming his cheeks. With less than six months experience on the job, the calls still enthralled him, but he was a hard worker, knew his medical stuff, and had yet to have a scene bother him to the point that his focus was called into question. In all, Mark was one of the best partners Mitchel has had so far in his years of service. And for Mitchel, that says something about the kid.

Pulling the vehicle slightly to the right in order to avoid running over the arm-waving guy, Mitchel put on the brakes, threw it into park, and jumped out while Mark left his seat and moved towards the rear to grab their medical bags. Exiting out of the rear door, the audience that was now moving from the front of the building to the back had a first-hand look inside the emergency van. Murmurs, whispers, finger-pointing, and weaving all accompany crowds such as this and Mitchel and Mark both new to be wary of a crowd. You never know when some psycho is going to leap out of the middle of it and either try to steal emergency medical supplies, get into the middle of things, or do something absolutely *stupid* that causes to them to become the team's next victim.

Typically, rubberneckers point out the victim, or victims, so that emergency teams do not have to look too far to begin their work and this situation proved the same. As soon as Mark hit the pavement, bystanders were talking and pointing all at the same time. Holding up his hand in an effort to calm the people that were quickly surrounding him, like some kind of hero or famous actor in the spotlight, Mark weaved his way through the scantily-clad dancers and alcohol-smelling customers to find his victim.

Seeing that the person lay on their stomach, Mark began to note the obvious as he knelt down beside the body and pulled out a pair of latex gloves. You never touch a victim without gloves on for protection. These days, victims often turned into offenders, as many cannot verbally tell a medic if they are suffering from a disease, have some type of virus, or even if they are allergic to something. Caution and protection outweighed jumping right into life-saving tactics and Mark pulled on his gloves, stretching the rubbery material over each finger and his wrists in seconds.

Squatting, Mark mentally registered the pool of blood that spread from directly underneath the victim's right shoulder and circled around their motionless head. A hole, smaller than a silver dollar, had breached the person's black denim jacket at the shoulder level, causing the threading to explode into millions of tiny broken threads. Moving the person's red hair off of the face and to the opposite side, Mark was able to place two fingers at on the side of their neck, just under the chin and felt a faint pulse. Immediately, the process of caring for this person sped up considerably.

"Mitchel!" Mark shouted over his shoulder at his partner who was still gathering information from the crowd. "Got a live one! Get the stretcher!"

Grabbing his bag, Mark pulled it closer to him and sifted its contents. Efficiency and speed were high priority now, and even though this just looked like a shoulder wound from a bullet, Mark had no idea what other complications the victim may also be suffering from. Pulling sterile bandages, medical tape, and a pair of heavy steel scissors from the bag, Mark moved quickly as he could. From the bottom of the jacket, Mark cut the tough material up the center all the way to the collar as Mitchel quickly approached the victim from the opposite side. Wordlessly, Mitchel stretched a pair of gloves over his hands and help spread the jackets pieces away from the victims back.

The cotton t-shirt underneath was soaked in blood stemming from the bullet wound and as Mark pulled the tails of the shirt out of the victim's jeans, Mitchel prepared the bandages and got the tape ready for use. Using the same cutting procedure, Mark cut the t-shirt in half, lengthways, and pulled the material apart, to find a lacy cream colored bra underneath. Cutting the bra's back strap into two pieces as well, the wound was finally free to dress. Pouring an antibiotic ointment around the wound, Mitchel quickly covered it with a heavy thick bandage and secured it to the skin with medical tape.

Now for the other side. Both men, Mark pushing and Mitchel pulling, gently rolled the victim onto her back, and as Mark quickly removed the clothing covering the front, Mark briefly confirmed the gender of the victim, her possible age, and the fact that she was barely breathing.

This side of her, blanketed in her own blood, was more of a mess to deal with. Her neck, chest, and stomach were covered in blood and required more care medically speaking. Although the exit wound was in plain sight, jumping to conclusions would be a mistake. Bullets can be tricky and unpredictable and there may way more damage to the body than they can see firsthand. Their main objective now after dressing the wound is to get the woman to the hospital where more profound medical services can be administered.

"Stretcher?" Mark asked quickly, knowing that he did not have to ask full questions in order for Mitchel to understand what he is referring to.

"Yes", replied Mitchel, standing quickly to grab the board behind him that they would use to lay the victim on top of. Rolling the body towards his own, Mark gently held her in place by placing a firm grip on one shoulder and another on her hip. As he did, Mitchel immediately placed the hard board underneath her and helped his partner gently position her body into the center of the board. Once she was positioned safely, the board was lifted by both men and placed onto a stretcher and, each one taking a side, rose the stretcher to a standing position so that they could roll it quickly back to the ambulance. In all, their response time and procedural work took less than ten minutes.

Up until this point, neither medic took much notice of the scene as it continued to evolve around them. As they pushed the stretcher into the back of the vehicle, each noticed that several officers were now mixed in with the crowd; each doing their part to figure out what had happened here. While Mark worked at replacing both of their medical bags, and got himself positioned into the back of the ambulance so as to continuously monitor the victim's vitals and the flow of blood that was steadily seeping out of her wound, Mitchel quickly approached one of the cops. "Hey, we got the vic, taking her over to Mercy."

"Still alive?" The cop asked; his eyebrows rising as he glanced up at Mitchel from the notebook he had been taking notes in concerning the scene. Seeing the medic quickly nod his answer, he sensed urgency on the man's face. "We'll have someone over there as soon as possible."

Nodding at the cop again, Mitchel turned and hurried back to the emergency vehicle. Jumping back into the drivers' seat, he turned on the blaring sirens again and headed out of the parking lot towards the hospital. Saying a silent prayer, he hoped he wasn't going to end up delivering the dead as he headed off into traffic and moved swiftly around the idiotic drivers that just couldn't seem to get the hell out of the way.

Chapter Five

Detective Ian Sampson put his key in the lock that secured his two bedroom apartment at the same time the cell phone in his pocket began to ring. Hesitating with the key in place, he sighed heavily and closed his eyes and raised his face to the ceiling, wondering briefly if the cell phone would quit ringing if he just ignored it.

No such luck. The ringtone, a head banging mixture of electric guitars and drums, only seemed to grow louder and more irritating as he finished unlocking the door and stepped into the apartment's small entryway. Fishing the phone out of his jeans front pocket as he shut the door behind him—mindful to avoid slamming it—he flipped it open and demanded, "What??"

Obviously flustered, the voice on the other end hesitated a second before ensuring that she was in fact speaking to Detective Sampson, Homicide Division. Discovering immediately that the call was not in fact coming from his partner, Frank Colliatti, Ian cleared his throat and muttered an incoherent apology to the woman on the other end.

"Yea, Sampson here."

"Sir, this is Officer Hammels, we've got a request here from Captain Leary concerning your assistance at Mercy General Hospital, ASAP."

"Details?"

"Gunshot victim, female, current condition is unknown at this time."

"Has Detective Colliatti been notified?"

"Yes, Sir. He was contacted first and requested that I call you."

Sighing heavily again, Ian walked carefully through the small living room to the kitchen and checked the time on the microwave, the only thing illuminating in this area as he had yet to turn on any lights. The bright red digital numbers red 11:49; not all that late, but after a near twenty-four hour stint sitting in an unmarked car while monitoring movement in and out of a suspected drug house where a murder suspect was believed to be hiding out in, Ian was exhausted. Giving in, he knew that he had no choice, especially considering that the request originated from Captain Leary.

"Got it. Thanks, Officer…?"

"Hammels, Sir."

"Got it, Officer Hammels, thanks for the info." Snapping his phone shut, Ian reached over and flipped a switch, brightening the kitchen up considerably. Blinking against the sudden change from darkness to light, Ian took a moment to grab a bottle of water from the fridge and left the kitchen and headed towards his bedroom, turning additional lights on as he did. Emergency or not, he was determined to grab a shower and a change of clothes before heading out again.

Knowing if he sat anywhere in the apartment, he would not get back up; Ian quickly grabbed a clean pair of jeans, a white button down shirt, and fresh boxers and socks. Heading into the bathroom, he started the shower and drank greedily from the water bottle. A full day of nothing but coffee and soda made his body hungry for water and, before he stepped into the shower, the bottle was empty.

Fifteen minutes later, he was dressed, armed, and ready to go. Closing up the apartment, he silently prayed that the next time he stepped inside it; it would be for longer than twenty minutes. Heading down the hall, he rounded the corner, signaled for the elevator doors to open, and leaned against the back wall of the small compartment while it slowly crawled down four floors to the basement level, where his Dodge Ram was parked.

The Ram, his baby, was notably where a chunk of his income went. As he was unmarried, completely single in fact, he cared less for the apartment but more for what he drove. The apartment, nice in a homely, bachelor-pad sort of way, was not slept in, eaten in, or even relaxed in as much as his truck—as he only drove department issued vehicles when absolutely necessary, Ian took care and pride in his Ram. He could live in it if he had to.

Metallic black in color, the truck was decked out with leather seating, top of the line speakers, and a navigation center located above the center console. With seating for three in the back, the truck could fit up to six people if needed and sat upon twenty inch tires. It was top of the line—again, his *baby*, and as he pulled out of the garage and headed towards the hospital, he couldn't help but sink back into the leather seating and smile to himself.

The emergency parking lot located on the side of Mercy General was a mess of illegally parked cars, the wandering sick who looked lost and miserable, and a full parking area in which no one vehicle seemed to be parked in between the white lines. Exasperated from the obvious ignorance of the sick mixed in with a lack of sleep, Ian drove around until he found the entrance marked *Emergency Vehicles Only* and drove into the lot as if on a mission.

Before he even had the truck parked and alarmed in the only empty space, which was supposed to be designated for a *Doctor Halloway*, a security officer approached him from the south corner of the nearly enclosed lot. Hefting up his blue polyester pants, the guard looked as though he couldn't outrun a small child, and Ian flashed his badge quickly. Putting a stubby finger in the air, as if determined to argue that Ian's official badge had no meaning here, Ian put up one hand to stop the man from speaking.

"Detective Sampson, Homicide." Glancing over his shoulder quickly to read the Doctor's name that was stenciled in red on the wall facing the space he had just parked in, Ian added quickly, "I don't think the good Doctor Halloway will mind me parking here for a few minutes." Passing the dumbstruck guard, Ian smiled inwardly, only to have it stifled once he entered through the automatic doors that led into the emergency room.

People were everywhere. The seating area, facing a row of desks and cubicles, was jammed with the sick, family members trying to offer support, and judging by the look on some of the faces, the near-dead. Irritant cries from young voices indicated that many patients had failed to leave their children at home and the room smelled of sweat, mixed in with a touch of vomit and a pinch of urine. It was loud, obtrusive, and for a moment, caused Ian to reconsider his career options.

"Detective!"

Stopping quickly, Ian scanned the mass of future patients but couldn't find the person that belonged to the voice until he heard, "Detective Sampson!" coming from the opposite side of the large room. Seeing his partner, Ian made his way through the crowd hoping that he didn't catch anything along the way.

"Hey, Frank." Ian approached his partner and asked, "What do we got?"

Detective Frank Colliatti, an older, heavier man with more than twenty years on the job, smirked and replied, "Got a *stripper*." As if wanting to let that fact sink in, Frank paused for a moment before continuing, "Name's Amanda Pearson. She's got a bullet hole in her right shoulder, was found face-down in a parking lot. The docs are workin' on her now to repair it."

Refusing to comment on the connotation in his partner's voice concerning the stripper aspect of why they were there, Ian tried to focus on the details of the shooting instead. "You visit the scene?"

"Naw...couple of vice worked it pretty good. Just got the call that the girl was brought here, still alive but needing surgery. They found the bullet at the scene, Crime Scene is there now. Figured we could try to get a status report here, then head over. She worked at Lucky's Girls!" Eyebrows raised, Ian could only imagine what was going through his partner's mind.

Despite his cockiness and failure to act like an adult at times, Detective Coliatti had his moments when he appeared to be a diligent, respectable cop. Nearing retirement, however, such instances were becoming few and far between. And as much as Ian tried to overlook the faults in his partner, after four years together, it was getting harder instead of easier. Ian knew that the comment stressing that their victim was a stripper was meant to cause some kind of reaction out of him, and it probably wouldn't be the only remark to be made by Colliatti, but he wouldn't allow himself to get mixed up in such adolescent behavior.

Before Ian had the chance to respond in any way, however, the electronic double doors that led into the heart of the hospital's emergency department swung slowly open. Stepping back from them, both detectives immediately noticed the chaotic atmosphere that is common in most emergency rooms on any given Friday night. Nurses, dressed in scrubs varying in look and color, crossed paths between their stations and the semi-private rooms that housed the sick. Wandering in between were several doctor-looking types, mostly males, each seeming lost and overtired as they weaved in and out of the rooms visiting patients, concurring a diagnosis, and passing them on to one of the nurses for final instruction and releasing information. It was loud and confusing and as efficient as any form of managed chaos can actually be.

"Detectives??"

Peeling his eyes away from the array of medical personnel as they continued scrambling back and forth, Ian took notice of an official looking staff member standing just to the left of the opened corridor. Nodding, he introduced himself and Colliatti, and both men walked through the opening just as the wide double doors began to automatically close again.

"I'm Doctor Alice Sway." Taking a minute to shake both detectives' hands, the doctor smiled briefly as Ian sized her up silently. At least five-foot-seven, her blond hair was pulled back into a tight bun at the base of her neck and her white coat looked as though it had just come from the cleaners. Light blue eyes under long lashes graced her tanned face and she didn't look a day over twenty-one.

Great, Ian thought to himself, *all I need is to have Colliatti start droolin' over this one and we'll never get outta here!*

Turning her back on them as she lead them up the corridor, she gave them a detailed account of their victim by speaking loudly and glancing over her shoulder periodically to make sure she was being both heard and understood while both men made mental notes concerning her patient, Amanda Pearson.

"Ms. Pearson was brought in around 10:00 or so, suffering from a bullet wound in her right shoulder. She was unconscious...barely breathing, really...and we took her in to surgery immediately to repair the damage to the muscles. The bullet did not cause damage to anything major, thankfully, and it was a through and through." Meaning that it entered one area and exited out another, Ian noted to himself, immediately assuming that the fragment Frank said that the crime scene guys had found was probably their bullet.

"Is she awake?" Ian asked, causing the doctor to glance over her shoulder again.

"No, she wasn't when I came to meet you two. But, she may be now, she has been out of recovery for about a half hour and we only gave her a local anesthetic since the repairs to her shoulder required nothing in the way of vital organs and such."

Nodding, Ian glanced over at Frank and wondered briefly if he was going to ask any questions. The big man was quiet, eyeing the passing of staff and patients as they continued walking past the emergency rooms towards the rear of the corridor, where they were met with another set of wide double doors.

Sighing to himself, Ian took his partner's silence as a sign that he was going have to lead and carry through conversing with the victim's doctor by himself and asked, "Was there any word of how Ms. Pearson ended up with a bullet in her shoulder when she was brought in? Anything the medics relayed to your staff?"

"Not that I'm aware of." Doctor Sway shook her head as she lifted a security badge to a small digital gadget to the right of the closed double doors. Hearing a soft buzzing sound, the devise registered the doctor's clearance and as the doors began to slowly open, the group stepped back to make way. Continuing to lead the detectives through another section of the hospital, the noise level here was drastically lessened and once the double doors retracted and clicked closed behind them, Ian breathed a sigh of relief, thankful for the quiet.

Suddenly, another doctor-looking staff member ran up from behind the three of them, causing each to jump slightly. Before Ian could mutter a swear word at the frantic looking guy, Doctor Sway placed both hands on the guys forearms and started to question him.

"Your patient...in room 278, she's having some kind of panic attack! They've been trying to page you, Doctor Sway!" The guy, now looking less like a full-fledged doctor, but an intern or something of the sort, paused to take a breath has the heat in his cheeks rose to a bright red. He looked as though he had run a few miles before finding the doctor and Ian immediately wanted to find him a chair to sit down in before he collapsed.

"Okay, okay, Samuel. Calm down." Even though the doctor's voice was steady and calming, her pace quickened immediately and Ian and Frank found themselves nearing a slow jog in order to keep up.

"This our vic??" Ian asked quickly and seeing the doctor nod at him over her shoulder, his heart beginning to race a bit. Hoping that Ms. Pearson was not having some kind of cardiac arrest or something that would alter the course of her being interviewed, the two detectives managed to keep pace with the doctor. For the most part, victims who were rushed to emergency services after finding themselves on the wrong end of a bullet often couldn't, or wouldn't, give up vital information in order to help law enforcement build their case. Aside from watching cases fall apart due to lack of evidence and knowing that an offender could go free, this was the most aggravating part of the job.

Turning down another corridor, Ian immediately noticed an increase in activity as he quickly registered hospital staff hurrying in and out of a room near the middle of the wing they were now jogging down.

A woman's yell turned into a scream, causing staff to react at an even quicker pace and as Doctor Sway reached the room ahead of Ian and Frank, a dreadful feeling that their victim may not only be suffering from a gunshot wound fleeted across Ian's thoughts.

Reaching the room, both detectives slowed down; Frank breathing heavy and growing red in the face as he came to a stop. Ian, in much better shape than his partner, took a deep breath to steady his already tired nerves and steeled himself just before crossing the threshold that led into the patient's room as another blood curdling scream engulfed the entire wing.

Chapter Six

No, no, no, no!!!! Don't put me in the trunk....I don't want to go in the trunk!!!

It's so dark! Why can't I see??? He's holding me down...and I can't see!!!

Fight!! You've got to fight, Amanda!!

"Ms. Pearson!!!"

Oh, God—he knows my name!! My NAME!! How can he know that?? I didn't tell him—

"Ms. PEARSON!!! Open your eyes!! Come on, sweetie...relax!"

It's so dark...I'm in the trunk—wait—a woman's voice?? What???

The grip on my arms tightens, then releases slightly, and I know suddenly that I am coming out of the dark. But how? Where am I?? Trying to breathe, I feel my lungs expand, the tightness in my chest incomparable to the pain that is shooting from my right shoulder. My voice hurts. I was screaming...I know I was—the ringing of it still strong in my ears. But where—??

"What??" My voice sounds a million miles away and croaks as I force it out. "Where—??"

The female voice answers: "At Mercy General. In the hospital."

Squeezing my eyes closed one more time, I know that I have to open them. Swiftly, I pray that I am not being deceived, that I won't open them to find myself really in that trunk, hearing voices from that girl's make-shift grave. Chancing it, they slowly flutter open, but quickly squint against the light. Light!! I am surrounded by light! *Oh, God, am I dead??*

"Ms. Pearson?"

The female voice is calmer, gentler. And I think I can trust it. Blinking, I open my eyes, only to find myself looking into a woman's face. Her blue eyes look concerned. Maybe I'm not dead. Maybe I just had a bad dream...

"Ms. Pearson, I'm Doctor Sway."

Watching her carefully now, I sense that we are not alone but can't take my eyes from her young face in order to be sure. Doctor Sway, if that is really who she is, leans back from me, releasing her grip on my arms and I am suddenly aware of a scorching pain running across my shoulders and up through my neck. My *hair* seems to hurt. "Where...where am I?" my voice is creaking again, and I suddenly need water like there's no tomorrow.

I watch her breath heavily as she stands up from the side of the bed that I now realize I am laying on. Following her glance, I see two men standing just off to the side. Looking back at me, she starts to explain. "You were brought in a few hours ago, by ambulance. You are at Mercy General Hospital and we had to do some work on your shoulder in order to repair the damage from your gunshot wound."

"Gunshot???" Feeling more confused, I shook my head but had to stop moving it immediately as the pain in my neck ran upwards and pounded beneath both temples. "I was shot??"

Not offering me an explanation, the doctor looks again at the two men behind her, and steps to the side to offer me a better view of them. "Ms. Pearson, these are detectives. They are here to try to figure out what happened to you. I want to check your vitals and your wound, but once I am done you can decide if you are up to talking to them now or I can have them return later."

Eyeing each of the men, I notice the thinner one take a step forward, as if wanting to say something. Looking back at the doctor, I know that there is something that I need to tell them but right now, for the life of me, I can't remember what it is. Maybe if they start with their questions, I will remember. "No, it's ok. They can stay."

"Ok." Turning back to the detectives, I listen as she asks them to step outside the room for a few minutes. Returning to me, she leans over the upper half of my body and I try hard not to pull away from her as she unties the top of my hospital gown to check my shoulder, where the pain is now close to excruciating.

"Wait!!" Sitting up suddenly, I ignore the pain that screams at me. My swift movement causes Doctor Sway to stand up quickly and the look she gives me is full of concern. "Brighton!! Where's my daughter??"

"Your daughter?" Doctor's Sways voice goes from gentle to urgent in a second. "Was your daughter with you when this happened??"

"No—I mean—I don't think so", pausing I try to think but my thoughts are muddy and confusing. "Anna watches her when I work. Are they here??"

"Hold on one second, okay? I will go find out."

My heart pounded in my chest and all the pain I had been feeling was swept away, as if a strong wind had wound itself up from my heart and spread itself across my body. Watching the doctor leave the room in a hurry, I realized in an instant that firstly, she had no idea I had a daughter, and secondly, she really had no clue as to where she could be at this very moment. If I had been involved in some kind of gun fight—and nearly lost—who's to say that an innocent child wasn't out there suffering as well??

Racking my foggy brain, I managed to pull minor details from my memory, but none seemed to have any significance as to just how I ended up here. The bar. The greasy, drunk guy that tried to get me to sit on his lap in the VIP Lounge. Matt, coming to the rescue. Leaving the bar after getting dressed. All of these images flashed behind my eyes, but after that there was nothing. Just darkness. Looking around the room, I searched for clues in the stark white walls, the medical machinery that constantly monitored my heart rate, my blood pressure, and my temperature. The rough, scratchy bedding that I lay upon. Nothing offered any headway...it was if my mind had shut itself off and I had no idea as to how to get it up and running again.

As the doctor made her way back into the room, I tried to sit up but a wave of nausea circled through my stomach and stilled my shaky body. Seeing what I was trying to do, Doctor Sway hurried across the room to my bed and placed a gentle hand on my uninjured shoulder. "Don't try to get up", she warned, "you've only just started to fully awaken from the anesthesia, your body isn't ready for much movement yet."

"Where's my daughter?" Ignoring her, I refused to acknowledge just how sick I was feeling at that moment. "Is she here??"

"Ms. Pearson, those detectives are checking on it now. No one was with you when you were transported here, except the emergency technicians who brought you in. If your daughter was with you when this happened, they would have allowed her to ride along with you."

"What are you saying??" My heart began racing as she frowned down at me, looking almost as worried as I was becoming. Then, as if suddenly awakening, my memory began to slowly open its closed doors. As the doctor started her way around the bed to check the digital readouts that were offered by the machinery attached to my arm, I reached for her. "Wait—I don't think she was with me. I know I was at work when this happened and Brighton would have been at home with Anna—please, someone has to check on them!"

"Okay, okay, Ms. Pearson." Obviously trying to calm me down, she added, "The detectives who are waiting to talk to you are focusing on that now. I'm sure we will have word about your daughter soon. Now, I need to check your shoulder." Stepping closer to my right shoulder, she continued her original task of removing the corners of the gown I was dressed in. With a soft touch, she released the bandages that were fixed over my wound and began her examination wordlessly.

As she did this, my eyes never left the doorway of my room. Where are those detectives?? Why haven't they come in yet with information about Brighton. God, what time is it?? I should have been home hours ago and Anna and Brighton must be so worried!

Finally, one of the cops, the skinnier one, entered the room. Standing by the doorway, he awaited for Doctor Sway to finish her examination on me, only glanced in my direction briefly, as if he couldn't make eye contact. This only made me feel more anxious, as if he had something he needed to say, but didn't know how—or want to.

"Well??" I croaked, making him look at me.

Clearing his throat, Doctor Sway met his glance, and took her cue. With quick movements, she tied my gown again, punched a couple of buttons on the machine next to the bed, and gave me a small smile. "Everything looks good so far. You need to rest as much as possible tonight and tomorrow, we will see about sending you home as long as the surgical area remains free of infection and you are able to eat and drink without complication. I will send in a nurse with water but for now we need to wait a few hours before you can try eating. Right now, you are being administered Morphine through this tube", raising a small plastic tube that was attached by a needle in my arm to something unseen above and behind my head she explained, "and all you need to do is push this button when you need a small dose for the pain. After a couple of hours, I will have it removed and we will start you on Tylenol and see how your stomach takes to that. Any questions?"

Shaking my head at her, I didn't even thank her. The look on the cop's face had captured all of my attention and I refused to focus on anything else. Doctor Sway reminded me one more time of the emergency call button located on the side of the bed, requested that the detective stay for only a few minutes, and finally left the room.

"Well?!?" I demanded again.

Coming fully into the room, he remained quiet as he grabbed the back end of a worn-out looking armchair from the corner of the room opposite me and pulled it over to the side of the bed. I wanted to throttle him.

"Ms. Pearson, I am Detective Ian Sampson."

Like I care at this point what his name is!

"How long have you worked at Lucky's Girls?"

What?? What does that have to do with—shaking the argument from my thoughts before I could open my mouth, I took a deep breath. "Seven years, why?"

"As a dancer?"

"Yes!" Frustrated that he was giving me no information on my daughter, I glared at him.

"Did you have anything unusual happen tonight, before you left at 8:45?"

Unusual? *Unusual??* "Other than the fact sometime after I left I ended up with a bullet in my shoulder, no, nothing *unusual!*"

Giving me a look, the detective pulled a small notepad from the back pocket of his jeans and started to leaf through the first couple of pages. "What happened to cause you to leave your shift early tonight?"

Unable to hold his stare, his question caught me off guard and I had to think for a moment. "Um...some guy...a customer...had trouble keeping his hands to himself and I had him tossed. Where is my daughter??"

Ignoring my question, he continued as if I hadn't asked. "Did you get his name?"

"Mr. Grabby!!" Reaching a boiling point, I didn't care if he arrested me for being a smartass, all I was worried about was finding out where Brighton was. "Stop with the cloak and dagger shit, *Detective*, and tell me about my daughter!!"

Sighing, I watched as he ran a hand through his dark brown hair and for the first time, really saw him. Deep brown eyes carrying long lashes graced his strong face. He was tan, free from any facial hair, and looked to be in his thirties. His hair looked choppy, as if his last haircut had been done by a child, and the length of it ran along the collar of his button down shirt, giving him a boyish look—and, it was *almost* sexy when added to the obvious muscle structure that remain hidden underneath his pressed white shirt and blue jeans. Under other circumstances, I would have loved to dance for him; that is of course, if I really liked what I did for a living, which coincidently, I didn't.

"We sent a car to your listed address on file with your...um...*employer*." Glancing up at me, I suddenly wondered if he thought I was embarrassed by what I do. I wanted to explain that I wasn't—I didn't like it—but I wasn't embarrassed. "They went up to your apartment but no one was there."

"What—??" I was dumbfounded. "What do you mean, no one was there??"

Lips pursed, he stared back at me and I suddenly felt numb. No one was there? How is that possible?? Anna would never leave with Brighton, not without asking me first, unless—

Sensing where my thoughts were going, the detective continued drilling me with questions, interrupting my building panic. "Who do you have watch your daughter while you are at work?"

Unable to concentrate on his face, my eyes fell to my hands, searching them for answers. "Anna. She lives just down from me, but on the first floor." Then, suddenly, a thought! "Did they check at Anna's?? Maybe they are there!"

"They have talked to your neighbors, no has seen them. They are canvassing the rest of the building now, to see if anyone in your immediate area knows where they are and—"

"Ma???"

A soft voice coming from the doorway of my room cut off Detective Sampson. Turning quickly in his seat, I was able to catch a glimpse of my daughter. "Brighton!!" I yelled, not caring if the entire hospital heard me. Trying to get out of bed, I frantically fought with the tubes and needles in my arm, but was interrupted as the detective stopped me as gently as he could. Looking up at him, our eyes met and as my own filled with tears, I thought he was going to hug me or kiss me or something. Then as quickly as this feeling registered in my brain, it vanished as he let go of my hands and backed off with a warning. "Don't mess with those. You could end up hurting yourself."

"Ma!"

Interrupting our close encounter, my daughter bounded into the room and pushed the detective out of the way, catching him completely off guard and at first I thought he was going to yell at her, but he smiled instead. Reaching over, I grabbed my nine year old and pulled her thin body up and onto the bed with me, hugging her tightly to my chest. The pain in my shoulder swelled to new heights, but I didn't care. She was here, safe, and in my arms. That is all that mattered, I would dose up with Morphine later!

"Oh, God! I thought you were lost!! Are you ok??"

Gently, I pushed her small frame away from me so that I could search her face, which carried the biggest smile I think I have ever seen. Yes, she is ok, and I can breathe again.

"Amanda?"

Looking over Brighton's thin shoulder I saw Anna, my Godsend, bracing the entryway to the room with one hand. "Oh, God, Anna! Thank God you guys are alright!" Then, thinking further, I asked, "How did you guys get here??"

"Ginger...err, *Samantha* came to the apartment." Ginger was Samantha's stage name at the bar and my one close friend from work. "She said that you had been shot and were taken to the hospital. She's outside—wants to know if she can come in."

"Yes!" I said; laughing slightly only to have my happy thoughts cut off from the pain. "Yeah, Anna, she can come in." I said with a wince, still unwilling to let my daughter go. Anna quickly left the room and returned in a second, Samantha on her heels.

"Amanda! What the hell happened??" Concern covered her face, her usually perfect make-up looking a bit haphazard, as if she had run water over her face but failed to completely remove the eye shadow, mascara, and the deep red shade of lipstick she favored. "They said you had been shot!!"

"Um...I don't know." Shaking my head a bit, I admitted, "Everything is foggy."

"Well, at least you're alright!" Passing Detective Sampson as he made his way out of the room, cell phone to his ear, she stopped to give him a second glance before returning her attention to me. "Who is that??"

"A detective. He's here to ask me about what happened."

"Ooohhhh, do I have to take a bullet to get me one of those??" Her grin was insatiable and I couldn't help but smile as she winked at me. In her early thirties, Samantha was the absolute opposite of me. Her blond hair curled gently and was always in place around her thin face that held deep blue eyes and a gorgeous smile. Often referred to as 'Barbie', she lived up to the name through a strict diet, an intense work-out plan, and cosmetic surgery. And while many people in the business referred to her as "fake", her high maintenance lifestyle did not alter the fact that she was caring and compassionate; a true friend.

Clearing his throat, the detective had at some point reentered the room, and Samantha turned to give him another look, unabashed and simply shameless. Why is that my face reddened when I am not the one who made the comment?? Catching her gaze again, I shook my head at her, not wanting to say anything to egg her on; she'd probably end up getting date out of all this.

"Ms. Pearson, I really need to get some information from you." Detective Sampson stole a glance at Samantha before focusing on me and I suddenly felt like the odd one in the room. Giving Brighton another tight hug, I looked at her in the eye to make sure I had her attention. "Mommy has to talk to this gentleman right now. Can you go with Anna and Sam to get something to eat?"

Her round green eyes stared back at me, then over to Anna, who nodded and smiled at her as she held out her hand for Brighton to take. "It's ok, sweetie, let's go get some French fries or something, ok?" Saying nothing, Brighton relaxed her thin arms from around my chest, slid off the bed, and took Anna's hand. Then, looking at each of us, she gave us a soft, "bye", and left the room with her part-time caregiver. Samantha, looking for a more dramatic exit, sauntered past the detective and leaned to give me a kiss on the cheek. Whispering, she said, "Make sure he's gentle with you!" before straightening and turning around to leave the room. She looked as though she was walking a runway and I couldn't help but grin wide at her retreating back.

Surprisingly, the detective didn't give her a second glance, but instead pulled the chair he had been sitting in before my family reunion interrupted our interview closer to the side of the bed. Pulling out his ever-trusty notebook again, he sank into the chair and gave me a long look.

"Your daughter is..." Giving me a sideways glance, he looked as though he wasn't sure how to ask. I saved any uncertainty he was obviously feeling and finished the sentence for him. "Disabled.

"When she was four, we were in an awful accident. We were all injured pretty bad, but Brighton was sitting on the side of the car where we were hit and she had to have surgery. To make a long story short—she ended up with traumatic brain injury, despite the fact that she had been buckled up safely in the back seat. She struggles with speech and memory because of it and at times, her coordination is off."

"Oh." As if searching from something to say, he closed his mouth quickly and I tried to lighten the mood a bit. "But she's a great kid. We struggled a lot in the beginning, but she never let it stop her from learning everything she can. She loves to laugh and loves people. This whole thing has probably scared her to death, when she feels like that, she refuses to try to talk."

"And your husband...?"

Sounding like he was fishing, I gave him a questionable look and replied, "Decided that we were too much for him to handle. We left him before I he had a chance to leave us." Then, focusing on that statement longer than I should have, I added, "I'm sure his secretary was ecstatic over it all." Looking up at him, I realized that I had his full attention, and I suddenly felt flustered and out of place. "Sorry, I haven't thought about him for a while. It's just me and Brighton and I thank God for her every day."

Then, changing the subject, the detective shifted in his seat and opened the small notebook. "Let's go over what you remember from tonight, okay?"

"Yeah." I said, nodding slightly, shrugging inwardly. I should be used to people's reaction to Brighton by now...seemingly concerned in the beginning, until they know some of the details and then suddenly they are out of words, not knowing what to say to me. Despite the normal reaction I tend to get out of people who have just met her, he seemed to be bothered by the facts concerning my daughter and that, for some reason, bothered me. Pushing my thoughts aside, I gently shifted on the bed, giving him my full attention again. Now that I knew Brighton was safe, I was ready to pry the doors to my memory open, with a crowbar if necessary.

"Ok. So, you left work at about a quarter to nine. Did you leave out the front or the back of the building? Anyone escort you outside?"

Before I could answer, a loud mix of guitars and drums sounded off from the direction of his pants, and I almost choked on my spit. Heat rising in his cheeks, Detective Sampson leaned his body to the side and slid a thin phone out from his back pocket. Standing as he flipped it open and placed to his ear, he walked briskly out of the room, offering me a chance to checkout his backside. *Not bad*, I thought to myself, thinking swiftly of Sam's comments about the man.

As he reentered the room, I could tell something was wrong, and any further fantasizing I may have had about the detective was instantly given a cold shower. "What's wrong?" I asked, not sure if I could take anymore drama tonight.

"I'm sorry, Ms. Pearson. I am going to have to come back later. Something has come up."

"Everything okay?" I asked automatically despite the fact that whatever it was, it was none of my business.

"Umm...I'm not sure. They found something near the vicinity of where you were found."

"Something to do with what happened to me??" I leaned forward on the bed as my heart raced a bit faster. Watching him stuff his notebook and phone back into his jean pockets, I tried to catch his eye. "What did they find??"

Instead of answering, he hesitated before turning towards the doorway, and asked, "Do you remember seeing anything else in the parking lot? Another car perhaps? Or someone else??"

Starting to answer, I opened my mouth, feeling confused. "I...I...don't think so" and dropped my head to stare at my hands again. God, why can't I remember??? Looking up again, I wanted to add something more, but couldn't, as I suddenly found myself alone in the room. Leaning back again, I went to rub my throbbing shoulder, but caught myself quickly as my memory returned in the way of broken strands of dimly coherent thoughts.

The trunk of a car...

Blond hair....

An ugly scar....

What the hell????

Chapter Seven

Making his way out of Mercy General, Ian headed down the same corridors that had brought him in to see Amanda Pearson. Phone to his ear, he talked to his captain while searching the still frantically busy emergency room for his partner. Finding him leaning up against a vending machine near the rear of the large room, he finished his call and updated the detective, who was focusing on devouring a bag of Sour Cream and Onion potato chips.

"Hey, Frank, you talk to Captain Leary?"

"Yeah." Licking his thick fingers, Frank tossed the now empty bag into the nearest trash receptacle and followed Ian out the automatic double doors to the outside. "Got the information on the newest vic, you headed over there now?"

Ian sighed and ran his fingers through his hair. All he really wanted to do at that point was head home and crash. But, he knew that wouldn't be possible, not with what was waiting for them down by Lucky's Girls. Thinking of the bar, his thoughts turned to Amanda Pearson and he had to push them out of his head. Concentrating on her wasn't going to do him a bit of good and instead of lingering on that fact, he simply nodded at his partner. "Yeah, let's head over that way and see what they've got. Captain Leary said the crime scene unit was there now, they finished the parking lot about twenty minutes ago...didn't find much, though."

"Sounds good. There's a fast food joint on the way, I think. Gonna swing through the drive-thru and grab some dinner. You want anything?"

Immediately wanting to remind the detective that he had just polished off a large bag of chips, Ian thought better of it and just shook his head. Fast food was questionable, at best, and Ian would have to be absolutely *starving* before he would eat at any one of the joints around town. Trying to explain this point to Frank, however, would lead into a conversation that he had no energy for so he simply said his goodbyes to his partner, noted the location to where they were both needed at, and headed off towards the lot where his Ram was parked.

Once inside the truck, Ian pulled out of Doctor Halloway's parking spot and traveled in silence towards his next destination as thoughts of Ms. Pearson returned once again. Something about her just wouldn't let go; her vibrant red hair, sea green eyes, the obvious love and care she had for her disabled daughter...she held his attention the minute he had stepped into her room and despite how tired he was, he was having a hard time thinking about anything else.

Thoughts of her led to the scene that he was headed towards and he considered the fact that there may be some kind of connection. When he got the initial call from Captain Leary that was his first thought; his second being that if the two occurrences are connected, how did Amanda Pearson end up surviving?? Knowing his thoughts were turning back to the dancer again, he turned on the CD player and increased the volume considerably as Mick Jagger from the Rolling Stones complained in high-definition sound that he couldn't get any satisfaction.

"I know exactly how you feel, Mick." Ian muttered to himself as he drove away from the hospital and out into the dwindling traffic. Given the lateness of the hour, now going on two in the morning, the road was nearly empty, and he relaxed a bit in his seat.

Fifteen minutes later, he was pulling down a dark alleyway that eventually led to the parking lot that sat behind Lucky's Girls. Not seeing Frank's beat up Chevy sedan anywhere, he parked near the mouth of the alley and got out of the truck. Ahead of him, flashing red and blue lights lit up the narrow passageway and he noted at least three other police cruisers. Among them was the crime scene van, and as each vehicle he passed proved empty, he figured that everyone was located ahead of him, where the actual crime scene must be. Continuing to follow the sound of voices and the occasional white flash from a camera, he found the group halfway down from where everyone had parked.

Guys in crime scene attire were gathering evidence in small bags and plastic vials while uniformed police walked along the chain link fencing that ran the length of the alley on both the north and south sides. Trying to distinguish possible evidence from the pieces of broken concrete, scattered bits of gravel and rocks, empty food wrappers, busted liquor bottles and crushed beer cans, and used cigarette butts; every few minutes consisted of requests for more evidence bags and digital recording.

Amongst it all, was the body.

Obviously female, her body was laid out in the middle of the alley, arms across her bare chest and legs crossed at the ankles. She was completely nude, showed signs of trauma all over her thin body and judging from her face and height, must have been in her early twenties. Her long blond hair fanned out above her head, and from where Ian was standing, he could see that her eyes were closed. In all honesty, she looked peaceful, as if she were sleeping.

Nearing her final resting place, Ian knelt close to her body and began to mentally note the areas that he believed took the brunt of whatever it was that had killed her. Her wrists showed faded signs of ligature marks, like she had been tied up for some amount of time. On her ankles, the same marks were apparent, and Ian wondered just what hell the girl had been through before she breathed her final breath. As a crime scene technician gently lifted each hand and bagged them in plastic; in an effort to preserve any evidence under her fingernails; Ian counted at least four bullet holes that were scattered across her torso. She'd been shot several times and the lack of blood on her body suggested that the violent act may have occurred near or after death, or that she had been cleaned up before being dumped in the alley.

"Make sure to check for any bullet fragments or casings." Speaking to the tech that had finished bagging her hands and was now doing the same to her feet and ankles, Ian wanted to make sure nothing was overlooked. "Yes, Sir", was the guy's only reply.

"Hey, any ID?" Detective Colliatti finally joined the scene and Ian stood to go over what he had already suspected, including the fact that so far as he knew, no ID had been found that would offer them insight as to who this victim was. After discussing the marks on the girl's wrists and ankles and the wounds obviously caused by a gun, Colliatti muttered, "What a waste", and turned to speak to one of the other officers combing the area for evidence.

Taking a long look at the area that served as a probable dump site; the lack of blood around a body speaks volumes when it comes to considering this; Ian counted at least seven buildings whose back doors faced the alley. Even though there was fencing that ran along both sides of the alley, the backs of the buildings stood at least fifteen to twenty feet from the one side. The opposite side barred off desert plants, animals, anything else that may find its way across the dry wasteland south of them. Seeing no entry past the fence that would lead him to the actual buildings, Ian made a mental note to drive past the front parking lot in order to see what type of businesses these were. He knew this may not help make headway in solving the girl's death, but too much information is better than not enough.

Turning back to the scene of the crime, Ian noticed that the medical examiner had arrived and started in his direction. At fifty-something years old, the man stood tall and thin in his medical attire and was very in-tune with his job. After thirty years of working on bodies, he could smell foul play from a mile away and Ian was hoping that this scene would be no different for the man.

"Hey, Wilson." Ian extended his hand in greeting. The older man returned his offer with his own hand and gave him a grim look as the detective asked, "What do you think?"

"Well, I don't think she tied herself up, then shot herself four times in the chest."

Approaching the body, Wilson knelt down, careful not to disturb the immediate area around the young girl and Ian followed his lead. "Look here", the examiner started, "see these marks on the wrists and ankles? Similar markings and coloring on all four. She was obviously tied up for some time, but it's been a couple of days at least." Then, reaching out, he gently picked up one of the girls hands and, pointing to her wrist, added, "These wounds were starting to heal. See the discoloration?"

Nodding, Ian said nothing, silently encouraging Wilson to continue.

"The wounds to her chest seem more recent, but also look to be post mortem. The blood loss would be more evident if she were still alive when she was shot. Of course, we'll have a more accurate assessment after I get the girl back to the office, but right now, I'd guess she was tied up while still alive, endured whatever hell had come her way, then died, and *then* she was shot."

"Any sign of rape or other trauma?"

"Well, if it's all the same to you, I would prefer to perform that testing within closed quarters. Give the poor girl some dignity, you know?"

"Of course, Doctor. Thanks, you've been a great help already."

"Of course, you know me, Ian. I just hope you find the bastard that did this to her."

"Yea, doc, you and me both."

Standing, Ian left Wilson to continue with what work he needed to do before the body could be moved and went on a search to find his partner; last seen discussing something with one of the other uniforms on scene. Looking down one end of the alley, he didn't see him and as he turned to search down the other end, where everyone seemed to be using as a make-shift parking lot, he heard a hefty laugh coming from that direction. Knowing it was Frank's famous belly-laugh (the man sounded like Santa at Christmas time when he laughed) Ian headed off to find him, determined to let the remaining officers and the crime scene officials finish the processing procedures.

As he closed in on his partner's position, he could make out parts of the conversation occurring between Frank and another officer; who seemed to have nothing to do but stand around and bullshit each other. Overtired and frustrated as how his night had come to an end, Ian caught wind of what Frank was saying and stopped short before being seen.

"…a *stripper*, no less!!"

"Oh, man!!"

"Yeah, I tell ya', with that red hair o'hers…"

"Damn, Colliatti…"

"Oh, yeah, man! I'd like to fu—"

Blood boiling to the point of overheating in his veins, Ian dug his heels into the dirty floor of the alley and charged at his partner. Frank, caught completely off guard, had no time to defend himself as Ian's sudden attack pushed the big man up against the fence he was standing in front of, the links rattling as if an animal were trying to fight his way through.

"*SON-OF-A-BITCH!!*" Ian spat at Frank, pushing him harder against the chain link as his hands fisted around the zippered ends of the man's jacket.

"What—??" As his face turned a bright red, Frank tried pushing his partner off but to no avail. "GET THE *FUCK* OFF ME, SAMPSON!!"

Suddenly, Ian was being pulled backwards as a group of officers grabbed at his arms, trying to get him to release the detective. Relentless, Ian pulled against them, unwilling to let go of Frank's jacket. "You disrespecting *asshole*!!!"

"Oh yeah, Ian, like you weren't thinking the same thing!!!"

"She's a victim, Frank!! A fucking *victim*, you got no right—!!!"

Finally, enough men joined the mix and managed to pry Ian's fists off of his partner's clothing. Continuing to pull him backwards, Ian struggled, and then shoved them off. "Get off me!" Glancing at each officer quickly, he kept one eye on Frank to see if he was going to fight back. When he didn't, Ian took one more step towards the man and with hatred in his voice, declared himself done. Done at the scene. Done listening to his partner's shit day after day. Just…done.

Backing away completely, Ian shrugged off another hand or two belonging to his coworkers and turned to leave. Frank, now the bigger man of the two, continued to challenge him. "Yeah, walk away, Ian!! You know I'm right!! Yeah...we'll see won't we???"

Ignoring the taunting coming from Frank, Ian continued to walk back to his truck, flexing both fists in anger as he did. He knew Frank was an ass—but until now, had never heard him act like one so blatantly. And he meant what he said, he was done. Not caring that Frank only had a few months left until his official retirement, he was finished working with the man. Let them find someone else to put up with his shit—Ian had seen and heard enough.

Jumping into the truck, he gave the now thinning group one last look. He didn't have to stay and watch to know that Frank was now bullshitting his way into playing the victim of an inappropriate attack. Ian also knew that it wouldn't take long for his captain to catch wind of the event and demand that Ian present himself to his office immediately—with or without sleep. With that, Ian put the truck in reverse, spun the truck's tires as he pulled away from the mouth of the alley, and, instead of driving home, made a beeline back to the hospital. He was going to check on his victim, telling himself the whole way there that he was just being a good cop—and not acting like some infatuated, overgrown teenager, that couldn't get Amanda Pearson out of his head.

Chapter Eight

As the car's headlights flashed over the town limit sign, signaling that they were now leaving Red Rock, Lenny Nelson glanced over at his sleeping companion, David Orion. Leaning heavily on the passenger side window, it took a few moments for Lenny to realize that, yes, David was still sound asleep. Dumping their latest project in that alley had proven more exhausting then either of them had expected, and of course, David took the first shift devoid of driving so that he could sleep.

Glancing over at David again, Lenny sighed to himself and rubbed a heavy hand over his rough face, as he silently asked himself why he always had to let David call the shots. Friends since their junior year in high school, David was always the first to do anything; drink, get high, get laid...hell, he was even the first of the two to find himself expelled from school and ever since then has been the one to take charge, demand his ridiculous schemes be played out by Lenny alone, and was sure to continue to do so until the end of time.

Movement from the passenger seat caused Lenny to inhale sharply, as if David could hear his thoughts, and he waited for the tongue lashing to commence. Instead, the inside of the car remained quiet and Lenny stole another glance at David. His scar, running from the bottom of his left eye, crossing his cheekbone, and ending just above the man's jaw, twitched slightly as David muttered something in his sleep. Oh, and yeah, David was also the first of them to come so close to death that he could smell it. Not that Lenny was really jealous of *that* fact...but, come on, when's it gonna be his turn for a first??

Peering out over the steering wheel, Lenny tried to mentally change the subject as it continued to weigh on his mind but could see nothing past the headlights. While he was extremely comfortable with the area, looking out past the dim white lights produced by the car's headlamps he saw only darkness. Only occasionally did he pass the lights of an all-night gas station or fast food joint; the miles in between being home to only various cacti, huge boulders that led into the mountain ranges common in this area, and brown dirt—*lots* of brown dirt. Rain fall was scarce out here and the lack of humidity ensured that whatever small, single trees grew around here was almost as barren as the land itself.

Passing another green freeway sign marking the number of miles to the next town, Lenny glanced down at the fuel gauge and realized that they were getting close to the bottom of the tank. Looking over at David again, he quickly debated waking the man in order to update him on their whereabouts and the fact that they were going to have to stop again. Since leaving Tucson, they had stopped twice: once for food, and once to use a bathroom. Stopping was not supposed to be part of their agenda; once the deed was done in town, they were supposed to head right back to Queen Creek; a small, dried up town south of Phoenix.

"Dave", Lenny's voice came out as a squeak. "Hey...Dave."

Leaning over slightly, Lenny gently shook his friend's shoulder. David; the side of his head pushing up against the window; shrugged off Lenny's hand before opening his eyes for a second, trying to figure out where he was.

"We need gas." Lenny said simply.

"So, find somewhere to get some!" His reply rang loudly through the quiet car and out of habit, Lenny jumped slightly in the driver's seat. Then, as swiftly as his anger rose at being woke up, it dissipated, and David asked, "Where are we?"

"Just past Red Rock."

"God, you drive slow!"

"Well...you don't want a ticket do you??"

Staring hard at Lenny, who quickly regretted challenging David, he sneered at the younger, more fragile man, and said nothing. No, he didn't want to be pulled over, especially in this stolen piece of crap. "Just find something quick so we can get back on the road", he said through gritted teeth before leaning back into the passenger seat and closing his eyes again. "Don't wake me again until you do."

Letting his breath hiss swiftly through his thin lips, Lenny said a silent prayer of thanks that the verbal instructions were all he got in retaliation. *I'm so stupid*, he thought to himself and shook his head, *you'd think I'd have learned by now to just keep my comments to myself!*

Up ahead, Lenny noticed a barely lit service station and smoothly moved the car over to the right hand lane. The trucker, who had been behind him for the last few minutes, blew by the car and Lenny was surprised that the driver hadn't blown his horn at him as he passed. Even though he had known that the big rig had been traveling closely behind the car for at least five minutes, his refusal to move over one lane had not been done out of malice, rather it was a lack of paying attention—his concentration had been on Dave, not who was sharing the road with them.

A look in his rearview mirror told Lenny that they were once again alone on the interstate, but he signaled to exit anyway. On this long stretch of road, highway patrol was difficult to see at night, usually unnoticeable until you have already blown past a sitting patrol car and because of this, Lenny obeyed the laws of the road without question. Again, they didn't need to be pulled over.

The gas station, a broken down building offering four small gas islands, looked to be deserted, save the dimly lit entryway that lay underneath a concrete roof. Pulling up to one of the gas pumps, Lenny immediately noticed the outdated stature of the building; the digital age had definitely missed this place. The numerical readout on the pump was a rolling set of faded numbers and the chance to use a debit or credit card was not possible from here. Looking over to the right, he noted the aging look of the joint and questioned whether or not he should keep going to find a livelier looking place. Course, with this place, there is likely to be only one person manning the store—less of a chance of a problem with anyone occurring, no chance of being recognized by anyone, and the risk of any other form of trouble lessened greatly. With those thoughts,

Lenny opened the door to the stolen Capris they were driving in and set the gas pump up.

Hearing a door slam behind him, Lenny turned to see David exiting the car. Saying nothing to Lenny, he headed into the store as he eyed their surroundings. Lenny followed him, wanting to pick up a pack of cigarettes and something to drink.

Inside, the station looked as ancient as the outside. Three shelves of outdated grocery items and emergency road supplies filled the small room. In the back, two refrigerated sections with grimy glass covered doors stored cold drinks, pints of milk, and beer. Choosing a bottle of Pepsi from one of the coolers, Lenny immediately felt like he needed to wash his hands after touching the door handle and he rubbed them along the front of his black jeans as he made his way to the counter located at the front of the store.

Bearded with coarse, gray hair, the clerk looked as old as the establishment and he silently rang up Lenny's drink and cigarettes on a rusty looking metal cash register. Noting a small sign taped to the hard counter that screamed, *"CASH ONLY!!"* Lenny pulled a fifty out of his front pocket and requested the change be rung up for gas.

"Hey, pay for the paper too."

Turning, Lenny noticed David by the door of the store reading the front page of a newspaper. Not waiting for the Lenny to respond, David leaned his back against the glass door, pushed it open, and said, "Gotta go hit the head", as he went out. After paying for the paper and giving the silent clerk one last look, Lenny followed suit and filled the car with gas before getting back into the drivers' seat.

Opening the bottle of cold soda, he took a long drink out of it and briefly considered going back into the store and buying another one. With at least another hour and a half until they reached Queen Creek, he knew that he would want another one but also knew that if he made another stop, David would have his head on a platter.

Suddenly, the passenger side door was pulled open violently and Lenny jumped in his seat, choking on the liquid that he had been in the middle of swallowing. Looking over as tears filled his eyes and his throat reddened with pain, he looked over as David jumped into the front seat, tossing his cell phone onto the dash with enough force that it bounced off it and fell onto the floor of the car. "GO!!" he demanded as he slammed the door closed, not caring that his driver was now gasping to take a breath. "Dammit, Lenny, drive!!"

Starting the car, Lenny somehow managed to get his coughing fit under control and with a scratchy voice asked, "What's wrong??"

"Head back! Now!! Get this piece of shit car back on the highway and head back to Tucson!"

Confused, Lenny pulled away from the service station and made his way under the interstate overpass to find the onramp that would head them in the opposite direction. Once back on the road, he cleared his still-burning throat and asked David again what was going on. Ignoring him, David rocked back and forth in the passenger seat and began to rant.

"That girl!!!! That *fucking* girl!"

Lenny, wanting to interrupt David's little meltdown, held his tongue instead, knowing that it would get him nowhere. Over the past ten years, he has seen David behave this way only a few times, and it never ended pretty. Driving Lenny's thoughts home, David suddenly reached across the middle console and punched Lenny hard in the forearm. The sudden impact caused Lenny to swerve, rubber squealing as the front tires protested against the sudden force of it.

"Shit!! Dave—c'mon!! I'm trying to drive! What the hell, man??"

"Well driver faster, dammit! We need to get back now!"

"Why?!"

"Coz that girl...that *fucking* redheaded girl survived, Lenny!!"

"What girl??" Then, as the realization of who David was screaming about hit him harder than the punch to the arm he had just endured, Lenny whispered, "Oh, shit", and punched the gas pedal, uncaring if they ended up getting pulled over for speeding now or not.

Chapter Nine

Waking up to a throbbing pain that ran across my shoulder and down my right arm all the way to my fingertips, I awoke with tears building in my eyes. Shifting as carefully as I could on the bed, I tried to remember what I could about the night before but my thoughts were still foggy and out of reach. Trying to clear my head, I forced my body off of my left side and tried to sit up, only to discover that I wasn't the only person in the room. Sitting sideways in a chair, with his heavy looking hiking boots resting on the bottom corner of my bed, was the cop.

Detective...*Sampson*...right??

Confused as to when he had returned to my room—and why—I grabbed hold of the bed controls and slowly raised the top half of the bed until I came to a sitting position. At that moment, he shifted in the chair and woke up suddenly. Looking as lost as I felt, his eyes flew open and he glanced questionably around the room. Seeing me staring at him, his face relaxed, as if he now knew why he had found himself sleeping in a chair.

"Hi" he greeted me softly as he removed his feet from the bottom of the bed and sat up, wincing slightly. "Wow, they really need to do something about these sleeping accommodations."

Looking him sideways, I couldn't help but smile.

"How are you feeling?" His question seemed full of genuine concern and my confusion as to his presence here began to build rapidly.

"What are you doing here?" Ignoring his question, I asked one of my own, really wanting to know if he was here out of some sense of duty or something else. Not that I needed any sort of relationship at this point in my life, but I had to admit, the curiosity was now killing more than the pain in my shoulder.

"Oh...um," he started, at first refusing to look at me. Then, "I never got that interview last night. I really need to get some information from you." When he finally looked me in the eye, the intensity of his brown eyes made my cheeks redden a bit and I suddenly knew that he was lying through his teeth. Instead of raising the issue with the man, however, I nodded and said nothing. I was probably misreading him anyways.

"You mind if I use your bathroom before we get started?" Standing as he asked, I noticed that he was wearing the same blue jeans and white, button-down shirt that he had on last night. Not waiting for a response he stretched briefly and a wave of brown hair fell across his forehead and I had the sudden urge to reach up and sweep it back from his face.

God, what is wrong with me??

Peeling my eyes away from his face, I looked down at my hands and tried to refocus my thoughts as the detective made his way to the small bathroom located in the rear corner of the room. Not looking up until I heard the door close, I breathed heavily and silently chastised myself for feeling like a schoolgirl.

As the water turned on in the bathroom, a nurse dressed in light blue scrubs entered the room carrying a tray of food and a small plastic cup with medicine-looking capsules in it. Smiling at me, she placed the tray on a bedside table that was off to one side of the room and began the task of checking my vitals as she made small talk. "Sleep okay?"

"Yes."

"How's the pain this morning?"

"Throbbing, but I'm okay. When can I go home?"

Smiling again, she seemed to understand exactly how I was feeling, as if she had dealt with this sort of thing daily. "I want to check your bandages, okay? I am also going to remove the morphine tube and the I.V. The doctor has prescribed Tylenol for the pain and we'll see how well you can keep down some food. When she comes in, she is going to want to examine you again and then will decide whether or not you need to stay another night or if you can be released."

"I need to go home...I have a young daughter." I tried to explain this without sounding too much like a child. I even had to fight the urge to pout.

"Yes, I'm sure the doctor is aware of this, but your health is priority here."

Sighing, I sat forward in the bed so that the nurse could check my wound and at that moment the bathroom door swung open and the detective walked out. The nurse, obviously unaware that anyone else was in the room, jumped slightly at his sudden appearance and frowned at him. Detective Sampson gave her a look as well, as if silently challenging her. The whole scene was comical, and I couldn't help but smile as I watched him return to the chair he had slept in.

"Well, this looks pretty good." The nurse admitted as she replaced the old bandages with new ones. Once finished she brought the bedside table over and adjusted it so that the table could be moved to sit above my waist. "Try to eat something but if you feel like you can't keep it down, let me know right away." Glancing at her hospital badge that was clipped to the front pocket of her smock I noted her name as being "Abby Hollestead, RN" and thanked her. After washing down the two pain pills with a small paper cup filled with luke-warm water, she seemed satisfied and left the room; frowning again at the detective as she left.

"Don't think she likes me." He said with a grin.

"I don't think she knew you were in the bathroom. Probably thinks we were up to something." The statement was out of my mouth before I could stop it and my face reddened again as the detective gave me a curious look. His mouth curved upwards slightly, as if trying to hide a smile and I tried desperately to save face. "That's not what I meant...um...I didn't mean...*that*!"

"Well, let's get started."

Gasping slightly, I looked up at him and it was his turn to correct himself. "With the interview, I mean." "Of course", I replied immediately, nodding at him as our eyes met and held for a brief second. Feeling foolish, I was first to break eye contact and glanced down at my hands again, now half hidden by the mobile table that held my food.

"Eat." He said, causing me to look up at him again. "You should eat while that is still hot, believe me, hospital food is no good cold." Smiling at me again, he reached over and took the lid off the food container, revealing a small mound of questionable looking eggs, a half piece of toasted bread, and a small sealed cup of applesauce. "You sure it's any good when it's hot??" I asked him, smiling back.

"No", he admitted as he pushed the tray closer to my chest so that I wouldn't have to lean forward any further. "How's the shoulder feeling?"

"Like I've been shot." Jokingly, I looked up at him and his smile had faded. His piercing brown eyes stared back at me, and again, I was filled with confusion. Why was he really here?? Why did he feel the need to come back, sometime in the middle of the night, and sleep in that uncomfortable looking chair when he could have been home sleeping with whomever was waiting for him; a wife or girlfriend or even a dog perhaps??

As if sensing the questions as they invaded my mind, he cleared his throat and said, "Um...ok, let's start with what happened after you left the bar. Your employer said that you normally work until closing on Fridays nights, why did you leave early?"

Taking a small bite of eggs, I forced myself to swallow them instead of following my first instinct—spitting them right back out onto the plastic dish. "I had an issue with a customer and hurt my ankle. Frank, the night manager, let me go home after it happened."

Hearing the name Frank seemed to irritate the detective and before I could ask anything about it, the expression on his face disappeared quickly and the interview continued. "What kind of issue?"

"A guy I was dancing for tried to get me to sit on him and I twisted my ankle when I tried to get him to let go."

His eyes on the notes he was scribbling in his notebook, I noticed his jaw clench at my explanation but relax quickly as soon as he looked back up at me. "Did you get the guy's name? Have you ever seen him before?"

Shaking my head in response, the detective noted it before asking, "Ok, so then what, you got dressed to leave, correct? Which door did you leave out of, the front or the back? Did anyone escort you out? Or did you notice anyone else leaving the bar at the same time you did?"

Sighing, my memory was still foggy, and I shook my head. "No, I don't think so. I left out the back—which we are really not supposed to do, especially at night. But I was pissed off and my ankle was really sore. I just wanted to get out of there and get home to Brighton."

"How's it now?"

"What?" His question caused a break in my concentration.

"You're ankle. How is it feeling now? Did you have anyone here take a look at it?"

"Oh—no, the pain in my shoulder has kind of taken up residence over anything else. You could probably break one of my legs and I wouldn't even feel it."

"Well, I'm not about to do anything like *that* to your legs." Flushing a bit, I stole a look at him and my heart raced beneath my chest. Jesus, I need to get a grip! Or...get *something*! Moving on, as if not noticing how flustered he was making me feel, he continued asking questions.

"Was your car in the back parking lot?"

Thinking back now, I nodded, "Yea, it was. I always park back there, and again, we're not supposed to at night, but it's easier to get out of the parking lot from the back then from the front. Especially on the weekend nights, the front parking lot is usually full and it's a pain to get out of it at times. My car was parked over on the right side of the lot, almost directly behind the building."

"Any other vehicles there that you noticed?"

Again, I nodded and explained that there were just a couple of them, but now I couldn't remember what type they were or what they looked like. After that, my brain went muddy again and I sank back into the hospital bed, frustrated. "I can't remember anything else! Ugh...it's so frustrating! The next thing I remember is waking up here."

"Close your eyes."

"What—??" It wasn't until I looked up from my hands that I noticed him standing over me. Swiftly, he pulled the bed table away from the bed and turned back to look down at me. I had the sudden urge to pull him down to me, screaming shoulder or not. Having him sit on the edge of the bed, close to my thighs, did nothing to hinder that urge either. Steeling myself, I said nothing and eyed him carefully as I wondered just what he was going to do.

"Close your eyes. We will walk through this one step at a time and try to jog your memory."

"Okay", I said softly, and took one last long look at his handsome face before closing my eyes. Trying to control my breathing I focused on the last thing I remembered from the night before. An image of walking out the back door swiftly flew across my memory and I felt tension build behind my eyes as I tried to concentrate.

Remembering that the parking lot was dark once the back door slammed shut behind me, I tried to think about what I could see. Feeling my lips tighten, I felt like my head was going to explode. Shaking it slightly I was about to admit that his suggestion wasn't going to work when I suddenly felt his hands on the sides of my face. Starting to open my eyes in surprise, he said quietly, "Keep your eyes closed. Relax your body and breathe."

Yessir, officer, whatever you say!

The thought burst through all the others that I was having at that moment. As his fingers gently massaged my temples, I felt the tension quickly leave my head and my lips parted slightly at the sudden release of it all. "What do you see?" he asked, again in a soft tone.

"The parking lot."

"Where is your car?"

"Close. Maybe twenty feet away from where I am. But it's dark..."

"Yes, but you're okay, nothing is going to hurt you." Continuing to massage my temples, his fingers made circular motions and suddenly, his thumbs were on my chin, just under my lower lip. If I hadn't been in such a state of relaxation, I probably would have had to fight the desire to bite one of them. Instead, the movement of fingers as they worked along the bottom of my chin and across my jawbone and over my cheekbones was almost hypnotic.

"What are you doing now?"

"Walking to my car. But...I can't find my keys...they're somewhere in my bag, I think. I need to find them." Then the flood gates opened and, "another car is driving past me. I don't know why, but I'm scared. I can't find my keys!"

"It's okay, Amanda. Relax. Nothing is going to hurt you." Pressing slightly on my temples, his fingers shifted swiftly and he began to massage the area right around the lobes of my ears and I felt the tension leave my body once again. As if sensing it himself, he exhaled softly and continued, "Now what is happening? Where did the other car go?"

"To the back of the lot", I answered, unconsciously nodding my head at the same time. "I found my keys. And I'm getting in the car. I want to get out of here and go home." Hesitating, another image focused itself in my mind's eye and I gasped slightly. "But...I can't leave, I don't know why, but I want to hide in my car. Those guys are fighting...something is in their trunk...I...I don't know what it is!"

"Amanda", he said, tension now building in his own voice, "Calm down, just tell me what you see. Remember that no one can hurt you. I am here with you and no one can hurt you—"

"Oh, God, someone is outside my car! I know it's them, those two guys that were in the back of the lot...I can see a gun...he's gonna break the glass!" Now shouting, I have no more control over my voice and my breathing speeds up as my heart pounds against my chest. Then, "He broke the glass!! My hair...he's gonna get me—HE'S GOT MY HAIR!!!"

Suddenly, my eyes flew open and I was in Detective Sampson's strong arms as my own hands flew to the back of my head, as if feeling the pain of being dragged out of my car by my hair all over again. The feeling of relaxation now gone, my body shook as the tears rolled freely down my face. At that point, I didn't want to remember anything else. I didn't care if whoever shot me was out there, shooting or killing other women, I just knew I couldn't do this again.

"Hey...hey, it's ok." Trying to calm me, the detective didn't move as I crumbled against his chest. Stroking the back of my hair, he muttered more to himself than to me, "That's why they found glass in your hair when you were brought in."

"Excuse me?! What is going on here??"

Letting me go, Detective Sampson turned to look over his shoulder only to see Nurse Hollestead standing in the doorway of my room. Ignoring her, he looked back at me and asked, "You okay now?" Nodding at him, my eyes dried up as the rest of my body calmed down a bit. Sniffling, I suddenly felt a bit embarrassed and felt sure that he felt the same as he stood up from the side of the bed and headed towards the bathroom. Looking at the nurse, I noted her frown but explained nothing to her—it was none of her business—whatever the hell *it* was, that is. My emotions felt raw and I didn't know if what had just happened did so because he wanted to be that close to me, or if he was just trying to be a good detective and help me to remember whatever I could. Whichever it was, I wasn't going to forget the feel of his hands on my face or the strength in his arms as he held me for quite some time. The nurse can frown all she wants—she couldn't take that from me.

Moving over to the bed, she explained in a stiff voice that she had overheard my yelling a few moments ago and wanted to check to make sure that I was okay. Giving the closed bathroom door a scoff, she looked at me, waiting for an answer.

"I'm fine. It was nothing...I'm sorry if I disturbed anyone else."

As if wanting to say more, she chewed on the inside of her cheek briefly. Deciding to let it go, she sighed heavily and explained that my doctor would be in to see me in a few minutes. "Please let the detective know that Doctor Sway will need to speak to him as well."

"Oh, okay." The question rose in my voice, but Nurse Hollestead gave me no explanation as to why my doctor would want to speak to Detective Sampson. Instead, she turned on her heel and stalked from the room, as if still pissed to find me in the middle of an embrace instead of lying back on the bed, resting my tormented body.

As if on cue, Detective Sampson opened the bathroom door as soon as the nurse's thick white soles squeaked out of the room. "Wow...I *know* she doesn't like me." Before I could offer any comment on that obvious fact, Doctor Sway entered the room, her blond hair gathered up in a ponytail bouncing lightly. Offering the detective a small smile she walked over to me and asked how I was feeling.

"Fine, I'm okay, really. Just ready to get home."

His cell phone interrupting us, Detective Sampson quickly pulled it out of his pocket and left the room. Turning back to me the doctor asked, "How are the pain meds working? I see you haven't eaten much." Eyeing the small mobile table that was sitting off to the side, she looked at me questionably.

"I just wasn't all that hungry. But the meds are working pretty well; not feeling too much pain."

"Good. Let me check your bandages."

Sitting forward a bit, the doctor removed the wrappings from my shoulder and examined my wound as I kept both eyes on the doorway to the room, wondering if Detective Sampson was planning on returning or not. "Well, this looks good. I'd say we'll have you out of here in about an hour. I am going to write up some pain medication for you to take and also a script to ensure that no infection builds up. You will need to have your regular doctor check your wound in about a week, but if anything changes make sure you come back here. You want to watch for any redness around the wound and if any bleeding occurs, do not hesitate, get back here quickly. Your sutures are dissolvable, so you are not going to have to have them removed, but your doctor will need to do a follow-up. Understood?"

Her blue eyes held mine steadily, as if to ensure I knew the importance of following her instructions. I nodded, just thankful that I wasn't going to have to spend another night here. I really want to be home with Brighton tonight.

"Ok, I am going to go write up your scripts and get going on your release paperwork. Do you have someone to drive you home?"

"Yes, she does."

Until that moment, neither Doctor Sway nor I had realized that Detective Sampson had reentered the room. Looking over at him, the doctor's lips pressed into a firm line and I thought she was going to argue with him. Looking between the both of them, I wanted it known that I was not a child—I am perfectly capable of finding myself a way home. Since my car was still in the parking lot of Lucky's (at least I think it still is!) I could call Samantha to come pick me up and drop me off there. Starting to open my mouth, I shut it quickly as the look on the detective's face clearly challenged the doctor's frown.

"Remember my instructions, Amanda. Take care of the wound, and of yourself."

That said, the doctor secured my bandages and left the room. Alone again, I watched Detective Sampson sink back into the chair he had spent the night in and noticed just how tired he seemed to be. "You don't have to take me home; I can call someone to pick me up and take me to my car."

"Your car's been impounded for evidence. And I don't mind—I'm off today."

"Oh", sinking against the bed, I realized that I was running out of options. Then his statement about being off today sunk in. "You're off today? Really? Then why did you sleep in that chair last night instead of going home after finishing whatever it is you detectives do on the job?" I challenged, teasing him a bit, but very curious as to what his answer would be.

"I, uh, just wanted to check on you, that's all."

"Look, Detective Samp—"

"Ian."

"Huh??"

"My name is Ian—Ian Sampson—you can call me Ian."

"Ok...*Ian*. I'm not sure if you offer all your victims a ride home from the hospital, but—"

"Nope, just you."

The look on his face shut me up immediately and as my heart fluttered against my chest; I knew that there was nothing I could say to make him change his mind. And I suddenly didn't want him to. A young, handsome—no, *sexy*—detective is *wanting* to take me home and I'll be damned if I am going to get in his way. Even if this goes nowhere; if his intentions are purely innocent and he is just trying to be a decent human being; I can relish in the fact that this man may possibly be interested in me...interested, despite the fact that he is under no influence of alcohol, is not under the effect of how differently I look under the florescent lighting of the bar, and has yet to see me dancing in the middle of a stage, half naked...stress the word...*yet*...

Chapter Ten

Almost two hours later, I was being helped up into Ian's Dodge Ram truck, prescription paperwork and extra gauze and medical tape packaged into a large bag in my hands, thanks to the generosity of Doctor Sway. My clothes, scrubs donated by one of the nurses who had looked in on me through the night, hung loosely around my waist and despite their uncomfortably large fit, I was thankful that the top had some give due to the pain in my shoulder. The Tylenol helped immensely however, it was no match for the morphine—which I would have given my whole arm for a truckload of if the hospital would have been ever so giving.

Watching Detect—err, Ian—hurry around the front of the pickup and climb into the driver's seat, reminded me of a kid on his first date and the thought of this colored my cheeks heavily. Still confused as to his true intentions, I thought better of asking and decided to just be thankful for the ride. Not that I wouldn't have called Sam for a lift, but Ian's truck was much more comfortable than her small, red Fiat Spider, and I knew that I was not up to enduring the game of twenty-questions that she is famous for when it comes to her being left in the dark about anything.

"You okay? Comfortable?" Ian glanced at me as he started the truck.

"Yes, very, thanks again for the ride."

"My pleasure."

His smile played on his lips and I was again tempted to question him about why he was really here. Playing the cat-and-mouse or catch-me-if-you-can types of games that many people play when they are attracted to each other (but are not ready to really do anything more about it) are not concepts that I am familiar with. I am more of a straight arrow when it comes to relationships— not that I have been in many, mind you—but I'd rather hear it straight from the horse's mouth instead of teasing and tempting back and forth.

But, in fear that I was reading his signals completely wrong, I held fast, not wanting to end up embarrassing myself to no end. So, instead of risking such an event, I watched the desert landscape pass by looking out the passenger side window as we drove through the hospital grounds, anxious to get home to see Brighton. After calling Anna, to let her know that I was coming home and that I had a ride, I was feeling better but still couldn't wait to get there.

"Where do you go to fill prescriptions?" Ian asked, interrupting my thoughts.

"Oh...um...I'll get those filled later." Not looking at him for fear that he will see right through my lie, I kept my eyes on the parked cars we were moving steadily past.

"Nonsense." His intense reply made me really want to turn to look at him, but I refused. "Amanda, you need those filled. Where do we need to go to fill them? A Walgreens? A CVS? Where??"

Sighing, I knew that he wasn't going to let it drop. "Nowhere, okay?" Now, having to look at him, the embarrassing feeling that I was afraid was going to occur was now creeping up quickly, before I even had the chance to stifle it. "I don't have any insurance. And the only money that I made yesterday has to go towards other things."

Suddenly, Ian pulled the truck over to the side, blocking a parked car to our right; not caring that the driver of that car had been a few seconds away from pulling out of the parking space. Honking his horn, I eyed the angry driver before returning my attention back to Ian. "You gonna move and let this guy out or what?" Anger building faster than I expected, I justified it by reminding myself that my money and my insurance problems were none of his business.

"Yes...as soon as you explain to me why you cannot fill these prescriptions. What's your money going for, Amanda??"

Ignoring him, I turned my eyes back towards the driver that we were still blocking and smirked as he gave us the finger. Then, in a fit of anger, the guy put his car in reverse and peeled backwards out of the space and I quickly wondered if he had even looked in his review mirror to see if there was anything parked in the space directly behind him.

"Amanda!"

"What, Ian??" I nearly shouted at him and his raised eyebrows caused me to put my temper in check. Sighing, I shook my head and bit my lower lip before explaining. "Look, the money I have has to go towards getting food. And Brighton needs a new pair of shoes on top of that. Last night sucked for tips and because I left early and ended up in the hospital overnight, I couldn't work this afternoon to try to make it up. I don't have the money to pay for any prescriptions. I will just deal with it, okay??"

Saying nothing in return, his brown eyes pierced my green ones and I waited for him to challenge me. When he didn't, I said in a calmer voice, "I appreciate your concern, Ian, really. But this is my problem. Lucky doesn't offer health insurance and I can't afford to get it on my own. It's nothing new, and something that I'm used to dealing   with."

"What about Brighton?" He asked, his eyes softening but never leaving my own.

"She is insured through the state. She gets all the care she needs and that is what is most important. I have some samples of Tylenol that the doctor gave me; I will be fine, I promise. Now, can we please go before you piss off another driver and they decide to take it out on your truck? I really don't want to spend another night here."

Shaking his head at me, he tried desperately to hide his smile and I knew that I had won that argument. I had no clue as to why he felt the need to argue with me when he hasn't even known me for twenty-four hours. All I did know was that the next couple of days were going to be very painful without any real pain medication, but I will get through it. When it comes down to buying milk and bread or prescription pain meds, I will always choose the milk and bread. It's the way it has always been during times like these and it will continue to be that way until the end of time.

"So, you want to tell me where I am going?"

"Oh—yea, I guess you need that information, huh??"

Tension gone, Ian seemed more relaxed as I gave him directions on how to find my apartment, which was only about twenty minutes away from the hospital. Heading past the dry, brown surroundings that this part of Arizona is famous for, I suddenly had a desire to see something greener. Maybe, if and when I can get back on my feet, Brighton and I could take a trip to someplace green. Somewhere we can see the ocean and real trees. Thinking on that for a moment, I smiled to myself and wondered just what kind of reaction she would have at having soft beach sand pressed under her toes as blue ocean water foamed around her feet.

"What are you thinking?" Ian, noticing my smile, gave me a curious look. "You don't look like someone who has just lived through a gun battle."

Laughing slightly, I winced as a sharp needle of pain spread across my shoulder blade but ignored it as best I could. Hoping Ian hadn't noticed, I said, "Just wondering what it would be like to go see the ocean. Brighton and I have never been out of Arizona and a vacation sounds really good right about now."

"Have you lived here your whole life?"

Nodding at him, I told him to turn left at the next corner before returning to our conversation. "I've always wanted to see the ocean, and I don't care if it's the Pacific or the Atlantic. I would love to see Brighton's face as she took it all in and be able to build sandcastles with her! I could also go for a little greenery too..." My thoughts drifted off a bit but I managed to focus again as the familiar signs of our small neighborhood came into view.

The convenience store on one corner boasted the cheapest, and best, coffee in town while a Burger King across from it claimed to serve homemade French fries. Heading down past the next block, the houses were small and unkempt. Littered yards filled with children's toys, broken down vehicles, and overgrown weeds led the way to the small apartment complex Brighton and I called home. With less than twenty apartments in all, the two story structure faced the street and included an eight foot electronic fence that encased the perimeter. On the other side of the building, there was a small playground with three swings, a metal slide that couldn't be touched during the summer for fear of it burning the skin, and a small, five-foot deep swimming pool that was never free from debris. Despite the look on the outside, I tried my hardest to make if feel like home on the inside, for Brighton's sake.

Giving Ian the code that would unlock the gate and allow us to pass, I directed him to the area of the complex that I lived in and he pulled into an empty spot. Turning to thank him once again for bringing me home, I stopped short when he turned off the truck.

"Which apartment is yours?" He asked peering out through the windshield.

"Really, you've done enough; you don't have to walk me up."

"I want to." He said simply. "It will give me a chance to say hi to your daughter and make sure that you both have everything you need for tonight."

Sinking back into the leather seat, I went to open the passenger door and then stopped; knowing that now was as best a time as any put an end to his chivalry. Knowing that I was probably going to be greatly disappointed; I didn't believe that there was a 'Mr. Right' out there for me and I figured that I needed to face that fact now more than ever. Looking over at Ian, I realized that he was watching me carefully, as if wondering if I was going to get out of the truck or continue to sit there in silence.

"Look, Ian—err, Detective Sampson," *yea, use his official title—that'll starve off any rejection!* "I know that you are doing all of this out of kindness, and I really do appreciate it, but I'm fine. I will be fine. Thank you."

Getting that out as quickly as I could, I bounded out of the truck swiftly, not giving him the chance to respond. It wasn't until I rounded the front that I realized he had gotten out of the driver's seat and was coming around at the same time to face me. Probably wants to set me straight before heading off to his next case.

Refusing to look him in the eye, I fumbled with the package that held my medical supplies when the sides of my face were suddenly in his hands, yet again. Gently forcing me to look up, he brushed aside the locks of red hair that surrounded my cheeks and I gasped slightly at the familiar look of desire as it spread across his unshaven face; a look that I have seen in so many different men's eyes in my seven years of dancing; and then, his mouth suddenly grazed mine.

At first hesitant, as if unsure of my reaction...or of himself, for that matter... his lips barely pressed against mine. Then, the kiss intensified and as my mind warned against it, my body said something else. Opening my mouth, I accepted his fully and he groaned slightly in return, the vibration of it causing heat to rise up from my belly. He tasted warm, but sweet, like honey dipped in coffee and it was all I could do not to quiver. Feeling his fingers leave the side of my face, his left arm circled around my waist and he pulled me closer so that my body pressed against his. The thin fabric of the scrubs did nothing to protect me from his hardened chest and I felt them rub and move easily against his clothing, which in turn made me ache. Then, as suddenly as it had started, it was over, and he pulled away slightly only to come in for one more, close-mouthed, seal of a kiss.

I felt dizzy, out of control and out of breath. As we parted, he held my face in both hands again and gave me an intense brown-eyed look as he tucked my red hair behind my ears. "Does that answer all of your questions as to what my intentions are, Amanda?"

The sound of my name as it rolled affectionately out of his mouth made my knees weak and at first I couldn't do or say anything...just stood there staring back into his eyes as I held onto his arms for support. Finally, I whispered, "Yes", and before my head spun more out of control over the whole thing, he backed up, took the bag of supplies out of my hands, and stepped aside; offering for me to take the lead up to my apartment.

Surprised that I was able to stand after that kiss, I stumbled over the curb and Ian reached out instinctively and placed a strong hand on my side. "Careful", he warned, seeming to be more worried about me falling and further injuring my shoulder than anything else. "Hmmm…" was all I could muster in reply.

The entrances to the apartments were all located on the other side, facing the pool and the playground, and as I rounded the back corner of the building, I ran smack dab into Anna. Surprise and pain spread across my face and before I could even think of asking her what the heck she was doing out here, I heard a small voice coming from behind her. Brighton, looking scared and confused, looked up at me and recognized me immediately.

"Ma!" Her small voice filled my heart instantly and it felt like I hadn't seen her in a month. Letting go of Anna's hand, she jumped into my arms as I knelt down to hug her and I ignored the screaming pain in my shoulder. Glancing up an Anna, I started to raise my concern at having Brighton out here, the both of them alone, but stopped as a look of dread spread across her face. Standing immediately, I asked, "What's wrong??"

"Amanda…" breathing heavily, I must have startled her as much as she had scared me and she placed a small hand over her forehead, pushing back her thin black bangs as she did. "Your apartment…God! Someone broke into your apartment!"

"What?? When??"

Not waiting for an explanation, Ian suddenly sprang into action. "Stay here", was his only demand and while I hugged Brighton against me tightly, I watched him dart around the three of us and head towards the stairs. "What apartment?" He called from over his shoulder and I answered, "17—second floor!"

Taking the metal stairs two at a time, he reached the top railing in seconds. Stepping cautiously onto the concrete walkway that ran along the length of the building I held my breath as he reached behind his body and pulled a gun out of the waist of his jeans. As we watched him close in on my apartment door, Anna stepped closer to me, placing a hand on the middle of my back.

Whispering, I asked her if she had seen anyone coming or going from my apartment.

"No", she whispered back. "I had Brighton over at my place last night and hadn't been to yours until a few minutes ago. We were going to clean up and get your bed ready for you so that you could lie down and rest once you got here. But as soon as we got to your door, I knew something was wrong. It was open a crack, Amanda. Whoever broke in left the door open when they were done.

"I saw the door and brought Brighton back downstairs. We didn't go in. I was too scared that whoever broke in was still in there." Before she could continue, I tensed as Ian came out from inside the apartment, cell phone to his ear as he requested that someone get over here quickly. Looking at Anna, I told her to stay here with Brighton and I left the two of them to head upstairs. Reaching the top landing, Ian put out a hand to stop me, but I pushed it aside, wanting to see the damage for myself. Frowning at me, I told him I wouldn't touch anything as his attention turned back to whomever he was talking to on the phone.

The door was wide open and I stepped over the threshold carefully. The place, usually clean and in order, was ransacked. The small kitchen that was just to the right of the front door was trashed. Food from the refrigerator had been pulled out and tossed everywhere. The cupboards, swung open, were nearly empty as their contents had been strewn all over the floor; broken pieces of my dishes and drinking cups were everywhere and crunched in protest underneath my shoes.

Turning my shocked face away from the kitchen, I spun around slowly to check the living room, which was only large enough to host a small loveseat, two small wooden end tables, and an old television set that barely worked. These things...*our* things...were just as trashed as the kitchen. The television had been pulled off of the table it usually sat upon and looked as though someone had kicked a soccer ball through the middle of it. The end tables were on their sides, their legs having been broken off and tossed across the room and the couch looked as though it had lost a fight with a lawnmower or a pair of shears or something. Covered in long tears, the stuffing that made up the inside of it had been pulled out through the cuts in the fabric and covered everything in sight.

Feeling as though I was going to be sick, I hunched over slightly as tears built up in my eyes when a hand suddenly squeezed my good shoulder. Standing up straight automatically, I cried out in surprise. Turning quickly, I took a deep breath as Ian quickly released my shoulder and took a step back. "Shit, Ian! You scared me!"

"Sorry!" He exclaimed, grabbing my hand and holding it tightly. "C'mon, you can't be in here. There are some guys from vice on their way here now."

"I want to see my bedroom," I said, shaking my head at him and added, "and Brighton's room."

"Amanda..." he started, but stopped when catching my eye.

Walking around him, I lead the way to my daughter's room and immediately wished that I had listened to Ian. The room was just as trashed as the rest of the apartment, her bedding suffering the same cuts and tears as the couch and every piece of clothing from her dresser and closet were pulled out, cut and torn, and strewn all over the room. The pink and purple flower wall hangings that I had bought to brighten her room were torn from the walls. Her small bookcase was upturned, her favorite books missing their covers and pages.

Anger steamrolled over my feeling of helplessness and hot tears flowed freely down my cheeks. Turning away from her room, I figured that I may as well see mine, thinking that it couldn't be any worse than the rest of the place.

But I was wrong...my room had taken the brunt of the assault. My bed, a twin, was pulled apart, the mattress leaning off the box spring haphazardly and cut up beyond recognition. Everything I owned in the room was either trashed beyond repair, or covered in some kind of wet substance...at that point I didn't even want to think about what that could be, but a strong stench of urine assured my unwanted thoughts. My clothes, like Brighton's, were flung and torn, but also included black smudges on the lot of them and as the smell of burnt fabric mixed in with the urine smell, I knew instantly that my clothes had been set on fire and left to burn.

Covering my mouth with my hand, Ian tried to pull me out of the room, but I held fast as my gaze fell upon the intruder's final message; left solely for my benefit. On the wall, above where my bed had been originally positioned was a single sentence, scrawled out in something red and sticky-looking. As the meaning behind it clarified itself in my scrambling mind, I felt Ian's body tense behind mine as he too read:

Next time I won't miss!

I didn't need to see his face to know that he was more than angry....he was *pissed*. The message also did something else...it opened a floodgate of memories that I had been trying unsuccessfully to unlock. And as the images of what had actually happened to me in between the time that I had been drug out of my car by my hair and when I awoke to find myself in the hospital, my strength seeped out of my body and I was engulfed in darkness; the message on my wall instantly burning its place in my mind's eye before going completely black.

Chapter Eleven

"What the hell are you doing here, Sampson??"

Captain Leary eyed the detective and waited for an answer while a team of investigators, including those from the crime scene unit, entered Amanda Pearson's apartment. Ian, watching the show from the sidelines, felt his anger soar as Detective Colliatti swept past the two men, a sneer etched across his thick face. "What the hell is *he* doing here, Captain??"

"This is his case, Ian." The captain, a veteran of the force with almost thirty-five years under his belt, stared back at his detective, waiting for him to challenge his directive. When he didn't, Captain Leary added, "*You* left me no choice, after pulling your little stunt last night in the alley and disappearing until this morning. When I called you this morning, I thought you understood that your suspension was effective immediately."

Shaking his head in fury, Ian opened his mouth to respond, then chose to close it. He needed to get his temper under control and his thoughts in order. If he didn't he was likely to move past the week suspension he had been handed down for pulling his little "stunt" and lose his job completely instead. Leaning heavily against the wall adjourning the row of apartments on the second floor, Ian sighed and ran his hand through his disheveled hair.

"Look, go get something to eat. Go get drunk. Go get laid. I don't care. But get the hell out of here and don't think about returning to work until you hear from me, you got it??"

Ian, as if seeing at his captain for the first time since he had arrived on the scene, tried to refute. "Captain, Colliatti is an *ass*. He shouldn't be here, on this case. And he wouldn't be if you had heard the things he was saying about Aman—the victim."

Stepping closer to Ian, the captain's anger rose to a higher level. "And if you would have brought your issues concerning your partner to me instead of trying to resolve them in the a middle of a crime scene", pausing as he stopped Ian from walking away by placing his two hands on the man's chest and pushing him back towards the wall, he continued through clenched teeth, "with six other officers as witnesses...you would be in there running the case instead of him. I know Colliatti is a piece of shit. But he's a good cop and he's nearing retirement."

Shoving the captain off, Ian stalked away—not caring whatsoever about his job at this point. Reaching the stairs that would lead him to the first floor of apartments, he made himself stop and look back at Captain Leary, who shouted, "Stay off this case, Sampson! And stay away from the victim!"

Yeah, like that's gonna happen! He thought angrily as he moved quickly down the stairs and headed to the left, where Anna's apartment was located. Her front door closed, he knocked hard against the thin wood of the door as he tried to get his breathing back under control. A medic, one of the ones who had been brought in to check on Amanda, answered the door and stepped aside when seeing Ian standing on top of the threshold.

"How is she?" He asked, not giving the medic any other type of greeting.

"Good. She's awake, in that back room there."

Following the medic's gesture that pointed him down a small hallway, Ian found Anna and Brighton kneeling on one side of a small bed, Amanda, lying on top of it, was holding her daughter's hands in her own. Seeing Ian in the doorway, Anna immediately stood, flushed, and walked past him as she left the room. Brighton, watching Ian with wide eyes, inched closer to her mother, as if unsure of who this man was or why he was here.

God, what have I gotten myself into?? Ian wondered briefly; then, looking into Amanda's tear stained face, he had his answer. Looking back at Brighton, he asked gently, "Hey kiddo, can I come in?" The young girl, silent and wary, looked back at her mother who gave her a small smile, and then she nodded slowly at Ian. "Thanks."

Not wanting to scare Brighton before he even got a chance to get to know her, Ian stepped slowly into the room and, seeing a small, straight back chair in one corner, walked over to it and sat down. "How are you feeling?" His question was directed at Amanda, but it was Brighton he was watching carefully. Still unclear as to the extent of her disability, he did not want to do anything to upset the girl, whose long red hair and green eyes matched her mother's perfectly.

Rolling onto her back, Amanda peered up at the ceiling and Ian had to fight the urge to crawl into bed with her and hold her. Looking over at her daughter, Amanda asked her if she was hungry. Hesitant, Brighton gave a short nod in answer and Ian listened as Amanda told her to go out to Anna and ask her for something to eat. Curious, due to the fact that the he has yet to hear any other word out of the little girl's mouth aside from "Ma" and "Bye", he watched the interaction between mother and daughter with extreme interest.

Nodding at Amanda, Brighton leaned over and, obviously wanting a kiss, steadied her small head just below her mother's chin. Raising her stiff neck and shoulders up off of the pillow she had been laying on, Amanda squeezed her eyes closed, as if trying to shut out the obvious pain she was feeling, and gently kissed Brighton's crown. Satisfied, Brighton looked up and gave her mother a wide smile, and then stood up from the bed. Looking over at Ian, her smile didn't falter, instead it grew a bit in his opinion and he felt his heart swell with pride, a feeling that took him off guard.

Once her daughter was out of the room, and out of earshot, Amanda could no longer hold in her tears. Shuddering, she turned away from Ian and covered her face with her hands and sobbed into them. Ian, reacting immediately, left the opposite corner of the room and approached her by walking to the side of the bed that she was now facing and kneeling down in front of her. Wrapping one arm around her thin waist, the other went to the top of her head and his fingers gently caressed her long hair as they pushed the thick, wavy strands of red away from her eyes.

"Ssshhh...it's okay, Amanda." Trying to console her, he suddenly felt out of place. Never in is life had he ever felt this way about a woman. Oh sure, he'd had his fair share of relationships, but they always sizzled out...as if once the fun stopped, the sex had been had, and things looked to be turning a bit more serious, either the woman or himself found the need to walk away. The story of his life, his parents often joked that he would have been better off joining the priesthood—priests don't marry and have children, whereas cops are almost expected to.

"No—it's not the apartment—it's not that—"

Hiccupping as her sobs slowed, Amanda remain hidden behind her hands. Ian, wanting to see her face, gently coaxed her to move her hands away. Waiting for her to continue on her own terms, he just knelt there and slowly wiped the tears from her cheeks.

"I remember."

Cocking his head to the side a bit, he asked, "Remember what?"

"What actually happened last night...before I was shot."

Tensing a bit, this is exactly what he was hoping for, just not under these circumstances. His cop mode kicking in, he quickly reminded himself that he was on suspension for the rest of the week and he stopped her from saying anything else. Explaining, he said, "I need to get one of the other officers in here to talk to you then."

Seeing him start to stand, Amanda reached out quickly and stopped him. Her hand on his forearm left a heated impression that ran swiftly across his body and for a moment he froze, not wanting to the desire he was now feeling tampered with. But, duty calls. And if he were to remain here any longer, he knew he was going to cross a line that he had no business crossing. Forcing himself to stand and step out of her grasp, he said, "You can't talk to me about this. I've been taken off the case. I need to get someone else in here so that this remains by the book."

"What?" Amanda tried to rise from the bed, but quickly thought better of it. "Why aren't you working my case anymore?? Because of me?"

"No", he lied. "I just....I fuc---err, messed up last night and am on suspension. I lied earlier when I said I have the day off...I actually have the whole week off."

Raising her eyebrows at him, Ian knew that he couldn't lie if she demanded to know exactly what happened to cause his suspension. Clamping his mouth shut, he turned suddenly from the room in search of someone to take Amanda's statement—someone other than Colliatti, that is. Suspension or no suspension, he would NOT allow his EX-partner near her. He'd go to jail before he'd allow that to happen.

Stepping out of Anna's apartment, he found just the person he was thinking of. Detective Marie Gonzalez was just coming down the stairs from the second floor and he caught her eye. Silently nodding his head at her, she understood the signal and walked towards him. Leading her by the elbow, Ian noticed a small opening in one corner of the building, a U-shaped hideaway where someone could view most of the area in front of the building without being obvious. Guiding Detective Gonzalez over to it, he knew that he could talk to her without causing any attention to themselves.

"Hey, Gonzalez."

"Sampson...what the hell is going on??"

"I've been suspended."

"Yea, that news is already all over the airwaves, my friend. What happened?"

"I'll give you the details later. I need you to do something for me."

"Anything" After three years of working together, Gonzalez trusted Ian as much as she did her own brother—with her life—and anything he needed; she would gladly do her best to comply. "What's up?"

"Amanda Pearson is in Apartment 9, her friends place, and she needs to make a statement about what happened to her last night. I need you to take that statement, please."

"What about Colliatti??"

"*Fuck* Colliatti."

"Now Ian...you know me better than that...I'd have to be dead before something like that would happen!" Smirking at Ian, Gonzalez glanced over his shoulder and inhaled sharply. "Ian— Colliati's coming our way..."

Straightening immediately, Ian turned to find Colliatti gazing smartly in his direction. Then, as the statement, "Boy, Sampson, you're really starting to think with your dick, aren't ya??" left Colliati's rotten mouth, Ian turned away from Gonzalez and rushed at him, wanting nothing more than to finish what he had started last night as his blood heated to the boiling point. Gonzalez, darting quickly, managed to get in front of Ian, yelling at him the entire time. "Stop, Ian!!! He's not worth it, man! *STOP!!*"

"HEY!!! What the HELL is going on here???!!!"

Captain Leary, who had overheard Colliati's remark, jumped from the bottom rungs of the metal staircase and placed his body effectively between Ian and Colliati. Fuming at both men, he first addressed Colliati. "If I ever hear you speak to another officer like that again, you won't make it to retirement!! Expect a report in your jacket by the end of the day—", pausing for a second as Colliatti started to argue in return, the captain cut him off immediately. "— for today's remark and the shit you pulled last night in the alley! Now, if you want this case, you work it as a professional and nothing less! You got me, Colliatti??"

Colliati's chest rose in anger, but he said nothing as he turned from the captain and stalked away. Now, turning on Ian, the man in charge yelled, "And what the hell are you still doing here?? I instructed you to leave a half hour ago, Sampson! If you still want a job after your suspension is lifted, you'd best turn your ass around and leave!"

That said, the captain ran a hand over his reddened face as he stood for a second and pondered his own retirement. Then, seeing that the situation had been halted for the time being, he turned to leave, giving last minute instructions to the men heading up the stairs to continue processing Amanda's apartment. Ian, stepping back from Gonzalez, took a deep breath and placed both hands on his hips.

"You alright?" Gonzalez asked, also seeming to be out of breath.

"Yeah. Look, will you take her statement. Please? I don't want Colliatti near her and she may open up to you—being that your female. When you're done, give her friend Anna my cell phone number and make sure she calls me."

"Ian...what are you doin'???"

Holding up a shaky hand, he stopped Gonzalez before she could continue with her warning. "Just do it, please Gonzalez?? For me?" Sighing back at Ian, Gonzalez surrendered and shrugged her shoulders. "Alright, but it's your career your screwin' around with, you know that, right??"

Hanging his head for a brief moment, Ian nodded once at Gonzalez, then turned and headed back to the parking lot where he had left his truck. Getting in, he started it, and looked around for Colliatti. Seeing no one, he put the truck in reverse and pulled out, passed through the gate that was now standing open and ended up at the Burger King on the next corner up from the apartment complex. Sitting inside the restaurant, he forced himself to eat the greasy meal that he had ordered without even realizing what he was doing and tried his best to put his head back on straight.

Was she worth his career??

Contemplating Gonzalez's demanding question as it rolled over in his mind, he couldn't stop the image of Amanda's red hair and deep emerald green eyes from invading his thoughts. Unconsciously, he popped a golden fry into this mouth and slowly sucked the salt from it before chewing it softly. Giving in, he admitted to himself that yes, maybe she was worth it. Her *and* her daughter, whose silent characteristics only intrigued him more. Seeing her wide smile in his mind's eye, he felt himself smile as well, and knew that these two women were not something he could just walk away from.

But what about Amanda? Did she feel the same? Sighing at himself, he was suddenly reminded of her reaction to his kiss. At first he had thought that she was going to push him away—angry with him because of it. But she hadn't. She leaned into him instead and that had to account for something...didn't it?? Her hands on his arms, the feel of her warm touch, the taste of her mouth...the memories of the moment they shared just before having it shattered by the violation of her apartment sent a shiver up his spine as heat spurred up from his belly. Shifting on the hard stool he was sitting on, he tried to think about something else, but didn't have to as a voice from behind caught him off guard.

"Man—your girl is somethin' else, Sampson."

Jumping at the voice, Ian stopped himself from sliding off the stool by grabbing the side of the bar he was seated at that overlooked the parking lot. Not seeing that Gonzalez had come in from one of the side entrances, he nearly laughed at himself...she about scared him half to death! "Jesus, Gonzalez—where did you come from?"

"Got one of those for me??" Eyeing the fries on the table, Gonzalez propped herself on the stool next to Ian and grabbed a small handful. "So, you want the good news or the bad news?"

"Just give it to me straight, Gonzalez."

"Okay...you asked for it." Pausing as she finished chewing on a couple of fries, she continued after a moment. "Everything that happened last night, she remembers. And in detail. She is the most amazing witness that I think I have ever met. It's really too bad that she didn't remember it all immediately after it happened, we may have had a head start on those two shitheads before now."

"Wait—what??" Confused, Ian had no idea what she was talking about. "What shitheads? What are you talking about??"

"That's right…" nodding at Ian now, Gonzalez understood his confusion, "…you and Colliatti haven't been following the serial case we got. You guys were on the Johnston drug investigation, right?"

Looking at her sideways, Ian waited for her to eat another fry when all he wanted to do was take the bunch away from her and throw them out—if it would get her to talk faster, that is. "Gonzalez, what are you talking about? What serial?"

"Over the past three months, we've had four bodies found around town, all female. I think your girlfriend was witness to number four." Staring Ian in the eye, she made sure she had his attention before continuing. She did. "The girls found are all unidentified so far, blond, raped and tortured, shot, and then dumped without any evidence found. No DNA, no prints, no semen, no *nothing*. When Amanda left the bar last night, she saw another car pulling into the lot."

"Yeah, she remembered that this morning when we talked at the hospital."

Ignoring that fact that she knew that the last place Ian should have been this morning was to see Ms. Pearson, she continued on, "Well, basically, she was attacked by two guys. After they parked in the back of the lot she said that they had went to the trunk and shot into it. After that, she tried to hide in her car, but they caught her and dragged her out and pulled her across the lot to their car. Sampson, she *swears* she saw blond hair coming out of the open trunk.

"She also said", pausing, she gave Ian a grim look, "that one of them tried to rape her on the back end of the trunk. She said that the other guy did nothing to stop it, like he was taking orders from the one aiming to rape her or something—"

"What—was she raped???" Cutting off Gonzalez, Ian's brown eyes hardened with anger.

"No, no, she wasn't. She fought back and managed to get away from them. That's when one of them shot her in the shoulder. She was running back towards the entrance to the parking lot at the same time another car was driving in. That's when she went down. That's all she remembers before waking up to your gorgeous face in the hospital.

"Now, considering the look of her apartment and the message that was left on her bedroom wall, we can assume that—"

"That they know she survived."

"Yeah, that and they somehow found out where she lives. And now they know that she has a daughter." Considering this, Gonzalez frowned for a second before adding, "How could they have found out where she lived?? The press wasn't let in on the incident; until now no one even knew there may be a connection between what happened to her, the girl she saw in the trunk, and the other girls that have been found over the last few months."

"It's like they've got someone on the inside, isn't it?? Someone feeding them information about the cases you guys have been investigating."

Nodding at Ian, Gonzalez shifted on her stool, as if suddenly uncomfortable. "If this is the same two guys, how did they know to come looking for her at her apartment? How did they know that she survived? It hasn't even been twenty-four hours since this happened."

"And if the bodies found so far are all tied together, these two aren't likely to stop now."

Nodding, Gonzalez considered the facts for a moment before responding. "But, we haven't heard anything from the M.E. concerning the woman found in the alley yet. She may not be these guys' fourth victim—her case may be entirely separate."

"True, but she fits. Blond, nude, ligature marks on hands and ankles, shot...it matches your previous victims. She could very well be the woman Amanda saw."

Calculating each factor as Ian ticked them off to her, Gonzalez shook her head for a moment. "But, that's a bit of a coincidence, don't you think? I mean, granted there was no other vehicle in the parking lot except Ms. Pearson's when she was found and there was no other body found anywhere near the scene, but for her attackers to turn around and leave the body a few blocks away in the alley?? That's a stretch, Sampson."

Muttering a, "yeah, maybe", Ian looked out the window they were seated in front of, now lost in his own thoughts. Not hearing Gonzalez stand up, it took her touch on his shoulder to bring him around. "Hey, you be careful, you hear? I don't need you fired from the job just because of Colliati. And if you leave me alone, working with that prick until he *retires*...Sampson, I will come after your ass!"

Smiling at Gonzalez, Ian stood and gave her a brief hug, thankful that he had at least one person to trust on his side. "I'll keep that in mind."

Turning away from him, Gonzalez stopped and called over her shoulder, "Oh, and Sampson? Don't bother getting all pissy because you didn't get a call from your girl's friend...I told them both that I knew exactly where to find you and that you would be on your way once we were done." Looking at him sideways, Gonzalez gave him a wide smile and then left the restaurant.

Cleaning off the bar, Ian emptied his trash into the bin nearest the exit and walked back to his truck. Getting in and turning it over, he hesitated, wondering if the cops had all cleared out at the apartment complex yet. Shrugging at himself, he immediately decided that Amanda was worth the risk and he pulled away from his parking space and headed back towards her place, a new mission set in stone in his mind.

Chapter Twelve

Pulling into a Circle K parking lot, David jumped out of the passenger's side of the car before Lenny had a chance to come to a complete stop and put it into park. Knowing his best friend was hyped up to the gills as the adrenaline from trashing the dancer's apartment was still running high in his veins, Lenny said nothing, not wanting to stifle David's good mood.

As Lenny watched from the driver's seat, David pulled out some change from his pocket and picked up the handset from one of the last payphones this side of Mexico. Nowadays, everyone carried a cell phone and because of it, more and more businesses were clearing their walls of pay phone stations and replacing them with cell phone packages, calling cards, and other communicative accessories. As David had ordered Lenny to dump their last set of burn phones, their only option in connecting with their employer was by using a pay phone, or stealing someone else's mobile phone which was not a good idea due to the attention it could cause.

Listening to the numbers on the face of the pay phone beep loudly in his ear as he pressed each button that would complete his call, David did some sort of happy dance. The thrill of getting so close to that redheaded stripper was almost too much for him to handle. Sifting through her clothes, slashing her bedding, and burning whatever he felt like at the time was more than a rush…it was a lifeline. Realizing the other end of the line had been picked up, David forced himself to calm down, seriousness was called for when dealing with the employer.

"Protected?" Was David's only question and over the next few minutes anyone walking past who overheard his part of the conversation, they would have just shaken their head in confusion— the whole point to the coded lingo. The term "protected" was code for *is this a protected, or private, line?* And since David had worked for this particular employer for over three months now, decoding what he heard and coding his responses came easy.

"Go." *Is the job complete?*

"Goose is cooked." *Yes, the job is complete...*

"Dinner?" *Any complications?*

"Potatoes and gravy." *Under no suspicion...*

"Dessert." *Good work...*

"Your place or mine?" *Is the payment ready?*

"Neither." *There is a second part of the job...*

"Empty fridge." *More supplies are needed...*

"How many times has the Broadway production, Chicago, been performed on stage since 1975?" *Find the answer, decipher the hidden message, and you'll get your supplies...*

With that, the conversation ended and David hung up the receiver. The last part, concerning the question about the Broadway show, was always the longest part of the conversation and the only one that needed further investigating on his part—which was Lenny's job to complete. In order for David to retrieve the additional supplies and instructions that were waiting for him, they needed to find the answer to the question and decipher it from there. Already understanding that the 'Broadway' reference in the clue represented an actual street name, David knew that they were almost home free and did nothing to hide his smile as he climbed back into the passenger seat.

Twenty minutes later, David instructed Lenny to pull into a small coffee-focused café that offered free Wi-Fi. Stepping out of the car, they headed in together and found an out-of-the-way circular table to set their laptop computer on. Buying flavored coffee, if only to appear to blend in with the crowd and not necessarily to drink, Lenny worked his magic on the laptop while David eyed the crowd.

Made up of mostly college girls, David found himself in no hurry to leave. A mixture of blonds, brunettes, redheads, and a few that couldn't decide just what hair color suited them best, sauntered around the coffee bar, sipping their orders from the Styrofoam cups the place was famous for, and never gave him or Lenny a second glance.

"Got it."

Lenny's brief statement brought David back around and for a second he could have slapped the man. Sitting here, sipping his ungodly expensive coffee while watching the young girls come in and out of the joint, was something he could have done all day—well not *all* day, at some point he would've had to fulfill the need that was slowly making its way up from below his belt. On the other hand, that need; to take one of these blond headed beauties out back somewhere and have his way with her; would likely distract him enough to steer him off course.

"Got what?" David asked, trying to hide his irritation.

"The answer."

"Good. Let's get the hell outta here."

Closing the laptop, Lenny followed David out of the coffee bar, never noticing the temptations that David was enthralled with. Opposite of the ringleader of the duo, Lenny was not sexually deviant—that part belonged to David. Shy, awkward, and extremely unsure of himself, Lenny preferred to remain hidden in the background and although he found some satisfaction in watching, he could never see himself playing a more direct part. What set him further apart from David however, was his ability to research, work his fingers around any piece of technology, and the ability to take instruction (in whatever form it may come) and follow it through without question. And this attribute, in a way, made Lenny more dangerous than David.

"Where we headed?" Once in the car and safely out of earshot, David turned to Lenny, eyebrows raised. "You got the address right?"

"Of course." Mixed with a bit of surprise, Lenny wanted to stress that he always got the address right, no matter how difficult the clue, but bit his tongue instead. Again—one of his few qualities that made him effective—the knowing of when to shut up and let David think what he wants overrode his desire to tell the man off; which isn't something he would do anyways.

"What the hell are we still sitting here for then??"

The question directing Lenny to head towards the place where they will pick up the supplies needed to do whatever job David had lined up with their 'employer' was enough instruction. Starting the car and pulling out of the parking lot, Lenny headed west from their location, on a road that would eventually lead them away from the center of city, but not too far out of civilization.

Tucson, a large metropolis, was home to well over four hundred thousand and despite the mountain ranges that surrounded the area, it was widely spread out. Passing through the traffic as the made their way to the location that Lenny had unraveled using both his laptop and the extensive amount of knowledge that constantly swirled around in his brain, he took notice of the various cacti and desert plants that covered the landscape.

Thick saguaros, with arms that leaned every which way, offered small amounts of shade to the multitude of prickly pear, cholla, agave, palo verde trees, and yucca shrubs that were common here. Needing very little water to survive, the patches of bone dry dirt that lay in between the plant life made Lenny suddenly thirsty and for a moment, he was thankful the stolen car they were traveling in had air conditioning. With heat rising each summer over one hundred degrees, he couldn't imagine crossing these desert areas like many illegal immigrants do year after year, commonly beginning their journey in Mexico. Every year, more and more dead bodies were found lying in waste due to heat exposure and lack of water and this fact only further confused Lenny. How anyone could choose to cross such land as this was beyond him.

As the road narrowed and wound around a small mountain pass, Lenny cleared his thoughts. Every now then, they would pass a house, tucked away from the road, with only a solid, southwestern-style mailbox marking its place. Watching addresses, Lenny found the one they were looking for and made a left off of the paved road and as the tires of the car tried to make their mark on the dirt driveway they were now heading up, Lenny slowed down considerably.

Approximately a half mile down the dirt road, they came upon a one story, concrete building. Looking more like a garage than an actual home, the walls looked to be constructed out of stucco and appeared to be thick and strong. On one side, two large metal doors that were also white in color ran from the roof of the structure down to the dirt covered floor, and Lenny assumed they opened up into a large garage of some sort. On the other side, double steel doors looked unwelcoming and Lenny was immediately thankful that he was instructed to remain in the car as David climbed out of the passenger seat.

Making his way to the doors of the place, David took a slow look around him, as if trying to see anything, or anyone, that may be hidden from his view. Listening, he stood still, halfway from the car to the door but heard nothing out of the ordinary. A hot breeze made its way around the building in front of him and swept through the itchy looking desert life that surrounded the area. Refocusing his eyes to the metal doors, he was starting to sweat and silently cursed the gods who had thought that desert heat was sustainable for human dwelling.

Before he even knocked, one side of the doors was pulled open and he heard the unmistakable squeak of rubber against unpolished porcelain. He didn't have to look down to know that the flooring inside the building was some sort of tile and that rubber matting stretched across the bottom of the door. Curious as to whether or not this was actually someone's home; he hesitated over the threshold, waiting to see who was behind the door.

A tall, lanky man was suddenly in front of him and as they eyed each other carefully, a voice called from further inside. "Let the man in, Ryan."

"Sir." Was all Ryan replied as he stepped back and pulled the door further open with ease.

"Come in, David. Where is your partner in crime?"

Unwilling to say anything yet, David stepped past Ryan and walked into a large, empty room. Confused, he took a moment to look around, noting immediately that there were no furnishings, no materials, no supplies or equipment of any kind. It was literally empty, save Ryan and the guy who was now addressing him. "You're partner??" The man asked of him again.

"Waiting outside." David said, still unsure of this meeting place and the two people before him. "He don't do well with meeting others."

"Ah...I see. Well, I assume you solved the puzzle."

"No, we just drove around knocking on doors, until we found the weirdest one." His sarcasm caused the other man to smirk and as David sized up the short, heavy-set man with thinning hair, he knew that this was not his employer. "My supplies??" He asked, wanting nothing more but to get back to the job at hand.

"Of course, David, my apologies. Ryan?"

Nodding, Ryan silently left the room by way of a thin hallway that led him away from the large room. Peering after him, David still saw that nothing seemed to be housed here and he wondered if this place was even owned by anyone. Maybe these guys just go around to empty buildings or houses in the middle of nowhere and set up shop for a few hours, never calling anything home. Whatever the reasoning, David was past interested.

After a few more moments of silence, Ryan returned, carrying a large black nylon bag with him. Handing it to the guy that was giving the instructions, David watched carefully as the bag was unzipped and inspected briefly. Then, handing the bag back to Ryan, the man said, "I trust you will find everything you need. Make contact when the contract is complete."

Handing the bag over to David, he hesitated before taking it. Going down in history as the strangest meeting and exchange in his criminal history, David was not sure whether or not this was all legit. "Mind if I check the contents?"

"By all means...please."

Kneeling, David kept a steady eye on both men as he took the bag and unzipped it. Feeling around, he noted the weaponry, boxes of ammunition, something thin and small—another burn phone perhaps—and, what he was really after, a heavily bounded stack of cold, hard, cash. Smiling, he zipped the bag closed and stood to make his exit. "Well, our work here is done. Don't have too much fun, *boys*."

"Oh, I'm sure you'll be the one having all the fun...what with your history with women, David."

Turning on his heel at the remark, David gave the man a shocked look, then remembering the redhead that was probably still a priority to his employer; he suddenly understood the meaning behind the statement and grinned wide as he reached up and caressed the scar that draped down the side of his face before turning to leave.

Chapter Thirteen

"I *have* to go to work, Anna."

"Amanda... *really*???"

"Yes!" Sitting here over an hour arguing with Anna about whether or not I should return to work for a few hours, I was getting agitated. "My apartment is trashed, Anna, *trashed*!! There is nothing left! We have no food, no clothes, *nothing* was salvageable!"

"What if they come back???"

Anna's question brought me around and I bit my lip, unsure now of what I should do. I had no money, no family, no place to go to, and no car. With no idea as to how long my vehicle was going to be impounded as evidence, as Ian had explained earlier, we couldn't even sleep in it if it came down to that. Exhausted and frustrated, I sank into one of Anna's kitchen chairs and watched Brighton color in a Disney Princess coloring book.

"What about that guy...the detective??" Obviously referring to Ian, I felt heat rise in my cheeks and immediately shook my head. "Why not??" Anna demanded, "He acts like he wants to help you!"

"Because, Anna, I don't need that right now. What I need to do is make sure that Brighton is safe and get back to work so that I can start replacing the stuff we will need over the next few days. If I let Ian get involved..." Refusing to let anything further leave my mouth, I stopped talking and looked down at my hands.

"What, you may find some kind of happiness in all this??"

"I am happy, Anna, I have Brighton. And I have you. I don't need a man."

"Well, I know that! But he sure does seem like the one you need to relieve some of that tension you've been building up!" Smirking back at me, Anna pointed a finger in my direction and I suppressed a giggle as I gasped at her.

"Anna!!"

"It's true...and you know it!"

"Ok...ok...look, Ian is out of the question. I've got to do this on my own. But in order to do so, I have to go to work! I'm sure Lucky will let me cocktail for a while until my stupid shoulder heals and I can get back to dancing."

Shaking her head at me, our argument was suddenly stifled as a soft knock came from the other side of the closed front door. Standing immediately, the chair I was sitting in skid backwards across the floor and Brighton looked up at me questionably. "Shshsh..." Anna pressed a thin finger to her lips as she crept to the door. Since the cops had already finished the initial investigation of my apartment, we both knew that it had to be someone else at the door.

Peering through the peephole that was positioned high on the door, Anna suddenly stood back and gave me a smirk as she unlocked it and swung it open, allowing Ian to walk in freely. All this talk about not needing the man and she lets him come in to her apartment as if nothing I had said mattered! I could have killed her.

"Hey." He said to Anna and then looked past her, giving Brighton a smile before meeting my eyes.

"What are you doing here?" I asked, sounding irritated without really meaning to. Giving me a hard look, Anna stepped up to the plate and quickly spilled the beans to Ian concerning my intention of heading into work. At that point...I almost did kill her!

"What?? You're not going to work!" Ian looked at me incredulously.

"See what you've started??" Glaring at Anna, I knew that I was going to lose this fight.

"Tell her she's not going to work! Brighton and Amanda can stay here for a while." Anna pointed out her side of the argument as if I wasn't even in the room but glared back at me swiftly with her hands on her hips. "I have everything you need here, you can borrow some clothes for now, there's food in the fridge, and I even have some of Brighton's stuff here."

"And if staying here puts you in some kind of trouble??" I shot back and the room suddenly went quiet. Anna had no retort and Ian leaned up against the fridge said nothing. I was right and I knew it. "If whoever is behind this can find me in less than a day, I am sure he can find you, Anna, especially if Brighton and I are here. I'm not going to put anyone else in danger."

"She's right."

Anna and I both looked at Ian, who was staring at the floor with his hands in his pockets. Anna, clearly frustrated with the both of us, left the kitchen in a huff and headed back to her bedroom. Sighing, I glanced at Brighton, who was still coloring as if the tension in the room had not registered in her mind, and swept past Ian to talk to Anna some more.

Stopping me quickly, he gently grabbed my elbow and said, "But I agree with Anna on the work thing, you shouldn't be working right now, especially since that is where this all began."

"Ha!! See, I knew he would take my side!!"

Anna, who was coming out of her bedroom and down the hall yelled in triumph. In her hands was a bright pink gym bag, the phrase *"Put down that donut and pick up a dumbbell!"* scrawled across it in black lettering. "I do have a question concerning where you and Brighton are going to stay however."

With his hand still on my elbow; he didn't seem to want to let go; Ian and I both turned to look at Anna, who was now sinking into her overstuffed, Simmons brand loveseat. Watching me carefully, she hesitated before continuing. "I want to take Brighton to my parents."

Stepping forward with an, *are you kidding me,* look on my face, Anna stopped me from saying anything in return by jumping ahead with her idea. "You know she loves it there. She will be safe and taken care of. Just until this thing blows over."

"Anna....no." Shaking my head at her, I was beside myself that she would even suggest separating me and my daughter. "You know that I have to stay here, the cops requested it just in case something comes up on my case. But I cannot let Brighton go, just like that. What if she needed me? Or something happened and I couldn't get to her? No, Anna. I'm sorry, but no."

"Amanda—" Ian tried to butt in but I cut him off immediately.

"Ian, NO! What kind of mother do you two think I am??? I am not leaving my daughter on someone else's doorstep!! No, it's out of the question!" Even though Anna's parents had retired to Green Valley, Arizona a few years ago and they only lived about thirty minutes away, I was dead set against being away from my daughter for any extended amount of time.

"Ma?"

"Oh, honey," immediately lowering my voice as Brighton's wide eyes searched mine, I realized that I had startled her and bent down to where she was sitting at the kitchen table as I said, "it's okay, sweetie. Mommy and Anna and the detective are just talking. Everything is okay. Go ahead and color some more."

Watching her do so, I waited by her side to make sure she was okay, then stood and glared at Anna and Ian before walking out the front door and closing it firmly behind me. Walking over to the fenced in pool, I leaned my arms over the top of the four foot enclosure and began to cry.

How did I ever get into this mess?? And how am I going to get out of it in one piece??

Suddenly knowing that I wasn't alone, I sniffled and turned my head to look over my left shoulder. Ian had followed me out of Anna's apartment and stood back only a few feet, as if unsure whether or not he should approach me. Turning away from him, I dried my tears using the neck of the scrub top I was still dressed in before managing to croak out an apology for yelling at him and Anna.

"I just don't know what to do at this point." I admitted my back still facing him.

Hearing his steps crush the gravel underneath his feet as he walked to one side of me and leaned on the fence as well, he gave me a strong look before speaking. "Look, I know that you would do anything to protect Brighton. Even though I have only just met you, it's not hard to see the love you have for her. But right now, you've got to realize that someone out there is pining for you, and if they find you, I have a feeling that they are not going to care that you have a daughter.

"Your life is in danger, Amanda; you've got the bullet wound to prove it and now a trashed apartment. Anna said that her parents don't live that far away and you know you can trust her to take care of Brighton the same way that you do."

"Yes, but..."

"No buts, Amanda. I'm sorry to say this, but what other choice do you have if you want to be sure she is safe and being taken care of. If whoever is out there finds you, they will find her. On top of that, they could very well use her to get to you...and keeping her here with Anna in her apartment also poses a danger, they already know where you live, it won't take long for them to figure out where the people closest to you live as well." Taking a breath, he paused briefly before reaching out and gently moving a strand of red hair from the side of my face. Pushing it back, his fingers grazed my cheekbone and I flushed at his touch and closed my eyes.

"And where am I supposed to go?? I have no money for a hotel room and my car is still unavailable, as far as I know. I'm sure Lucky will let me serve drinks for now and that is the only way that I know to get some money so that I can get Brighton what she needs."

Despite my ranting, my emotions betrayed me and I found myself unable to focus as his fingers found their way to the back of my neck and he began to slowly work his magic over my tense muscles. Trying hard not to concentrate on his touch, but on the matter at hand, I turned away from him as I admitted, "You're making it really hard to be angry at you right now!"

"It's because you know that I am right", he said and I could hear the smile in his voice.

Taking a breath, I whispered, "No, it's not", still unwilling to look at him.

Stepping around me, Ian forced me to look at him again and before I could turn away again or say anything in protest, he lifted my chin and his mouth pressed hard against mine. Caught off guard, I grabbed the top of the fence railing and took a small step back, only to find myself trapped between his strong body and the chain link. Then, as our mouths opened simultaneously, I let my body take over and I pushed forward, off of the fence so that it pressed against his. He groaned, and as his fingers worked their way through my hair, pulling gently at first and then tugging harder seconds later, a small moan escaped my mouth and filled his own. Unlike the intensity of our first kiss just a few hours ago, this one set my toes on fire.

Desire filled my insides and I ached all over as we continued, our tongues meeting over and over again. Then, suddenly, he moved his mouth to my neck as his fingers pulled harder on my hair, causing my face to turn towards the open sky. Responding to the desperate feeling I was now having, I wrapped my arms around his waist and pulled him closer to me, wrapping one leg around him as I did, as if welcoming him from below. His breath hissed against my neck and I shuddered, bringing my head down and meeting his lips with my own once again.

"Amanda..." His voice hoarse, the hold Ian had on me tightened as he let go of my hair and brought both hands down my back to the middle of my waist. The scrubs I was wearing were thin, offering my body the chance to feel every rub...every touch...until I thought I was going to explode.

Then, suddenly, and for some unknown reason, I opened my eyes and remembered exactly where we were standing. "Ian", I started as his lips moved from my own, finding their mark along my chin, my cheekbone, then to my ear, causing my body to tense. "Ian...oh, God...Ian...stop. Ian, we've got to stop."

Slowing down a bit, I forced my leg to release him and moved my hands from the base of his spine to his chest. God, I didn't want to stop, but I was not about to surrender to him out here in the open...twenty feet from the door to the apartment where Brighton was tucked safely inside. One look from Anna's small living room window would have given her an eyeful and I couldn't live with that.

"Come home with me." Ian whispered against my ear, breathing hard as he did.

"No." My response was immediate and was out of my mouth before I could think twice about it.

"Please...Amanda...*please*, come home with me."

Pushing against his chest with trembling hands, I forced him to stop moving against me in an instant. Confused, his brown eyes searched my green ones and he opened his mouth to speak and then closed it immediately. Pressing his forehead against mine, he closed his eyes and shuddered as his breathing slowed down. Then, nodding as he understood, he said, "Okay, okay. I'm sorry."

"I'm not."

Startled, Ian opened his eyes and looked at me but before he could respond I said, "Wait for me here? Please?" Now confused, Ian just nodded and separated himself from me. Leaning against the fence, he rubbed his face with both hands, as if attempting to get himself under control again.

Leaving him there, I walked back to Anna's apartment, questioning myself the entire way. Was I doing the right thing? *Yes*, I thought, *it has to be this way.* And before my emotions could argue with the logic that my mind was forcing me to consider, I opened Anna's door and walked inside.

Giving me a huge smile under bright eyes, I knew that Anna had seen us.

"Don't." I warned, not wanting her to say anything just yet.

Finding Brighton still sitting in the kitchen, I suddenly felt as if I'd betrayed her or something. Shame centered itself over my heart and I didn't know how I could have been so careless. I have never acted out in such a sexual way; not even with my ex-husband when we were dating or after we were married; and at that moment, I felt embarrassed and as though I had just disgraced myself in some way. Never wanting Brighton to think such things of me, I was careful of how I spoke around her, acted, and portrayed myself and it was such a concern that I was conscious of these factors even when she was not with me.

Completely unsure with myself, I turned from my daughter and went to Anna, hugging her so quickly that I caught her off guard, ignoring the throbbing pain in my shoulder. "Hey, Amanda, what's wrong??"

"I don't know what to do...right now I am so confused I don't know which way is up and which way is down. But, God! He makes me feel so good!"

"So, run with it, honey!"

"I can't, Anna, I just can't."

"Why?? Because he's a gorgeous guy...a cop, no less...who is interested in you before he has even seen you naked??"

"And Brighton, what does that tell her, huh??"

"Amanda, you have spent her whole life taking care of her. Making sure she has the best life any kid could ask for. You deserve a little down time...know what I mean??? Let me take her to my folks in Green Valley, please. It will be like our little adventure. I can't stay here, I am going with or without her, but I want to keep her as safe as possible, just like you."

"Ian asked me to go home with him."

"And..."

"I said no."

"What did he say?"

"He said 'okay'."

"Good God girl, you need to marry that man!!" Slapping me on the arm as she said it...the one connected to my injured shoulder...I winced in pain and Anna raised both hands to her mouth, instantly sorry and angry with herself. "Oh, shit!!! Oh, Amanda, I'm so sorry, are you okay??"

"Jeeze, Anna, kill me why don't you!"

"Oh, God, I'm sorry! I forgot!!"

"It's ok, Anna, I'm okay. It just woke me up that's all." Trying to laugh it off, I turned as tears stung my eyes and changed the subject. "You sure about taking Brighton with you?"

"Of course! I have already spoken to Mom and Dad and they are excited to have her. They love her like a granddaughter, you know that. And they know that having her there will let you get some rest...*or something else*...and that you both will be safer. At least for tonight, you can drive out to their place tomorrow and we will decide what to do from there."

"I don't have anything to send with her." Knowing I was caving; and not for the reasons that she may think; I second guessed the decision immediately. Having nothing to send with her, Brighton was going to be at Anna's mercy, and Anna didn't have that much money either.

"Amanda." Anna said sternly, pulling my attention back around. "You know that neither my parents nor I are going to let that precious girl go without, even if it is for just one night!"

"Okay...okay...just, let me go talk to her first, okay?"

Walking into the kitchen, I pulled a chair out from the other side of the table and sat down next to her. Looking up at me,

Brighton smiled, and my heart warmed. "Brighton, I need to ask you something." Dropping her crayon, she looked up at me and I knew I had her attention. "Anna wants to take you out to Nana and Papa's house, just for the night. Would you like to go?"

Anna's parents have known me since I was a kid, having lived next door to them as a little girl. Anna and I grew up together and were literally the best of friends. When her parents decided to move back east for a while after we both graduated from high school, Anna and I shared an apartment up until the time I married my ex-husband. During the four years I was married to the jackass, Anna and I drifted apart some, but not enough to cause a hindrance on our friendship. After I left Alex, taking Brighton with me, Anna found an empty apartment upstairs from where she was living...the apartment that now looks like a psychotic had endured a meltdown in it.

Anna's parents moved back to Arizona shortly thereafter and wrapped Brighton and me back into the family mold. They were the only grandparents she knew of and she loved them as much as they loved her. There was no question that she would be taken care of in their home, no matter how old she got, how bad her disability may grow to be, no matter what.

"Yes!" Brighton's excitement caught me off guard and as she leaped into my arms, I laughed despite the pain my shoulder was now giving me. Leaving me suddenly, she ran from the kitchen and jumped into Anna's waiting arms.

"Okay...okay, I give in..."

"Yeah!!!!" They both squealed at me.

Then, suddenly it was a race to grab everything they would need for a night out of town. Pajamas, shorts, a t-shirt with Minnie Mouse waving on the front, clean socks and underwear, and her shoes tossed into a bag and she was ready! Anna grabbed her keys, her purse, and her overnight bag...which mysteriously was already packed...and passed me the pink gym bag that she had brought out earlier. Looking at her questionably, she explained with a wink and a smile, "I knew you were going to change your mind!"

Opening the front door, Anna and Brighton walked out before me and I hesitated over the threshold, watching Ian as he leaned against the fence, looking sexy as all hell. Seeing us exiting the apartment, he pushed himself away from the fence and stuffed his hands in the front pockets of his jeans, as if nervous.

Tearing my eyes away from his as Anna touched my arm, I turned to listen to her. "We are going to head out so that we can get to my parents' house before supper. Call me if you need anything; but especially if you end up having second thoughts about you-know-what!" Giving me a knowing look, I shook my head at her and kneeled down to say goodbye to Brighton.

"Okay, you be a good girl. And you know that I love you more than life, right??"

"Yes." Struggling with her words, she added, "Ma."

Hugging her hard, I couldn't help but wonder again if this was the right thing to do. I knew that I would worry about her, but I also knew that she was going to be safe. "I will see you tomorrow okay? Have fun and listen to Anna and Nana and Papa."

Nodding her response, she hugged me tightly again and then took Anna's hand, skipping along the way to the parking lot. Standing, I turned to Ian, who hadn't moved from his spot. Watching Anna leave with Brighton with questions burning in his eyes, he turned his gaze towards me and gave me a long look before walking in my direction. Meeting him halfway, I held up one hand, stopping him before he got to close and I chickened out with what I was about to say.

With about a foot of space in between our bodies, I paused, watching him carefully and swallowed hard. I could still feel the electricity that his body had caused in mine and the thought of us locked together, bodies pressed so tightly against each other that we moved as one up against the fence, speed dialed its way into my subconscious and I fought myself to stand still. Pressing my eyelids closed for a brief second, I looked at Ian and said, "Will you please...*please*...loan me the money so that I can get my prescriptions filled??? I don't think I will survive spending the night with you if you don't."

Chapter Fourteen

Pulling into a nearby Walgreens Drug Store, Ian found a close spot in which to park and helped me out of the truck, handling me with kid gloves as he did. As if believing that any sudden movement would cause me to turn and run in the opposite direction, he was slow in responding, careful when having to touch me, and seemed to be always sure that there were at least several inches in between us, like he was avoiding any contact whatsoever. If not for the two immensely intense moments that we had already shared, I would have begun to wonder if he was having second thoughts.

The pharmacy was busy and as we approached the end of the line that would eventually lead us to the counter, Ian reached over and took the two prescriptions out of my hands. Giving him a questionable look, he smiled and said, "I've got these."

Not knowing what to say, I simply stood there. Yes, I did ask him for help in paying for these, but I meant it as a loan—not something he was just going to take care of for me per say. I would have been more comfortable standing in line with the money I needed in my hands instead of in his wallet. I have never been one to ask someone else for help, for anything, with exception to Anna, that is. I could ask her for anything and she the same of me. We relied on each other like no one else, and we rarely let the other one down. If she were a man—and I was even remotely attracted to her—I would have married her a long time ago.

"You hungry?"

Bringing my attention around, I considered answering Ian's question with a lie; I was sure to owe him a lot of money after these two prescriptions were filled, especially considering the fact that I have no insurance. Having my stomach awaken at the simple question however forced me to nod my head at him.

Looking around, he said, "Well, I'm not eating here—what kind of food do you like?"

Immediately tempted to tease him a bit; if nothing else but to have him relax around me a bit; I stopped myself, as it would surely cause a scene. Keeping my answer clean and to the point, I said, "Italian."

"Really??" He looked surprised and explained, "I would have figured you for a vegetarian or something."

"Why do you say that??"

"Because you're so skinny!"

Flushing, I looked down at myself and said, "It's just the scrubs, they are at least ten sizes too big and they make me look skinny."

"I really doubt it's that alone", his eyes meeting mine and I thought I was going to melt.

*Well, you'll find out for yourself soon enough...*wanting to say this, but biting my tongue hard, the line in front of us finally moved forward a bit and I sent a speedy prayer of thanks to the Man upstairs.

"Italian is good, anywhere in particular?"

"Anything cheap will be fine."

Giving me a hard look, he opened his mouth to argue and I raised my eyebrows at him, silently daring him to challenge me here, in the middle of the pharmacy; and he quickly closed it. As the line moved ahead again, he suddenly placed one hand over the small of back and gently guided me forward as he leaned down. Mouth over my ear, he whispered smoothly, "Amanda, honey, you will never be a cheap date."

Before I realized what I was doing, I reached back with one hand and found his right thigh and gave it a tight squeeze. Then, immediately chastising myself, went to remove it as Ian's body tensed behind my own. Grasping my hand, he thread his strong fingers through mine and tightened his grip as we finally reached the front of the line.

The clerk, a bouncy looking blond dressed in a white smock and tan pants, took one look at my face, then glanced over at Ian and flushed before asking how she could be of help. Explaining what we needed, the clerk, whose name tag read Christine, took the paperwork from Ian and cleared her throat loudly.

God, is it that obvious??

Thinking to myself as Christine's fingers began typing feverously on the keyboard that was attached to her computer screen, I felt my cheeks redden slightly. Answering her questions concerning my address, my phone number (which I had none and Ian offered his own), and my date of birth, she completed my order and stated that it would take at least two hours before it would be ready for pick up. Ian, obviously teasing her, piped up and said, "I'm sure we can find something to do while we wait."

Choking on my spit as Christine turned bright red—not something she minded too terribly judging by the wide grin on her face—I dropped Ian's hand and left the counter as quickly as I could, weaving in and out of the other customers standing by for their orders.

Catching up to me as I neared the cosmetics aisle, Ian grabbed my elbow, worried that he had just offended me. "Amanda, wait—I'm sorry! I just couldn't help it! Did you see her eyeing us the minute we got to the counter??"

Looking back at him, I gave him a comical look and he relaxed. Then, unable to swallow my laughter any longer, tears soaked at the corners of my eyes, in a loud tone exclaimed, "Ian! You are terrible!!"

"C'mon, let's go eat." He said; the laughter in his voice unmistakable. Leading me out of the drug store, he held my hand tightly and the schoolgirl feeling drenched over me once again. Unfamiliar with the emotions swirling around in my insides, I wondered if he was feeling the same. Knowing nothing about this man, I was suddenly scared, not just for me, but for Brighton as well. If I allowed him to get close, to let him fully into my life, it would have a great effect on my daughter. And if it didn't work out between us in the end, I wasn't sure who would end up hurt more—me or her—and I immediately wondered if this was really a risk I was willing to take.

My smile vanishing as these thoughts invaded my happy ones; I stepped up into the passenger seat and buckled myself in. Noticing my worried look right away, Ian hesitated before closing my door. "You okay?"

"My shoulder is just sore." I said, lying through my teeth.

"Do you want to wait here for your meds to be ready? We can go eat after if you'd like."

Stomach acting on cue again, I shook my head. "I'm hungry and I should probably get something in my stomach before taking any medication anyways."

"True." Agreeing with me, he gave me a steady look that told me he knew that my shoulder wasn't the only problem here. Forcing a smile that did not reach my eyes, I knew he saw right through me but he said nothing as he closed my door.

Driving out of the parking lot we sat in silence, Ian concentrating on the road ahead of us and me staring out the passenger's side window. Taking a chance every few minutes, I studied his profile, wanting to know what he was thinking but every time I opened my mouth to ask, I chickened out and returned my eyes to the passing scenery.

The sun was just starting to set, the sky a brilliant mix of orange and red to the west of us. A few clouds floated overhead and their heavy, darkened look heeding the warning of the nearing monsoon season that is common out here. While there were a million things that I absolutely hated about Arizona, the heat sitting currently at the number one spot, the monsoon season was one that I could tolerate. During this particular part of the year, storm clouds were known to move in without warning, dumping their heavy weight of rain upon the area so fast that extreme flooding was common and forewarned on a daily basis.

The aftermath is what I really loved; the smell of the rain as it dies down, the coolness in the air just before the humidity rose to the point that air conditioning was needed, and the green smell that covered the ground was enough to keep me here—for now, that is. Someday, Brighton and I will get out of here; begin a new adventure someplace else. What would make this daydream even better would be if we had someone to share it all with and for a brief moment, I wondered if Ian was the certain someone. Frowning at my wishful thinking, I thought better of if, not willing to hold my breath in fear that I may end up suffocating myself.

Pulling into an Olive Garden parking lot, I looked over at Ian in surprise. "This isn't cheap, Ian." I said, knowing that a table for two could end up being well over forty dollars.

"Amanda—don't take this the wrong way—but...shut up."

Scoffing at him, I tried to argue, but he was out of the truck before I could even think of a rebuttal. Opening my door, he stood to the side and looked at me without even a hint of a smile. "C'mon, get out of the truck."

Looking at him sideways, I considered refusing but thought better of it. Figuring he would end up making me leave the confines of the Dodge whether I came willingly or not, I caved. Heading across the parking lot, I shook my head slightly, and then thought, *well, he can make you come in, but he can't make you eat.*

But of course, the minute he opened the large, heavy door to the restaurant, the aroma hit me like a ton of bricks and I lost my will to fight him about it. Olive oil, baked cheese, and general sense of Italy wrapped around my senses and my mouth salivated in an instant. *Okay, okay, I'll eat,* I thought as we were led to a small, intimate table in the back of one of the side rooms.

Ordering drinks, Ian picked up a menu and asked me what I liked. Soup, salad, breadsticks, chicken marsala, five-cheese pasta, meat lasagna...whatever, I'm not picky...but I didn't want to seem piggish in front of him so I settled for minestrone soup with salad and breadsticks on the side.

"That's it??"

"What?" I asked, innocently.

"That's all you're going to eat?"

"That's enough."

"No, it's not", he said looking sideways at me. "What about dessert?"

"What about it??"

"Do you like anything they have here for dessert?"

Are you on the menu?? SHII!!! Stop it!!!

"I'll be fine, Ian, really...and if I am still hungry, I can always order more soup or salad."

"Well, you'd better. Need to fatten you up a bit, if you ask me." Muttering, I suddenly felt like we were an old married couple; unable to get through a single conversation without having some kind of argument about something that is not worth arguing about. This thought, however comical, opened the doors to our conversation as our drinks and salad arrived and I slowly sipped my Diet Pepsi as he poured sugar into his iced tea.

"Can I ask you a question?" I started.

"Anything."

"How come you're not married? Or...are you and your wife is home wondering what you are doing right now?" I asked, unable to hide my smirk.

"I'm not married, never had the pleasure."

"Oh", taking a small bite of salad that Ian had just dished out to me, I continued prying. "No kids?"

Smiling, he answered as he swallowed a bit of salad himself, "No."

"Brothers or sisters?"

"Nope, only child. My parents are teachers and I think after they had me, they were satisfied with the kids they taught and the one they raised."

"What made you want to be a cop?" Putting his fork down, he suddenly got serious and I quickly regretted asking. "You don't have to tell me if you don't want to."

"No, it's not that. When I was in college, my mother was attacked as she left the mall one night. She was okay, and they didn't hurt her too bad, but the anger I felt over it really did a number on me. Finally, one of my guidance counselors from the university sat me down and suggested that I rethink my degree options."

"So you decided to become a cop?"

"Withdrew from school the next day."

"What was your degree supposed to be in?"

"Engineering. I like trying to figure things out, take things apart and put them back together and the science and technology that is involved in a lot of that is..." pausing, he found the word he was looking for, "intriguing."

Nodding, I finished what was left of my salad just as our waiter brought our meals. Adding extra, freshly grated, parmesan to my soup and then to Ian's seafood and pasta, the waiter asked if we needed anything else and went on his way.

"Ok, my turn." Ian took a small bite of his food; melted cheese stringing itself from the plate to his mouth and as he automatically wrapped the length of it around one finger and sucked it off, I had to look down for second and catch my breath.

"Why do you dance?"

Looking up, the heat left my face and I shrugged. "The money, I guess," then reconsidering for a moment, I added "the attention at times."

"You have a desire for attention?"

"I said sometimes...we're being honest here, aren't we??" Defending myself, Ian gave me an amusing look as I clarified, "Really, it's for Brighton. I've worked regular jobs before, but when I can make more money in one shift than in forty hours, it's hard to pass up. There are way more times when I can't stand what I do, and I never want Brighton to know, but every once in a while, the girls and I have fun and it makes it a little easier to do."

"Would you ever quit?"

"Under the right circumstances, yes."

"Just like that?"

Thinking about it, I answered with a strong, "Absolutely."

"Have you ever dated anyone you danced for?"

"No."

"Why not? I'm sure there are a lot of guys that have...met you... who would give you anything you want." Smiling back at me, I tried to explain. "I don't want date anyone who has seen me half naked before they even know my last name."

Raising his eyes to meet mine, he stopped moving, mid-bite as his fork hovered an inch before his opened mouth. Then, taking the bite slowly, he chewed and swallowed before saying, "so you mean I've got a chance, huh??"

"A chance at what?" I challenged, unable to stop myself.

"A chance to make you happy", he said not missing a beat and then, the feeling was gone, swallowed up by the ringing of his cell phone. Breathing deeply, I went back to my soup and tried to take this opportunity to clear my thoughts. He was making me dizzy and I knew that I couldn't keep going back and forth in my mind, avoiding making a decision about tonight—or any night or day thereafter—for much longer. It wasn't fair; to him or to myself. And just as I came to that conclusion, the tone in Ian's voice changed drastically and I looked up at him, a feeling of dread spreading across my chest.

"When??" Listening to the person on the other end, he said, "How long ago??"

Then, standing up, he gestured for me to do the same as alarm darkened his eyes. Instantly my body started to shake and as Brighton's beautiful face entered my brain, I had to sit down again. Was she okay? Were her and Anna in an accident?? What??? I wanted to scream at him to put down the phone and tell me what was going on but held fast, knowing that he was still getting information.

Sensing that he was hesitating for a moment before responding to a question or comment that I couldn't hear, he suddenly said, "Yes!" and hissed out a strong breath of air. Then, calming a bit, said, "Okay, okay, Gonzalez. Thanks for the call." And, finally, "We're on our way."

Shutting the phone closed, he quickly scanned the table for anything that should not be left behind and then reached over and grabbed my hand. Pulling me up, he said nothing as he led me out towards the hostess's podium located at the front of the building. The hostess, seeing us coming in a hurry, started to question our actions and Ian spoke over her quickly.

"I'm sorry. Police emergency, we need to leave. This should cover the check and the tip." Pulling a couple of twenty dollar bills out of his wallet, he stuffed them in the shocked hostess's hands and turned me around by my elbow to leave. Wanting nothing more but to yank away from his tight grasp and demand that he tell me what was happening, I never had the chance. In seconds we were outside, consumed by the early evening heat, and practically running towards his truck.

Reaching it in record time, I caught my breath enough to pull away from him as he unlocked my side of the truck and yanked open the passenger door. "What the hell, Ian?? What is going on?!" Nearly yelling, a couple passing the truck paused to look at us.

"Get in, Amanda." Avoiding my demand for answers, he glared at me.

Taken back for a moment, I inhaled quickly and searched his face for any hint of the man that I had found myself falling for. *"Ian??"* Whispering, I watched as he ran a hand over his face and remorse quickly replaced the look he had given me.

"I'm sorry, hon, really. But we have to go."

Trying to stand firm, I waited, refusing to move, my anger rising to new heights.

"Amanda," he said, giving in, "it's your apartment. It's been set on fire and...and...Amanda, they think there may have been someone inside."

Chapter Fifteen

As the understanding of what he was saying registered in my already fragile mind, I felt my face go numb and as the feeling rushed down my body, I could no longer hold myself up in a standing position. Legs collapsing, I felt my knees bend but could do nothing to stop myself from falling. It was like I was suspended in air, just for a moment, and then Ian's strong arms grabbed me around the waist, stopping my body from crashing to the ground.

"Amanda!!"

He sounded distant, and I blinked a few times, trying to focus my eyes on the surprised look on his face. "What??" My voice left my dry lips in a whisper and for the life of me I couldn't swallow; there was no moisture in my mouth. It was as if it had deserted that area only to end up behind my eyes in the form of tears. "Brighton..."

Immediately understanding what I was trying to say, but couldn't, he held me up and gently pushed me back towards the side of the truck's leather seat. "She left before us remember?? She is with Anna. Amanda, look at me!"

Keeping a tight grasp on my forearms as my body relaxed against the soft leather of the seat, he gave me a slight shake and I slowly came out of the trance-like state I was in and nodded. "It's not Brighton, is it???" Then, as my green eyes overflowed with tears, I cried, *"Oh, God, Ian, tell me it's not my daughter!!!"*

Knowing that he could not tell me for sure...they may have been a million reasons why Anna had to turn back to Tucson, even if she was minutes away from Green Valley...he gave me no answer. My brain scrambling for something to hold on to, scenarios of what would have brought Anna and Brighton back home flooded my mind's eye. Anna could have forgotten something at her apartment, or felt the need to try to find something in my demolished one. She had a key and in the past, that is exactly what she has done—start to head out somewhere with Brighton, only to realize that my daughter needed something from our apartment and in returning, used her key to unlock my front door and let herself in.

As the thoughts ran through me like hot flames, the top half of my body launched forward without warning and I automatically covered my mouth with one hand. Then, unable to stop it from happening, I gained use of my arms and legs again and sprang out of Ian's arms as I pushed him out of the way. Making it to the rear of the truck, I bent suddenly at the waist and vomited my soup, salad, and breadsticks all over the ground, barely missing the tennis shoes that Anna had loaned me.

Suddenly at my side, Ian reached forward and gathered my long red hair, fisting it off of my neck and back from my face as the spasms continued to rock my body until I was spent. Waiting a few minutes, the nauseated feeling wouldn't let up and I closed my eyes to try to starve off the dry heaving. Giving myself a few minutes before trying to stand up straight again, I heard an "Oh, God!" from somewhere in front of me and then Ian's voice, "Sorry folks, it's not the   food...really!   She's...um...she's...pregnant,   you know...ahh...morning sickness!!!"

And with that, the dam broke. Hysteria rattled though my body and shook it like an angry, caged animal. Stumbling from my place of desecration, I collided into Ian's body, catching him completely off guard and he automatically took a few steps back to brace my body against his. Unguarded tears smothered my cheeks and my laughter rose to an all-time scary level. The only coherent thought I had at that very moment was that morning sickness usually occurred in the *morning* and the idea that I had been miraculously impregnated despite the fact that I hadn't had sex in years set me off into La-La Land.

Then, as suddenly as the wave of hilarity had hit me, my emotions twisted again and I was crying heavily against Ian's chest. Saying nothing, his body tensed while I leaned on him harder and worked through my meltdown.

"I...don't....I don't...think I...can...take this..." My body shuddered as I sobbed, the air heaving within my lungs and I felt like I was gasping to take a breath. "I...just...can't..."

"Shshshsh...." Trying to comfort me, his hands ran the length of my back, his left one stopping just shy of my wounded shoulder as my sobbing finally slowed down; my body too exhausted to continue. "Look," he started; putting one hand on my face he raised it to look me in the eye, "we are going to get through this. First, I want to call Anna—"

Breathing in sharp enough to cut him off, I stared up at him as terror once again appeared in my eyes. "You don't think that—"

"No!" Then more calmly, "No, I don't think that Anna was in your apartment, Brighton either, but I want to double check with her to be sure that everything is okay where they are at. Secondly, we need to get you out of those clothes."

Leaning back, I gaped at him and then realized why he had said what he did. When I pulled back, the top of the scrubs I was still dressed in clung to his white shirt...glued to it in a way, the contents of my stomach working as an adhesive and I didn't have to look down to see the mess I had created to know it was true.

"Oh...God...Oh, God, Ian, I'm sorry!" I exclaimed as another dry heave suddenly threatened to surface and I reacted without thinking, knowing that I just had to get out of these clothes. Reaching down to immediately tear off the top, Ian stopped me. "Whoa....hang on, Amanda!"

Reaching into the opened side of the truck, he grabbed Anna's pink gym back and unzipped it as fast as he could. Tossing the contents back and forth, his found what he was looking for and pulled a black t-shirt and a pair of blue jeans out of the bag. Turning back to me, it was his turn to gape at me.

Standing there, in the middle of the Olive Garden parking lot, I had stripped down, leaving only a matching bra and panties on as coverage...again compliments of Anna, who had purchased the set of soft pink, lacy garments months ago but had never even taken the tags off...he hesitated for a second, as if suddenly at a loss for words. Reaching out I took the shirt out of his stilled hands and pulled it over my head and then reached for the jeans and as carefully as I could from a standing position, pulled them on one leg at a time. Not until this was done, did I stop and look at him. "What??"

"Amanda, you know I could arrest you for that??"

"Why, I wasn't *naked*, and if anyone passing by had seen me—which no one did by the way—you could have just explained that I was getting ready to dive into the little Italian fountain they have in front of the restaurant." Then, allowing myself to give him a half smile I added, "It would've gone well with the pregnancy line...I could be overdosing on prenatal pills and losing my mind..."

Shaking his head at me, he muttered, "You're funny." Pulling a bottle of water out from inside the truck, he handed to me so that I could rinse my mouth out and then pulled out his cell phone and asked for Anna's number. Giving it to him, I tried to breathe evenly as he waited for her to pick up. Finally, after at least ten rings, someone picked up and he said, "Anna?" as he let out a breath. "Are you and Brighton okay? Amanda and I are just checking."

Nodding at me, I bent over and inhaled deeply before finishing off the bottle of water. Hearing him tell Anna that I wanted to talk to her, I stood and took the phone from him. Swallowing back my tears of relief, I assured her that everything was okay...that I was okay. Hearing the tease in her voice as she asked how I was doing with Ian (I KNOW she really meant to say 'what are you *doing* with Ian?) I smiled and told her we were both fine and I fought back the tears and hoped she couldn't hear how close I was to crying from relief.

After she explained that Brighton had eaten, taken a shower, helped Nana feed their two dogs, and had a story read to her, she was sound asleep. Not wanting Anna to wake her, I said my goodbyes, promising that Ian and I would drive out to Green Valley tomorrow afternoon and closed the phone to end the call.

As I had been slowly pacing in the parking lot, I never noticed that Ian had removed his soiled shirt and was now sifting through the contents in the back seat of his truck, obviously looking for a shirt to wear. Standing still with my mouth hanging slightly open, I soaked in as much as I could before he found a shirt to pull on and ruined my examination. His back muscles looked hard and solid, yet shifted and moved smoothly as his arms and hands worked around whatever was lying on the seat. Wide in the shoulders, my eyes continued their sweep across his bare back and I could tell that the man worked out...a lot. Tight and firm at his sides, he looked to be free of any love handles and under the dull light of the street lights that surrounded the parking area outside the Olive Garden his skin looked as though it carried a deep tan.

No wonder I can hardly concentrate around the guy!

Turning around before I could close my mouth, Ian immediately noticed my stare and froze. Wanting him so bad I could taste it, I tried to force myself to chalk it up to the insanely crazy weekend I was having so far. Taking a step forward, our eyes locked, and he slowly pulled a thin-looking blue shirt over his head, as if not sure he really wanted to or not.

"We should go." Speaking softly, he closed the back door to the truck without taking his eyes off of mine. Still a few feet apart, I couldn't stop myself from asking, "Why are you really here?"

Cocking his head to one side, he gave me a confused look.

"You could be anywhere right now. With *anyone*. Why are you here with me?"

"You know, I could ask you the same question."

"I'm here because...*you* brought me here." I answered smartly, giving him a half smile.

"And I will continue to take you wherever you want to go, Amanda."

Nodding as if this answered all of my questions, I simply said, "Okay."

"But first, we should really get over to your apartment."

The drive back to my apartment was spent in silence. Ian's right hand covered mine as he drove with the other. Leaning my head back in the seat, I closed my eyes and tried not to think about what we were going to find when we got there by concentrating on his touch. Using the pad side of his thumb, he rubbed small circles around the backside of my hand, pressing hard as if trying to work out any tension. Simultaneously, his remaining four fingers did the same, only in the opposite direction, on my palm. Every few seconds, his fingers moved up my small hand and massaged each finger, one at a time, pulling on the length of them before starting all over again.

The feeling was relaxing, yet highly erotic. I had never known any who had that kind of power in one hand and before I could stop it, flushed at the thought what both of his hands could do to the rest of me and an inescapable groan floated through my slightly parted lips. I was drifting...not to sleep, but to someplace a bit more heavenly.

Feeling the truck turn a corner and then come to an immediate stop, I sighed heavily as my daydream lifted and I came back to earth. Opening my eyes, I didn't recognize anything outside my window and wondered quickly if Ian had taken a wrong turn at some point. Looking over at him, his intense stare caused my breath to catch in my throat.

"I need to say something." His brown eyes deepening in color, I answered with a shaky, "Okay".

"You asked me why I was here...with you...and I need to clarify some things."

And suddenly my heart deflated and I knew what was coming. He has had a change of heart—no, not heart, he didn't know me enough to go through that yet, right?? The attraction was gone—that sounds more accurate—that or, in the short amount of time he had decided he had no time for the dramatics that having Brighton and myself around would be sure to cause—I mean, shit— look at what has been going on in my life in less than twenty four hours.

Deciding that any one of those reasons will be what I would hear in the next few seconds, I frowned, and opened my mouth to tell him that it was ok, he didn't need to give me any type of explanation or excuse. Just drop me off at whatever is left of my apartment and be on your way. I'll be fine. Brighton will be fine. Like I mentioned to Anna earlier in the day, I don't need a man.

"Stop it!"

Taken back, I demanded, "Stop what??"

"Doing that!"

"Doing what??" *This was getting us nowhere!*

"Automatically assuming I am just going to dump you off at your apartment and walk away!"

Jesus, can he *hear* my thoughts???

"Well, isn't that what you are about to do?? Ian—I—"

Putting two warm fingers to my lips, he said firmly, "Shut. Up.", nodding his head as he stressed each word and I raised both eyebrows at him. "Now, I am going to remove my fingers from your mouth." Glancing down at my lips, he hesitated, as if losing his concentration, then his eyes flew upward to meet mine again. "Will you please stop assuming and let me say what I need to say?"

Unable to speak, and not because of where his fingers were positioned, I simply nodded.

"Thank you." Removing his fingers, he inhaled deeply before continuing. "I don't know where this going to end up. You may end up hating me and walking out; it's seems to be the trend with women I have had relationships with in the past."

Starting to speak again, he gave me a look and said, "Amanda...shut it..."

Giving me a moment to do so, I clamped my mouth shut and began chewing on the inside of my cheek, feeling as if it was going to kill me not to say *something*.

"I know you have a daughter and that you are probably looking out for her interests more than your own. I am not familiar with kids; never got involved with someone who had any, but I do know that I am not only intrigued by you, but by Brighton as well. Watching the two of you together, in what little time I have been able, has opened up a door that I don't want to close.

"Watching you, alone, on the other hand, has made me more than just curious. I don't do one-night-stands. And I don't begin relationships on the pretense that I am just passing time until the next one comes along. Yes, I...*want*... you. I want you in the worst way and I think that point is abundantly clear. But, I can safely say that I also want more than that. I can't promise you that this will work out the way I want it to in the end, but I can promise you that when I give myself to someone it's not halfheartedly. I want to take care of you. Of Brighton. And whatever it is waiting for you at your apartment, I will not allow you to go through it—or anything else from this point on—alone, as long as this is also what *you* want."

Covered in goose bumps, the tears that had been building as he spoke spilled over the bottoms of my eyelids and I did nothing to stop them. No one has ever given me a speech such as this and I felt a bit overwhelmed. But more than that, I felt relieved, I now know exactly what his intensions are and I honestly felt that every word he spoke was the truth. I wasn't being played with, nor did I feel that he was going to have his way with me and then hit the road running. The question that now faced me, however, was whether or not I felt the same.

And in answering that very question, not only for Ian but for myself as well, I reached out and grabbed a fistful of his dark brown hair, pulling him to me. Hearing his breath exhale quickly, I knew that he had been holding it, waiting for my response. And in giving it to him, I pressed my mouth over his and in the next few seconds, reached heaven's gates once again.

Chapter Sixteen

Floored by the response he had gotten from Amanda only seconds after admitting his feelings for her and her daughter off his chest, Ian had to consciously monitor his speed as he drove down her street. A fire truck passing them from the opposite direction, silent and moving slowly, told Ian that the fire had been extinguished. Looking over at Amanda, he noticed the stress returning as she leaned forward in her seat, and ran a hand through her long red hair.

Wanting to tell her again that everything was going to be okay, but with no proof, he decided keep his mouth closed. Nearing the end of the road, he caught a glimpse of a news van as it pulled away from the curb, obviously done with getting their story, two marked police cruisers, a crime scene van, and an ambulance. Flashing red and blue lights lit up the front of the complex; running on silent mode. Neighbors, the majority probably being evacuated tenants, were strewn about, some watching intently as the scene unfolded in front of their eyes while the others wandered around the parking, looking lost.

Pulling up to a curb close to the opened electronic fence, Ian parked the truck and hesitated before getting out. Searching for Detective Gonzalez, he waited until he had eyes on her before looking over at Amanda, who was now sitting back in her seat with an unreadable expression on her face.

"Give me a minute, okay, I'm going to go find out what happened."

Giving him a short nod, he almost thought twice about leaving her, but knew he didn't want her in earshot of whatever information Detective Gonzalez had for him. When Gonzalez phoned him to tell him what was going on, while he and Amanda were sitting at the Olive Garden, she had mentioned that it looked like the fire department was pulling a body out of the burning inferno. Until he knew all the facts and could relay them to Amanda, he wanted her out of the middle of things, if nothing else but to protect her.

Leaving the truck, he made his way through the spectators and approached the female detective, who caught his eye and finished discussing things with a member of the crime scene team. Reaching Ian, she pulled him aside and said, "She still with you??"

Hardening his jaw, Ian simply said, "Yes."

"Well, good." Gonzalez gave him a second to allow her surprising remark to sink in before adding, "If she had been here, Ian, her goose would have been cooked. And not only hers, but that little girl's as well."

"How is that you are here, Gonzalez, where's Colliatti??" Wanting to know if they should be having this conversation away from the scene, especially since he was still under suspension and had blown off his captain's orders to stay away from Amanda, he looked around nervously.

"Colliati's off the case."

Gaping at her, Ian said, "No shit???"

"No shit. Captain lit into him when he got back to the station. Wish you coulda' been there, man, it was *classic*!"

"Well, good, the bastard deserved it!"

"Yea, I know that's right!"

Refocusing his attention on the scene, Ian asked, "So what's the word here? What happened?"

"Not sure yet, but it's definitely arson. We're still waiting for the fire marshal to check out the apartment, but we do know that there was an accelerant used and that the woman inside was an older adult. She didn't make it and it looks like she was dead before the blaze even got started, but again, we are going to have to wait on that too. As for the place itself, it's a goner. By the time the fire department was called, the fire had spread to one of the adjoining apartments."

"Anyone else hurt??"

"No, just the victim they found inside."

"Any apartments on the first floor damaged?"

"Not that I know of."

Sighing in relief in knowing that Anna's apartment had been spared and that no one else was hurt, he had another thought, "But whatever evidence that was still inside the apartment from the vandalism is now gone."

"Yep." Pursing her lips together, Gonzalez added, "And now, I'm the lead detective on this thing and we've got nothing to go on, except for the fact that someone out there is trying to kill your girl and from the looks of it, they aren't caring too much about anyone who may get in their way."

Nodding, Ian thought about that for a moment, then asked, "So what now?"

"Keep her with you, and don't tell anyone else but me."

Giving the detective a surprised look, he said, "You do believe that someone is working this from the inside." Seeing her nod, he then asked, "Any ideas who??"

"Not at this point. But we don't need any further interference from anyone until we can get this under control. Where's her daughter?"

"Safe."

"Good. Make sure you keep it that way."

"You know how to reach me."

"Yessir, I sure do. And as soon as I hear anything—especially concerning this new victim—I will contact you. Be safe, Ian, and don't do anything I wouldn't do."

Smiling at her last remark, Ian watched the detective head back to the stairs that led up to what was left of Amanda's apartment. Turning, he knew he had made the right choice in getting Gonzalez involved. Not only did she pass his test concerning the whereabouts of Brighton...by taking him on his word that she was safe and leaving it at that...but he also knew that she would work diligently until the bastard, or bastards, were caught and behind bars. The only thing that did worry him now was the fact that he didn't know if there was anyone else he could trust.

Getting back into the truck, he gave Amanda the rundown on what was going, leaving out the probability that there may be someone close to her involved. Feeling that she had had enough for one day, they pulled away from the curb and, looking over at her once more, noticed silent tears run down her cheeks. Reaching over, he grasped her hand and gave it a tight squeeze, knowing that nothing he said or did was going to make it better at the moment.

Twenty minutes later, he pulled into the Walgreens drive thru lane to pick up Amanda's prescriptions and realized that she hadn't been complaining much about her shoulder. Softly asking her about it, she looked over at him and blinked, as if trying to focus on his question.

"Um...it's pretty much a constant throbbing."

Nodding at her, Ian figured that she has had way too much happen today to probably even notice it hurting. Then, thinking more about it all, began the task of detailing what he was going to need to do to make sure she was taken care of in the coming days and made a mental list of things in his mind as he waited for the car in front of them to finish up at the window and get out of his way.

Medications, supplies to clean and dress her wound, clothes for her and Brighton, toiletries, food for his apartment, making contact with Anna and her parents to make arrangements for Brighton if needed....the list went on and on...and he was suddenly thankful for the suspension he was under. He now had the time he would need to take care of everything he possibly could.

Finally reaching the window, Ian leaned over the side of the driver's side window and spoke into a small device that housed a microphone, located below a huge picture window that offered him an inside look of the pharmacy. Giving the clerk—not the one from earlier, thankfully—Amanda's information, he waited while the guy left his view and pulled her order out of the mix. Giving Ian a total of $248.56, Ian did not hesitate as he chose a credit card out of his wallet, placed inside a small tubular container, and sent it back through the long tube, hearing the all familiar suction sound as it went.

Glancing over at Amanda, he was waiting for her argument concerning the cost of her prescriptions, but her focal point was concentrated on something outside her window and she said nothing. Leaving her to her thoughts for the time being, he focused on retrieving her order and drove away, now heading to his part of town.

Living on the east side of Tucson, Ian had all the convenience of home within a three mile radius. A Safeway grocery store, several fast food restaurants (neither of which he had yet to step inside in during the fifteen years he had lived in this area), a couple of places to get work done on his truck, and a Wal-Mart Supercenter. Pulling into the Wal-Mart, he chose a spot close to the one of the entrances and turned off the engine. Asking Amanda if she wanted to come in with him, she shook her head.

Not wanting to leave her alone too long, he quickly entered the big box store and grabbed a cart. Heading for food, he grabbed the essentials needed for the next couple of days; eggs, milk, bread, meat, cheese, fresh vegetables, a large package of bottled water, and then headed to the Health and Beauty section and grabbed extra toiletries for his guest bathroom that included what he hoped was kid's shampoo and conditioner, toothpaste and extra tooth brushes, and whatever else he could think of. On the way out of that department, he paused, thinking for a moment and turned the cart around. Grabbing a package of condoms, he hesitated—wondering if they were even going to be needed with everything else going on—but decided to go against his better judgment and tossed the box into the cart.

Then, into Bedding and Home Furnishings, and in minutes had loaded up with enough blankets, extra sheets, a girly-looking comforter, and new pillows that would dress up more than just one room. Then turning around another aisle, found a truckload of other accessories that would make any little girl happy. Wanting to then grab clothes, shoes, and whatever other items a woman and her daughter may need, he remembered that he had no idea of what sizes to get and decided that in the next day or two, he would drag Amanda back here if that's what it took for him to shop for her and Brighton.

Satisfied with his purchases, he checked out one of the counters; not even blinking at the total cost of it all; and made his way back out of the store to the truck. Reaching the front of it, he stopped in his tracks.

The passenger side of the truck was empty.

Turning around immediately, he searched the area right around the truck but didn't see her. Heart thundering against his chest, he yelled, "AMANDA!!" but only received curious looks from a family of four that was passing by. Stepping towards them in a hurry, the only male in the group stretched a tattooed arm across the smaller members of the group, stopping each of them from moving.

"Have you seen a young woman?! Long, red hair...wearing a pair of blue jeans and t-shirt?!"

"Nope, haven't seen anyone!" The guy with the tattoos hollered back, obviously out of sorts caused by Ian's sudden advance on his family. Then, more calmly added, "But we just pulled in to the parking lot a couple of minutes ago."

"Okay...thank you." Panicked, Ian raced back towards his truck and, beginning to pull the bags of groceries out of the cart, he yanked open the door behind the driver's seat and, froze immediately. Curled up in the backseat of the truck was Amanda, sleeping softly with one arm tucked under her head.

"Oh, Jesus!!" Huffing out a breath of air, he placed a heavy arm on the inside of the opened door and dropped his head. Closing his eyes, he laughed at himself before opening them again to give her another long look.

Laying on her side, she looked peaceful and content. Her chest moved up and down smoothly as she breathed and she shifted slightly as Ian reached above her face to move a soft layer of long hair away from the side of her face. Taking a deep breath, he gave himself another minute or two to let his heart return to its normal speed of beating and then closed the backseat door softly but firmly.

Loading up his purchases into the front passenger's side of the truck, he returned the cart to the front of the store, got back into the truck, and drove to his apartment. Once he was parked in the garage area, he had to decide what to move first, the three hundred dollars' worth of merchandise or Amanda's sleeping body.

Choosing to get Amanda up to his apartment and settled in first, he stowed his wallet and keys into his front pocket, pulled his weapon out of its holding place by his seat and tucked it into the back of his jeans (checking to ensure the safety was on first, of course!), and gently lifted Amanda out of the backseat of the truck, hoping that he would not wake her.

Using one hip to close the truck door, he shifted her body so that he had one arm cradling her head and the other holding up her from beneath her knees. Realizing just how light she was in weight, he decided that he was going to force her to start eating more as he made his way to the elevator.

Arriving on his floor, he stepped out of the elevator and made his way to his apartment, careful to not disturb her in any way if possible. Reaching his door, he remember that his keys were still in his front pocket and debated swiftly as to how to fish them out without dropping Amanda. Then, hearing a door open down the hall from him saw Mrs. Lange poke her head out of her open doorway, peering down the hall at him.

"Mrs. Lange!" He called in a low voice. "Can you come help me??"

"OH! Mr. Sampson! I didn't realize that was you!!"

Hurrying down the hall, Mrs. Lange stopped short when realizing just what Ian was carrying in his arms. "Detective......" she said coolly, "is she a criminal??" Then, eyeing him, asked, "*Did you have to taze her*???"

Laughing at the old woman, Ian shook his head and explained his dilemma. Turning a hip towards Mrs. Lange, he felt her arthritic fingers sift through his front pocket as they searched for his keys. The seconds flying by, he was tempted to ask her if she was enjoying herself—her fingers feeling around the inside of his pocket, feeling all they could while stuffed in there.

"Ah!! Got 'em!"She cried out in glee and he tried hard to suppress a grin. Leave it to Mrs. Lange to try to cop a feel before the woman in his arms had even a chance!

Unlocking his door, the woman stepped into the apartment ahead of him and searched for a light switch to flip on. Still sleeping in his arms, Amanda barely stirred when she did and bright white light covered her face.

"Thanks, Mrs. Lange", Ian said, relieved that he had Amanda inside.

"Ohhh....you can call me Edna, *Detective*!" Then, after offering a wink and a smile, she headed towards the opened door to leave. Pausing quickly before exiting she turned and gave Ian a suggestive look. "Now, you get her right to bed, and no hanky panky! You're much too young to have a bunch of kids runnin' around, especially before you are married!! But...if unable to wait, young man...you'd better protect the both of ya!"

Unable to stifle his laughter, Ian nodded at his neighbor, said thank you, and shut the door using his back to make sure it closed all the way. Then, heading down the hall, he stopped in front of the guest bedroom, but decided against it. Amanda wouldn't stay in there until it was cleaned up, brightened, and included fresh bedding.

Turning, he carried her to his bedroom instead and leaning carefully, was able to pull the black comforter with matching top sheet back enough to lay her down on top of the fitted one. Stepping towards her feet, he undressed them, tossing her shoes on the floor by the bed and stripping her of her socks, glanced at her painted pink toes. Breathing deep, his eyes took in the rest of her and he debated whether or not he should try to get the rest of her clothing off.

Deciding against it due to the fact that if she woke in the middle of it, she may get upset—or it may lead to something else, and at that point, they both needed to sleep; he pulled the covers over her body and held his breath as she turned in her sleep. Quietly leaving the room, he made the perilous journey back down to the garage and brought up the Wal-Mart bags and Amanda's gym bag before constructing a make-shift bed out of his couch and collapsing upon it...asleep before his head even hit the pillow.

Chapter Seventeen

It's so dark....why is it so dark?? Why can't I see anything??

There is something on top of my... (Trying to sit up, I banged my head on something solid) I can't sit up! It's cold in here...why is it so cold???

Oh, God, it's moving! Whatever I am laying in, its' moving...what...?? Oh, GOD!! Oh, no! I'm in the trunk—they got me and I AM IN THE TRUN—

Eyes flying open, I literally felt my scream vibrate over my lips as it echoed through the darkness that surrounded my body. Looking around immediately, I saw nothing but dark shadows and my heart pounded in my ears so hard that I couldn't hear anything over it. Then, suddenly, a pair of hands grabbed my shoulders and I fought back as hard as I could, grunting and yelling as I pushed against them with all my might as my heels dug into whatever it was that I was lying on.

It's the trunk!! I'M STILL IN THE TRUNK!! My mind screamed at me and I screamed out loud again, ignoring the soreness already building in my throat.

"AMANDA!!!"

Hearing my name did nothing to slow me down, and then—I was FREE! The hands that were holding me released their grip on my arms and I scrambled to get away. Then, the darkness was gone as a soft white light immediately took its place and I threw my hands up, protecting my eyes from the sudden change. At the exact same time, the hands returned and gripped my wrists, pulling them down to get me to lower my arms, and I fought for a second longer before forcing my eyes open to look up at my attacker.

Ian instantly let up on his grip when he saw that my eyes were open and I could see that he was sweating and out of breath. I relaxed my arms immediately and searched his face as I choked back a sob and he swiftly cradled my upper body into his arms. Giving in, my body shook as I wept into his arms; my head pressed against his bare chest and I was unable to speak.

"It's okay, baby, it's okay…it's all over. It was just a dream…a bad dream."

His voice shook slightly as he spoke and I knew that I must have scared him almost as much as I had scared myself. Blinking rapidly, I could hardly see through the river of tears as they continued to run over my eyelids. Pushing against him for a second, I raised my fingers tried to dry them but hands were too shaky to be effective.

Feeling Ian release my body for a second, he grabbed a box of Kleenex from somewhere and brought to my side. "Here", he whispered as he pulled a couple of tissues from the box and said, "Look at me."

Complying, I raised my eyes to meet his and he gently wiped the tears from my face while his other hand centered on the middle of my back, as if trying to hold me upright in a sitting position. Then, seeing clearly for the first time, I turned my eyes towards my surroundings and looked around. The room I was in was small in size, but offered enough space for the bed that I now knew I was sitting on, a tall dresser that sat in one corner, and a small end table located at the head of the bed.

"Where are we?" My throat sore, my voice creaked as I spoke.

"My apartment", he answered softly.

"And this is your room?"

Then before I could ask anything further, like how I got here because the last thing I remembered was crawling into the backseat of his truck to lay down while he went into Wal-Mart, hot pain shot across my shoulders and ran down the middle of my back, causing me to inhale sharply and straighten my upper body.

Seeing the pain register on my face, Ian left me on the bed and hurried out of the room. Returning seconds later, he had two pill bottles and a bottle of water. Dishing out the prescribed amount of pain and antibiotic medicine that I was to take, he handed me the pills and opened the water bottle for me to drink from.

Once I was finished, he looked less tense, as if taking my medication had been a high priority to him. Now, standing by the bed, he gave me a worried look as I drank more water, the pain in my shoulder beginning to subside just a bit as I sat as still as possible on the backs of my heels.

"You should eat something."

Thinking, I nodded slowly.

"Amanda? You okay?"

"Yea", I said quietly, "it's just been a hellava day, you know??"

"Well, c'mon, let me show you the place, so that you know where everything is, and then make you something to eat. You don't need to get sick because you took those pills on an empty stomach."

"Okay. Mind if I change first??" Still wearing jeans and a t-shirt, I felt like I needed to get into something more comfortable in order to relax.

"Of course. Your bag is on the dresser", motioning to it, he paused for a second, "and the bathroom is just down the hall on the right." Then, heading towards the bedroom door, he said, "Make yourself at home, Amanda."

Leaving me, he softly closed the door behind him and I took a moment to try to take it all in. In less than forty-eight hours, I have been shot, had my apartment vandalized—then burned to the point that it is probably unlivable—found out that someone was in it at the time and died, and amid all that—may have found the man of my dreams! Good, God, I hope things calm down a bit after all this!! Then, rethinking it, I admitted to myself that if *some* things heated up a bit...I'd survive.

Getting off the bed took some effort. The pain in my shoulder making it difficult to move my arm very much, I crawled to the edge of the queen sized bed using only my left arm for support. Grabbing the bag Anna had packed for me, I carried it out of the bedroom and down the hall to where Ian had said the bathroom was. Stepping in and turning on the light, I found myself amused at the look of it.

Small in size, the bathroom consisted of a short counter with sink, small square-sized mirror positioned on the wall, the toilet immediately to the left of the counter with a short towel rack above it, and a half-sized shower across from it; minus a tub. A tall hamper sat between the door and the shower and took up most of the space in the room. Although everything was clean, even the toilet, it represented bachelorhood to a tee. There were no decorations on the walls, it was painted a dull white, and the counter was free of anything feminine; rather reeked of masculinity—of *Ian*.

Sorting through the bag after moving the hamper down to give me some room, I realized that Anna did not know the meaning of "comfy" sleeping attire. Finding a lacy red nightgown that had spaghetti straps instead of sleeves and a low neckline, the shortness of it wouldn't have covered half of my bottom. Another sexy outfit, black in color, was a two piece short set, and by short...I mean SHORT...with a halter top to match, both made out of satin.

Aside from those options, there was another pair of jeans, a green tank top, another brand new bra and panty set with the tags still attached, and a couple pair of socks. Oh....I was so ready to strangle that woman!! Sighing, I decided to just stay in the clothes I was wearing for now and when trying to sleep again later, would change into one of her selections. I wasn't about to face Ian in one of these outfits just yet, especially when knowing that I needed to eat something before I did anything else.

Finding a small travel case of toothpaste, a toothbrush, deodorant, and a hairbrush, I brushed my teeth, gave myself a quick sponge bath using the hand towel from the rack and a bar of green colored soap that was on the counter. Brushing through my hair, I had to do this left handed and it was awkward, I smoothed out tangles as best I could. My red hair, all one length, traveled halfway down my back and I suddenly decided it may be time for a change. With everything going on, a visit to a hair salon may be just what I needed to escape real life—even if only for an hour or so.

Leaving the bag on the floor of the bathroom, I left the room and wandered down the rest of the short hallway to find Ian. Coming to a small living room, I noticed that a dining area sat to the left of it and led the way to a box-shaped kitchen. Ian, wearing nothing but a pair of dark blue pajama pants, was at the stove. Steeling myself from speaking, I took in the sight of him and couldn't stop my eyebrows from rising slightly.

Granted, I had seen him shirtless in the Olive Garden parking lot, that moment didn't do him justice. His shoulders, broad and wide, looked thick and gave way to a strong muscle structure that ran the length of both arms. The part of his chest I could see, looked tight, or "cut" as they say in the gym world and I knew that his stomach muscles were likely to be reminiscent of a washboard. He was built, but not overly muscular or veiny—like those guys you see on Muscle and Fitness magazines. Ignoring the sudden desire to run a hand over the curves of his arms, I blinked a few times to regain my focus.

"Hey." I approached him softly, not wanting to scare him twice in fifteen minutes.

Turning from the stove, he smiled and noticed that I was still in my jeans and t-shirt. Giving me a questionable look, I entered the kitchen and leaned against the counter opposite him and somehow managed to keep my eyes level with his face instead of allowing them the opportunity to drift down his chest. "Anna has a sense of humor."

"Huh??" Turning to look at me again, I could see that he was stirring something in a small pot and the smell coming from it was mouthwatering.

"The bag she packed me?" He nodded, understanding what I was referring to and I went on. "Had nothing…to sleep in packed in it. She…um…must have forgotten to pack that stuff." Feeling my face turn red, I turned from him to study the few magnets he had on his refrigerator.

Nodding again while he continued to stir the contents on the stove, he replied absently, "Well, if you don't mine men's clothes, I have a couple pair of shorts or sweats and some t-shirts if you want. They will probably fall right off of you, but you're welcome to them."

Sensing no sexual innuendos in his comment about his clothes falling right off of me, my face became a deeper shade of red when I heard it, I thanked him for the offer and, after turning off the stove; he left the kitchen and returned a few minutes later with a pair of gray shorts and a white t-shirt. Changing in the bathroom, I returned only to find my dinner on the table…minestrone soup and a small plate of Saltine crackers. Alongside it, a can of Diet Pepsi. I smiled in knowing that he had remembered what I had eaten at the Olive Garden.

Ian held the dining room chair out for me to sit in and I suddenly felt spoiled. While I've been on a few dates since my divorce, never had I met a man who was so conscious of my needs and I knew then that this one was different from the rest.

While I ate, Ian sat across from me, and we made small talk about Brighton, his job, the bar, and his parents. When I had finished, he cleared the table and set the dishes in the dishwasher. Only then, did he turn and discuss sleeping arrangements.

"I have a spare bedroom, across from mine and it's yours but it needs to be cleaned first. I don't usually have any reason to use it so right now it's just extra storage space for me. Tomorrow— err, *later today*, after we see Brighton and decide what to do from there, I can get it ready for you if you want to stay here for a while. But for now, you take the bed and I'll take the couch."

Sounding firm in his decision, I thought twice about arguing. I didn't want to put him out and didn't mind sleeping on his couch but knew that saying as much probably wouldn't get me anywhere, so I kept my mouth shut and just nodded.

"I picked up some stuff at Wal-Mart; stuff for the bathroom and such. It's already in there, in the medicine cabinet for you to use. And there are towels in the hall closet across from the bathroom, use the shower whenever you need. Just...make yourself at home, okay?"

"Okay." Not knowing what else to say, I followed him back to his bedroom as he flicked off light switches along the way, leaving the rest of the apartment in the dark. Reentering the room, he straightened the bedding for me, showed me how to turn off the small lamp on the night stand, and asked if I needed anything else.

Hesitating, my heart started pounding in my chest...I knew what I wanted, but wasn't really sure if I could just come out and say it. Staring at him as he took another look around the room while waiting for my answer, he went to take a step but stopped immediately when catching my eye. Feeling an ache rush through my body, I prayed that he understood the look on my face. He did...

Cocking his head to the side, he gave me a look of warning and he said, "Amanda, don't look at me like that. You're overtired, sore, and probably aren't thinking straight—"

Cutting him off, I whispered, "Yes, I am."

Crossing the room, he reached me in less than a second and placed his hands on the sides of my face, his deep brown eyes never leaving mine. "I don't want to hurt you—you're shoulder..." His voice now husky, I bit my lip and whispered his name and, reaching around, placed my palms on his lower back, pulling him to me. His mouth suddenly on mine, he groaned slightly as I surrendered my tongue, my lips, my *everything*.

And in that quick moment, our kiss became more than just passionate; it became urgent, and he put an arm around my waist and guided me as he slowly walked backwards to the edge of the bed. Breaking our embrace, he searched my face for any sign of uncertainty and, upon finding none, sat on the edge of the bed and I took a step forward, looking down at him as I did.

Raising my shirt just short of my breasts, he put a hand on my lower back, pulling me even closer, then with his mouth, worked his way across my stomach and my ribs, teasing just above the waist band of his shorts that I was wearing, causing fresh goose bumps to cover my body. Cradling his head in my hands as he flicked his tongue across my skin and I closed my eyes and leaned my head back.

In seconds, I wanted more, and got his attention as I released his hair from my fingers and, reaching, dragged my nails up his back and felt his body tense as a result. Groaning again as his mouth continued to work its way around my belly, I slowly turned in my place, giving him access to my side and then my back. Now with his hands at my front, I covered both with my own and took charge of them as I guided them up my body to my chest. Moving over my breasts, his fingers pulled and teased, causing me to arch my back and then, I was suddenly on his lap, my back facing his chest.

With an open invitation to my neck, Ian whispered my name and a wave of electricity ran through my body. Moving my hair to the side, he nipped at the side of my neck and moved his way up towards my ear. Inhaling sharply, I suddenly felt desperate for him and carefully pulled my shirt over my head, taking extra care of my shoulder as I did. The bandages still in their place over my wounds, he paused for a moment and I thought he was going to force us to stop. Instead, he moved my hair, from left side of my neck to the right and began the process all over again. His hands took up their exploration once more and as they pressed against my skin my body began moving on its own, grinding gently on his lap as he tried to move underneath me.

Pulling his hands aside, I suddenly stood, wanting to be free of anything obstructing the feel of his skin on mine. Keeping my back to him, knowing he was watching me, I dipped my fingers into the insides of the shorts he had given me and the lacy panties I had on underneath and slid both down to my feet, bending at the waist as I did. Hearing him inhale sharply, I stood, stepped out of them, and turned to face him, completely naked and unabashed.

Mouth open, his eyes drank in the sight of me for a moment before returning to meet mine. Whispering, "You're beautiful", I had the sudden urge to turn away from him. Not used to this kind of attention; unfueled by alcohol, loud music, or florescent lighting, I bit my lip as I stared down at him.

As if hearing my thoughts, he stood, gathered me into his muscular arms and said, "I mean it, Amanda, you are *beautiful.*"

Kissing me again, slowly—as if making love to my mouth—I let myself go, allowing my body to act on its own free will. Using both hands, I slid my fingers beneath the waistband of his pants and, breaking the lock his mouth had over mine, took a small step back to watch his face. Pushing down on his pants, I freed him from them, slowly lowering myself to my knees as I did. Wanting to pleasure him in every way I knew how, I gasped when he pulled me back to my feet without warning.

"No." His intense stare surprised me and I suddenly wondered what I had done wrong. Then, turning me so that my back was to the bed, he said, "Save that for some other time, I want to focus on you tonight."

"Oh", my response barely audible, I felt my knees weaken as my insides began to ache with need. And when he told me to lie down on the bed, on my back, I thought I was going to melt. Positioning myself, our eyes locked; his deep in color with desire. Near my feet, he was the first to break eye contact as he focused on my legs. Starting just above my ankles, he began, touching, kissing, and teasing as he took turns with the both of them and slowly worked his way up my body. Feeling an ache center in between my legs, I tried to sit up, wanting to grab him and pull him up to me but at the same time I didn't want him to stop.

"Oh...Ian—" Gasping as he reached my inner thighs, I reached and grabbed a fistful of his hair. "Come here..." Ignoring me, he continued, his mouth trained on my skin and I felt like I was going to explode before he was even inside me.

Then, suddenly, he pushed my legs apart and my knees bent as he buried his mouth where I needed it. My center shuddered and he groaned against my softest part and I felt the effect of it vibrate through my hips. Working his tongue expertly, he tasted and teased at first, then pulling my skin through his teeth gently, I rocked my hips forward and pushed on the back of his head, wanting him to go even deeper as my insides rattling uncontrollably. Then he found my spot and feverishly working to pleasure me, he pushed his hands under my backside and pulled up on my hips, causing me to arch my back at the same time. My fingers, still in his hair, fisted tightly and I felt his arms tense underneath my body.

"Oh, shit, Ian....come here!"

Yanking on his hair, I fought to get him to do what I wanted, and he as he gave my center one final flick of his tongue, he pulled himself up onto his knees and looked at me, seeming satisfied with himself before he suddenly left the bed.

"What—??? Where are you...??" Unable to spit a normal sentence out, my breath caught in my throat when he returned, a package of condoms in his hand. Lying there, I gave him a sideways look and, smiling, said, "Oh....were you planning on getting some tonight??"

"No—but I have to say that I was hoping." Admitting this to me with a smile, he kept his focus on me as his fingers worked to get the package open and pulled one out and tossed the remainder aside. Palming the wrapped condom, he decided that he was not done with me yet and climbed back onto the bed, repositioning his body in between my legs. Holding himself up, as if getting ready to do a push-up, he kissed my mouth and I could taste myself on his tongue and the knowledge of this nearly drove me out of my mind. Breaking the kiss, he eyed me for a moment and smiled softly.

"Want more??" He asked, teasing me with a look.

"I want you..." I replied and felt his body tense again, as if hearing this was enough to turn him on. Then, propped up on his elbows, he said, "This okay? Not too much on your shoulder?"

The hell with my shoulder! I wanted to yell at him, but nodded instead, waiting for whatever he was going to do next. Kissing my lips again, I felt more of his weight on me and my body reacted immediately. Wrapping my legs around his waist, I could feel how hard he was and I moaned against his mouth. Moving his body down a bit, I released the hold my legs had on his hips, and he left my mouth and found my taut nipples.

Caressing with his tongue, he focused on one and then moved to the other and my body rocked underneath his still one. His skin felt warm and I shifted my hips as the deep ache returned and danced across my belly before moving down to my core. I wanted—no *needed*—him inside me...the ache beginning to hurt.

"Ian—*please*..."

Continuing to work his mouth around my breasts, he murmured softly.

"Please, Ian, I need you..."

Breathing heavy on my skin, he pulled one nipple through his teeth and my breath hissed as I exhaled. Then, he raised himself forward, eye level with me again and, watching my face, adjusted himself once more, fitting perfectly between my legs.

"I want this to last as long as possible." He muttered as he nipped at my neck again. "If I enter you, I won't be able to control myself."

Whimpering at his words, I raised my head up, sinking into the soft pillow underneath it. "I want to come...Ian, please," then, looking at him, I demanded, "make me come."

Groaning as his mouth pressed against mine, he surrendered to my request. Kissing me softly, he made on of his own, "Tell me how you want it."

"On top."

Pushing his hands underneath my body, so that his palms held my back, he rolled suddenly, pulling me with him at the same time. Now on top, I took over. Lying flat on top of him, I positioned my body right where I needed it. Moving freely now, I let myself go, not wanting my moment to end too quickly, but at the same time, desperate to have it flow through my body. Rock hard underneath my body, Ian quivered slightly and a heat wave fluttered through me in an instant.

Grabbing his hands, I laced my fingers in between his and brought them up above his head. Moving slowly, I ground myself against him, and shuddered as a deep moan left my lips. Seeming shocked, Ian forced to free his fingers, and placed both hands firmly on my backside, pushing me down onto him. Feeling him harden even more as my body took over and moved faster against him, I could feel myself getting ready to explode.

"Come on, Amanda..."

Even closer, I gasped, "Can you feel it?? Feel me??"

"God—YES!"

Gripping his shoulders, I pushed myself up, and arched my back, and as I yelled his name, I finally found release. Rocking hard against him, my orgasm fluttered through my insides and I held on to it as long as I could.

As one final shudder escaped through my tingling skin, I let go of his shoulders, feeling my nails release their pressure on him and I collapsed against him. Kissing the top of my head, Ian held me tightly against him and I could feel the pounding of his heart against my chest. When I was finally able to move and my burning ache had cooled down, I raised my head to look at him.

"Oh my God—that felt GOOD!!!"

Laughing slightly, he gave me a look and replied, "*You* felt good."

Then, kissing him, it took no time at all for us to heat up again, my only intention now being to make him feel as good as he had made me feel. "What do you want?" I asked softly.

"You" was his only reply.

"*How* do you want me?" I muttered against his mouth as his hands began moving across my back. "Anything you want, Ian...tell me..."

Feeling him start to sit up, I did the same and as we moved together towards the edge of the bed, my heart began racing again.

Scooting so that the backs of his knees met the edge, he put both hands on my shins and repositioned them so that I was straddling his lap; my legs wrapped Indian-style around his lower back. Then, pausing, he gently pushed me back and I watched as he grabbed the condom and tore the package open.

Sheathing himself, he then placed his hands on my sides and raised me up off of him only to bring me back down and filled me with himself. His mouth found my breasts and he focused on them again as I began moving at the direction of his hands. Pulling, pushing, and pulling my hips back again, I let him guide my body for me.

"Amanda..." He groaned against one nipple, biting at it as he did. "You feel so good..."

The sound of his voice, husky and drenched with desire, caused my body to tense against his and he wrapped his long arms around my waist and pulled me even closer, as if not wanting anything to get between us and raised his head to kiss my chin, my neck, and my mouth.

Reaching around with one hand, I slipped it beneath my bottom, trying to feel him as he moved inside me. The act caused him to inhale sharply and he spread his legs slightly, allowing me more access. Cupping him, I squeezed gently as our mouths continued working on each other and as his lower half moved faster, I leaned back slightly and cried out his name.

Feeling him harden even more, I looked at him, watching the pleasure spread across his face and said, "Come, Ian...c'mon...give it to me" and his eyes closed as his head rolled back. Then, suddenly, his arms tightened around my body and after two sudden jerks from below, he emptied himself in me, swearing as he did.

Slowing down immediately, he held me close as he dragged his fingers through my hair, massaging my scalp. Sitting in this position, I pressed my forehead against his and closed my eyes while I breathed in the scent of our lovemaking as it drifted through the air and felt his heart slow down along with mine. Only when we were finally able to breathe normally did I raise my body up, releasing him and crawled across him to lie fully on the bed.

With my back to him, I felt the bed shift as he left it and headed out of the bedroom to the bathroom. Lying there, alone and suddenly emotional, I felt tears build up behind my eyes and wondered if this one night was going to the first of many or if, for whatever reason, this was all I was going to get.

And as Ian crawled back into bed, still free of clothes, but now smelling like soap, he adjusted the bedding so that it covered the two of us. Stretching over my body to turn off the light, he then pulled me close and wrapped one arm around my waist, spooning me. Finding much comfort in this position, I pushed the thoughts out of my head, deciding that whatever happened from this point on, I would deal with it as it came, thankful for this one night at least. Drifting off, I felt Ian breathe evenly against my neck and weakly whispered, "Thank you, Ian" and, not fully registering his reply, thought I heard, "I love you, Amanda", before sleep quickly took over.

Chapter Eighteen

David watched in quiet fascination as the car Lenny and him had been using was positioned into the crusher. Stripped of all its valuable parts and emptied of all fluids, the skeletal metal structure was now ready to be flattened. Observing from the salvage yards wide office window, he watched as a one of the yard workers positioned the arms of the loader he was operating to the side of the vehicle in order to hold it in place. Hear the creaking and moaning of the crusher as it spurred to life he continued to watch as the roof of the machine slowly cranked its way down onto the roof of the car.

Whining loudly, as if in protest, the frame of the vehicle began to flatten and as the windows shattered, David took an automatic step back; forgetting momentarily that he was safely inside the confines of the office. Obviously feeling that the vehicle was not going to come jutting out of the crusher during the process, the loader was backed up and parked at one end of the yard.

Hearing a door open behind him minutes later, David turned around swiftly, ready to pounce if needed but relaxed when seeing the operator enter the small room. Turning back to the operation now in full force, he gazed out the window and nearly drooled at the sight. The roof of the crusher rose up slightly, then lowering on one end, came crashing down on the hood of the car. Flattening itself again, it evened out and with one final push downward, the process was complete. In less than five minutes, any evidence left by David or Lenny had been squashed and the knowledge of this caused goose bumps to blanket his arms as a wide grin spread across his face.

Turning from the window, David went to leave when the operator stopped him. "Wait—you have a call coming in." Almost immediately, the phone on the desk began to ring, a shrilling annoyance that caused David to lose his smile. Picking up, the operator answered with a simple, "Yes", before handing the receiver over to David.

Hesitating for a second, David reminded himself that other than his employer, no one knew that he and Lenny were here. Slowly taking the phone, he narrowed his eyes at the man before him, preparing to attack if at all necessary. The operator, a burly man in his forties, stared back at David, as if daring him to act. Feeling that he could have the scarred man out of his office and drug out to the crusher in seconds if he so desired, the loader operator was not intimidated as he watched David put the phone to his ear and listened.

"You fucked up", the voice on the phone accused.

Waiting, David said nothing.

"You missed the girl", the caller went on, anger building in his voice.

Still quiet, David was not intimidated, just curious if he and Lenny were done or if there would be further instructions. Thinking back to the redhead, the one who had seen his face, he decided right there and then that he would find her either way. He would pull a freebie if his employer ended his contract now; he wasn't about to just walk away with a witness still out there who could identify him.

"—continue the deal." Turning his attention back to the caller, David missed part of what was being said, but did not ask for clarification. Focusing instead on the conversation now; he could pull the missing pieced together if needed. "Continue to hold your supplies", meaning the bag that he had obtained the day before out in the middle of nowhere. "Further instructions are soon to come. Fuck up again and that is the end."

With that, the caller disconnected and David knew that he was still in business. Hanging up the phone, David gave the operator one last look, then left the office to find Lenny. Waiting outside, the lanky man was sitting on a wooden bench to the right of the exit, watching the desert awaken as the sun breached the mountains to the east. A bead of sweat forming above his upper lip due to the quickly building heat, Lenny absently wiped it away as he waited for David to instruct him on where they were going to next...and how they were going to get there. The demolished car had yet to be replaced by any other transportation and despite David's power over him, he was not about to walk the fifty or so miles it would take to get back into town.

Just then, the entrance to the office that ran the scrap yard opened and the operator stepped out. Heavy boots kicking the dirt floor underneath them, the man approached David, handing him a set of keys. Following the man's gaze, Lenny noticed a Ford Excursion parked in the lot ahead of him. Understanding that this was their next mode of transportation, Lenny stood and waited to see if there would be any other interaction between David and the yard worker. There was none.

Heading to the dark blue SUV, Lenny automatically went for the driver's seat but David beat him to it. "I got this", he said, instructing Lenny to stow their supply bag in the backseat. Lenny, surprised, said nothing, did as he was told, and got into the passenger seat.

Pealing out of the dirt lot, David grinned wide as a whirlwind of dust and rocks flew up from the back tires. Looking up into the review mirror, his grin turned into a laugh as the loader operator flung open the entrance door and charged the yard, obviously pissed-off at David's dramatic exit.

A half hour later, the pair was nearing the other side of Tucson, passing through the south side, or South Tucson, as it is commonly referred to by the locals. Influenced largely by a strong Catholic and Hispanic heritage, this part of town consisted greatly of small single family homes; often found built close together, fenced in, and many in disarray; entrepreneurship forms of businesses offering everything from spicy Mexican-born entrees to family-owned automotive repair shops, hair stylists, and small grocery markets; many of them displaying pride in not only their heritage, but also in their faith in their showcasing of statues and monuments depicting Christ, the Virgin Mary, and a few other biblical characters that were unrecognizable to either Lenny or David.

Turning into one of the neighborhoods, Lenny eyed the landscape carefully, wondering just where they were headed as David had not spoken a word to him once leaving the scrap yard. Rows of houses, junked cars, and overgrown yards full of weeds and the occasional desert plant or tree slipped past his view as David steered down the street. Every couple of houses, children would be out to play, dressed in dirt-covered shorts and loose fitting t-shirts, Lenny wondered how some of them could be out playing barefoot; as if the heat from the morning sun had no effect on their tiny feet.

Suddenly, David turned down an adjourning side street and, heading towards the end of it, pulled into a driveway free of any other vehicles, children, or movement....the place actually looked deserted. Turning off the engine, David stepped out and pocketed the keys as Lenny followed suite; still unsure if he should ask any questions or not.

Following David through the front yard, they headed towards the back of the one story house. Constructed from stucco, the walls of the home were white-washed, giving it an industrial feel in a way. A large picture window faced the front yard but looked to be covered with heavy drapery on the inside, concealing whatever lie within. The side that they used reach the back of the house was heavily weeded with bits of gravel strewn about.

Reaching the back of the house, Lenny noticed a multitude of empty beer cans, crumbled food wrappings, and used cigarette butts tossed this way and that around the yard. Weeds being thicker here, it looked as though the trash had been here long before the wild plants had grown up and immediately wondered again, why they were here.

A large, heavy looking wooden door closed off the house from the broken concrete flooring that made up the porch. David, reaching it first, raised one fist and knocked three times, pausing in between each before taking a few steps back.

Within minutes, the door swung inward and they were met by a small, Hispanic woman, dressed in a long wrap-around outfit that ran from the top of her neckline to the tops of her toes. Decorated in a reddish pattern of Chinese dragons, Lenny immediately thought she looked a bit strange. Her long black hair, twirled up into a bun that sat near the top of her head, gave way to a thin face, drenched in makeup and age lines. Her eyes, almost charcoal in color, looked tired and weary, as if she hadn't slept in days and her thin body looked as though she had missed more just one meal.

Recognizing David right off, her exhausted look vanished, replaced by a large grin that showed off her bright white teeth. Speaking to him in Spanish, David replied easily in the same language, as he made his way into the house. Lenny, still following behind, had no idea as to what they were speaking of and became self-conscious and uneasy as David pointed to him over his shoulder and the woman gave him a once-over, her smile growing wider as she did.

Then, with a single, sharp clap of her hands, the trio was joined by a group of scantily-clad women, each of their own shape and size. David, eyeing a familiar face in one that wore her black hair down to the middle of her back, continued his foreign conversation with the mistress of the house. Frowning for a second, the woman nodded, and said something to the dark haired beauty behind her. Leaving the room, the girl gave David a pouty look, and Lenny suddenly realized what was going on.

This was a brothel....of sorts, he guessed, now feeling embarrassed and uneasy.

But before he could voice his concerns with David, a redhead joined the group, coming from a long hallway of rooms that let away from the living area they were standing in. With shoulder length hair, the girls green eyes looked nervously between her mistress and David and it was clear to Lenny that she couldn't understand the language that was being spoken around them either.

Taking a moment to study her, Lenny noted her high cheekbones, soft full lips, and thin body. She was wearing a long white, lacy gown that hugged her breasts tightly and curved around her small waist and Lenny felt the attraction to her almost immediately. Smiling shyly as he caught her eye, the girl refused to return one as she turned her own eyes to the floor. This bothered

Lenny for some reason but before he could do anything about it, David turned to him and instructed, "Don't waste my money."

Then, reaching into the front pocket of his jeans, David pulled a wad of cash out and handed it to the mistress; obviously pre-counted and reserved for this pit stop. Then, the mistress turned to the redhead, gave her instructions in broken English and stepped aside so that David could follow the girl down to one of the rooms.

Turning to Lenny, the woman said, "Which you like?"

Immediately Lenny felt his face turn bright red and, unable to avoid it, eyed the back of his partner as he turned into one room behind the redhead. Angry that once again, David got what he wanted without even thinking about him, Lenny glared at the remaining selection of girls for a few moments before shrugging his shoulders, unable to pick a replacement for himself.

The mistress then chose for him; another black-haired girl looking to be in her twenties. Wearing a red laced bra with matching hot pants, the girl nodded at her employer and started down the hall, expecting Lenny to follow.

Debating for a moment, he quickly wondered if he would even be able to perform under such feelings of irritation. Then, doing as David had demanded, he decided that he wasn't going to waste his money; more out of fear of the man than anything else and he followed the young woman ahead of him into one of the rooms.

Closing the door behind him, Lenny watched as the girl sauntered over to a twin-sized bed and crawled on top of it. "How you like it?" she asked, sounding routine-like and uninterested.

Suddenly, a scream coming from outside the room stopped Lenny's heart and as he listened, wondered just what the hell David was doing to the redhead. As far as he knew, they were the only men here, and knowing David's appetite for sex and pain, figured that the scream must have come from the girl he was renting for the hour. Hearing nothing following it in the seconds that past, he looked down at the dark haired girl and thought that, yes, maybe he could be more like David….take his building anger and use it to his advantage.

And has he stripped himself of his clothes, heard another muffled scream from outside the room, this one sounding tear-soaked and full of pain. Jaw clenched, he approached the bed, covered the girl with his body, now hardened in all the right places. Ramming himself into her without offering any warning, he heard her stifle a whimper and this turned him on even more. Then focusing on that and the cries that continued to come from David's rented room down the hall, closed his eyes and let his rage guide his need, no longer caring about the girl underneath him.

Chapter Nineteen

"Ian!!"

Listening, I hesitated before shaking him again.

Hearing a door close from somewhere down the hall, I automatically sat up, and my heart pounded against my chest. Shaking, I focused on the bedroom's open doorway, waiting for whomever was in Ian's apartment to come crashing in, killing us both.

Shoes clicking on the tiled floor, I realized it sounded far away and I thought back to the night before and remembered feeling carpet under my bare feet when I had left the bedroom and walked the short hallway to the bathroom; which was the only other room tiled—I think. The living room was carpet, I was positive. So that meant that whoever was in here, wanting to do us harm was either in the kitchen or in the bathroom.

Frantic now, I gave Ian a hard shove and hearing him murmur in protest, leaned close to his ear and whispered loudly, *"Ian!!! There's someone in the apartment!!!"*

His brown eyes flew open and I knew that I had finally broken his sleep. Propping up on one elbow, he listened, saying nothing. Somewhere a cupboard door slammed shut, scaring us both and Ian reacted immediately. Jumping out of bed, naked, he made it to the closet door in three long, deathly quiet strides. Sitting there, breathing heavily, I didn't know what to do—hide under the covers? Stuff myself under the bed?? Climb into the closet and try to find coverage in the clothes probably hanging from the rack???

Now nearing hysterics, I tried to catch Ian's eye, but too late, he was dressed in jeans and shirt and out of the bedroom, gun in hand, before I could even speak. Suddenly, the silence around me broke as I heard a woman's scream, a curse from Ian, and the crashing sound of something heavy and made of glass.

Bounding out of bed, I searched for the clothes I was wearing last night and, finding them at the end of the bed on the floor, pulled them on as fast as I could. Trying to ignore the pain in my shoulder as it fired up uncontrollably, I ran out of the bedroom and down the hall where I found Ian, holding his upper body up with both hands as they formed a tight grip over one of the backs of his dining room chairs. His weapon was on the table and I was suddenly confused.

"Good Lord in Heaven, Ian!!!! What we're you going to do…*SHOOT ME*?!"

Approaching the kitchen carefully, I made eyes on an older woman with short brown wavy hair and wide eyes. Seeing me instantly, she cried "Oh!!", and backed into the side of the counter.

Hearing her exclamation, Ian quickly looked up at her and then followed her stare to find me, only to turn back to her. Breathing heavily, he exclaimed, "I could have very well shot you!!! What are you doing here, Mom??!!"

Mom????

Staring back at her son, mouth open, her face suddenly relaxed as a hand covered her breast, as if to try to calm herself. Swallowing, she explained, "I—we—you're father and I were wanting to take you to breakfast…but", giving me an interesting look, "it looks like you may have already had yours."

"Mom!!!"

Oh, my God!!!

Suddenly floored by the teasing look she then gave her son, his mother suddenly turned to me and walked past him, taking my hands into her own. "And who might you be, my dear?" She asked; her interest obviously piqued at this point.

"Um…" Suddenly at a loss for words, I couldn't remember my own name and I just stared back into her brown eyes. "I…um…"

"Mom, this is Amanda. Amanda, this is my mom, Josie." Turning to the both of us as he made introductions, he pulled his fingers through his thick brown hair and I could immediately see the resemblance between mother and son.

"Amanda...." Saying my name as if it were dipped in honey, she smiled brightly at me. "And how long have you and my son, been...um....*knowing* each other???" Dipping her head at me, my face turned red and I stifled a nervous laugh, completely unsure if this woman was for real or if I was actually dreaming and still in bed.

"Mom—where is Dad??" Interjecting immediately, Ian gave me a look and I knew that I needed to keep my mouth shut for the time being. Not sure what his mother's feelings would be in knowing that for one, their son was getting himself involved with a topless dancer and two, we had only met two days ago; I had a feeling she would not react in the way that most normal mother's would react—but anything was possible at this point.

"What—oh!!" She exclaimed, dropping my hands as she turned to Ian. "Oh, he's waiting in the car downstairs. I told him I would be right down, seeing as how I had a key and you usually have nothing to eat in this apartment. I didn't figure that I would have caught you—err—*indisposed*, honey."

"You didn't catch us *indisposed*, Mom," Ian said tensely, "but don't you think you should get going since he is waiting?"

"Well..." sounding as if she didn't want to leave, she turned back to me, then back at her son. "I suppose you're too busy to come to breakfast but make sure you bring Amanda to dinner tomorrow night." Ignoring her son's exasperated sigh, she turned to me once more and said, "It was absolutely *wonderful* to meet you dear, please make him bring you to dinner! I want to know all about you!!"

"Okay..." I answered with a laugh, absolutely beside myself at this woman's flagrant disregard for embarrassing her son; who was turning redder in the face by the second. Imagining just what Ian's mother was going to say to his father once back in their car, I couldn't help by smile at her.

"It's settled then! I'll give Ian the time and find out what you like to eat later on today." Then stepping to the door, she looked back, gave me a wink and said, "Make sure you get to eat *your* breakfast too, now dear!"

"MOM!!!"

Another exclamation from Ian sent her gliding out the door and as soon as it was closed behind her, I burst into laughter—unable to hold it in any longer. Listening to me, Ian finally caved, laughing as he sank his body into the chair he had been bracing himself on when I first came into the kitchen. Holding his face in his hands, his laughter finally subdued and he sight deeply.

"Oh, God...I'm so sorry, Amanda!! I had no idea she was going to show up this morning!"

Still laughing, I couldn't answer; just sank my body into his couch as I tried to control the tears that were now running down my face. Then, lying down across it to stretch, my laughter finally began to slow down. Looking up at the ceiling, I sighed, the air leaving my body in short bursts until I was finally able to control it again.

Not hearing Ian leave his chair, he was suddenly looking down at me from a standing position. "I think she likes you." He said with a smile and as my laughter threatened to return, I made myself sit up and moved over to give him space. Taking the empty spot, he sank into the soft fabric and brought my legs over his own bent ones. Softly massaging the area below my knees, he eyed the front door for moment, as if wondering if his mother was going to return for some reason. Then, looking over at me, he asked, "You okay?"

Nodding, and comfortable, I closed my eyes as fingers moved across my ankles, down to my feet. "Does your mom pop in often?" I asked, still amused at her unabashed display towards the woman she thinks her son is sleeping with...oh, who we kidding...he is sleeping with me! There's just no word yet as to how *long* he will continue to sleep with me.

"Not usually and she does call first, most of the time." Then, thinking, he added, "But things have been a bit hectic around here.

She may have called to set something up, then not hearing back from me, just decided to come on over and make herself at home."

"What was she doing in the kitchen?" And then, remembering hearing a crashing sound when Ian found her in the kitchen, raised my head and asked, "What broke?"

"She was emptying my dishwasher...don't ask me why...when my dad was downstairs waiting for her to return with me to go to breakfast. When I came around the corner of the dining room, I scared her and she dropped a glass that she was holding." Then, considering the situation even more, he admitted, "And she's lucky I just didn't come around the corner and start shooting; what with all that's happened since—"

Cutting himself off, he stopped before saying it. Opening my eyes, I gave him a look and finished for him, "Since you met me." Lying there for a half second longer, I picked my legs up off of his, and stood up from the couch.

"Amanda, wait...that's not what I meant!"

"Yes, it is, Ian, and I don't blame you for saying it. Everything that has happened since Friday night is because of me. I have not only put myself in danger, but my daughter, my best friend, and now, you. I shouldn't be here, Ian."

Leaving the room, I headed back to his bedroom, my sole plan now to shower quickly, change my bandages, and get out of here before the next person that comes into Ian's apartment unannounced is someone aiming to kill me or anyone who stands in their way. I was not going to be the cause of anybody's wellbeing— with exception to my daughter; she was the only person I aim to be responsible for from this point on. And if anyone tried to get at her, they'd have to kill me first.

"Amanda, STOP!!"

Reaching the bedroom doorway, I obliged to his demand. Forcing myself not to turn around, I spoke before he did; feeling his eyes on me while I said what I needed. "Ian, we both know that I should not be here. It's not fair to you. And it's not fair to my daughter. I should be with her right now, making sure she is protected and safe.

"I come with a lot of baggage, Ian. I have a daughter who needs me way more than other kids her age need their mothers. You know nothing about us. And I don't think it's right to drag you into all of this; especially when the neither of us know what is going to happen next. No...it's best if I just leave. Get your job back, go back to work, and find the bastard that is trying to hunt me down. But do it without dealing with the complication of having me here.

"And who's to say that this would even work, Ian. Girls like me are like a novelty to most men, you know...'fuck the stripper and mark a point off on your bucket list'? I'm not a novelty and I cannot stay here hoping that this will all work out, no one will get hurt, or *killed*, because of me, or that you will wake one morning to discover that the novelty has run its course."

The tears were running down my face now, and I did nothing to stop them. My heart was breaking; I knew this; but I also knew that I could not stay here in good conscious. Hearing no response from him, I walked over the threshold and grabbed my bag off of his dresser. Looking at the bed, remembering our night together and just how damn good he had made me feel, I almost changed my mind. Shaking my head against it, I tore my eyes away from the room and walked out, heading to the bathroom. Not seeing Ian, I assumed he had accepted my decision, and shut the door behind me.

Looking at myself in the mirror, I studied my face as I again questioned what I was doing. Then, becoming angry with myself, I turned away from it and undressed carefully. My shoulder was killing me and I had yet to take any pain killers or have anything to eat. But at that point, I took it as punishment. Punishment for putting this good man at risk, for allowing him to get close to me...punishment for the last forty-eight hours including the choice to send my daughter out of town so that I could get laid.

Turning on the water to the shower, I carefully peeled back the bandages from my shoulder. The medical tape sticking to my skin, I winced as it pulled unforgivingly on it, but I finally got it to let go. Tossing the mess into the garbage, I hesitated before looking at myself again in the mirror and gasped when I finally did.

My wound, sewn shut with some kind of medical threading, was red, puffy, and ugly. Turning to try to see the other side of it, I could tell that the back of my shoulder matched the front. Praying that it wasn't infected...and I didn't know what to look for to see if it was...I stepped into the shower and carefully let the warm water wash over it. Finding a bottle of woman's shampoo and conditioner, I wondered if this was one of the items Ian had purchased for me last night.

Thinking of him, I paused, mid-shampoo, and allowed myself to break down. Standing there, under the rainfall of water, I shuddered and pressed my head against the wall as my body shook with sobs. I didn't want to leave Ian; felt rather that if I stayed and gave this a chance I may come to find love again. But who's to say he would? While, thinking back to last night, I could have sworn that I heard him say 'I love you' before I feel asleep, but it was a dream....all a dream...and I was really kidding myself.

Forcing myself to push Ian out of my mind, I worked instead on carefully washing my body. The heat from the shower was magically killing some of the pain in my shoulder and I could move a bit more freely. The first thing I needed to do when I leave, I decided as I washed my legs, is eat and take two more pills. With no health insurance, I was relying on my body to heal itself the way that it should. I wouldn't have anyone to prescribe me anymore antibiotics or pain killers and I didn't want to forgo this part of the treatment while I had it.

Finishing, I turned off the water and stepped out, grabbing the towel off of the rack above the toilet to dry my body with since I had forgotten to get one out of the hall closet before locking myself in here. Once dried, I got myself half-way dressed in the bra and panty set courtesy of Anna and worked to attach fresh bandages to my wound.

The wound above my right breast was easy to doctor, the matching one my back was a great challenge though and I ended up giving up, unable to secure the adhesive to make the bandage stay put. Frustrated, I finished dressing in the jeans and tank that were packed in the bag and dressed my feet with fresh socks. Not seeing my shoes in the bag, I realized that they were probably in Ian's bedroom and I was going to have to face entering that room one last time. Running a brush through my hair, I figured it would air dry in about ten minutes once the Arizona sun beat down on it, I took one last look around the small room to make sure I wasn't forgetting anything. I wasn't.

Pausing before opening the bathroom door, I closed my eyes and took a breath. Not wanting to cry again, I decided that the best way out of this was to leave the restroom, find my shoes, and head for the front door. My decision was not up for discussion. I was doing the absolute best thing by leaving Ian and going to get Brighton. Where we ended up from there, I had no clue, but that's the way it was going to be. No backing down.

Leaving the bathroom, I stepped to the left and quickly walked back to Ian's bedroom. Finding it empty I searched the floor for my shoes and found them near the closet door. Sitting on the floor to put them on—I wasn't going to sit on his bed at this point—I tied them and stood up, grabbing my bag as I did. Starting to head out, I stopped short. Ian was standing in the doorway.

"I need to show you something." Making eye contact immediately, I had a hard time breaking it.

"No." Trying to stay strong, my voice betrayed me and my answer came out soft and questionable.

"Please, Amanda?" Taking a step towards me, I stopped myself from taking one back. Even if I did, I had nowhere to go. Ian's strong body took up most of the doorway and I knew I wouldn't make it past him without us touching...and if we touched; my decision would fly right out the window.

Taking a breath as the tears threatened to fall again; I simply nodded but stood my ground.

"It's not in here." He said quietly, and I hesitated before taking a step forward. Then, forcing my feet to work right, I walked towards him, keeping a careful eye on his hands.

Turning, he immediately faced another door; this one closed and not one that I remembered seeing before now. Wondering what was behind the door, I had my answer when Ian turned the handle and pushed it inward and stepped to the side to allow me access.

Gasping, I never felt the strap of my bag slide from my hand. Taking small steps to enter the room, I knew that my mouth was hanging open and those tears that had been threatening to fall, were now doing so under their own free will.

The room, light blue in color, was set up for a little girl. A twin bed sat in one corner and was dressed in a pink and purple comforter with matching pillow case and I'm assuming sheets, as I could not see those. Next to the bed was a small white nightstand and on it a lamp with butterflies painted on its base and on the shade.

On the floor, a large pink butterfly rug, big enough to lie on and looking soft enough to sleep on. Opposite the bed was a white dresser that matched the night stand. On it sat a small stack of coloring books, *Disney Princess* coloring books, a large box of crayons, three empty picture frames with butterfly décor, and a pink journal with matching pen to write thoughts down in.

The closet was empty, but on the outer door hung a poster depicting a mystical scene of green trees, brightly colored flowerbeds, and a gleaming white haired unicorn standing before a waterfall. Turning around slowly in the room, I then noticed the walls, covered with wall art—butterflies, pictures of each Disney Princess in their gowns, and additional photo frames waiting for their pictures hung from small nails in the walls. Turning again, I was truly in awe.

Watching me from the doorway, Ian admired his handiwork and smiled as I walked through room, touching the bedding, the lamp, and the things on the dresser. "Ian, I—"

"Don't say anything."

Stopping, I looked at him, silently offering him the floor.

"I don't want you to leave. I want you to bring Brighton here." Sensing my argument, he cocked his head at me and I closed my mouth, allowing him to continue. "I didn't buy all of this stuff last night because I thought you were a novelty. I will never, *never* treat you as one either.

"As for my job—I put my life on the line every time I go to work—for people that I don't even know. I would like the opportunity to do the same for someone that I love. I can't promise you that you being here won't put me in danger, but I don't care. Let them come. I will protect you and Brighton with my life if I have to. Because I *want* to. Do you understand that??"

"But you talk like you love *me*. *Love* me, Ian??? You don't even know me! Do *you* understand how crazy that is?!" And then it dawned on me...that is *exactly* what I heard him say last night before falling asleep! I was suddenly flabbergasted and didn't know what else to say to him.

"Then give me the chance to know for sure. Hell, give yourself the chance to discover it as well!"

"But, Brighton, Ian! I can't do that to Brighton...if this doesn't work out, and she gets attached to you...what will happen then, huh?? You gonna just stick around because of her? End up resenting me, her, or even yourself when you find out how unhappy you are?! NO...I don't care about me, but I won't do that to my daughter!"

"Give me a chance, Amanda, please!! At least give Brighton a chance to get to know me!"

Wanting to end this conversation now, I grabbed up my bag and swung it over my left shoulder. Staring at him one last time, I knew that if I didn't get my body moving, I was never going to leave. Seeing what he had done here to make Brighton comfortable and happy was throwing me for a loop. I needed to get away...if nothing else to think.

But even then, I knew that this was never going to work. He says that he loves me, but men throw that word around so much that it really has no meaning anymore. And I knew that the way I felt was not going to be fixed by a beautifully decorated girls' room, for a girl that two days ago had no meaning to Ian.

These thoughts running through my head, I stood up straight and, pushing past him, I was barely able to choke out the words, "I'm sorry, Ian, I just can't", before I walked out his apartment and his life forever.

Chapter Twenty

Wanting to take the stairs instead of the elevator, I quickly moved down the hall that I found myself standing in after walking out of Ian's front door. Overwhelmed and emotional, the tears continued to run down my face as I reached the end of the corridor and, looking up, saw a low hanging sign marking the emergency exit.

Pushing through a door, I found the stairs and bolted down the three flights that led to the first floor of the building but, not knowing exactly where I was, stopped short as I came into a small lobby. Reminding myself that I had been asleep when Ian had first brought me here, I steeled myself for a second, wanting to avoid running around in circles like a dog chasing its tail. I knew that Ian wasn't going to just let me go. It was obvious in his pleas and I read it all over his face just before I had left him standing in the bedroom he had created for Brighton.

Following the exit signs above my head, I thought of her again and really questioned what I was doing. We have no money, no home, no clothing, and no food and I just walked out on the one good thing that may have been able to help me turn our lives around.

No turning back!

My mind screamed at me, while my heart said something entirely different.

Then, as if a sign from above, the double-glass doors that marked the entryway to the apartment building came into view and I ran for them and pushed them out of my way as I went through. A blast of heat hit me in the face as soon as I hit the sidewalk, instantly causing small beads of sweat to cover my forehead. Looking around, I still had no idea as to where I was exactly, and making a rash decision, headed off to the right.

Coming up to a corner, I stole a look behind me to see if I could see Ian's Dodge, wondering how close he may actually be behind me, or if he had too, given up on us the minute I walked out the door. Seeing nothing coming my way that remotely resembled his large black truck, I turned the corner and kept going.

Reaching the next corner, the street name offered me some idea of where I was; I came to a bus stop and sat down on the rotting looking bench available for customers to sit on while waiting for public transportation to pick them up. Sifting through Anna's gym bag again, I prayed that I would find enough change in it to pay for a ride. Being that Anna often used this bag to carry her work-out clothes and purse in when deciding to hit the gym, I was hoping that some of her lose change had ended up in the bottom of it over time.

Finding a small zippered compartment positioned in the inner lining of the bag that I hadn't seen before; I unzipped it and pulled out a white, sealed envelope. Turning it over to look at the front cover, I saw that there was a message:

In Case You Decide to Run!!

Written by Anna's hand, I whispered, "God bless you, Anna...you know me all too well..."

Tearing the flap open, I took a nervous look around; not for Ian, but for any prying eyes belonging to anyone not needing to know that I may have a hidden treasure in my pocket. Peering into the envelope, without pulling out the contents, I counted at least six twenty dollar bills. Her emergency stash....

Deciding against the bus, I hid the envelope back into the zipper compartment of the bag, closed it back up and stood to walk again. *The heck with the bus*, I thought, *I need a cab!* Heading in the same direction that had found me the bus stop, I eyed passing vehicles for a taxi, hoping that I would find one before having to stop to use a payphone somewhere.

As luck would have it, there was one parked on the next block and after knocking on the guy's closed window and asking him if he was on duty, I jumped into the back seat when he nodded silently at me. Instructing him to take me to *Lucky's Girls!*, I put my head back against the tough leather seat and closed my eyes, trying to breath and get Ian's broken-hearted look out of my mind at the same time.

Twenty minutes later, and almost thirty dollars broker, the cabbie dropped me off in front of the bar. Being a Sunday—early Sunday—Lucky's was not open yet, but I knew that he would be in there somewhere making sure that the guys were getting ready for the afternoon shift to start. Sunday is the only day that we open later than usual. On every other day, we open at 11:00 in the morning and offer lunch specials to the guys that come in on their lunch breaks. On Sunday however, we open at 3:00, offer nothing in the way of lunch but run drink specials during the day and on through the night.

Coming to the locked doors that marked the entrance to the bar, I banged one fist against the large metal barrier and prayed that someone inside would hear me. Waiting a few minutes, I banged again, and suddenly heard the lock being keyed open. The door being pushed outward, I stepped back and found Matt staring back at me.

"Amanda!!" He looked startled, as if he was generally shocked to see me. "What—what are you doing here?"

"Hey, Matt, Lucky around?" Giving the bouncer an odd look, I stepped past him to enter. The lights were on in the bar and being that I was so used to dancing in the near-dark here, it took a minute to for my eyes to adjust to the unexpected light.

"Um…Amanda…can I talk to you??"

Feeling Matt's hand on my arm, he squeezed, as if trying to stop me from going any further. Wanting to immediately ask him what his problem was, I was cut off before I got the chance when I heard, "Amanda!!! Darling….come, come!!" Turning back to Matt, I gave him a look and he immediately released my arm and gave me a frown before turning away.

"Hey, Lucky, you got a minute?" I asked the short, chunky man.

Wearing a dark blue suit with matching tie, Lucky's best attribute was his laugh—well, that and his money if you ask some of the other girls—his bubbly personality made him a hit around the bar scene and his money made him even more popular. Guiding me to the bar, he stepped behind it and offered to pour me a drink.

"No thanks, Lucky, I'm fine", I answered as I propped myself up onto a bar stool. "I need to ask a favor though."

"Oh...anything for my favorite girl!"

Yeah right, your favorites are the ones that bring in the most regulars and I do not fall under that category! Wanting to say this, I held my tongue, and pressed the issue that I was facing instead. "I need to work, Lucky, but with this wound on my shoulder, don't think that I should return to dancing right away."

Nodding his head at me as he made himself a mixed drink, he said nothing, allowing me to continue. "I was thinking of cocktailing for now...at least until my shoulder heals the whole way. If I can just serve drinks for a couple of weeks, it will still allow me to bring in some tips to take care of Brighton."

Leaning on the bar, he took a drink before answering. "How is Brighton, she doing okay?"

"Yea, she's fine, I've got her out at a friend's house for right now."

"And you, my sweet Amanda, how are you holding up with all this terrible business??"

"I'm okay. Look, Lucky, I've got to get out to Green Valley tonight, but still have to figure out a way there. What do you think about my idea?" Suddenly wanting to get outta there, I had a weird feeling in the pit of my stomach but, attributing it to hunger pains, I pushed it aside.

Thinking, Lucky paused for a moment and then said, "Sure, sure, you can cocktail for me. Start tomorrow night, okay? Same shift?"

Instantly relieved, I felt some of the tension leave my body. Rubbing my temples for a moment, my thoughts streamlined their way to Ian and the day he interviewed me in my hospital room. His fingers on my temples, circling the tension right out of my head, came into focus and I suddenly missed him terribly.

Shaking the feelings off, I stood and grabbed up the gym bag. "Thanks, Lucky, I really appreciate it." Turning to leave out the same way I had entered as there was no way that I was leaving out the back door ever again, Lucky called me back to the bar.

"You were saying that you need to get to Green Valley??"

Pausing, I said, "Yea..." hearing the question strong in my voice.

"Lemme get Matt to take you. Least I can do after all that's happened."

As the image of Matt's hand on my arm just a few moments ago thundered in my head, I started to protest, explaining to Lucky that I could take a cab out there.

"Oh—don't speak of it, Amanda!! A cab ride would cost you way too much!" Then, calling over his shoulder, he yelled, "Matt! Come!"

Abiding by his boss's demand, Matt came out of the booth he sat in when the doors were open, checking the identification of everyone who entered and ensuring that no one was let in that shouldn't be allowed, he walked stiffly to the bar.

"Yes, Boss?"

"Take Amanda out to Green Valley, anywhere she needs to go. Take the van."

The van, as Lucky referred to it as, was a cargo special that could fit up to eight people. During holiday weekends, Lucky promoted free rides for customers who found themselves heavy from the sauce in order to keep them in their seats at the bar and be under no risk by allowing them to drive themselves home. The free ride was available to any customer during these special nights and the driver that Lucky usually hired on for that role specifically took each passenger to wherever their home was located, no questions asked.

"You sure, Boss?" Eyeing me for a minute, I suddenly felt uncomfortable and moved away from the bar to head back to the front doors. Trying not to listen, I heard Lucky's voice raise an octave as he instructed Matt to drive me anywhere I needed to go.

That said, Matt obliged but did not look happy about. In fact, he looked a bit green in the face and when I asked him if he was alright, he simply nodded and waved off my question. Leaving the bar, I heard Lucky yell, "Drive safe, Matt! See you tomorrow evening, Amanda...say 'hi' to Brighton for me!!" followed by Lucky's classic roll of his belly as we left out the front door.

Not understanding the joke, I quickly wondered how many drinks Lucky had put down before adding the one he had chugged down while we were talking at the bar.

The van parked in the back lot, I followed Matt about halfway there before abruptly coming to a dead stop as the images of my attack came back, full force. Heart pounding, my memory left nothing to question and I suddenly felt as though I couldn't breathe. Sensing that he was walking alone, Matt stopped up ahead of me and turned around. "Amanda?" Not fully hearing him, the look on my face must have told him something was wrong and he walked back to me in quick strides.

"Hey, Amanda? You okay??"

Taking a deep breath, I softly replied, "I...um...I don't think that I...c-can go back there."

Following my stare towards the back lot, it dawned on him as to why. "Huh?" Then, "Oh, shit, Amanda, I'm sorry! I wasn't even thinking...stay here, I'll go get the van and bring it to you."

"Hmmm..." was all I could reply, my mind lost in the events of Friday night. Remembering the attack, the man with the scar sneered his way across my mind's eye and I knew that if I ever saw him again, I would know it in a heartbeat. Stepping to the side, I placed my back against the solid wall of the bar and closed my eyes, trying to focus.

The other guy that was here that night...I couldn't get a fix on his face; I just remembered that he was standoffish...the weak one...the sidekick. It was the other guy, the one with the black evil eyes and the damaged face, he's the one that gave me my wound—I just knew it.

Eyes still pressed tightly together, I was lost in the memory and felt like I could *smell* him; his breath on my check as he violently yanked my head back, threatening to make my life a living hell. He was sweaty—but not like he had just been out in the hot air for an hour or two—no, it was like he had *bathed* in sweat, as if he hadn't showered in a month...but then, the stench...*his stench*...was covered up by something else...something familiar but I couldn't place it.

But before I could concentrate on it further, the sound of the van's engine coming to life caused my eyes to open quickly and the picture was gone; replaced by the white van with the bar logo stretched across its side. Stopping in front of me, I rounded the front of the van and got into the passenger seat. Suddenly missing my car, I briefly thought about contacting Ian to see if he could find out when it would be ready, but immediately changed my mind. Contacting him for anything would lead me to a world of trouble and being that I have set my mind to walk away, that would not be a good idea.

As Matt drove out of the parking lot and headed towards the Interstate that would eventually lead us into Green Valley, neither of us spoke until he reached the exit I gave him. Heading east from that point on, I instructed him on which turns to make as we weaved our way out towards the outskirts of the retirement community.

Offering residents the opportunity to enjoy their retirement living in splendor, Green Valley had more varieties of churches that I have ever seen, a million options when it came to health care and related issues, two grocery stores, a couple of Walgreens pharmacies, and various out-doorsie types of activities to keep their citizens in the best health possible.

There were no malls, no movie theaters, not even an automated car washing business. Everything here encouraged one to get up off their couch, get outside, and do things for themselves. It was small, a bit quaint, and really had nothing to offer families with children—or single moms with a disabled child for that matter. Despite all this, I loved spending time out here, especially in the company of Anna and her parents; who were big on hiking the nearby Madera Canyon, traveling along the desert paths that this area was covered in, and in offering Brighton different ways in which to spend her time, which in turn promoted her to learning new things with every visit she had.

Asking Matt to take the next left turn, we left the paved road behind. Traveling on dirt now, he slowed the van down and carefully guided it as we crossed over the bumps and holes that were famous in these areas. Occasionally passing a home, some of them mobile homes and other made of brick or some type of stone work, he came to the end. Anna's parents lived in a brick-styled one story home, surrounded by brown desert, green cacti, and the occasional shrub or tree. Pulling to the front of the house, Ian drove in a half-circle, following the prints of tires made over the years by vehicles that have come and gone before us. Pulling to a stop, he put the van in park and glanced over my shoulder to view the front of the house.

"Thanks, Matt—and thank Lucky for me one more time."

Then, as I opened the door to step out, he reached out, touching my hand gently. "Amanda, wait. There's something you should—"

"Ma!!!!!"

Hearing Brighton's excited voice calling from the enclosed porch, Matt was cut off instantly and I jumped out of van. "Hey!!!!" I called, watching her leave the enclosed area and, bounding off the steps, she raced for me. Reaching me, she jumped into my waiting arms and I scooped her up, tears in my eyes. Feeling as though it had been years since I'd seen her, I hugged her to me and bent to pick up my bag. Peering in at Matt, I laughed and thanked him for the ride before shutting the passenger door.

Heading back to the house; where Anna now stood with her parents watching us and smiling; I turned my back to the van—never noticing the look Matt was giving us through the review mirror or the fact that he continued to sit there, alone in his thoughts, for a few minutes until putting the van back into drive and speeding back down the dirt road towards civilization; kicking up dust and rocks as he did.

Not willing to let Brighton go until I made it to the steps of the porch, I set her down on her feet and followed her happy laugh up the stairs and through the wide screen door. On the porch, I received gentle hugs from Anna's parents; Sylvia and Austin Yearling. Assuring them both that I was doing okay, Anna grabbed my arm and said, "My turn!!" and hugged me tight. In my ear, she whispered, "We need to talk" and I knew instantly that Ian had called her.

Ignoring her request, I followed Sylvia and Austin into the house, Brighton excitedly bounding in behind us, leaving Anna to bring up the rear. The next half hour was filled with Brighton's display of artwork that she had completed while visiting, a quick tour of Sylvia's small garden out back, a brief discussion of my wound with Austin, and the orders to stow what belongings I had in their spare room...I was told that I would be staying for the night, no arguments or protests allowed.

Once emptying my bag of what little clothes I had in my temporary bedroom, I discovered that Brighton had been given her own room for the time being. With five bedrooms and three baths, the Yearling home had enough room for everyone and the one set up for Brighton was perfect for her. With a twin bed in one corner, her Nana and Papa had set up a desk for her to write and color at, a large bookshelf with all her favorite stories waiting to be read, a small flat screen TV that was positioned on the wall opposite the bed, and a matching dresser and night stand carved out of oak.

It was perfect for her and while I greatly appreciated the love the Yearlings bestowed on my daughter, it was still missing something. Thinking back to Ian's decorating efforts, I smiled as I thought of the many butterflies and princess depictions that he had carefully positioned around the room. The bedding, posters, rug, and lamp had Brighton's name written all over them and as I stood there, reminiscing, the differences between the rooms became easily understood: the one I was standing in now reminded me of something a grandma and grandpa would create for their grandchild....Ian's version was more of what a father would give his daughter...

Causing my breath to catch in my throat as this sank in, I swallowed hard, cursing the lump in my throat and blinked back a few tears.

"There you are!"

Turning quickly, I caught Anna's eye as she entered the room. Unable to hide anything from her, she gave me a look of understanding and wrapped her arms around me, careful of my shoulder, whose pain I had endured all day to the point that I'd come to just flat out ignore. Unable to stop, I shuddered against her as the tears began to fall.

Giving me my moment, Anna said nothing, just stood there, holding me as I cried. Finally, after several minutes, I was spent...my eyes burning and tired from the state my emotions had been in over the last two days.

Pushing me back to look me in the face, Anna finally spoke. "What happened??"

"Oh..." frustrated now, I turned away from her and faced the window, looking out at the brown desert as I tried to come up with a reasonable explanation for my actions. "I—just got scared, I guess."

"Scared of what??"

"Of Ian—of what I was feeling" I paused, considering more, "Of him getting hurt or killed because of me."

"Don't you think that he has a say in this decision? "

"Shit, I knew he had called you!" Giving her a glare over my shoulder, I turned back to the window to see a jackrabbit bound into the yard, his ears standing on end and a twitch bouncing in his nose.

"Yes....a few times! He's worried about you, Amanda." Approaching me from the side, she said, "You should call him."

"No", voice firm, I refused to look at her.

"For God's sakes, why not???"

Sighing heavily at her, I turned from the window in frustration. "Because, Anna, if I do, I won't stand my ground! I'll end up running back to him and I can't do that!!"

"This has nothing to do with the psycho that is out there, does it??" Accusing me, Anna faced me again, making me look her in the eye. "This is because you're your scared of finding out that he may actually love you!!"

"God—what the hell did he say to you on the phone?!"

"Did you sleep with him???"

Taken aback, I stuttered, caught off guard. "I—that—it's none of your business!!" I yelled at her, face turning beat red as I did.

"You did!!! Oh....here we go....now this is all making sense!!!" Continuing, she lectured me without giving me a word in edgewise. "You made love to him! And I bet that he made you feel like you've never felt before in your life!!! And now, your running away with your tail between your legs, coz you can't get it through your thick, red head that there may be a man out there who can love you *and* Brighton without any strings attached or false promises!!"

Breathing heavy, Anna gave me an angry look to which I matched with my own. "Are you done, Anna???"

Taking a minute to cool her jets, she said a bit more calmly, "No, I am not done. You are throwing away something that you haven't even allowed to start. And I, for one am not going to stand by and watch you do this. I love you, sister, but I am giving you one day—ONE DAY—", she stressed, "to call Ian and give him back the chance you took. He loves you, Amanda. I could hear it the first time he called me, frantic that you took off on foot with no money to get you anywhere...*hell*, I saw it the first time I saw you two in the same room together! Now it may not last, it may not end up being what the either of you want—but I'll be damned if I am watch you throw it all away before giving it a shot. Nope, ain't gonna do it! You have one day...then I'm calling Ian myself."

Huffing at her a bit, I shook my head, thinking about everything she had just pointed out. Was she right? Am I just running away because I'm scared of feeling anything...or did I really run because I don't want him in danger because of me? Now, uncertain, I sighed heavily, resigning to Anna's one-day rule that she has bestowed upon me.

"God, Anna, I hate you." I muttered.

Pulling me close to hug me, she laughed and said, "I hate you too, Amanda."

Then, leaving Brighton's room together, we commenced with doing whatever it was Brighton and her parents wanted to do for the evening: BBQ on the front porch, watering the plants and garden with my daughter, playing a game of Scrabble at the table, and finally, sitting down together to watch Sleeping Beauty as one, big family.

And all through this, as the night wore on...my mind silently clicked away the minutes...counting down the hours until my one full day was run completely out of time and I would have to face Ian...and myself, for that matter...

Chapter Twenty-One

Waking up on the couch, Ian stared up at the ceiling, cursing the seven hundred dollar overstuffed piece of furniture as he tried to lay as still as possible. Already feeling the kink in his neck and a mother of a headache building behind his brow, he knew he had to move in order to work it all out, but at the moment was happier lying there in misery.

Unable to sleep in his bed last night, Ian thought back to the look on Amanda's face just before she had walked out on him; a look that nearly killed him. Remembering her argument, he continued to lie there, questioning his sanity.

Is it crazy to think that someone can fall in love after only a few days??

Is there such thing as love at first sight—because thinking back, the first sight he caught of her lying in that hospital bed had caused his heart to race, his palms to sweat, and his way of thinking to go out the window.

How in the world is he going to get her back???

The last question brought him to a seated position, and he wondered if it was even possible as he rolled his head back and forth in an effort to rid it of the stiffness. Her final words, adamant and to the point, had shocked him as soon as they were out of her mouth. And when he went to react, to stop her in some way, she was already gone.

Yes, he did go after her, but after scrambling for his shoes, his wallet, and his keys, he had been too late. Not knowing which direction she had went after leaving his building, he drove around in circles trying to find her, but to no avail. He ended up coming home, drank himself into a stupor, and passed out on the couch when the sight of his bed made his heart ache even more.

Forcing himself up, he did the only thing he could think of at that moment. He left the living room for the bathroom, turned the shower on as cold as he could handle it as a form of punishment for letting her get away, and drowned his thoughts and his tears under the strong current of water as it poured over his body.

Twenty minutes later he was dried and dressed and wandering around the apartment as if lost. Not knowing what to do with himself, he considered calling Anna again to get some word on Amanda, but hesitated. In the five calls he'd made the day before, he had made himself out to be some lovesick puppy. He didn't want to add 'psychotic stocker' to the bottom of that list. No, he had to respect Amanda's wishes and leave her alone.

So...that left...going to see his parents which he quickly rejected when figuring that the first thing his mother would do would be to ask about the whereabouts of Amanda. She was already expecting them for dinner; a dinner he intended to skip. A night of twenty questions was not something he intended to endure, at least not tonight.

He couldn't go to work because of the suspension. He had no real close friends that weren't on the job and either working or spending the day with their families. And at this point, he was doing nothing in the way of making himself feel better. As every option he had was not possible right then and there, he continued walking from room to room, until he ended up at his bedroom again.

Turning from it, he faced the closed door that should have opened up to Brighton's room. Considering entering it and taking it all apart; repacking the bedding and re-boxing the decorations; he could take it all back to Wal-Mart and request his money back. But he didn't want to do that either. Frustrated with himself, he stalked away from both bedrooms and headed towards the fridge, thinking that another drinking binge was on the horizon. Reaching the door to the appliance, he froze when hearing his cell phone ring. Not wanting to get his hopes up, he forced himself to let it ring a few times; the obnoxious ringtone setting his nerves on fire until he gave up and answered it.

"Sampson—you busy??"

Sighing heavily, he eyed the fridge when he said, "No, Captain, what's up?"

"I need you back...you ready to come back?"

Jumping at the chance, Ian didn't think twice about answering. "Yes! I can come in now!"

"Good, get down here. I'm putting you with Gonzalez for now. Colliatti is on an extended vacation as of yesterday and I need an extra hand in handling the serial we are looking at. I got Marlow and Green working a couple of robberies where the clerks were each gunned down and Snider and Frankford are working a missing person's case that just got reported. The remaining crew is working on other cases as they come up. That leaves you helping Gonzalez. Think you can keep it professional from here on out??"

*Hell, with Colliatti outta the way; my problems have disappeared! Well...only one of my problems, that is...*Thinking to himself, he realized that the Captain was asking if he was still on the line. "Yea, I'm here, Cap—I'll be there in about thirty minutes, tell Gonzalez I'm on my way."

"Will do that, Sampson, see you soon."

With that the line went dead and Ian had a new purpose that would, if nothing else, help keep Amanda out of his head, even if it's just during the drive to work being that he was returning to help out with her case and try to figure out how it may be tied to the serial that Gonzalez has been focusing on.

Holstering his weapon and pocketing his badge and cell phone, Ian took one last look around the apartment before locking it up and heading down the elevator to the garage. Moments later he pulled out onto the street and cranked his stereo up high, preparing himself for the job; all the while hoping that he may be able to shed some light on what Gonzalez was working on and have some kind of excuse to get a hold of Amanda—even if it took him a month to do it.

Located in the heart of downtown Tucson, Ian's workplace was on the second floor of a large, rustic building, originally constructed during the 1940's. Four floors in total, the first of these were dedicated to community resource liaisons, meeting rooms commonly used for city officials, law enforcement informational gatherings, and the official offices of the chief of police and his entourage of aides and city workers. In general, it was the main base for general information and resources through which the public could effectively educate themselves.

The second floor housed the main squad room and included offices for Captain Leary and his minion of officers and detectives, including the lieutenant, while the third and fourth floors of the building housed additional meeting rooms, the technology divisions, human resource departments, and compliance and complaint offices and were areas commonly avoided by officers unless absolutely necessary.

As the city jail was operated outside of this building, in one of its own adjacent to the police department, offenders facing arrest were held in the basement level for a brief amount of time as common procedure required their transport to the city jail within twenty-four hours of arrest. As such, Ian's building also included ten holding cells, all on the lower level—technically the basement of the building—and were manned with officers and personal to ensure that the rights of the accused were upheld until transport to the city jail was complete.

Entering through a rear entrance, Ian jogged up the flight of stairs that would take him to the second floor. Upon entering, he hesitated for a second and took it all in, feeling like it had been months since he last stepped on the floor to work instead of a few days. The squad room was a mess of warm bodies, desks covered in paperwork, computer systems, and telephones that never seemed to stop ringing. The noise level was normally high, and today was no exception.

Wading through the sea of bodies, Ian nodded at those he knew and was met with claps on the back, words of encouragement, and a few, "Glad you're back, Sampson!" exclamations. His desk, located near the rear of the large room, was the only thing in the building that seemed clear of clutter. Suffering from a small case of OCD, Ian never left the building after each shift without making sure everything was in its place and cleared away. In his eyes, there was nothing worse than a messy desk, and he often chastised his fellow officers for not keeping their areas clean and organized. How can anyone expect to do their jobs effectively if they can't find anything on their desks?

"Sampson!!"

A call from behind brought his attention around and he nodded at Detective Marie Gonzalez, who was leaning out of a doorway that led into one of the examination rooms they used to display information on a particular case.

Grabbing a couple of pens and a large yellow notepad out of one of the desk drawers, Ian made his way to where the detective had set up shop. Entering, he closed the door behind him, effectively killing the noise level, and found that Gonzalez was alone.

"We the only two on this one?" He asked, hoping that she would say yes.

"Yep, with Colliatti on leave, we are even more shorthanded and personally, I prefer it this way."

"Agreed", he said, nodding at her. The less hands in the pot, the less chance of mistakes or miscommunication occurring. When they needed some help, they would go to Captain Leary. Nodding to a white board that ran the length of one wall, he asked, "What are we looking at?"

"Ok, here we go." Gonzalez took a deep breath, knowing that Ian was coming in uninformed. Addressing four glossy 8x10 photos that were taped near the top of the white board, Gonzalez started with first of the victims.

"Victim One; found April 13; was discovered just west of the Interstate, coordinates here," pointing to a large map of the city, the location was marked with a push pin and labeled in black marker as 'Number 1', "one-point-three miles off of Sabrina Trail. Victim Two: found May 1; was discovered here; Victim Three: on June 27th, and, finally, Victim Four: found on July 16th, in the alley."

As she spoke, Gonzalez pointed to each of the victim's pictures, all taken after death while in the custody of the medical examiner, and Ian followed her moves, matching each picture with the marked location indicating where they were found on the map. The final victim, number four, was the one that he had started to investigate just before getting himself suspended for his tiff with Colliatti.

"We have been able to identify each victim, all based on dental records, but the first two have been also identified by family. Victim Number One is Sherry McDonald, 22 years old, originally from Cleveland, left home in November of last year, on her way to New Mexico, but never met up with her aunt and uncle who were waiting for her arrival. Victim Two is Marsha Reynolds, twenty-three and from Phoenix, left one morning in late December to go to work, but was never seen again. Victim Three is Angela Ford, nineteen. She was reported missing in January by her parents in Pinetop and her boyfriend in Tempe, said she was supposed to drive down for a weekend with him but never made it.

"Number four—you're victim from the alley—just got identified late yesterday, but nothing else yet. Her name is Georgia Sweeny and I am in the midst of trying to run background on her. Similarities between these four women include that they were all found nude, arms across their chests and legs crossed at the ankles. Ligature marks found on all four indicate that they were bound by some type of thick cord; located at the wrists and ankles. Doc says that each woman had to have been restrained for some time, but because all the wounds to the skin appeared to be healing when death occurred, something in the past two to three days of these girls' lives changed in the way they were being held. Also, each was sexually assaulted prior to death and bruising and abrasions covering the face, arms, thighs, and calves are consistent with all four.

"All four women were shot, four times, all between the neck and the abdominal area. Ballistics from the first three matches, so we know that the same weapon was used, but we are still waiting for the results from our fourth victim. I have a sinking feeling that the fragments found in Ms. Ford are going to match as well. Oh...and one more thing...their tongues are missing."

Ian looked up, disgusted and growing angrier by the second. "Missing??? As if—"

"As if cut out of their mouths."

"*Jesus*", he muttered. No wonder why Leary called him in, canceling his suspension.

"That's pretty much all I got right now. With everything that has been going on around here and being shorthanded, I haven't had much time to take each girl and run a more comprehensive background check. I have files started on each and those begin with the most recent information so we are ready to run this backward to get a clearer picture on each. I'm hoping that the further back we investigate, there may be a link between the four other than the blond hair, ethnicity, and violent way that each one died."

Taking it all in, Ian sank into one of the leather bound chairs surrounding the long conference table that was centered in the room. Carefully, he eyed each photograph, as if trying to commit each victim memory, noting similarities and differences between the four as he did.

"Any evidence found on any of the bodies?" He asked after a few quiet minutes passed.

"Nothing. No semen, nothing under any of the girl's nails and nothing on their bodies that offered any evidence. All he's got really is the information on the wounds and abrasions, but can't give a definitive answer as to what was used, just that it had to be some kind of blunt object, maybe a pipe or bat or something. Hopefully when we come up with a weapon, he can match it to what he's collected and documented."

Gonzalez sighed as if exhausted and walked the length of the white board again, staring at each victim individually for a moment, then the map, then walked to the opposite side of the room to see the whole picture—wanting to take it all in at once to see if something sparked. Nothing did.

"The one thing that I am confused about is your girl, Amanda Pearson", she admitted.

Not wanting to correct Gonzalez (Amanda was no longer *his* girl) he turned his eyes from the white board and gave her his full attention. "What's that?"

"Her statement."

Saying nothing, Ian gave a Gonzalez a small shrug of his shoulders and shook his head slightly as a frown spread across his mouth, indicating that he wasn't sure he knew what she was talking about.

"Has she talked to you about everything that happened to her Friday night??"

Eyeing her now, he said, "I only know what you told me on Saturday."

Detective Gonzalez grabbed a file from the stack that was piled up at the end of the table, glanced at the tab to be sure that it was the right one, and took the seat across from Ian. Watching her do this, he quickly became agitated, knowing that she suspected something concerning Amanda but didn't come right out and say it.

"Marie!" Addressing the detective by her first name was something he rarely did, the same true for anyone he worked with. Communication between officers was commonly performed by addressing each other using their last name. But sometimes...the use of an officer's first name was called for...this being one of those times. When she didn't respond, instead focusing on the contents of the file now open in front of her, Ian said loudly, "Marie!! What are you not telling me?!"

"Just....bare with me okay??" Her question was more of a demand than anything else.

Sinking back into the hard chair he was in, Ian clamped his mouth shut as Detective Gonzalez thumbed through the first few pages in the file. Looking to the side tab, he could see Amanda's first and last name listed, as well as her date of birth, and the date the file was created; all typed neatly on a white sticker that was attached to the tab itself. Seeing this made his mind wander a bit and the events that led up to her leaving the day before ran through his mind, causing him to feel anxious and depressed all over again.

"You with me??" Looking up, he caught Gonzalez's stare and cleared his throat and nodded.

"Ok, Friday night, Ms. Pearson reported leaving Lucky's Girls just after 8:30. She talked to the manager on duty about some injury—"

"—her ankle", Ian interjected, causing Gonzalez to give him a look.

"She talked to the manager about her *ankle*, then dressed and left out the back door. Once in the back parking lot, she remembers seeing a few other cars parked, but nothing else. She heads towards her car, but forgets that her keys are still in her bag. Kneeling on the driver's side of the car, she found them in her bag and entered the vehicle. At that point, she notices another car coming into the lot, said their lights lit up the parking area pretty well.

"Then, she said the lights cut off...before the car had parked in a space. According to her, the car drove past hers, went to the very back of the lot, and parked as she got into hers. She then said she saw two guys exit the vehicle and move towards the trunk. Hearing them argue, she got scared, and instead of starting her car and leaving, she froze.

"Next thing she hears is the sound of gunfire, four rounds being fired off—she was adamant about how many. That caused her to lie down in the front seat of her vehicle. Now, she's not sure how long she lay there, but she said there was a sudden knocking sound on the driver's side. Said she looked up and could see the butt of a gun being hit against it." Pausing just then, Gonzalez looked up from the typed statement and eyed Ian. His jaw set hard, she could see that he was clenching his teeth and his brown eyes looked as though they were going to start shooting out flames any second.

"Do you want to read this for yourself?" She asked him.

"Just keep going, Gonzalez."

"Okay...." Looking down to find where she left off, she continued, "Ms. Pearson said the gun was then used to break the window and she was pulled from the vehicle by her hair. Said when she started screaming and tried to get away, the guy holding on to her basically said he was going to kill her if she didn't shut up. She was then dragged to the other vehicle. She gave me a really good description of the guy who had pulled her out of the car—hair color, eyes, and the most important detail...a scar that ran from the bottom of his left eye and down the side of his face.

"The other guy she didn't get a good look at, but did mention that the one with the scar seemed like he was the one in charge. The other guy didn't say anything, do anything, or get involved unless he was told to. After being pulled to the car, the one with the scar made the other one shut the trunk—that's when she said she saw blond hair coming from it and said that there was a strong odor coming from it, because it almost made her puke.

"From there, the one holding her pushed her down onto the top of the trunk and told the other guy to hold her down. Figuring that she was about to be raped, she fought back and managed to get away from the both of them. She said she took off running towards the front of the parking lot when another car turned in and she went down. That is when she was shot from behind."

Saying nothing, Ian sat, staring off into space and Gonzalez knew him well enough to know not to say anything more just yet. She imagined that he was taking it all in, visualizing the scene in his head, and it didn't help that he had an emotional connection to the victim. It made things worse, in fact, and was frowned upon so greatly that such situations had been known to ruin an officer's career in the past.

"Witness statements?"

Looking through the file again, Gonzalez answered, "Yea, quite a few that were not of much help. But the officers on scene were able to get a statement from the guy that had pulled into the parking lot when it all happened...a...Marcus Fletcher. According to this," referring to a typed statement that Gonzalez had just pulled from the file, "Fletcher drove into the lot and went to park in the back when he saw Ms. Pearson running towards him. He slams on the brakes and she goes down. Said he saw a flash from the back end of the lot and automatically believed that someone was firing a gun and he hid for cover in the front seat.

"When he sat up again, he said, quote "there was someone lying on the ground in front of my car". He managed to pull around her and parked, then got out, checked to see if she was breathing, saw the blood and called 911. Said he never saw another car leave the lot, just waited there until emergency showed up and by then other customers had come out of the bar and the word had spread. Guess when the responders go there, everyone in the bar was outside of it, rubbernecking. Other statements were collected but no one said anything concerning the other vehicle or the two guys that Ms. Pearson says she fought with."

"You think she's lying??" Ian looked accusing at Gonzalez, causing the detective to hold up both hands in a defensive manner.

"Hey, I'm not saying anything! She didn't shoot herself...and personally, after talking to her, I believe that someone else was in that parking lot. Plus, when she was brought into emergency, the doctors had to pull shards of glass out of her hair. Her injuries match her statement."

"But...." Ian gave her a look, encouraging her to explain what she was thinking.

"But...how did the other car leave the parking lot without the guy that drove up on the scene seeing them leave? Where did the other car go??"

"Have you walked the scene yet?"

"No, haven't had the chance with everything else going on."

"Let's go." Standing immediately, Ian waited for Gonzalez to put Amanda's file back together and, taking one more look at each of the victim's pictures pasted to the white board, left the room and checked in with his captain before heading out with Gonzalez; hoping that visiting the scene of where Amanda was attacked would shed some light on what they were facing and if everything really was connected in some way.

Chapter Twenty-Two

The parking lot in the back of the topless bar was still marked off with yellow crime scene tape, warning anyone that tried to enter that this area was still being investigated. Parking just outside the tape, Ian followed Detective Gonzalez under the thin strip and walked towards the middle of the lot. Using crime scene photos taken the night of Amanda's assault, Gonzalez marked significant areas within the area with small orange cones that she had pulled out of the trunk of the unmarked police car they had driven in together.

The spot where Amanda had been found when the medics arrived was apparent due to the blood-stained ground and as Ian stood and stared at it, he could visualize how she must have looked. According to the reports submitted by the medical emergency team and the officers that responded to the call, she was on her stomach, arms bent at the elbows with her hands near her head, as if she had known she was going to fall forward and tried to brace herself for it. The blood from her wound had covered both her back and her chest and spread outward from underneath her body.

In figuring just how far the shooter had been at the time the trigger on the weapon was pulled, the crime scene unit had calculated the trajectory of the bullet; based on the angle of the entry wound and the damage it caused to the skin upon entering and exiting and this information had already been submitted to Gonzalez and with it, she marked the shooter's location with another cone.

Knowing that Amanda had been shot from behind, Ian studied the distance between where she fell and the area that Gonzalez had just marked. Walking towards Gonzalez, he calculated about fifty feet or so between the two areas and noted that as the distance was not too far, and if the shooter was in fact tied to the other four murdered women...why did he miss? If the shooter had been aiming for Amanda's heart, or her head for that matter, how is it he missed and got her in the right shoulder instead? This brought about a whole series of additional questions that had yet to be considered and voicing them out loud to Gonzalez, he ran through them one by one.

"If the shooter was experienced, why did he aim for Amanda's shoulder?"

"Good question..." Gonzalez answered, thinking about it now herself. "Maybe he's not experienced with shooting a moving target?"

"Okay...possible; but the other four victims have similar shots, right? Two in the stomach and two in the chest...what's the exact position of the wounds on the four girls, are they close in location?"

"Yeah, actually, now that I think about. They don't really appear to be random, but pretty spot on if you look at each victim's wounds all together."

"Okay, so that would tell us that the shooter is pretty experienced with a weapon and is comfortable. Then why did he miss?" Wanting Gonzalez's take on what has been bothering him the most since they started picking apart the scene, he voiced his concerns.

"Huh??"

"Why did he miss?? Think about it...you're the shooter, right? A serial killer who has killed four victims so far. You've just discovered that someone has witnessed you kill your latest victim. You really gonna let her live?? Let her walk away...especially when you know that she can identify your face??? Doesn't make sense..."

Thinking for a moment, Gonzalez took a few minutes to answer. "Maybe he didn't realize he had missed. It was dark, practically no moon that night, and from what I see", turning in a circle, Gonzalez raised her eyes, searching for any light posts that would have lit up the parking lot that night and only found one and, pointing it out to Ian, continued, "there is only that one post that would have offered any light. If it was working, I think it would have still been pretty dark where Ms. Pearson was at the time of being shot."

Nodding, he understood her point.

"That and, the other car..."

Looking at her for clarification, Ian let her explain with interrupting.

"Ms. Pearson said that when she fought them off, she ran towards the front of the lot and another car was just pulling in to park. In all that panic, the shooter might have just made the shot automatically and not taken the time to line it up or anything. When she went down, the other driver then became involved, and the shooter decided to take off immediately."

"Okay, that makes sense. But if that's the case, where did he go?"

Turning and facing the back of the lot, the two detectives took a closer look at the chain link fence that wrapped around the perimeter. Finding a gate attached to the south end of the fence that would have offered enough room for a car to pass through if opened up wide enough, they found it secured with a heavy duty padlock; requiring a key to unlock it; and both Ian and Gonzalez stole a look at each other.

"Wonder if this is always locked??" Gonzalez thought out loud, eyebrows raised.

"Wonder who carries the key??" Ian offered in return.

"Think it's time we pay Mr. Lucky a visit." Gonzalez suggested and Ian replied, "Oh...I'm looking forward to this", as the pair headed towards the front of the building.

Having just recently opened for the day, the inside of the bar was dark, loud, and practically empty of customers. Entering the building, Ian and Gonzalez were met with empty podium; where the doorman would typically be positioned in order to greet customers as they came in, check their identification to ensure proper age, and collect the entrance fee if one was required during the time of the visit. During the day, there was no entrance fee, however at night a ten dollar cover charge was in effect. Surprised to find the entrance unguarded, Ian didn't wait for a doorman to show but instead held the long black curtain that separated the inner bar from the entryway (hung with the purpose to disallow a potential customer from seeing the inside of the bar prior to meeting barroom requirements) for himself and Gonzalez to step through.

Dark in setting, Ian stood still for a moment, allowing his eyes to adjust while *Queen's "Fat Bottom Girls"* assaulted his hearing. Feeling the vibration of the drums and bass from the song creep up through his boots, Ian noted a blond haired dancer who was busy strutting her stuff on the back stage. Seeming tall and thin from where he stood, he glanced over her bare chest, plaid school-girl mini skirt, and thigh-high black boots and counted at least six other girls sitting around the bar area; each looking bored and lonely.

Heading in the direction of the bar, Ian waited on the sidelines as Gonzalez sized up the bartender, a short frizzy haired brunette who looked as though she had seen better days. Bags under her eyes, she leaned over the bar to ask Gonzalez if she wanted a drink; who returned with a short shake of her head, requesting to see the owner instead.

"Hey there handsome, would you care for a dance?"

Breaking his train of thought, Ian turned at the sound of a voice dripping with sweetness, and found himself staring in the blue eyes of a young looking blond. Eyeing him behind long lashes, she gave him a painted smile as she twirled a strand of hair around a thin finger. Wanting instead to ask her just how old she was, Ian shook his head and turned away. Dropping her innocent act immediately, she frowned and stalked away, muttering 'asshole' as she went and he couldn't help but smile. On the job made no difference; he was not a frequent customer of topless bars and refused to spend money on a three minute dance that would probably just leave him sexually frustrated and feeling more alone than he felt on normal days.

Watching Gonzalez say something to the bartender, he took a step towards her but stopped instantly when a bright light invaded the darkness of the bar from the back of the house. Turning his eyes towards it, his breath caught in his throat when seeing Amanda walk through a door that obviously led to the back rooms of the bar. As the door closed behind her, the light was cut off and his eyes readjusted, only to now focus on the coloring of her outfit as the bar's florescent lighting made her appear to glow. Wearing a white top that showed off her thin stomach and hid her bandaged shoulder, her short black skirt barely covered her rear and Ian's heart began to suddenly race as he watched her make her way to the bar from the opposite side.

Carrying a circular tray, Ian unknowingly sighed in relief. She was here to serve drinks...nothing more. Despite the fact that she had walked out of his life and was no longer his concern, the thought of her dancing for some drunk, removing her top for a few bucks in the process, made his blood boil. And not knowing if it was jealousy or something else that made him feel this way, he tried to pry his eyes away from her, but could not.

"Hey—you okay??" Approaching him from the side, Gonzalez followed his gaze and, seeing Amanda, said, *"Okay...?* What's up, Sampson...you look—" Seeing the tension build in his jaw, she stopped herself short.

Knowing that Gonzalez had no clue about what transpired between Amanda and him over the weekend, he said nothing; wishing to avoid having to explain that just when things seemed to be going great between him and Amanda, everything blew up in his face. He wasn't ready to rehash that event with anyone. Instead, he silently watched as Amanda made her way up to the side of the bar, obviously setting up her tray to serve whatever customers came in during her shift. As if sensing that she was being watched, she suddenly looked up and immediately locked eyes with Ian; causing his heart to flip and butterflies to flutter within his stomach.

Mouth slightly open, all he wanted to do at that moment was wrap his arms around her and kiss her, but held fast again. The look she was giving him was pure surprise and she froze, tray in midair. Then, as if coming out of a daze, she lowered it slowly to the bar's counter and glanced around, as if wanting to see if anyone else in the bar was paying attention. No one; with exception to Gonzalez; was.

Waiting to see if she was going to stay right where she was, move towards him, or run back to the back of the house screaming her beautiful head off; Ian stood in his place for a few seconds. Then, seeing that she was choosing to stay put, he decided to chance it and walked towards her; eyes on hers the entire way. Reaching her, he tried to smile as if nothing was amiss between them, but failed miserably and the look he gave her instead caused her to bite her lip and look down at her tray, unable to maintain eye contact.

"Hey." Ian started, not sure what else to say. By now, the other girls sitting between the bar and the back stage had woken up and were paying attention. "How are you doing?"

Nodding her head, Amanda kept her eyes down and muttered, "I'm alright." Then, as if building courage, she sighed heavily and finally looked up at him. "I was supposed to call you."

Cocking his head at her, he said nothing.

Sighing again, she rolled her eyes and gave him a comical look. "Anna. When she found out that I...um...did what I did, she chewed me a new one. Said she was going to give me one day to call you, then she was going to call you for me."

Raising his eyebrows at her, he smiled and said, "Really??"

Laughing slightly, Amanda cleared her throat and gave him a look, as if suddenly out of words.

Nodding, as if fully understanding, Ian replied, "But...you didn't call", and his smile disappeared. Then, wanting to make her feel better about her decision, he took a small step backwards and said, "and its ok, Amanda, really. I know that I probably moved way too fast and I'm sorry. I've never been one to avoid saying what I feel."

Opening her mouth to reply, Amanda closed it quickly as Gonzalez reached Ian's side. "Sampson, the owner is available to see us. Ms. Pearson." Nodding at Amanda, Gonzalez left the two of them and headed towards the back of the bar where the owner, Lucky was standing, eyeing the detectives carefully.

"I'd better get back to work." Amanda said, noting that Lucky was also giving her a look.

"Yeah." Turning to follow Gonzalez, Ian stopped quickly to face Amanda one more time. Leaning in close, he felt her body tense as he whispered, "But know that when you are ready, I will be there. I'm not giving up so easy, Amanda. I *have* fallen in love with you... and I can say that without question." Then, straightening, he searched her wide green eyes for a moment before saying, "I hope you and Brighton are doing well, please call me if either of you need anything."

And with that, he walked away, which felt like the single-most difficult thing he had yet to do in his life. He wanted her back—badly—and knew that even though they had spent only one weekend together, she was not going to be easy to get over if she decided never to call. Ignoring the stares he was getting from the other dancers on the floor, he greeted the owner of the bar with a handshake and a flash of his badge and then followed him and Gonzalez back through the door that led them past the liquor storage room, a set of employee bathrooms, and small-sized offices to a larger one where they could conduct their interview without the interference of the music, the half-naked girls, or Amanda.

Sitting himself behind a large wooden desk, the owner once again introduced himself as Lucky Serifino while offering seats to Ian and Gonzalez. Pulling out a small notebook and pen, Ian sat silently, offering Gonzalez to lead the conversation—this was her investigation after all.

"How long has Lucky's Girls been in business?" Starting general, Gonzalez wanted to get a feel for the owner while working her way up to more direct questions essential to the case.

"Ten years." Lucky answered, sinking into his office chair, a sign that he was at ease.

"How long has Amanda Pearson been employed here?"

"About seven of those ten."

"Any problems with her employment? Issues with customers or the law during this time?"

"Oh, no! Amanda is one of my best girls. She comes to work on time, is always happy to be here", pausing for a second, Ian caught the owner's eye and wondered if he was trying to make a point being that Ian was just seen talking privately with the dancer, "she always seems to like what she does."

Moving ahead, Gonzalez discussed Friday's incident. "Why did Ms. Pearson leave early on Friday night? She was scheduled to work until closing, correct?"

Breaking eye contact with Ian, Lucky turned his attention to Gonzalez and answered, "She had a problem with a customer. Apparently, they were in the VIP Lounge, where dances cost a bit more, and the customer tried to pull her down on top of him. She twisted her ankle and my bouncer stepped in and escorted the customer from the building. Amanda had my night manager check her ankle and requested to go home for the night. She was allowed to leave."

Hearing exactly what had happened to cause Amanda to leave early that night, Ian suddenly found himself angry and spoke up. "Do you often serve customers who can't keep their hands to themselves??"

Giving Ian a look, Lucky paused before answering. "The touching of my girls is not only against the house rules, it against the law. My girls all know that if they encourage a customer to get more personally involved while here, they face discharge as well. Amanda does not fall into this class of girls; she has always conducted herself as a professional while under my employment."

Hearing Lucky refer to Amanda as one of 'his girls' did nothing to calm Ian's nerves and he suddenly thought that maybe working with Gonzalez on this was not a good idea; if he couldn't keep himself biased as the investigation ran its course, he may have to consider requesting a different assignment.

As if sensing the tension building in the room, Gonzalez took the reins again, causing both men to turn their attention back to her. "When Ms. Pearson left for the evening, she did so out the back door, is this common being that no one is usually stationed out there?"

"No, it is discouraged" Lucky admitted, but added quickly, "but we have never had a violent act committed on these premises. I believe that if Amanda believed herself in danger, she would have asked Matt to escort her to her vehicle."

"And Matt is....?"

"My door man and head bouncer. He ensures that no one enters my establishment that should not, keeps an eye on my girls, and, generally...keeps the peace when needed."

"And is Matt available for us to speak to?"

"No...actually, Matt is...indisposed at the time..."

Noting the hesitation in answering to Gonzalez's question pertaining to the bouncer, Ian sat up in his seat and asked, "Indisposed???"

Giving Ian a hard look, Lucky frowned when saying, "Yes, detective, he is indisposed at the time. I believe you would refer to it as 'out for the day'....Matt is using some personal time at the moment."

"Hmm..." was all Ian responded with, suddenly feeling that the bar owner was not being upfront about something. Then switching gears before Gonzalez could continue on with her questions, he asked, "So, who holds the key to the locked gate out back??"

Giving Ian a look, Gonzalez did not let it linger and immediately returned her focus to Lucky, who shifted in his seat before answering; another sign that the man was becoming uncomfortable with the line of questioning.

"That gate is always locked."

"You're ignoring the question", Ian accused automatically.

"No...I am pointing out that there has never been an instance when that gate was unlocked."

"So, who holds the key??" Pressing the point, Ian leaned forward in his seat a bit; causing Lucky to straighten his back in his; as if on the defense. "Mr. Sarifino, we can either continue this interview here or we can head down to our offices and finish it there. Your choice."

"Matt." Clearly agitated with Ian, Lucky turned away from him and focused on Gonzalez. "Matt keeps the key on his ring that also holds all the keys to the building, the offices, and the liquor room."

"Really???" Skepticism building in his voice, Ian grinned as Lucky refused to look him in the face. "So, can you say without reservation that the key was not used this past Friday night, say...to open the gate wide enough to allow a vehicle to pass through to the alley?"

Forced to look at Ian, Lucky clenched his teeth, causing his jaw to tighten dramatically and both Ian and Gonzalez knew that this topic was not one the owner was expecting to come up. "Yes. I can positively *guarantee* that that gate has never been opened." Then, standing from his seat, addressed both detectives when saying, "I believe this conversation is over. If you will excuse me, I have a bar to run. Any further questions may be referred to my attorney."

Glancing over at Gonzalez, Ian did nothing to hide his smile, who matched it with a smirk of her own. Standing, Gonzalez, said sweetly, "Thank you for your time, Mr. Serifino and if we do have more questions, you can be damned sure that we will contact your lawyer."

Following Lucky out, Ian was surprised when the short man directed them to the back door instead of walking them through the bar to the front entrance. Turning back to Ian, he said, "I would prefer it if you left my girls alone, Detective Sampson. What happened to Amanda was tragic of course, but the event has nothing to do with my bar, my employees, or myself. We are all just thankful that she came out of it with her life intact."

That said, the man turned from Ian and Gonzalez and headed towards the bar area; leaving them to exit out the back themselves, but was forced to turn around again when Ian asked one more question, "You got security cameras out back, Serifino??"

"Yes, in fact I do...regrettably; however, the camera that monitors the back part of our parking area was not in working order this past weekend."

"Oh...of course it wasn't." Ian prompted, trying to egg on the owner into losing his cool and saying something incriminating against himself. Lucky, unwilling to play such a game with the detective scoffed slightly and turned his back on Ian, this time making it through the door that led to the bar without further interruption.

Following Gonzalez back out into the heat of the day, Ian couldn't no longer hide his anger. "That son-of-a-bitch is hiding something."

"You think??" Gonzalez replied as they made their way through the lot gathering the orange cones she had placed prior to entering the bar. "And what the hell is up with you, Sampson??"

"What???" Giving her a questionable look, Ian stood his ground.

"With Ms. Pearson?? When she came into the bar, you looked like you were going to fall over! What's up with you two...what'd you sleep with her or something??" Then, noticing the look that covered Ian's face said, "Oh, *SHIT*, Sampson...really?!"

"It's none of your business, Gonzalez", Ian warned.

"It is if it is going to interfere with this investigation!"

"It's not!!!"

"Really?? I saw the way you looked at her, Ian! If Captain Leary finds out that you slept with a victim whose case is not only still open, but is being investigated by you, he'll have your balls in a vice before you know it!"

"He's not going to find out!" Glaring at Gonzalez, he finally admitted what he had been struggling to accept all along. "There's nothing there, anyways...it was over before it even got started."

Sighing heavily, Gonzalez had no retort. Then, seeing the hurt look on Ian's face, said, "I'm sorry, Sampson. But you've got to know that is was never a good idea to get involved with her in the first place."

"Yea, I know..." Ian muttered. Then, wanting to change the subject, said "Let's just get outta here, okay? I don't think there is anything else we can do here at this point."

Nodding at him, Gonzalez followed him back to the car. Leaving the parking lot, Ian stole one last glance at the entrance to the bar using the review mirror, wondering if Amanda felt the same as Gonzalez—that it wasn't a good idea that their relationship had gone as far as it did—did she feel that she had made a huge mistake? Because, if you asked Ian, he would never admit to it; instead would admit that not only was it worth it, he would do it all over again if he had the chance.

Chapter Twenty-Three

The squad room was no quieter when Ian and Gonzalez returned then it had been when they left—in fact it seemed even busier and louder. Heading back to the conference room where Gonzalez had originally set up all the information she had gathered on the four murder victims, they closed themselves off from the rest of the world to discuss Amanda's case in private.

"Alright...let's see what we got." Gonzalez said, sitting herself at the large oak table after pouring herself a cup of stale coffee.

Ian, sitting across from her, pulled out his notebook and pen and opened it to the pages that detailed all the information for this particular case. Reviewing them quickly, he silently hoped that the attempt on Amanda's life had been an isolated incident, but something in his gut told him otherwise and at this point, he voiced his concerns to Gonzalez.

"I've got the same feeling, Sampson. These have got to be tied somehow—based on her statement, she saw strands of blond hair coming out of the trunk, that and the fact that prior to being attacked, the two men from the car opened fire on whoever it was in the trunk. All of our victims are blond and had been shot. Something tells me that this is no coincidence."

"And the bar owner...Lucky. He's at the top of my list."

"You just saying that coz you can't stand him or for some other reason??" Gonzalez prompted Ian to continue; already feeling that he was right, but needing to know his reasoning behind it.

"His reaction when I asked him about the locked gate. He got real defensive and his body language screamed guilty if you ask me. If the man is not involved directly then he knows more than he is letting on. I've got the feeling that him blaming Matt the Bouncer

215

for keeping track of the key was just a ruse…get the heat off of himself for the moment."

"Agree." Gonzalez was feeling better about bringing Ian in on this already; despite the obvious friction between him and Ms. Pearson and the knowledge that the two had become to know each other on a more 'religious' basis.

"Okay", Ian stood and addressed the four victims photographs, still taped to the white board. "if our fourth victim, Georgia Sweeny, was the girl that Amand—err, *Ms. Pearson*," wanting to keep this completely professional, he corrected his usage of her first name, "saw in the trunk on the night of her attack, then we've got a lead on our murder suspects."

"Yes…but the main details we've got are only on the shooter, she didn't get a good look at the second guy. The shooter, she believes was at least a foot taller that she is, is described as strong in build, dark, shaggy looking hair, eyes dark in color, and has a scar running from under his right eye that spreads down the side of his face." Then, looking up at Ian, Gonzalez asked, "You think she could sit with a sketch artist??"

"Possibly, if she remembers all those details, we should be able to get some kind of composite."

"Good, let's set that up—you want to or would you rather I do it??"

"Nope, I got it." Determined to prove to Gonzalez that he could remain completely professional from here on out, did not hesitate when answering. "I have contact information for Anna, Ms. Pearson's best friend, and can get a message to her that way."

"Okay, good. Now, there's something that's got to tie these girls together. The similarities between the four of them are just too great for these to be random kills." Then, turning towards the mapped locations indicating where each victim was last seen and where their bodies were found, Gonzalez suggested, "How 'bout you take two girls and I take the other two—lets split this up. We need more background information on each of these girls, hopefully something will come up that will give us an idea as to how they ended up spending their last days on Earth being tortured and murdered." Looking over her shoulder at Ian, he nodded at her and she continued, "I'll take the first two victims, Sherry McDonald and Marsha Reynolds, you take Angela Ford and Georgia Sweeny. Also, I'll dig up what I can on Lucky Serifino and you try to find what you can on Matt the Bouncer—starting with his last name."

"Sounds like a plan, Gonzalez. You want to brief Captain Leary, or should I??"

"I can do it." Gathering up the files on each victim, Gonzalez handed Ian what she had on the two latest women and muttered, "Looks like it's gonna be a long night", as she did. Ian, stifling a yawn already, simply nodded but was silently thankful for the work. Anything to keep him out of his apartment and away from his bed—where he knew he would just end up depressed and probably drunk knowing that Amanda wasn't going to come back.

Leaving the conference room, Ian closed the door tightly behind him and headed for his desk while Gonzalez went in to brief their captain. Turning on his computer, he sat, gathered a couple of pens and regular sized notebooks on top of his desk and started with Victim Number Three; Angela Ford, only stopping when he needed another bottled water or when he could no longer avoid using the restroom.

Five hours into it, Ian was starting to see the similarities between his victims and tabled them out on separate sheets of paper so that he could review them side-by-side and pick out the commonalities between the two. Aside from the obvious way that the two had been found and the injuries to their bodies, Ian found that both had outstanding increases in income during the later months of their disappearances and that the last victim, Ms. Sweeny, had been employed by a topless bar in Phoenix. To top that, both girls were also found with similar drugs in their systems; heroin, cocaine, and gamma-hydroxybutyrate, or GHB, a drug known for its ability to knock out the user and completely make them unaware of what was happening around them, or to them for that matter.

Sitting back in his chair, Ian rubbed his eyes, thankful that this part of the process was nearly complete. When it had come to gaining information on the fourth victim, Georgia Sweeny, he had been forced to contact her parents. Offering to make the drive to visit with them in person, Mr. Sweeny rejected Ian's offer, believing that in order to save time, he could answer any of the detective's questions over the phone. In doing so, Ian could not judge the father's body language or facial expressions to ensure that his answers were truthful. Too many cases have come across Ian's desk in which the perpetrator was a relative to the victim and judging their reaction to questions often led to his gut shooting of warning signals.

In this case, however, Ian abided by the father's wish, conducted the interview over the phone, and paused only when hearing who he assumed was Mrs. Sweeny wail in agony in the background as her husband answered questions about their murdered daughter and at that point he didn't know what would have been worse—witnessing the mother's breakdown in person, or listening to it over the phone as her husband tried to console her in between answering questions.

Standing to take a quick break, Ian noticed for the first time that he was one of the only officers left in the room. Looking towards the wide windows that looked out over downtown, he saw that the sun had set, leaving behind a moonless night. Yawning, he suddenly realized how tired he was and turned from the windows to see the captain's light still on in his office. Approaching the closed door, he knocked once and entered upon hearing the captain yell, "Yeah?!" from behind his desk.

"Hey, Cap." Ian greeted the man with a small smile.

"Sampson—how's the case going?"

"Making some headway—found a couple of similarities between the last two victims—just waiting to see what Gonzalez has dug up so we can compare all four."

"And what about this bar owner...this...Serifino guy...anything on him??" Eyes raised, Ian's first reaction was to question how the captain knew that he and Gonzalez were looking at the owner of Lucky's Girls, but then stopped when remembering that Gonzalez had briefed the captain hours ago about their theories and progress thus far. Shrugging his shoulders, he answered, "Not sure, Gonzalez is looking at him. I am going to take a look at the bouncer, Matt somethingorother..."

Giving him a questionable look, Ian explained, "Don't know the bouncers last name yet. Gonna dig into him in the morning I think."

"Ahh...got it. Yeah, Sampson, go home. You've put in enough hours for one day; and if you see Gonzalez out there, send her home too, will ya?? You two don't need to start racking up the overtime and get Brass down here on my ass about it!"

Smiling, Ian nodded and said goodnight before stepping out of the captain's office to look for Gonzalez. Finding her back in the conference room, he stepped inside, this time leaving the door open behind him being that they were pretty much the only two left on the floor.

"Hey, how'd it go?? Any information on the first two victims?" Ian asked, sitting on top of the table as he did. Gonzalez, who was jotting notes down on the white board under the first two victims pictures answered without turning around.

"Yeah...was able to find some similarities between the two. Large bank account deposits right around the time of disappearance. Prior drug use between the two—oh, and the ME found similar drugs in their systems at the time of death—um...coke and GH—".

"GHB???" Cutting her off, Ian quickly explained that his two victims had the same drugs in their systems as well, plus the bank account activity between the two. Turning to face him, Gonzalez slowly nodded her head, admitting that these victims had more in common than originally thought.

"HEY!!! You two go home!"

Jumping at the sound of Captain Leary's voice as it boomed through the empty squad room, Ian turned around instantly and then relaxed, forgetting that he had left the conference room door open. Peering into the room, the captain said, "Go home, now!

Leave this stuff up for the night, I'll make sure the door is locked up and you guys get a fresh start tomorrow morning."

"Sure thing, Cap." Gonzalez swept up her information that was spread out on the table and gathered it into one pile while Ian stepped out of the room and grabbed his notes off of his desk. Bringing them to Gonzalez, she added the information to the pile, then taking one last look around the room, she followed Ian out.

"Hey, Ian, want to go grab some food?" Knowing that Ian hadn't taken any breaks to eat during the last five or six hours, Gonzalez offered to buy him dinner. Considering it for a moment, Ian shook his head, saying that he was just going to head home and eat there.

As if knowing he was lying, Gonzalez did her best to hide her smile, and shook her head at him. Somehow she knew just where he was headed—back to Lucky's to see Amanda—and while she wanted to say something about what a horrible decision it would be, she left it alone, bid him goodnight and left the squad room.

Heading out, Ian climbed into his truck and sat for a moment, thinking. Should he go back to the bar? Would Amanda even talk to him? What other excuse could he give her for showing up other than, 'I just wanted to see you'?? Then, deciding, he started the truck and headed back to Lucky's; now realizing that there was one reason that he could use to see her...the bouncer. He needed information on Matt the Bouncer and, in knowing that he wouldn't get anywhere with the owner, thought he would try his luck with Amanda.

Chapter Twenty-Four

Twenty minutes later, Ian pulled into the parking lot of Lucky's Girls and found a spot up front, near the entrance. Sitting there, he watched the clock and the door, suddenly realizing that he had no idea what time she was supposed to get off. Debating whether or not to just go into the joint, he figured 'what the hell' and got out of his truck. He was off duty, did not have to ask permission from anyone to enter it—despite the warning from the owner—and figured that if she was there, he would stay and buy a drink and if she was already gone, he would just leave.

Finding a female working the door, Ian submitted his driver's license for her to review and paid the ten dollar cover fee to enter. As the woman held back the back curtain, the loud music once again vibrated through his body as he made his way across the large room and found an empty table off to the right side of the bar. Sitting, his eyes finally adjusted and he took a look around.

A small crowd of men sat around the back stage; the front stage empty of both dancer and customer. The bar itself was full, guys crammed in sitting on small round stools only to tear their eyes away from the stage long enough to take a swig from their drinks.

On stage, a tall thin brunette was working the crowd, on her knees, grinding her body away to the sound of some metal band that he didn't recognize. Her costume, lit up brightly by the florescent lights, was a two piece bathing suit-looking ensemble that barely offered any coverage. Big-breasted, Ian shook his head, wondering if the money she had spent on an obvious breast enhancement was worth the backaches she probably endured on a daily basis.

"Ian??"

Hearing his name, he turned, and found a confused looking Amanda walking towards him, dressed in the same outfit she had been wearing this afternoon and carrying her empty tray in one hand. Taking a deep breath, he waited to respond to see just how angry she was that he was here.

"What are you doing here??" She demanded, her voice rising in volume in order to be heard over the loud music.

"I need to talk to you about something." Ian's voice matching hers, he suddenly felt as if they were yelling at each other.

"Ian...I can't do this—"

"It's not what you think," he cut her off; now wondering if this really was a mistake. "I need some information about one of your coworkers and you're the only one I could think of to ask."

"What about Lucky??? Or...ask the coworker yourself!" Starting to turn away from him, Ian knew she was pissed but held out a hand to stop her anyway.

"I can't. Your boss won't give us any information and as far as I can tell, the employee I am looking for isn't here."

Turning to face him, she asked, "Who is it you're looking for??"

"A bouncer named Matt."

Recognizing the name, Amanda's face turned a bit dark and she looked down at her tray, fumbling with the surface of it that was covered in a rough looking material probably meant to keep the beer bottles and glasses of liquor from sliding across is as they were delivered. Watching her pick at it for a moment, he reached out and covered her hand with his own, stopping her.

Looking up at him, Ian's body tensed as her emerald green eyes searched his own. "What is it??" He asked, again raising his voice so that she could hear him.

"I don't know..." she said, looking around for a minute before continuing, as if seeing if anyone close by was listening. "I saw him yesterday afternoon. He was acting kind of weird. Lucky made him drive me out to Green Valley and he dropped me off at Anna's parents' house."

An alarm going off in his head, Ian trusted his instinct even if he had no idea what it was trying to tell him. "Is there any way you can leave??"

"No!" Giving him a look, she took a deep breath, trying to calm herself. "I am on until eleven and I need the money." Then switching gears, she said, "Speaking of which, what can I get you?"

Knowing what he wanted to come back with, he bit his tongue before ordering a bottle of Budweiser. Watching her walk to the bar to fill his order, he decided that if she was not willing to leave early, he wasn't going to leave either. He would stay until closing if he had to, just to make sure she was safe. Not knowing if his gut was fired up due to feeling jealous over the bouncer that had taken Amanda out to Anna's parents' house or something else, he wasn't going to just ignore it.

"Hi, how you doing tonight?"

Tearing his eyes off of Amanda, he looked into the bright blue ones of one of her coworkers—a redheaded bombshell of a woman wearing a farmer-john type of dress with matching cowboy boots. Starting to explain that he was fine, but not interested in getting a dance, he didn't have the chance to speak as Amanda was suddenly at his table again, delivering his drink.

Eyeing her, he tried to judge the look on her face; pursed lips and lowered eyes; she looked as though she believed she was invading the dancer's territory in some way. Making her stand there while he slowly worked his wallet out of the back pocket of his jeans, he asked the dancer loudly, "How much for a dance?"

Smiling sweetly, she answered, "Ten bucks for down here, but if you'd like the *VIP treatment*, it's twenty a song." Starting to sit in the empty stool across from Ian, she gave him a wanted look.

"Oh…I'm sorry…" Ian corrected himself, watching Amanda intensely, "I meant, how much for a dance from the waitress??"

Looking up immediately, the shock on Amanda's face was priceless. Staring back at Ian, her mouth dropped slightly and Ian smiled at her, his brown eyes piercing her green ones and neither of them saw the other dancer stand up and leave them; frustrated that her potential customer obviously had no real taste in women.

"I'm not dancing tonight." Amanda said, so softly that he almost didn't hear her as the songs being played switched from metal to classic rock.

"How much??" Determined, he asked her again.

"Typically, if a customer wants a dance from a waitress, he has to pay fifty bucks for it."

"Well, I want a dance."

"Ian—"

"I'm serious, Amanda, I want a dance. Go clear it with whomever you need to and meet me in the VIP room, or whatever it's called!" Then, taking his beer, he dropped a ten spot on her tray and stood up, looking for the entrance to the room.

"It's up there", Amanda said, pointing, "up that ramp."

"Okay, don't keep me waiting...you've got money to earn."

"*Ian!*" Knowing she was getting angry with him, he smiled and turned away from her. Heading up the ramp, he found three other guys who were busy getting dances from other girls and, finding a leather bound loveseat positioned against the back wall, sank himself into it.

As the current song ended, another one started right up and the other three customers paid for their dances and followed each other back down the ramp. The room to himself, Ian propped his chin on one hand, placing one finger across his upper lip, as if studying something important.

A few minutes later, Amanda appeared at the bottom of the ramp and, looking up, sighed heavily before walking up it. Entering the room, which was still empty, she stopped in the middle of the room, facing Ian.

"Why are you doing this?" She demanded, hands on her hips.

"Because I want a dance." Amused at her stance, Ian fought back a smile.

"Bullshit." She replied, and he raised his eyebrows at her.

"Look, you can either sit with me for an entire song and take the fifty bucks in the end, or you can earn it and dance for me." Giving her the choice, Ian realized suddenly that he wasn't' sure which he would prefer at that moment, a dance from Amanda or the chance to sit and just talk to her.

"Fine." Was her only response, and as the next song started up, she walked towards him, her five inch black heels making her seem really tall as they accented her long legs. Bending slightly, she placed a hand on each of his knees and pushed them apart, giving her enough room to step in between them and he sank deeper into the soft leather.

Leaning forward over him, she was suddenly face to face with him, eyeing him carefully as she held herself up by placing both palms against the mirrored wall behind his head. "Now...you cannot touch me. You cannot touch yourself. If you do, I'll have your ass thrown out of here so fast you won't know what hit you. Got it??"

Grinning at her, Ian's heart did a flip and he nodded slowly, unwilling to break eye contact. Then, she added, "And I'm not taking my top off."

"I don't want you to." He replied, his voice husky. "I've already seen what you look like naked."

Biting her lip, she gave him an intense look before pushing herself off of wall and standing up straight again. Starting to dance, she moved graceful, and Ian found himself enthralled with every move that she made. Turning her back on him, she suddenly put both hands on his knees, and sat on his lap gently. Surprised, Ian shifted underneath her, causing her body to rise with his, and said, "I thought you weren't allowed to touch me."

Turning her head, she gave him a look from over her shoulder and said, "No...I said *you* can't touch *me*...I can do what I want—within reason, of course."

"Of course..." Ian's voice came out in a whisper and seeing her smile, he knew that she was doing this on purpose. And as her face turned away from him, she looked up towards the ceiling, giving her head a little shake; the effect being to get the back of her hair to lift gently off of her back before falling into place again. Because of its length, the ends of her red hair trailed softly across his waist, causing his body to tense and his fingers to tighten their grip on the arms of the chair. Giving his lap a soft grind, he inhaled sharply, his body responding immediately to the pressure.

Then she was up, off of his lap, straightening her back before bending forward, her fingers traveling down the sides of her legs until she touched her ankles. Her black skirt, short to begin with, lifted as she did this and Ian caught a clear glance of the matching black thong underneath, causing him to think back to the first time they had been together sexually—she had performed the same move...only stripped herself from her clothes that night. Despite that difference, the effect the move had on him was the same and desire quickly heated its way up his body.

Then, standing again, she turned to face him and he immediately noticed the hardness in her eyes as her cherry colored lips turned up in a smile. As the song came to an end, she placed her hands on her hips and cocked her head at him. "Had enough?"

"No", he whispered, barely audible as the DJ introduced the next girl to the stage.

"Ian—"

"No, I would like another...please." Ian locked eyes with her, and she clamped her mouth shut as she began to move again to the next song being played; country in genre but with a rock twist to it. Bending over him, as she did when she explained the rules, he inhaled her fruit-flavored perfume and eyed her tempting neck, wanting nothing more but to bite at it.

Leaning now, she pressed her upper body against his and the feel of her made him harden quickly. Shifting again, his fingers gripped the chair even harder and he wondered just how much more of this he could take. As if sensing his desire, Amanda turned her face towards the side of his and whispered, "Remember...keep your hands to yourself."

"You're not playing fair", he complained, to which she responded, "You're paying for it..." and her breath in his ear caused an ache to center itself below his belt.

Sliding down his body, Amanda bent her knees and knelt in between his thighs. Her hands traveled down his legs and he could feel their pressure despite the thickness of his jeans. Pulling back from him, she gripped his knees as she moved, resting her bottom on the backs of her heels, and laid her head back; offering him a full view of her exposed neck and the tops of her breasts as the top she was wearing was a low cut number that buttoned down the front. Coming around again, she gave him a wanted look as she got up on her knees once more and pressed her midsection against his manhood and looked down—giving the immediate impression that she was performing an oral act on him.

Suddenly wanting to push her away, Ian's anger surprised him; he wasn't expecting her to behave in this way—anyone walking by would have thought that Amanda was doing more than just dance at that very moment. Believing that she was purposely looking to degrade herself just to piss him off, and before he could think twice about, he took a hold of her shoulders and pushed her back slightly, causing her to look up at him, a surprised expression on her face.

"Stop", he demanded.

"Why—you wanted a dance!"

"Is this what you do??" He asked, his voice growing louder over the music.

Giving him a damning look, Amanda leaned back on her heels. "No, this is not what I do. I did it because you...you...pissed me off!!"

"Oh—I pissed you off?? And how do you figure that I did that, huh??"

"Because you got my head all scrambled that's why!!"

Breathing heavy, Amanda stood suddenly and sank her body into the chair next to Ian. Looking up she noticed the female bouncer that had taken Ian's money at the door looking up into the lounge, a worried look covering her face. "Everything's alright Jody, no problems."

"Okay, kiddo, just checkin'", the bouncer replied before tucking her body back behind the curtain to card the next customer that walked through the door.

Head in her hands, Amanda gave Ian a sideways glance as her breathing slowed down.

"Amanda, in all fairness...you've got my head scrambled too." Ian, leaning over to move her hair away from her face, he gave her a soft look as his anger dissipated quickly. "I really did just come in here to talk to you. I wasn't planning on...this..."

"So, what do we do now??" Sighing, Amanda stared down at her heels, not really expecting an answer from him.

"Well, you could quit this place for the night and come with me. I do owe you a hundred bucks and I'd say that's some pretty decent earnings for one night.

Thinking, Amanda turned her attention to the bottom floor of the bar, chewing on her lip as she did and Ian couldn't believe that she was actually thinking it over. Standing he grabbed his wallet and took two one hundred dollar bills out of it. Taking Amanda's hand, he brought her to her feet and stuffed the rolled up bills into her hand as he said, "No strings attached, no promises, or even planning involved. All I want to do is talk to you, mainly about this guy Matt and then I will take you back out to Anna's, no questions asked."

Eyeing him carefully, Amanda took a step backwards and said, "Finish your beer, Ian, I hate to see anything go to waste." And then, after a pause, added, "I'll meet you out front."

Nodding, he followed her down the ramp and as she headed towards the back of the house, he went to the table he had been seated at and chugged the remainder of his beer. Taking one last look around, he did not see another bouncer that could have passed for Matt; just the customers, dancers, the DJ, and the bartender; and headed towards the entrance.

Saying goodnight to the woman still sitting at the door, he stepped outside and met the heat of the night head on. Heading towards his truck, he got in, started it, and cranked up the air conditioning as he waited for Amanda.

A half hour later, Ian was starting to wonder if Amanda had in fact either changed her mind or was unable to leave an hour early. Eyeing the entrance to the bar one more time, he hesitated before turning the truck off to go back inside and check on her when she finally exited the building. Breathing deeply, he took a long look at her bare legs, noting the short red summer dress she was wearing.

Opening the passenger door, Amanda peered in at him and said, "You overpaid me."

"No I didn't." Waiting to see if she was going to actually get in or just continue to stand there, he added, "You are worth every penny."

Standing there for another second, Amanda seemed to contemplate his answer, then pulled herself into the truck, tossing her gym bag on the floor as she did. Pulling out of the lot, she asked him, "Can we go to your apartment?" and Ian fought himself from slamming the gas pedal down to the floor. Glancing over at her, he didn't answer, waiting for a reason and hoping that it was one he was wanting.

"I left my prescriptions on your nightstand. I haven't had any pain pills for almost two days, and I am really hurting right now."

"Oh...of course!" Not expecting that as a reason, he drove normally through town and made it to his building less than twenty minutes later. Heading up the elevator, neither of them spoke. The events that led up to Amanda leaving him in the room he had made for Brighton ran through Ian's head and he consciously reminded himself that the only reason she was back was to get her pills.

Heading into the apartment, Ian switched on the lights as Amanda made her way down the hall to the bedroom, as if feeling right at home and the sight of her here made Ian's heart ache; wanting her to stay for good.

"Got 'em." She announced as she came back down the hall to the living room. "Can I get some water?"

"Please...help yourself." Ian responded, meaning it wholeheartedly.

Once her pills were taken, he entered the kitchen and asked, "Do you want to talk here, or somewhere else?"

"Ummmm...I think we should head back to Green Valley. I called Anna to let her know that you were taking me home, if that's okay??"

Heart sinking, Ian nodded and began turning off lights again as Amanda reached to open the front door. Then, without warning, she closed it tightly and turned around to face him.

Confused, Ian had just reached out to turn off the kitchen light and froze. Peering at Amanda, he waited for her to speak first, not wanting to interrupt whatever it was she was going to say.

"I'm scared, Ian."

"Of what??"

"Of you...of how you make me feel." Then crossing her arms over her chest as if protecting herself she turned her eyes towards the floor as she continued, "I've never met anyone who made me feel the way you do—not even my ex-husband. After I left here, I found that I can't get you out of my head. Of course, it doesn't help that Anna brings you up every chance she gets!" Raising her head to meet Ian's eyes, she gave him a small smile.

"But I have to consider my daughter. I will not allow Brighton to get hurt—by anyone. It was really hard to leave you yesterday morning but..." pausing, she bit her lip and Ian saw her eyes begin to water, "...but I had to...for Brighton's sake. I can't just think about myself, I have to consider her as well. You say that you love me, and a big part of me wants to believe you. But what it really comes down to is Brighton."

Facing her, Ian forced himself to stand still as he answered her, not wanting to step towards her and cause her to run screaming from the apartment. "Amanda, I understand that— honest to God, I do. And, I am sorry for moving too fast. Like I said before, I don't hide my feelings, and I don't sugarcoat. I know how I feel, and whatever you decide to do from here on out, I will respect that."

"So...if I said that I will not be bringing Brighton here...that I am going to say with Anna's parents until I find a place for us again...you'd accept that??"

"Of course!" Surprised at her question, Ian suddenly realized just how forward he must have come off when presenting Amanda with Brighton's room...but then, it was the only way he could figure to show Amanda just how serious he was about them staying here at the time. Then, giving her a sideways glance, he asked, "Do I have to take Brighton's stuff back??"

Laughing, Amanda relaxed, dropping her arms to her sides. "No...no, you can leave them where they are. But I would like to take this a bit slow for her sake. You know...give her the chance to get to know you before anything too serious comes about."

"Anything you want." Ian's heart was pounding in his chest and he took a minute to get his breathing under control. He couldn't believe that she was giving him a chance to prove how he felt...giving him the chance to not only get to know her better, but get to know Brighton as well. And at that moment, he knew that he would do anything not to screw up that chance.

"Ian?"

"Huh??" Looking up at her, he realized that she hadn't moved from her spot at the door. Her look making him swallow hard, he held her stare.

"Did you know that make-up sex is supposed to be the best feeling in the world with exception to the first time two people make love to each other??"

And with that, Ian crossed the floor in two giant steps and took Amanda into his arms.

Chapter Twenty-Five

Covering my mouth with his, the kiss he gave me was intense and hot desire flashed through me like lightning. Pushing me up against the door, his hands cupped my bottom and I was suddenly lifted into the air and I wrapped my arms around his neck tightly as the center of our bodies came together like two pieces of a puzzle, fitting together perfectly.

Feeling his jeans rubbing against my center, I moaned loudly, not wanting to hold anything back. Knowing that I was making the right decision, I wanted to give him all of me without hesitation. Then, suddenly he was moving backwards, away from the door and, carrying me in this position, he made his way back to his bedroom as our mouths continued exploring each other; as if for the first time.

In the dark, he walked slowly to the edge of the bed, then set me down gently on my feet. Taking my head into his hands, he whispered, "I love you, Amanda", and my response caught in my throat. I wasn't ready to say it back and, seeming to understand this, he gently covered my mouth with his, kissing me so softly that my body felt weak against his.

Then, breaking the kiss, he reached down and grabbed the bottom of my sundress, lifting it up and over my head and then bent down a bit as he worked his mouth over my neck and his hands moved slowly across my back.

At that point, I wanted to be made love to—and wanted to make love to him in return. While the heat between our bodies made me feel frantic, I did not want this to feel like it was just sex between the two of us and that there was no real feeling or emotion. Slowly pulling the bottom of his shirt out of his jeans, I helped him out of it and worked my own mouth across his strong chest; feeling and tasting every ripple of his muscle structure as I did. Hearing him groan in pleasure, I stopped and looked up at him and softly told him exactly what I wanted.

"Make love to me, Ian." I whispered, as I watched his eyes intently.

"I was hoping you'd say that, Amanda..."

Gently stripping me of my bra and panties, he then lowered me to the bed only to stand before me to remove the rest of his clothing and I couldn't help but bite my lip. He was beautiful...and I ached for him immediately.

Turning from the bed, he found the box of condoms that had been hastily tossed aside the last time we were here and he pulled one out, tore it open and sheathed himself quickly. Lowering himself onto me, he entered me immediately and I closed my eyes as a deep moan escaped his lips.

Gasping as he worked slowly, I wrapped my legs around his waist, feeling a bit dizzy and beside myself. Closing his eyes for a second, I knew that he was fighting off the urge to finish, and whispered, "Ian..." as my body reacted on its own.

Feeling my climax build, our eyes met and I begged him not to stop, but to move faster. Then, kissing him again, I felt it closing in and tightened my legs around him as my hands worked to push him deeper inside me.

Panting now, Ian called my name and as I yelled his in return, my orgasm took over and I demanded that he join me in doing this same. Complying without hesitation, we were both spent and it was the most romantic feeling that I had ever had in my life; even though the entire act took less time than I had originally wanted.

Never knowing that making love to someone could be this good; I did nothing to stop the tears as they silently fell from my eyes and slid down the sides of my face as my body shuddered once more under his. Raising his forehead off of my collar bone, Ian reacted to my tears immediately. "Amanda?! God, did I hurt you??" Then starting to move off of me, I shook my head, tightening my grip around his waist, but couldn't speak just yet.

Really crying now, and unable to stop it, I buried my head into his shoulder while he continued to hold himself up, now looking confused.

"I just...I'm sorry..." trying to breathe, I wiped at my eyes and looked at him through my wet lashes. "I don't know, I guess I've never felt quite this way before. It was a bit...overwhelming..."

Giving me a look, Ian asked, "You've never been made love to before??"

Embarrassed, I tried to turn my head away from him, but after propping himself with one elbow, he used his other hand to turn my face towards his again.

"Amanda??" He asked me again, and I shook my head in answer. "Not like this", I admitted quietly and he replied as he kissed the tip of my nose, "Okay...well, anytime you have the need to be made love to...you just let me know; I will be *more* than happy to oblige."

Smiling up at him, my heart fluttered beneath my chest and I felt more than content...I felt *loved* and I knew instantly that I never wanted that feeling to go away. As long as Brighton was happy, I would do my best to make this work and to this, I made myself that solemn promise.

My thoughts broken by the sound of his cell phone going off somewhere on the floor, Ian sighed deeply and I took his face in my hands and whispered, "Don't answer it."

"I have to—"

Cutting him off as I moved slightly underneath him, I tightened the grip I had around his waist again, my body stirring and wanting more. Even though the making love part was over, I didn't want to stop but unsure if Ian was the type of lover that could be ready again so soon after finding release, I tested the waters carefully. Running my fingers up and down his back, I raised my head off of the bed worked my mouth around his chest. Hearing him groan slightly, I unlocked my ankles from around him and, bending my knees, used my feet to lift my midsection and at the same time used my hands to push down on his lower back; wanting to take in as much as I could of him.

Giving in, Ian relaxed his body over mine and the weight of him bore down on me, causing my desire to increase tenfold. Then, suddenly, he pushed his hands under my back and, holding on to me, rolled over onto his back. With me now on top, I moved freely and, feeling him harden once again from the inside of my body, a wave of ecstasy shivered through my body.

His cell phone ringing again, both of us ignored it as I continued to move; slowly at first, then gained speed when hearing him mutter my name. His hands gripped the sides of my waist tightly, then released them and grabbing my arms, he suddenly pulled me down so that I was lying on top of him. Automatically pushing my calves under his legs, he gave me a pleasure filled look and said, "Come for me..."

"Yeah??" I asked; breathing heavy as my center fluttered around him.

"Yes...oh, God, Amanda...yes, come for me", he demanded and I suddenly became so turned on that I cried out loudly. And then, it hit me....hard. Gasping as a second deep orgasmic wave rushed through me; I raised myself up using his shoulders and threw my head back, completely engulfed in the moment. Watching me, Ian smiled as I shuddered deeply as the tingling feeling slowly dissipated and brought my head back down to look at him.

"Feel better??" He asked, teasing me.

"What do you think?"

"I think that if you don't....at some point you're gonna kill me."

Smiling wide at him, I said, "Well, we wouldn't want that now would we??"

"I'd die an extremely happy man..." he admitted.

"Yea, but I really wouldn't want to have to explain that to 911!"

Laughing, he wrapped his arms around me and pulled me down onto him, hugging me as he breathed in deeply. Laying there for a few minutes, I asked, "Don't you need to…um…*finish*??"

"No…that was strictly for your enjoyment."

"Oh…well, thank you very much, Detective Sampson!" I said with a smile.

"You are so welcome, Ms. Pearson!"

And with another call coming in on his phone, he sighed and said, "I'd better find out who it is that's trying so desperately to get a hold of me."

Forcing myself to move, I sat up and lifted myself off of him. Lying down on the bed next to him, I watched as he moved over to the bottom of the bed and pulled his cell phone out of his jeans pocket. Lying on his back, he answered it while I quietly admired his naked body and after a few moments of listening to the caller, Ian suddenly sat up on the bed, alarming me in an instant as I listened to his end of the conversation.

"In the shower…" followed by, "Are you sure?!" followed by, "*Shit!!*", and then, finally, "Yea, I'll meet you there, text me the location." Call ended, he flipped his phone closed and, sitting on the edge of the bed, started to gather his clothes.

Understanding that something was wrong, I moved off of the bed and grabbed my undergarments and my sundress. Dressing quickly, I waited for him to speak; not wanting to sound like I was prying by asking him what was going on—I would much rather allow him to tell me on his own.

Process finished, I left the room and headed towards the kitchen and, finding my two prescription bottles, stuffed them into my bag. Feeling a bit more at ease here, I took a bottle of water out of the refrigerator and took a drink while waiting for Ian to emerge from the bedroom and wondered briefly if he was going to have time to run me all the way out to Green Valley. Thinking of calling Anna, my thoughts were interrupted as Ian came around the corner;

smelling strongly of clean soap mixed in with a subtle hint of cologne.

"You...ahhh...remember me asking you about one of the bouncers that works at the bar?" He asked quietly, running a hand over his face.

Turning, I studied his dark eyes before answering, knowing that whatever he was going to say, it wasn't going to be good. "Yes..." I finally answered, putting the bottle of water down onto the counter.

"Well, whatever you can tell me about him would be really helpful."

"Why...Ian, what's going on??"

"That was Detective Gonzalez on the phone. They just found a body out towards Madera Canyon. The identification that was found with it gave the name Matthew Duncan...and there was a Lucky's Girls business card in his wallet, naming him as head bouncer."

Mouth dropping, I leaned heavily against the kitchen counter, not believing at first that he was talking about Matt. "Are they sure???" I asked as my eyes started to water.

Walking towards me, Ian held his arms out for me to succumb to as a look of shock covered my face. Granted...I didn't know Matt all that well, but after working with someone for over six years, you can't help but come to care about them.

"And...he's *dead*???"

"I'm sorry, Amanda."

Then, suddenly my brain went into overdrive and I pulled away from Ian to look him in the face. "Ian, Matt drove me out to Anna's parent's house...he knew where Brighton and I are staying...and..."

Cutting me off, Ian nodded quickly, "And, if it's the same person Gonzalez is talking about, he's dead...and whoever killed him may now know where you and Brighton are hiding out. Come on, Amanda, let's go."

Heart beating faster now, I grabbed my bag while he stuffed his wallet into his back pocket and grabbed his keys. Flipping off the kitchen light, we headed out the door quickly and practically ran to the elevator while Ian pulled out his cell phone.

Dialing a number as we entered the elevator, I pushed the button marked for the parking garage and heard him say, "Anna??" into the phone and I held my breath immediately. "It's Ian. Everything okay there??"

Then, nodding at me, I sighed heavily in relief as he continued talking to Anna, "I'm bringing Amanda home now. Do me a favor and make sure all the windows and doors are locked....*please*, just do it. We'll explain when we get there." Listening to Anna for a second longer, he said "See you soon" and hung up as the elevator dinged loudly and the doors widened, allowing us to exit.

Getting into his truck, Ian pulled out of the parking garage and headed towards the Interstate. Watching as he ran a hand over his tired-looking face, I asked, "Are you okay?"

Looking over at me, he nodded. "Yea, just really tired. I'm not planning on getting any sleep now...not with what's going on out by Madera."

"Did...did they say how Matt was killed?" Not sure I really wanted to know, I forced the question out of my mouth. "Was it an accident maybe??"

"Honestly, I don't know. I won't know anything until I get out there." Then, after a moment, said, "If it does look like foul play, I am going to request that you and Brighton and Anna and her parents be put up someplace safe until we figure out what is going on."

"You really think Matt was killed don't you??"

"I don't know what to think right now...but knowing that he took you up to Anna parents' house yesterday...and, now he's dead...I don't know. Something doesn't feel right about the whole thing and I would rather waste the state's money in putting you all up somewhere safe than risk having any of you put in danger." Then, adding, "What I'd really like right now is to know more about your boss, Lucky Serifino."

"Lucky??? You can't seriously think he's involved in any of this?!"

Giving me a grim look, I knew immediately that he did. Gawking at him for a second, I argued with him, "Lucky is way too goofy for this kind of stuff! Yeah, he can run the bar, and usually does okay with running it, but the only reason his business does any good is because of the girls—he's strict with us, especially about the laws, but his main forte is hiring good looking girls and keeping his shelves stocked with alcohol—I can't imagine him being involved in all this!"

Nodding, Ian refused to look my way, keeping his focus on the road ahead of us.

"You don't believe me, do you??"

Glancing at me quickly, he said "It's not that I don't believe you—I do—there's just something about him that didn't sit right when we interviewed him."

Sitting back in the soft leather of the seat, I shrugged, figuring we could just agree to disagree. I would never believe in a million years that Lucky...short, balding, obnoxious laughing Lucky...could be involved in something so...*horrific*!

"Oh, hey, do you think you could sit with a sketch artist and describe what they guys who attacked you looked like? Say...tomorrow morning??"

Sensing that he was changing the subject, I said, "Sure. But I only got a good look at one of them. The other one was always in the background."

"That's okay. You never know when one sketch may lead to an identity or an arrest, for that matter. I'll pick you up if you want."

"Oh—you don't have to drive out to Green Valley twice like that! That's a lot of gas, Ian. I can ask Anna to bring me into town."

"Amanda, I don't mind. I wouldn't have offered if I did."

Still trying to get used to Ian wanting to fill my every need, I said, "Okay" and left it at that.

"Besides, I may still be out your way come morning; depending on how long the initial investigation into this is."

"Yeah, but when are you going to sleep??"

"When I'm dead." Smiling over at me, I shook my head at him. Then, seeing our exit coming up, I directed him off of the Interstate and down the road that would lead us to my temporary home.

Pulling onto the dirt road that led to the house, I turned to thank him for giving me a ride.

"Amanda—stop thanking me. Even if I wasn't already heading out this way, I would have given you a ride." Pulling to a stop outside the enclosed porch, he put the truck in park and looked at me. "Isn't this what couples do for each other, give each other rides when needed??"

Knowing that he was speaking honestly, I couldn't help but consider the sexual context that his statement offered and I turned away from him, not wanting him to see my face heat up as I quickly chastised myself. *God...what is wrong with me?!* I thought...wondering if all the sex I've had since Saturday has done damage to my brain or something.

"Amanda?? You okay??"

Clearing my throat, I turned back to him and asked, "So we're a couple now??"

Eyeing me carefully, he said, "If that is what you want." Then hesitating for a moment, he added, "Personally, I would love to be more than that, but I'll take you any way I can get you."

Lord Almighty…he definitely cuts to the chase!!

Nodding, I said, "I think that's a good place to start."

"Good."

Then, before the either of us could say anything else, a loud knocking on my closed window caused the both of us to jump. "Jesus!!!" I yelled, as I turned to find Anna staring at us through the window. Rolling it down automatically, I had to fight the urge to smack her upside the head. "Anna!! You scared the crap outta me!!!"

"What's going on??" She asked innocently, her smile widening immediately.

"Nothin' that I'm gonna tell you about, Ms. Nosey!!"

"Ian—am I going to have to drag all the juicy details out of you??" Anna teased, flashing him a bright smile. "I can be very persuasive, I'll have you know!"

Laughing softly, Ian leaned forward to get a good look at Anna and said, "Yeah, I'll bet!! But sorry sweetie, I'm already taken!"

Scoffing at him, I said, "By who?!"

"Hmmmm…don't think you know her…."

Nodding, I couldn't avoid smiling at him as he leaned in to kiss me. Hearing Anna whistle softly, I knew that Ian wasn't going to be the only one not to get any sleep tonight—Anna won't let me close an eye until I fess up about how I went from walking out on Ian to ending up being driven home by him.

Turning back to Anna, I switched topics, "Brighton sleeping?"

"Like a baby! We had so much fun tonight!! I'll let her tell you all about it in the morning."

Then, from the area of the porch, we heard, "Anna?? That you out there? Who you talking to???" Answering her father, Anna leaned to the side so she could see her dad from over the hood of the truck. "Its' just Amanda, Dad!"

"Oh—that cop with her???"

"Yes, Dad, he brought her home!"

"Oh!"

Then, hearing her dad's heavy footsteps leave the porch and cross the dirt covered yard, Anna poked her head back through my window, addressing Ian. "Sorry, Ian, but you're not getting out of here just yet."

Smiling, he looked as if he understood and rolled down his window.

"Detective Sampson, right??" Mr. Yearling gave Ian a serious look, as if trying to judge him just by the look on his face. Before he responded, Ian carefully opened his door and stepped out of the truck while Anna and I shared a curious look.

"Please, call me Ian", he requested, shaking Mr. Yearling's hand while he spoke.

"Well—it's good to meet you, Ian. Anna's told us a bit about you."

Giving Anna a hard look, I wanted to remind her that I didn't need her father questioning my dates, but held fast in knowing that he was doing it because he cared about me—even though I was feeling about sixteen years old right at that moment.

Hearing the two men continue to talk briefly about Ian's job, the terrible mess I was in over the weekend, and how the local fishing was down by one of the lakes further south, I suddenly knew that if I didn't rescue Ian, he was never going to get out of here.

"Hey, Dad?" For years, I have addressed Anna's father as 'dad' and wasn't about to stop now in front of Ian, "Ian's got a call to get to."

"Oh—goodness!! Don't let me keep you from your job!!" Then, stopping short, he asked, "Wait; a job out here?? Someone's been killed? Anna told us you were some kind of homicide detective."

"Yes, Sir. But it's nothing to worry about. I just hope that I can help close it up in a few hours so that I can get back to Tucson and get some sleep."

"You've gotta drive back to Tucson?? Tonight?? Son...it's nearly one in the morning now!!"

Hearing Anna's father call Ian "son" after only just met him made me relax even more about deciding to give us a chance. With some kind of sixth sense that is usually spot on about people, I knew that if Mr. Yearling had any reservation about his 'adopted daughter' dating Ian, he would have voiced them within a minute or two after shaking his hand. What I didn't expect was Mr. Yearling's offer that Ian come back here after he finished with his 'cop business' to get some sleep in one of the spare bedrooms.

"Then you can see Brighton in the morning!!" Mr. Yearling had this all figured out from the start and I suspected that Anna was not so innocent in all of this. "No...you come back here after you are finished with your work. We have plenty of space; there's no need for you to try to drive all the way back to Tucson, especially when going on such little sleep!" Then giving me a knowing look, I had no choice but to turn away from him, slightly embarrassed.

Jeeze...what has Anna told her father about us?!

Glancing over at me, Ian caught my eye and I knew that he had no idea as to what to say in return to Mr. Yearling's insistence that he spend the night here. Trying to save him from having to say anything, I finally spoke up. "Dad...I'm sure Ian would probably feel better sleeping in his own bed, especially since he's been working nonstop—" Cut off by the expression on Ian's face, I looked at him questionably.

"Mr. Yearling, I appreciate the offer, but I have no idea when I will be done in Green Valley. I don't want to end up waking your whole household by returning at the crack of dawn.

"Nonsense!! If I know these two girls", nodding at Anna and me as he spoke, "they will still be up at the crack of dawn!" Then, shaking his head, he decided for Ian himself, "Nope, I will not have you risking your life by driving on no sleep. You call Anna's cell phone when you get here and she can let you in and we will have one of the other guest bedrooms set up for you. There—it's settled, now you go do your job and be careful."

That said, Mr. Yearling took Anna's arm and led her back to the house, as if wanting to give Ian and I a moment alone before he left. As soon as they were out of earshot, Ian broke out into laughter, obviously shocked at the welcoming treatment he had received from Anna's father. "Wow...is Anna's father always this way?"

"Well," I explained, shrugging my shoulders slightly; "he's known me since I was a kid. I practically grew up at their house...I guess he sees me more like a daughter than just Anna's best friend. He loves Brighton like a granddaughter, even refers to her as one. Maybe he's trying to marry me off or something! I'm sure he'll get started on Anna's love life as soon as he decides that Brighton and I are taken care of!!"

Joking, I watched Mr. Yearling enter the house, turning on the porch light for me as he shut the front door. Turning my attention back to Ian, my laughter died on my lips as my smile faded. The look he was giving me was filled with pure heat and I suddenly found myself having trouble to breathe.

Taking an automatic step back, Ian responded by pulling me back to him. Holding my face in his hands, he bent and softly placed his mouth over mine. Kissing him back, desire stirred in my belly and I pushed all other thoughts out of my head as his fingers worked their way through my hair while his tongue explored the inside of my mouth. Quickly, the passion between us built dramatically and before I could do anything about it, Ian broke off our kiss, whispering, "I've got to go. Gonzalez is gonna kill me if I don't get out of here."

"Okay", I said softly, nodding my head at him.

"Do you want me to come back?" Eyeing me, I knew that it was really my decision as to whether or not Ian came back here after he finished up his work or if he went back to his apartment instead. Before I could second guess myself, I admitted, "Yes", meeting his eyes as I did.

"Okay. I will see you in a while then." Offering me one final kiss, he released my head and I backed away from him so that he could get back into his truck. "Go get inside. Make sure everything is locked up tightly. I'll call Anna when I am done."

"Be careful, Ian." I said, watching him for a moment before turning towards the porch.

"Amanda??" Hearing him call me back, I turned again to find him still sitting in the same spot with the engine idling softly. "I do love you." Then he put the truck into reverse and slowly backed up, not waiting for me to respond as if knowing that I couldn't.

Whispering to no one, I said, "I know you do", and watched him turn the truck fully around to leave before heading up the porch and into the house only to find Anna and her parents sitting at their kitchen table; each eyeing me carefully. Suddenly feeling like a teenager, caught in the act of having her first kiss, my face reddened as I stared back at the three of them.

"Well???" Anna started, propping her elbows up on the table as she rested her chin on her hands. "Well, what??" I challenged back, dropping my bag by the front door before heading into the kitchen to grab a Diet Pepsi out of the fridge.

"Did you sleep with him again??" Pressing the subject, I gave her a shocked look, beside myself that she could bring up the topic of sex in front of her parents.

"C'mon, Alex, this is about to get X-Rated."

Giving me a wink, Sylvia Yearling stood up from the table, pulling up on her husband's arm as she did. Keeping his seat for a moment, Anna's father gave me a serious look and said, "He seems like a really good guy, Amanda. Any man that spends his days looking out for other people to make sure they are safe is alright in my book. That, and knowing how much he wants to get to know Brighton—you would do well not to let that one go just yet."

"Thanks, Dad." I replied, knowing right off that if he had any ill feelings about Ian, he would have voiced them outside, in front of him. Alex Yearling was never one to avoid saying exactly how he felt—reminding me immediately of Ian and I couldn't hide my smile. Then, watching him leave the room with his wife, I took the seat across from Anna, knowing that she was not going to let me get away without clueing her in on exactly where I stood when it came to Ian.

"So....." she started, her blue eyes wide with anticipation and I couldn't help but laugh.

"You know, I think you're the one who needs a man!"

"Naw...I'll just live vicariously through you!"

So, in order to indulge her and get her off my case, I detailed the events of tonight—leaving out the possibility that Ian was headed towards investigating the death of one of my coworkers—as she sat across from me, practically drooling. Ending with our final kiss of the night, admitting that I told him that, yes, I did want him to come back here when he was done, I sat back in my chair and crossed my arms over my chest. "There you have it. Can I go to bed now??"

Sighing at me softly, Anna stood from the table. "Yes, I suppose. You're gonna need some sleep before going another round with Ian when he gets back here!"

"Anna!! Like I could do *that* with my daughter right across the hall!" Then, adding, "Besides Dad said to put him in the spare room when he gets here!"

"Oh, yeah, I'll just go make sure that room is all ready for him!!" Anna replied smartly, locking her arm in mine as we headed down the hallway to our rooms. Stopping in front of mine, I gave her a hug, thankful that she had been my best friend through so many years. "Love you."

"Love you too, Manders." Calling me by my childhood nickname, I smiled and watched her walk down the hallway to her room. Then, thinking of Brighton I reached for the closed door directly opposite mine and opened it softly.

Approaching her sleeping body as quietly as I could, I pulled the covers up from her waist and placed them gently around her shoulders, tucking her in. Breathing heavily, I knew that she was sound asleep and I as I bent down to kiss her forehead, I whispered, "Love you, baby", then left the room.

And as I tucked myself into my temporary bed, in my temporary room, I drifted to sleep wondering what was going to happen to the both of us next. Had I really found love?? Someone who would accept the both of us for who we were and not abuse the either of us in any way? And as a picture of my ex-husband flashed through my memory, I shifted quickly, trying to get his awful face out of my head before sleep finally took over.

Chapter Twenty-Six

Staring at his reflection in the grimy-looking mirror, Lenny cringed at the sight of his face. Realizing now that he had missed some drops of blood on his forehead, he leaned over the stain colored sink and tried to scrub it off. David's latest kill had been frantic, unplanned really, and because of his reaction to it, the victim's blood had gotten everywhere.

Usually, David had a plan for everything. But this time, their instructions had been only to get information, not to kill unnecessarily; which was not David's forte so to speak. Once they had the bouncer out in the middle of nowhere however, David couldn't be stopped...even after getting the information he needed out of him.

Now, waiting here in this rundown, godforsaken motel room, Lenny knew that it was only a matter of time before David got word of their next assignment. Having already reported what they had learned from the bouncer—as he begged for his life through sobbing cries of pain—David was more anxious than ever and it was driving Lenny mad; although he would never dare voice his irritations to David. No, he'd rather hide out in this dingy bathroom that smelled of Clorox covered puke than do anything as stupid as that.

Sighing as he examined his face once again, he felt satisfied that he had finally gotten every last speck of blood off of his exposed skin. Now for his clothes. Looking down, he knew that his t-shirt and jeans were not salvageable. Blood mixed in with brain matter dotted all over his clothing and as he stripped off everything without no emotion whatsoever, he knew that he was finally getting used to David's appetite for making a mess when he worked. In the beginning working with the man had been difficult for Lenny—even made him sick on more than one occasion—but over time he had come to expect a messy exit for any one of the victims David ended up being contracted out for.

And you'd think that this habit of David's would have gotten him caught by now. Messy crime scenes commonly include not only the victims identifying factors but usually their attackers as well. But David was really too smart to leave anything behind; despite his behavior when working. While they both knew that their previous victims have each been found, there was nothing reported so far that the police had any clues as to their identity. And this fact really only encouraged David to be even more exuberant when it came to their next assignment. Believing that he was free to do what he wanted, David didn't hesitate. This behavior alone made Lenny more nervous than his partner's short temper or morbid fascination with death.

Grabbing a change of clothes out of his duffle bag, he piled his soiled clothing into a large black garbage bag and put on the fresh ones. Eyeing the shower while he dressed, he wondered briefly if he had time to really get clean but decided against it knowing that their next call could come at any time. Gathering the trash bag and his duffle, he took one last look at himself and left the bathroom, closing the door behind him.

The room, a small closet sized area that offered two twin beds covered in bedding that looked worn and faded, contained a small stand-alone dresser in one corner of the room and a bulking looking nineteen-inch television that didn't seem to want to work right. Watching David smack the side of the TV, Lenny jumped slightly where he stood, not sure if David was going to pick the thing up and throw it.

Moving slowly, Lenny dropped the bags in his hands on the side of the bed closest to him and went to sit down when David's cell phone rang suddenly. Crossing the short room with one large step, David pulled the phone out of his bag and answered by placing it to his ear, saying nothing in way of a greeting. Then, as if wanting Lenny to listen in freely on the conversation, David hit the speaker option on the phone and placed it on top of the television. Wanting to question this act; the conversations that occurred between David and their contact were usually off limits to Lenny; the lanky man said nothing.

"You boys really did a number in completing our last contract." The heavy male voice on the phone sounded tense and David immediately realized that this voice was a new one. "Your instructions were only to retrieve information; termination was not included in this part of the contract."

"Complications arose." David replied, pacing the small room while he did. Even though the contact spoke freely, David still had reservations about speaking without code.

"Did you retrieve the information?"

Stopping mid-step, David turned towards the phone as his irritation grew immensely as he had already relayed such information to another contact hours ago once the deed had been done. "Of course!"

"And??"

"The girl is staying in Green Valley, with a friend." *Don't these contacts communicate with each other???*

"Address??"

"*I have it*", David stressed, his irritation now churning into something more dangerous.

"Good. We will try to clean up the mess you left pertaining to the bouncer." Pausing, the caller then added, "You do know that if there is anything there that leads to you, you are on your own, yes??"

Scoffing, David was growing angrier with the caller, wanting to ask that if his employer thought him incompetent, why was he contacted in the first place, but only affirmed the question that had been asked with a curt "yes".

"Good." Then, after another pause, David's caller gave him his next set of instructions. "Take her tonight. Alive. She may be worth more alive than dead. Do you understand??? If there is another fuck up, your services will be undoubtedly terminated."

Tensing on the bed, Lenny knew that this last statement meant that if David did not follow the instructions, and in fact killed the girl, he would be hunted and killed as punishment for disobeying the order. And if they got to David, Lenny was sure to follow. Positive that David's employer knew that he was not working alone in this, Lenny would not be any safer than David if things got out of hand and the girl ended up dead. Waiting anxiously for David's reply, Lenny sat up straighter on the bed while David chuckled at the caller.

"You threatening me now??"

"No, this is not a threat. It is a promise. Your employer is not happy about what happened with the bouncer. You are paid to do as you're told. You'd be wise to remember that."

Chewing on the inside of his lip for a moment, David's anger rose and his face began to turn red. Beginning to pace again, he thought about telling the caller off and hanging up the phone. He had plenty of money left over from completing his last task and he didn't really need the work at the moment. Even if he gave Lenny half of what was left—and he wouldn't—he could make it back up to Northern Arizona and live somewhat comfortably for a while. Besides, there would be other jobs—there always seemed to be someone in need of his services.

"Does our contract stand??" The caller asked, as if sensing David's indecision.

Reminding himself that the redheaded girl was the one who got away, David closed his eyes and sighed evenly, his anger lessoning as he did. Opening them, his black eyes appearing glossy and dilated, he finally replied. "Yes. Contract stands. What are the terms??"

"Action to occur anytime from now until contract is complete. Once the girl is in your possession *unharmed*, you may make contact for further instructions."

Thinking about the prior attempts at completing his job, David asked, "And if the woman is not obtained?? If...complications arise??"

"Take provisions if needed—only those pertaining directly to the target. No one else is to be eliminated at this point. If your instructions change, you will be further contacted; however this is how it stands as of now. You have done enough of a screw up with the last two sections of your contract already."

Last two sections...??? And then it dawned on David—the bouncer was one and the girl in the apartment was the other. The redhead was the only figure in that part of the contract that was supposed to be *eliminated*; to use the word offered by this new contact. Understanding now, David nodded, as if the caller could see him. Then, remembering that he was on speaker, and not personally standing in the room, David answered him with a stern, "Understood."

"Any further supplies needed??"

"No."

"Good. Then our conversation is over." And with that, the caller disconnected, leaving David to stew in his mistakes that could have cost him not only the remainder of the job, but his life as well. Now in a pissed-off mood, he turned to Lenny and demanded, "Get the shit together. We've got some work to do before heading back to Green Valley."

Chapter Twenty-Seven

The sun rising over the Arizona desert is something that many people travel from across the nation to see. Like the sunsets common in this part of the world, watching the sky take on brilliant hues of oranges, reds, and even blues has a calming, yet mystifying, effect on many observers. Despite this, when those bright colors invade my sleeping, I often wish I lived anywhere but here.

Waking slowly as the room began to warm up considerably, I went to move up on the bed, hoping to grab a hold of the curtains that hung over the window above my bed and pull them tighter together to cut out the strip of bright light that was now growing larger across the room. Feeling something heavy across my waist however, I forced my eyes open as my desire to cut out the early morning light was obviously impossible.

Looking down, I half expected to find Brighton's thin arm draped over me (despite knowing that it couldn't be...her thin arms aren't nearly as heavy) but found Ian's instead. Turning my head, I found him sound asleep, the side of his face within an inch of my left shoulder. Not wanting to wake him, I wondered just what time it had been when he had called Anna at the same time I fought against moving a wave of brown hair as it draped softly over his forehead back from his handsome face.

Turning my gaze to the ceiling above my head, I listened and heard no activity beyond my closed bedroom door or outside the tightly secured bedroom window. Usually an early riser, I thought about Brighton, wondering if she was already out of bed, watering the plants with Nana or out walking the dogs with Papa. Closing my eyes again, I decided to take advantage of any extra minutes I could get before having to move Ian's warm arm in order to get up.

"Good morning, beautiful."

Turning back to Ian immediately, his sleepy brown eyes met mine and I smiled, turning to lie on my side to face him as his fingers grazed the side of my cheek. Swallowing, I was suddenly at a loss for words. It had been years since I woke to find a man in my bed and the feeling was not only overwhelming, it was a bit scary as well.

My thoughts interrupted suddenly by the sound of my daughter's laughter, my smile grew, now knowing that, yes, she was up, and from the sounds of it, was already having fun.

"I have to say that I could get used to that." Ian closed his eyes and whispered.

"Used to what?" I asked, whispering as well. Knowing that Brighton would not be likely to enter my room; especially when sounding like she was having fun at the moment; I didn't want her to hear Ian and I talking and decide to come in anyways. Finding me in bed with someone that she hardly knows was not something I was willing to risk; even if Ian was laying on top of the covers, fully dressed in the jeans and t-shirt he had been wearing last night.

"Hearing a kid's laughter first thing in the morning."

Biting my lip, I didn't know what to say as his eyes opened to meet mine again.

"I could also most definitely get used to waking up next to you every morning."

"Yeah well, give it time," I said automatically, "I'm sure at some point you'll change your mind."

Raising himself up on one elbow, his look made me regret my words as soon as they left my mouth. "Why do you do that??" He asked as his smile faded quickly.

Turning from him, I said, "Do what?? You said yourself that you don't know if this will work between us, and you really don't know anything about me, Ian. If you did—"

"When I do, I will love you even more, I'm sure of it." Cutting me off, he gently turned my face back around to look at him. "Look, I don't know what you've been through in the past. I don't know a whole lot about Brighten either. But that will all come eventually. Right now, can we just lie here together and not worry about all that??"

"Yes...yes, I'm sorry." Meaning it, I got comfortable on my side again and closed my eyes and ignored the pain in my shoulder as it ran swiftly down my arm.

"Don't be sorry", he said as he laid back down next to me, our noses inches apart again. "Just, don't kill my chance before I even get the opportunity to put my plan into action, okay?"

Opening my eyes, I narrowed my eyes at him and asked, "What plan??"

"My plan to make you fall deeply in love with me...so much that you allow me to dote on you night and day, whisk you and Brighton away to fantastic destinations, and take care of you both for the rest of my life."

Unable to stifle my giggle, I said in a loud whisper, "God— you sound like a game show host!"

"Really??? Well then, Ms. Pearson would like to know what's behind door number one or door number two??" Ian closed his eyes and smiled as he waited for my answer.

"Hmmmm...which one holds the better prize??" I asked, teasing him as I draped my free arm over his waist. "If I only get to choose one door, then I want it to be the one hiding the best prize!"

"Well, then, that would be door number three", he replied, his eyes opening again, he gave me a sexy look. Then, raising his head slightly, he kissed me, causing a flurry of butterflies to scurry within my stomach.

Breaking apart softly, my lips tingled for a moment and I whispered, "I'm glad I chose the right door", before rising up slightly to offer him my mouth again.

Hearing Brighton's laughter gaining in both volume and length, we broke apart again. Closing my eyes, I breathed deeply, wanting to stow away the stirrings in my belly before they became too much for me to handle.

"Think Anna's parents would mind if I showered quickly?" Ian's question brought my attention around again and I shook my head. Pointing to one of the closed doors opposite the bedroom door, I explained that I had my own bath.

"There are towels on the rack that are clean, but I don't have any manly stuff in there."

"Oh, well, I don't mind coming out smelling like you." Ian said with a smile, and I knew that if I didn't force myself to leave his arms, I was going to end up doing more than just kiss him. Thinking again of Brighton, I gave him a return smile and sat up to leave the bed; lowering the covers off of my warm body as I did; completely forgetting that I was half-naked.

"Oh...you're just being mean, now." Ian accused, eyeing the upper half of my body that was free from clothing. "You'd better get off this bed now, or I'm not going to be able to contain myself."

"Easy...cowboy", I said over my shoulder as I pulled the floral patterned sheet up to cover my bare chest, "may I remind you that you were the one to enter my bed in the middle of the night??"

"Yea, well, according to Anna this room was the only spare room left. She told me that it wasn't in use."

Turning to stare at him, I said, "She did not!"

"Oh...yes, she did!" Then sitting up, Ian gently moved my hair from my shoulder and kissed it. "It wasn't until I laid down on the bed that I realized you were even in here. And once I did, that was it...I wasn't moving."

"Oh, that woman's gonna drive me nuts!"

"You complaining??" Ian asked, in between his kisses on my shoulders that were starting to have a deep effect on my thinking.

"No", I said softly, not wanting him to stop, but knowing that I had to get dressed and check on Brighton. "I have a feeling she had been planning this before you dropped me off last night."

Then, as if knowing he needed to stop, he gave the side of my neck one final kiss and wrapped his arms around me, hugging me from behind. "I'd better shower", he said, sounding a little disappointed.

"I'll go check Brighton and help with breakfast. You hungry?"

Tightening his arms around me, he whispered into my ear, "What do you think?"

Smiling, I turned my head towards his, offering a side view of my face and said, "For food!"

"We can bring food into this if you really want to..." he said, nipping at my neck again, I almost forgot what I was supposed to be doing at that very moment.

"Ian..." I whispered, "You've got to stop..."

Then, suddenly, he did. "Your right. God, but I don't want to."

"Me neither", I admitted.

Feeling him move, he was off the bed in a second, backing away from it as he gave me an intense look. "Okay, now I need a cold shower", he admitted with a smile, then turned from me and headed towards the bathroom. Waiting for him to close the door behind him, I sat in the middle of the bed and closed my eyes and I tried to get myself under control again before getting off of it to dress and leave the room to find Brighton.

Finding her in the kitchen with Anna, I stood off to the side for a second to watch them. Mixing some kind of creamy-looking concoction in a large bowl, my best friend was sitting next to my daughter, slowly explaining why she needed to continue mixing whatever it was in the bowl in order to break apart any lumps.

"Now, we can add the chocolate chips!" Anna said joyfully, grabbing the large bag as she did.

"Oh...what are you making??" I interrupted and was awarded a bright smile from Brighton, her green eyes wide with excitement as she continued stirring vigorously.

"Ma!" She squealed. "Make...pan...cake!" Pausing in between her words, I could see how hard she was struggling with speaking and my heart ached immediately. Trying to push the feeling aside, I entered the kitchen and asked if I could help. "NO!" she yelled, still smiling and looked at Anna for support.

"Ms. Brighton and I are making you and our special guest breakfast this morning. You can just go away, Mom!" Anna piped up, offering me a wink and a smile. Then, giving me a knowing look, added, "Why don't you go check on our special guest??"

"Yes! Eee—onnn!" Trying hard to pronounce Ian's name, Brighton's face turned a slight shade of pink as she struggled. Then, concentrating on her stirring efforts again, her smile turned into a hard line as she worked the wooden spoon around the bowl.

"I am sure that our guest is just fine", I stated matter-of-factly. "May I enter the kitchen to get something to drink??" Teasing the both of them, I waited until I got the okay from Brighton before heading over to the refrigerator to get a glass of water. Needing to take my pain meds, I left the two of them and headed back to my room.

Out of the shower smelling very much like roses and vanilla, Ian was just stepping out of the bathroom as I reentered the bedroom. Eyeing him for a moment, I immediately noted that he was only dressed in a pair of blue boxers. "Needing something clean to wear??" I asked, unable to hide my awe as my eyes took him all in; knowing that I'd never get sick of looking at him.

"I've got some in that bag over there." Pointing at a small duffle bag that was sitting on the floor by the dresser, I placed my glass of water down and reached for it. "This?" I asked, handing it over to him when he nodded. Turning, I reached for my prescription bottles that were on the nightstand next to the bed and took two pain pills with a gulp of water.

"How's the shoulder feeling?" Ian asked as he sifted through his bag.

"Sore." I admitted. "It doesn't feel like it's getting better. Honestly, some days it feels worse than when I woke up in the hospital after it happened."

"Come here, let me take a look."

Crossing the room to where he was standing; still half naked and looking awfully tempting; I turned my back to him and moved my long hair out of way so that he could take a look. Wearing an oversized t-shirt with matching shorts, I felt him gently lift the back of the shirt up to the top of my shoulder; exposing my bare back in the process.

Seeing that side of my wound free from any bandages, Ian scolded me immediately.

"You need to keep this covered, hon."

Concentrating on his term of endearment instead of really listening, my thoughts traced back to the last time anyone had ever called me that but cringed inwardly at the memory and forced myself to pay attention to what Ian was saying.

"This could be infected, Amanda. Have you been taking both medications?"

Thinking, I shook my head. "No, just the one for pain. I don't like taking that crap."

"Well, there's a reason why the doctor prescribed it. If this is infected you could end up in worse pain and it won't heal right. Where are the bandages that the hospital gave you?"

"In the bathroom, under the sink."

"Take your shirt off."

Hesitating for a second, I gave him a look before complying.

"So that I can clean it and put new bandages on it..." He explained and I suddenly felt like a scolded teenager. Why is it that everything that comes out of his mouth causes me to turn it into something sexual??? *Because you haven't had feelings like this in YEARS—no, that's not right—you have NEVER had feelings like this!!* My mind answered and I had to agree with it.

Pulling off my shirt, I covered my chest with it and listened as he rummaged around in the bathroom. Sitting on the side of the bed, he finally emerged carrying a brown bottle of hydrogen peroxide, a small hand towel, and the bag of bandages and medical tape that the hospital had given me.

Sitting behind me, he positioned himself so that he had straight access to my wound. After pouring a small dose of the peroxide onto the towel, he gently cleaned it while I tried to avoid cringing against the cold feel it left on my exposed skin. Then, hearing him tear open the bandages and tape, he adjusted the soft cloth over it and secured it. His fingers pressed gently against the tape and every time they grazed my skin, I felt a burning sensation wave through my stomach and goose bumps rose slightly down both arms. Turned on by the mere touch of his hands, I wondered swiftly if these feelings were ever going to dissipate...thinking that this emotional state I was constantly finding myself in would probably not last.

It was just the feeling of a possible new love that tingled all over my body, wasn't it??

At some point, it would fade, right???

"Okay, turn around. Let me see the other side of the wound."

Saying nothing, I stood from the bed and sat down again, facing him this time.

Gently peeling the bandage off of the wound on the front of my shoulder, I winced slightly as the tape pulled on my skin. "Sorry", he muttered, concentrating on what he was doing.

"This side looks like it could be infected too." Then, following the same process of soaking the affected area with peroxide and fixing a new bandage to it, he doctored me up as tenderly as possible. Sitting back when he was done, he caught my eye, hesitating before speaking.

"We should clean your shoulder again tonight before bed."

Wanting to ask him if he was spending the night with me here again, I held fast. I wanted him here...that much I knew for sure. But his life was pretty much centered within Tucson, not out here in the sticks. Was it fair of me to ask him to travel back and forth just so that I could wake up next to him every morning?? I wasn't sure.

"BREAKFAST!!!"

Anna's voice carried down the hall and through my closed door, breaking any chance I had of asking Ian what his sleeping plans were from here on out. Pulling on my shirt gingerly, I stood from the bed and went to lead him out of the room.

"Aren't you forgetting something??" His strong voice called me back around.

"Huh?"

"Your antibiotics. You need to start taking those with your pain meds."

"Oh." I nodded, heading over to the nightstand; I opened the pill bottle and took one with the last of my water. Then, turning to leave again, Ian stopped me quickly before I reached the closed door. Turning me to face him, his mouth was suddenly on mine, kissing me gently. Melting where I stood, I had to catch my breath when we came apart.

"C'mon, let's go see what the cooks have come up with for breakfast." I said after finally finding my voice. Opening the door, we were met with the aroma of pancakes, warm butter, and sweet syrup. Heading into the dining area, I noticed Alex and Sylvia, already at their places around the table. Coming out of the kitchen, Anna followed Brighton; both carrying plates of food.

Upon seeing Ian, Brighton stopped suddenly, her expression unreadable and I was suddenly aware that everyone was watching her; as if waiting to see what her reaction would be to a new man in the house. Stepping around me, Ian approached her slowly, then bent down to her level. "Can I help you carry something to the table?" he asked, holding his hands out as if ready for her to put something in them.

Looking up at me, I said nothing in the way of directing her in what to do. I was not going to influence her decision in any way and as if understanding this, she gave me a small smile and then returned her eyes to Ian, studying him for a moment. Then, she nodded and it was if the tension was suddenly lifted from the room. Sylvia and Alex picked up their conversation of how well her flower garden was flourishing this year while Anna walked around Brighton to deliver the food she was carrying to the table. Once done, she turned and approached me, putting one arm around my shoulders while we watched the transaction between Ian and Brighton progress.

Brighton, carrying a bowl of assorted fruit, handed Ian the bowl and backed up a step. Standing, Ian turned and took it to the table, placing it in the center. Then, turning around, walked back to Brighton and asked, "What else?"

Smiling wide at him now, my daughter turned and reentered the kitchen, grabbing a stack of chocolate chip pancakes. Approaching Ian, she stood in front of him while he knelt down again and asked, "Did you make these?" Nodding at him, her smile faded slightly, as if unsure if he would be happy with her selection of baking. "Can I tell you a secret??" He said, lowering his voice as he did. Her eyes wide now, she nodded and leaned in to hear. "I LOVE chocolate chip pancakes!"

"You—", swallowing hard, Brighton struggled for a brief second and my heart ached for her again. "D—Do?!"

"Yes!" Ian gave her a huge smile, took the plate of pancakes from her and walked them to the table. Noting that he did not look awkward or uneasy in anyway, I bit my lip, as my eyes watered instantly. Leaning in to whisper in my ear, I knew that Anna had noticed the same and said, "You need to marry that man, Amanda!"

Turning towards her I gave her a look and shook my head, not willing in any way to say that she was right. Not only is there a lack of good, decent men on the planet who are willing to get involved with a single mom, but there are even less of those in existence who would do so when there was a disabled child in the picture. Knowing that Ian fell into the tiny percentage that was not only willing, but *wanting* to, added to the intensive attraction that I had to the man; I was shocked that I didn't just bend down on one knee and pop the question right then and there!

Once seated, Anna and Brighton served; who only stopped once to offer me a hug and kiss on the cheek. The conversation around the table was a mixture of subjects; Alex discussing Ian's past fishing expeditions with him, Anna joking around with Brighton, and Sylvia asking me about what Brighton may be needing for the upcoming school year. No one discussed my attack, the bar, the lunatic (or *lunatics*) who may be after me, or the fire that destroyed my apartment. Loud and periodically filled with Brighton's laughter, I sat back in my chair and listened to everyone; feeling every bit as part of the family as I had ever felt before.

Once everyone was finished, Alex and Ian helped clear the table while Anna and I were on dish duty. Out on the porch with Brighton, Sylvia helped her water the plants. Leaning over my shoulder, Anna glanced out the living room windows to make sure we were all out of earshot and asked, "So what's going on with the apartment?"

Looking over at Ian, I let him answer her. "It looks like the whole place was destroyed. Whoever did it did so in such a way that there was no evidence left of the vandalism. The detective running the case has got some working theories and I've been assigned to help her out."

Stopping, I gave him a surprised look and asked, "You're back to work??"

"Yeah, Captain Leary called me Sunday and asked if I would be willing to work with Gonzalez—that's the detective working on your case and one other at the same time. He lifted my suspension right away."

"Suspension??" Alex turned around, eyeing Ian carefully, as if wondering just what could have happened to cause Ian to get suspended.

Nodding at Alex, Ian explained, "My partner and I had a disagreement about how he was handling a case and it didn't end well. I got suspended right away, but from what I hear, he has been placed on some type of leave."

"Was the argument worth the suspension?" Alex asked, as if ready to judge Ian's response.

"Absolutely." Ian stressed his answer with a nod of his head. "The guy is getting ready to retire, is not as professional as I think all of us cops ought to be, and we finally just butted heads over it."

"So you were standing up for what you felt was right?" Alex asked, wanting clarification as he dried a glass and put it away.

"Yes. I was suspended because I didn't take the problem to my captain. I got to the point where I couldn't stand to listen to him anymore and I reacted without thinking. The suspension, shorter than what it was supposed to be, helped me clear my head." Glancing over at me, I turned away from him quickly, feeling my face redden immediately.

"Well, that's good then." Alex said, nodding at Ian. "You need to stand up for what you believe in! And if this other cop is as bad as you say, maybe they should just accept his retirement a bit early!"

"Yea, that would be great!" Ian agreed. Then, turning to me, said, "Speaking of which, we need to get to the station. You still willing to work with a sketch artist?"

"Oh!" Remembering what Ian had asked me last night on the way out here, I nodded, "Yes! You want to go now?"

Looking at the time posted on the digital clock on the microwave oven, Ian said, "We probably should. If we can get that done by this afternoon, maybe we can get back here by dinner."

So...he is planning on coming back out here tonight???

"Why don't you guys go get ready?" Taking my dish rag out of my hands, Anna jumped in and said, "I'll finish these, you two go on, get out of here. Maybe we can all go out to dinner tonight if you get back by late afternoon."

"That sounds good." Ian said, taking me by the hand. "Thank you, Mr. Yearling for allowing me to stay and thanks everyone for breakfast."

"You're welcome anytime—well, you are coming back tonight, aren't you?" Alex's question caused Ian to turn and give me a look.

Eyeing him, I wanted to give him the okay, but also wanted to wait and see what he would say without my influence. Searching my eyes for a moment, Ian nodded and turned back to Alex. "I'd love to, as long as I am not intruding or anything."

Waving his dish towel in the air, Alex scoffed. "Of course not! We'd love you to come back, wouldn't we Anna??"

"Absolutely, Dad!" Looking over her shoulder at me, she smiled wide and I felt like a school girl again. Wanting nothing more than to kick her, I made myself leave the kitchen and headed out to the porch to talk to Brighton, who was now sitting in one of the wooden rocking chairs that faced the driveway and desert area beyond; Sylvia seated in one right next to her.

"Brighton??" Getting her attention, she left her rocker and walked over to me. "Hey, kiddo, I've got to go to town with Ian but I can't take you with me."

Looking up at Ian who was standing behind me, Brighton looked a bit confused.

Coming around me, Ian stepped towards her and knelt down. "Hey, Brighton", he started, placing his hands on his knees as he continued, "you know that I am a police officer right?"

Nodding at him, Ian explained, "I need your mom to help me with something at my work. And I promise it won't take very long. In fact, I think we will be back before dinner time. That okay with you if Mommy comes with me for a bit??"

Her eyes once again searching his face, she suddenly nodded and looked at me. "Stay—Nana??" she asked, and I nodded as I bent to give her a tight hug. "Yes, you can stay with Nana and Papa and Anna, okay? You can help with the dogs and maybe get Anna to play a game with you."

"K", she said, happy to be staying and as she bounced back to the porch to sit with Sylvia I sighed heavily, wanting badly to stay put and spend the day with her.

"C'mon, I promise that this won't take long."

Taking my hand, Ian led me back to the bedroom, where I changed and grabbed my purse; packing my medication into it as I left the room. Ian, ahead of me, said his goodbyes to everyone and bent down to say goodbye to Brighton, thanking her for the pancakes she made for breakfast.

"We won't be long, kiddo. I promise." He said, sounding like he meant every word.

Suddenly, Brighton wrapped her thin arms around his neck and I thought he was going to fall backward from surprise. Laughing slightly, he hugged her back gently, as if not wanting to hurt her frail-looking body. Then, as quickly as she had hugged him, she let go and was off running to the kitchen. Standing, Ian gave me a surprised look and said, "Wow, I wasn't expecting that!"

"Neither was I!" I exclaimed, the laughter in my voice matching his.

Then, stopping he looked down at me and offered me a serious look. "One down...one to go..."

Cocking my head at him, I started to question him but then remembered what he had said this morning about making me fall in love with him so that he could take care of me and Brighton for the rest of our lives. Teasing him I said, "Well, she's the easier of the two of us; don't expect a response like that out of me just yet!"

"Now that sounds like a challenge, Ms. Pearson." Ian said as he stepped onto the porch.

"Take it any way you like, Detective Sampson."

"Trust me", he said, looking back at me, "I will."

And with that, we headed off the porch to his truck, our hands tightly locked together the whole way as my heart swelled with a feeling that was so unfamiliar, I had trouble breathing the rest of the day.

Chapter Twenty-Eight

Walking into the police station where Ian reported for work every day was like walking into a circus—just without the animals; although a couple of the potential arrestees were in the midst of acting as such. The noise level was loud and Ian said nothing as he weaved his way through the jungle of desks, officers, serious looking law personnel, and the occasional criminal-looking suspect. Every step I took seemed marked with a ringing telephone, loud yell, and even laughter. It was more than just overwhelming...it was a bit scary.

Wanting to hold on to Ian as we made our way through the large room; I resisted, not wanting anyone to get the wrong idea about us and land him in trouble. If any of his coworkers knew what was going on between us, I was positive that it would not go over well and I kept my arms folded across my chest to avoid grabbing onto any part of his body for protection.

Finally reaching the other end of the room, Ian brought me to a closed off room. Opening the door, he flicked on the lights and took a quick look around, as if ensuring that the room was not in use by anyone. Seeing it completely free of paperwork or any sign that someone would be returning to it for any reason, he held the door open for me. Sitting at the large oak conference table centered in the middle of the room, I waited as Ian left the room to check in with his captain.

After sitting alone for nearly twenty minutes, I was beginning to wonder if he was in fact ever coming back when the door to the room swung inward and a short, black haired woman walked in. Carrying a stack of files in her arms, she stopped suddenly when seeing me.

"Can I help you??" She asked, giving me a serious look, causing me to swallow hard.

"Um….Ia—err, Detective Sampson brought me in here. I'm Amanda Pearson…"

"Oh!" Giving me a surprised look, the woman set the stack of files on the table opposite me and held out her hand. "Detective Gonzalez, Ma'am. I thought you looked familiar…I've been looking into your case with the help of Detective Sampson."

Standing, I gave her a smile, thankful that she wasn't going to arrest me or yell at me or just plain beat me for being in this room, closed off from the rest of the station. Shaking her hand, I noticed that she had a strong grip and knew instantly that she gave the men around here a run for their money. "I remember you now; you're the one who I talked to at my apartment. Thank you for doing what you can to help me."

"Of course! I want these bastards as much as anyone around here!" Then, sitting across from me, she asked, "You here to work with the sketch artist?"

"Yes, but I'm not sure how much help I will be. I only got a good look at one of them and the other one I just remember a few features."

"Hey, anything you can remember will help! Sometimes, when we are dealing with more than one suspect, having details on just one of them helps nail the others as well."

Nodding, I watched her sort out the files that she had brought in, trying hard not to look too nosy. Seeing my name typed on one them, I had the urge to pull it to me and turn it around and open it, if nothing else but to see what kind of information was in it. Noting that the other files had names on them as well; all female from the looks of it; I wondered if they were somehow connected to my case. Had the two men who attacked me outside the bar done the same to other women around town?? Suddenly, a chill ran down my spine and I wasn't so sure that I wanted to know.

The door to the room opened again and as Ian walked in, I automatically sat up straighter in my seat. Greeting the female detective, he glanced my way briefly and gave me a small smile.

Then, turning, he addressed another woman as she also entered the room before turning back to me.

"Amanda, this is Dr. Cecelia Eland. She is here to work with you on creating a sketch." Then, turning to the doctor he said, "Dr. Eland...Amanda Pearson."

Standing, the two of us shook hands and I immediately felt a pang of jealousy spread across my chest. Absolutely beautiful, Dr. Eland was my height and muscular looking—but not in a gross, veiny way—rather exotic instead. Her hazel eyes blinked under long dark lashes and her shoulder length brown hair hinted with red highlights and the effect was mesmerizing in a way. Her cream colored suit seemed to enhance her bronze skin and thin frame and she immediately reminded me of one of the Coppertone commercial models—the ones that you'd wish you could look like even for just a day. In all seriousness, the woman made me sick just looking at her.

"Ms. Pearson, nice to meet you." She said with a smile and a slight accent curled around her words as she shook my hand. Then, turning to Ian, she asked, "Will you be sitting in on this or your partner?"

"Oh—um...Gonzalez?" As if not expecting to be asked to witness the process, Ian looked over at Detective Gonzalez after giving Dr. Eland a long look. "Do you want to sit in or do you want me to?"

Oh, yea, he thinks she's hot!!

My jealous streak hit the top of the meter and I raised an eyebrow at him; which went seemingly unnoticed and I made myself sit back down at the table before I opened my mouth and really made an ass out of myself. Looking down at my hands, I listened as Detective Gonzalez asked Ian to sit in as she was due in another department at that moment.

Sitting at the other end of the table, Ian positioned his chair so that it was facing the doctor and sank into it, brought his left ankle up to rest it on his right knee and propped on elbow up on the table. Placing his chin in his hand, he studied Dr. Eland as she gently set up a briefcase full of art supplies; obviously used in creating her sketches. Eyeing him for a moment, I had the sudden urge to stand up, walk over to him, and smack him hard on the back of his head in order to get him to snap out of it. Recognizing the look of interest and, quite possibly, desire on his face as he watched the doctor unpack her supplies that I had seen in most of the men that frequented the bar, I found myself getting angry. She was just a woman after all—albeit beautiful—but just a woman all the same.

"Ok, are you ready to start?"

Looking over at Dr. Eland, the expression on my face caught her off guard and she raised her eyebrows at me in surprise. "Ms. Pearson, are you alright?" She asked; her accent thickening as she spoke out of concern.

Immediately embarrassed, I cleared my throat and nodded, unable to speak at the moment. Stealing a glance at Ian as soon as the doctor turned her eyes away from me, I noticed that he hadn't moved an inch—his brown eyes glued to Dr. Eland's beautiful face.

"Okay, here's how this goes." Dr. Eland began and I forced my attention around to what she was explaining. "We are going to start with a blank page—the only time I am going to draw is when you give me a feature. We will start with the shape of the face and work from there to include such things as hair, eyes, nose, mouth, bone structure, and whatever other features that you may remember. Also, this is not always an exact science; I take what information you give me and do my best to sketch it so that in the end we have a composite that defines the person you saw. If there is something that I need to change, or doesn't look right, make sure you speak up so that I can fix it. Understand?"

"Yes", I nodded at her again, ready to be done and out of here. Ian's obvious attraction to this woman was getting under my skin. Try as I may to ignore it and remind myself that he is just a man and that any guy with a heartbeat would be drooling by now—I couldn't.

"Okay, let's start, shall we?" Pulling a chair next to mine, the doctor began. "Now, beginning with the shape of the face...."

Two hours into it, I was completely frustrated with myself and extremely pissed at Ian. The only main thing that I could remember about the guy that had pulled me out of my car was that he had a long, ugly scar and black eyes. The other features on his face were a blur and I couldn't force my memory to work right. Don't even ask me about the other guy—he was just a hazy memory now. Demanding a break, I stood from the table and walked out of the room, not caring at that point if Ian followed me or stayed behind to continue drooling over the sketch artist—I was done.

Stomping my way through the room, I swept past the officers standing around without really noticing anyone. Finding the stairs that Ian had originally led me up this morning, I practically ran down them, feeling as though I couldn't breathe as tears ran down my face. Not knowing why I was crying, I grew angrier with myself and felt as if the walls were closing in on me. I honestly couldn't get out of the building quick enough.

Reaching the first floor I took a right and headed for the large glass doors that led to the outside when a strong arm suddenly grabbed my forearm. Turned around quickly, I yanked my arm free, ignoring the throbbing pain that was shooting down it, before my mind registered the confused look on Ian's face.

"Amanda! What's wrong?!"

"Oh—like you don't know?!" I yelled at him, causing him to take a quick step backward. His eyes wide with surprise, he looked as though I had slapped him and he gave me a startled expression before asking in a quiet voice, "Are you alright?"

"No!" Still yelling, several people walking past in their business attire and briefcases stopped to look in my direction. Giving them a frown, I felt like telling everyone to mind their own business but bit my tongue instead and turned away from Ian, still needing to get out into the hot air that would surely meet me once I managed to get outside.

Hurriedly, I focused on the exit doors and reaching them, pushed one of them so hard forward that it shot back immediately, almost catching me in the face before I managed to stalk through it. Out in the open now, I took a couple more steps and gulped the air around me, not caring that I looked like I was having a heart attack or something.

Hands on my hips, I walked slowly away from the building and as I listened to the two lanes of traffic that bypassed the police headquarters and headed further downtown, I was finally able to breathe right. Seeing a large concrete block ahead of me that offered an overgrown green plant a place to lay roots, I turned towards it and leaned my back against it; immediately feeling the heat coming off of it as it warmed the middle of my back up considerably.

It wasn't until then that I noticed Ian approaching me carefully.

Giving him a hard look, I quickly debated whether or not I should say anything. Now feeling a bit more in control of myself, I wondered if the stress I had been under since my attack was finally catching up with me. One thing that I did know however was that I was not going back into that room. I couldn't remember everything about my attacker anyways, so this whole process seemed like a big waste of time—especially when knowing that I could be back at Sylvia and Alex's spending time with Brighton.

Turning away from the concerned look in Ian's eyes, I focused on the people that were walking past instead. A mixture of professional looking business people blended in with those who looked homeless and hungry and even others who looked like they had time-warped here from the 1970's. A common flavor of downtown; vagrants, penniless musicians and artists, peace lovers, bankers, and lawyers swept past each other without really seeing anything. Somewhere the horn from a vehicle blared loudly and as the red lights changed to green, groups of people from all walks of life traveled their way to their next destination. Under any other circumstances, I would have loved to just stand here and people-watch.

Wiping my fingers under my eyes, I dried what tears were left and finally found my voice. "I think I need to go home." Then, pausing for a second before Ian could even answer, I corrected myself with a laugh, "Oh—wait—I don't have a home."

"Amanda—"

"NO!" Glaring at him, I didn't want to hear what he had to say...didn't want him to promise that everything was going to be okay...that *Brighton and I* were going to be okay. Shaking my head at him, I accused, "you don't get it, Ian. I can't do this. Physically or mentally. I can't remember jack about the guy who shot me...can't get past his freaking scar to see anything else. Everything has just fallen apart and I don't know how to fix it." Then, wanting to add more, I stopped and looked away.

"*And...?*" As if knowing that there something else bothering me, he pressed me to continue.

"And...I'm not going back in there." Nodding my head at the building that I had just fled from, I looked at him, waiting to see if he was going to argue with me. When he said nothing, I immediately took it as a sign that he knew there was more to my reasoning—Ms. Exotic Sketch Artist 2012. Thinking of her made my anger build again and before I could stop myself, I said, "So you can go back in there and continue drooling over whatshername. I'm done."

I turned from him and headed in the direction of the main bus station, where all the city buses made stops to during their runs all over town. Planning on catching a bus to somewhere, I didn't about the fact that Tucson city busses don't travel all the way down to Green Valley. I just started walking; figuring instead that I was good at that—I'd take a bus as far as it would go and have her pick me up. Then I'd get Brighton, maybe borrow some money from Alex and Sylvia and go from there. Either way, I'd figure it out, on my own, and put this whole thing behind me.

"So is this what you're gonna do?? Run away???"

Hearing the anger building in Ian's voice, I kept walking. Making it a couple more steps I had to stop to let a guy in a wheelchair pass by me; ignoring the questionable look he gave me as he did. Taking a step forward, I was suddenly turned around again as Ian had finally caught up to me. "What?!" I yelled, pissed at him for catching me off-guard.

"Is this your answer for everything, Amanda?? Running away??" Breathing hard, his eyes bore into mine and I immediately looked away. Taking my chin into his hand, he forced me to face him again and said coolly, "And I wasn't 'drooling' over Dr. Eland. I was refusing to look at you because I didn't want to make you feel uncomfortable or nervous."

Scoffing at him, I tried to turn my back on him, but couldn't because of the grip he had on my arms, so I called him a liar instead. "I watched you in there—you were eyeing her like you wanted her down on the floor right then and there!"

"You want me to tell you that I think she is attractive?? Fine—she's attractive. But she is a *coworker*, Amanda! I'm not interested in her! If I would have concentrated on you in there, it could have affected what you remember and your concentration. The only reason an officer sits in on the process of sketching a composite is to make sure that nothing influences or taints the victim's memory. I couldn't look at you", he explained, releasing my arms as he took a deep breath before continuing, "I wouldn't have been able to show an unbiased disposition if I had concentrated on you."

Swallowing hard, I knew what he was saying made sense and I suddenly felt like I had just made a fool of myself. Stepping back from him, I bit my lip and turned my attention back to the people that were making their way around us before saying, "I just…the way that you were watching her…and I couldn't remember anything about that guy…I guess I just had to get out of there." Not apologizing for anything, I waited for Ian to say something. He didn't.

Taking my face into his hands, he kissed me gently before whispering, "You don't have anything to worry about. I'm not interested in Dr. Eland or anyone else." Pressing his forehead against mine for a second, he took another deep breath, then released my face and backed up a step. "You don't have to continue working with her if you don't want to. All I ask is that you take one final look at the sketch to see if there is anything you can add and that's it. I will take you back to Green Valley."

Thinking for a moment, I nodded, still feeling like an ass.

Turning back towards the police station, Ian took my hand and intertwined his fingers with mine as he led the way. Once we reached the glass doors to the building, I dropped his hand and he stopped to look at me before entering. "I don't want you to get into to trouble", I explained, meaning it.

Holding my gaze, he said, "I don't care".

"I do."

Shaking his head slightly at me, we entered the building and I followed him back up the stairs. Making it back to the room where Dr. Eland was sitting patiently at the conference table, I entered and apologized for walking out so abruptly. Giving me a sympathetic smile, she waved it off and asked if I would like to continue.

"Can I see what you've drawn so far?" I asked, wanting to see if Ian was right about possibly remembering other features at this point. Staring into the eyes of the man she had sketched, my brain scrambled to see if there was anything else I could add. There wasn't, and after explaining as such, she handed the sketch over to Ian and began the process of cleaning up her supplies.

"Detective Sampson?"

Looking towards the door, I smiled briefly at Detective Gonzalez as she poked her head over the threshold, catching Ian's attention. Walking to her, the two spoke quietly for a moment before Ian glanced at me over his shoulder. "You okay here for a minute?"

Confused, I simply nodded and sat back down at the table.

"I'll be back in a minute." Then, addressing Dr. Eland, he said, "Thanks Doc, we'll get this over the wire now and maybe we'll get lucky." Shaking her hand, he then hurried out of the room and headed off to wherever the other detective had gone to.

Alone in the room with the sketch artist, I silently watched her finish packing up her supplies. Giving me a brief smile, she turned to leave the room a few minutes later, but stopped just before crossing the threshold. Turning back to me she said quietly,

"I don't know if you know this or not, but I have worked with Detective Sampson for a couple of years."

Giving her a sideways glance, I said, "*Okay...*" unsure of what her point was.

Maintaining eye contact with me, she seemed to consider something for a moment and then said, "There are very few men in this world that are worth holding on to. When you find one, you'd do well not to let him go."

Chapter Twenty-Nine

With that, she turned around again and walked out of the room, leaving me feeling a bit flabbergasted. *How did she know that Ian and I had more going on that just a professional relationship? Was it that obvious?? Can other people see it just be looking at us???*

Suddenly embarrassed and slightly ashamed of my actions, I was thankful that no one else was in the room with me at that moment. Looking down at my hands, I thought about what Dr. Eland had said and knew that she was right. There are too few men in this world that are honest-to-God true men. Feeling that Ian was most definitely one of those few, I chastised myself for putting him through all my drama; if I continued behaving this way—he would be sure to walk away, wouldn't he?? Wouldn't anyone—and who could blame them??

My thoughts interrupted with the return of Ian, I stood automatically, believing that he was now going to take me back to Sylvia and Alex's house. Giving me a look however, I froze where I stood as Detective Gonzalez entered behind him and approached me.

"Ms. Pearson, we've got some developments on your case. If you don't mind, I need to ask you a few questions before you leave."

Staring back at her, I immediately took my seat again as she sat down across from me, another file folder in her hand. Putting it on the table that separated us, she crossed her arms on top of it and I looked over at Ian; trying to judge the look on his face as I wondered if whatever was in the file was good news or bad news. Sitting down near the end of the table, he gave me a sympathetic looking smile and I knew that it had to be bad.

"Ms. Pearson, do you know a Samantha Green?"

Hesitating for a moment, I stared back at Detective Gonzalez for a moment before saying, "Yes".

"How 'bout a Sam Buckley? Or a Felicia Buckley?"

Looking down, I searched my memory bank and finally shook my head at her; knowing that neither name sounded familiar. "What's going on?" I asked, not sure if I really wanted to know.

Giving Ian a quick look, Detective Gonzalez frowned at me when her eyes met mine again and asked, "How do you know Samantha Green?"

Growing frustrated at the fact that she answered my question with one of her own I said, "We work together. I've known Sam for about five or six years now. Why??"

"Are you two close?"

"I suppose...we've had lunch outside of the club a couple of times. She has met Brighton, my daughter, a few times...*why??*" Stressing my question, I looked from the detective to Ian and back to her again before demanding, "What is going on?? Why are you asking me about Sam?"

Taking her arms off of the file in front of her, I watched as Detective Gonzalez opened it just enough to pull out an 8x10 color photograph. Placing in the middle of the table, she pushed it towards me and asked, "Is this the Samantha Green that you know?"

Sam's bright blue eyes and gorgeous smile stared back at me and, looking up again, my confused look must have said it all because Detective Gonzalez nodded and she pulled the picture back and replaced it into the file. "Let's go back to this past Saturday evening", she said, changing topics on me again and my anger stirred quickly.

"No." I said, giving her a hard look. "How about you tell me what the hell is going on here?!"

"Ms. Pearson—" She started, but I cut her off immediately.

"Don't you even dare tell me to calm down!" At that point, Ian stood and I quickly glared at him. "I want to know why you're asking about Sam and I want to know now, otherwise you're gonna find yourself sitting at this table alone!" Standing for emphasis, I took a step back, pushing my chair backwards with the backs of my legs as I did.

"Are you aware that a body was found in your apartment this past Saturday night—the same night that it was set on fire??" Knowing that I probably wouldn't make good on my threat to walk out of the room after hearing her next question, the detective sank back in her chair and looked up at me.

Chewing on my lip, I knew she had me cornered. She knew what was going on and the only way I was going to be let in on whatever it was, I was going to have to continue answering her questions. Still standing, I said, "Yes, I was told that."

"The body, badly burned, has been identified through dental records."

And at that very moment, I didn't need to hear anything else. All the questions concerning Sam had been answered in that one statement. In one sudden blow, I knew that Sam's body had been the one found in my apartment...the detective didn't have to confirm it...and the realization of this knocked the wind out of me. Feeling myself fall, it wasn't until Ian grabbed a hold of me and gently sat me back into my chair that I managed to respond.

"Sam??" Tears immediately flooding my vision, the detective blurred in front of me as I asked, "You're telling me that Sam...*Samantha Green*...was in my apartment that night...and now...now she's...*dead*???"

Speaking barely above a whisper, I was surprised that the detective had heard me. Nodding her head at me, she seemed to be watching my every move. As the tears fell freely down my face, I shook my head at her; wanting to argue that she had made some mistake but my mouth was too dry to speak. Looking up at Ian, who was standing close by, I searched his face for something that would tell me that this was some kind of sick joke. They were testing me or something. This couldn't be real...

"It's her, Amanda." Ian said quietly, as if knowing exactly what I was thinking.

"We need to know when the last time was that you saw or spoke to Samantha Green." Detective Gonzalez spoke up and her voice seemed a bit softer.

"Ummm...." Turning my attention back to her, I blinked several times, trying to think. "I think...yeah, Friday night...she came to see me in the hospital...she brought Anna and Brighton to the hospital."

Noticing movement from Ian, I looked up at the right moment to see the nonverbal exchange between him and Detective Gonzalez. Knowing suddenly that he must have already told her that she had showed up at the hospital during the time that he was trying to interview me; my response just confirmed that.

"Where were you on Saturday night, at around seven?"

The detective's question caught me off guard and I had to concentrate. Then, remembering that I was with Ian that whole day after being released from the hospital, I glanced up at him quickly and felt my face redden slightly.

"Detective Sampson was kind enough to take me home after I was released from the hospital. My car had been picked up by the police and I had no other way to get home. Then, we found out that my place had been broken into...that's when you first interviewed me..." pausing for a second, the detective nodded, allowing me to continue, "...and later he took me to fill my medications that the doctor had given me and took me to get something to eat so that I could take them. When he was notified that someone had set my place on fire, we had just finished eating."

"Okay, so the only time that you were at your apartment that day was in that afternoon, correct?" Thankful that she didn't ask me any further questions pertaining to what had happened after we left my apartment the second time, I simply nodded, unable to stop the scarlet coloring of my face as the events that occurred between Ian and me later that night popped into my head.

"Do you remember seeing Ms. Green anywhere in the vicinity while at your apartment?"

"No", answering without hesitation, I added, "Brighton was with Anna, my best friend who lives in the same complex. When Ian took me home, she was the one who had told me the she had found my apartment door open and the place trashed. I don't remember seeing anyone else around at that time."

"And Anna is..."

"Anna Yearling. We grew up together. She takes care of Brighton so that I can work."

"Did you know that Samantha Green has several aliases?" Turning the tables on me again, I knew she was doing this to gauge my reaction, and the confusion on my face must have spoken volumes.

"Aliases?? What do you mean aliases??"

"I mean that she has used different names in the past." Looking down at the file folder, the detective opened it, put aside Sam's color photo and studied a piece of paper that from my view looked like a computer printout of information. "Sam Buckley...Felicia Buckley..."

Hearing the names again that she had initially asked me about, I shook my head at her; not fully understanding. "You mean that Sam used to go by other names??" I asked for clarification.

"That's exactly what I mean. According to her record, she has used these two names several times in the past and there may be more, we are still researching it."

"Wait—record??? What record? You're saying that Sam has a *police record*?? Like...she's been arrested before??" Again, my mind went off on a tangent, I couldn't believe what I was hearing. And on top of that—what else did the detective have in that file to spring on me?? Not sure I could take any more of this; I put my head in my hands and tried to control my breathing.

Not allowing my shock to alter the course of her questioning, Detective Gonzalez continued on, not missing a beat. "Prostitution...drug charges...fraud...those are just the tip of the iceberg. It seems your 'close' friend was into stuff that she chose not to discuss with you."

Not sure if she was asking a question or just making a point, I looked up and glared at her. "You think that I knew about all this, don't you?? Do you honestly think that I would associate myself— my *daughter*—with someone who was a criminal???" Growing angrier, I did nothing to control the volume of my voice.

"Honestly, I know nothing about you. The stuff I see day-to-day—nothing would surprise me. For all I know, you orchestrated this whole thing."

"Gonzalez—" The warning in Ian's voice went unheard as I stood immediately in defiance, cutting him off as I yelled at her, not caring who heard me, "I had nothing to do with this!! You think I set myself up to get shot?! That I not only put myself, but my daughter as well, in danger?! I not only nearly lost my job, but my car, my apartment, and almost my LIFE!!!"

"Maybe", she said coolly, looking up at me with an amusing look; as if I was suddenly entertaining her, "but I'm sure you will find ways to make it all back..."

My blood boiling, my face felt hot with anger and I leaned in at her and yelled, "FUCK YOU, *DETECTIVE*!!!" before shoving my chair out of the way and storming out of the room. Hearing her call, "We're not done here, Ms. Pearson!" I ignored her and kept walking, knowing that this time; I was not going to be talked into returning by anyone.

"Amanda!!"

Hearing Ian call me from behind, I did not stop until I reached the stairs. Crying heavily now, I knew that I couldn't take much more of anything at this point. My life was crumbling around me and I suddenly felt as if there was nothing that I could do to stop it. Putting my face in my hands, I cried into them and felt Ian's hand on my shoulder.

"She's just doing her job, Amanda." He said quietly and I nodded into my hands, refusing to look at him just yet as he continued trying to explain, "She has to ask these questions. If she didn't, she wouldn't be such a good cop. And Gonzalez is a *really* good cop."

"Ms. Pearson?"

Hearing the detective's voice, I had to force myself to look at her. Standing off to the side, she motioned to the room I had just run out of with one hand and raised her eyebrows at me. "Please??" she asked and I shook my head slightly and bit my lip; not sure what to do at this point. Having already stormed out of that room twice in the time that I had been here, I wondered what the third time might bring as I forced myself to nod at her, drying my eyes with shaky fingers.

"We're almost done", she promised as she led me back across the station floor and into the room. Turning back to me for a second, she asked, "Would you like to use the restroom? Want something to drink?" Her voice kinder now, I nodded, knowing that I should go rinse my face off and use the facilities.

Leading me back across the busy station floor, she pointed me in the direction of the ladies bathroom. Finding refuge in it, I entered one of the stalls and locked myself in. Sitting there, alone, exhausted, and completely overwhelmed, I put my face in my hands and had a good cry—feeling all of my energy drain from me as I sobbed into my hands.

Hearing the door to the restroom open, I knew that I was no longer alone and did my best to calm down. Using some toilet paper to dry my face, I breathed heavily, thankful that I had not chosen to wear any make-up today as it would have been beyond ruined at this point. Listening as the other occupant locked themselves in an adjourning stall, I finished up and opened my door and headed to the sinks. Washing my hands and face, I glanced at myself in the mirror.

My red hair flaring around my face, I looked hideous. Eyes red from crying, my skin looked raw and swollen. Wishing I had brought my bag with me, I tried my best to smooth out my long hair and straightened my t-shirt. Sighing heavily, I decided that this was the best I was going to look and left the bathroom quickly after hearing the other woman flush the toilet she was using and unlock the door. I really didn't need anyone else staring at me or questioning the upsetting look on my face. Knowing that whoever had been out on the station floor had bared witness to both of my escape attempts thus far was enough.

Heading back to the room where Ian and Detective Gonzalez were waiting for me, I paused before the door, noticing that it was cracked open slightly. Hearing them talking loudly, I stood and listened and knew immediately that they were arguing.

"Think what you want, Gonzalez...but I know she had nothing to do with any of this!" Ian's voice was full of anger and my heart skipped a beat in knowing that he was trying to stand up for me.

"Well, if you weren't *fucking* her on the side; maybe you would have a better perspective about this whole thing!" Gonzalez's accusation shot back at him in anger and I didn't need to see either of their faces know that they were pissed at each other.

"That's none of your damn business!!"

"Really?? Well when your behavior gets in the way of our investigation, it becomes my business!! We have to be sure that she is free and clear from everything concerning this case! You know that better than anyone, Sampson!"

"You want me off this case??" Ian's demand caused me to take a step back from the door as he continued, "I'll pull myself off if that's what you want!"

"I want you to back me up, that's what I want!!"

"I am backing you up...and I'm telling you that she has nothing to do with any of this!"

"Why—because she's good in bed?!"

"No, dammit!! Because she wasn't anywhere near the events as they occurred—her apartment vandalism, the fire, the bouncer's death or the death of her friend!!"

The room quiet for a second, I imagined that the detective was thinking. Then, in lowering her voice, I barely made out, "And where was she, Sampson??"

"She was with me!" He charged back, voice lowered as well, but still filled with anger.

Deathly quiet now, I wondered if I should just walk away and come back in a few minutes or go ahead and enter the room. Choosing the latter of the two, I knocked softly on the door before pushing it open and entering. Looking at me, both Ian and the detective stared at me and I'm sure that the shocked look on my face told them that I had heard everything that had just transpired between them. Swallowing hard, Ian held my eyes for a moment, then turned and walked towards the other end of the room while Gonzalez sighed heavily at me.

"Ms. Pearson...um...I think we are done here. If I have any other questions for you, I have contact information for your friend...Anna Yearling, is it??" Her voice considerably lower now, I could tell that she was trying hard to keep it together.

Nodding at her, I glanced over at Ian, whose back was still facing the rest of the room. Standing in the doorway, I debated what to do. I could just turn around and leave and hope that he would follow; if nothing else but to give me a ride back to Green Valley.

Noticing I was still there, Detective Gonzalez gave me a questionable look and asked, "Did you need anything else, Ms. Pearson?"

"Ummm...no, thank you." I muttered in reply before slowly stepping back out of the room. Looking around for a moment, I took one last look at the busy station before finally moving towards the stairs. Heading down them, I felt numb all of a sudden, believing in the possibility that the argument between Ian and the detective had woken him up to the dangers of being in a relationship with me. Not only could he lose his job; but at this point, I truly believed he could also lose his life. For some reason, people around me just kept dying.

Weaving through the mass of people that were making their way across the first floor of the building, I reached the outside and breathed in the hot air as soon as it hit me in the face, warming my skin in the process. Looking around, downtown was as busy as ever. Lanes of traffic moved slowly from one red light to the next and the sidewalks were a river of people, all trying to get somewhere quickly. Looking to my right, I noticed a Circle K sign; indicating that the popular convenience store was within walking distance and I headed towards it; a cold Diet Pepsi sounding really great at the moment.

"Hey! Amanda, wait!!"

Hearing my name, I turned around just before I reached the next intersection and took a deep breath as Ian made his way towards me. Looking a bit frazzled, I wondered what he was going to say to me. Would it be goodbye?? Another declaration of love— one that I was starting to enjoy hearing?? Unable to judge the look on his face, I waited for him to approach me first.

"Where are you going?" He asked, taking a deep breathe.

Pointing over my shoulder with one finger, I answered, "Circle K."

Then, offering me a smile, he said, "Wouldn't you rather have a ride? It is pretty hot out here."

"Well, yea. But I figured you still had work to do. I can find my own way home."

"I know you can, but I would feel so much better if I were the one to give you a ride."

Eyeing him cautiously, I immediately recognized the teasing hint in his voice and wondered what could have happened in the last ten minutes to make him seem so...carefree. Looking down, I noticed his open hand, held out for me to take and as I accepted it; his fingers intertwined with mine and gave them a slight squeeze.

Unable to ignore it, I said, "What's gotten into you all of sudden??" as we headed back towards the station where his truck was parked in the garage below.

"I just quit."

Coming to an abrupt halt, I pulled my hand out of his; causing him to turn around and face me. The smile on his face had me completely confused and I asked, "You just what??"

"Quit."

"You...*quit*. You quit your job??" Watching him nod at me with a huge smile on his face, I shook my head at him. "Why??"

"Because there are more important things in this world for me to be doing than butting heads with my coworkers", he stated matter-of-factly. Then, offering me a better explanation, he stuffed his hands in his jean pockets and shrugged his shoulders as he spoke. "In less than a week, I have fought with not just one detective, but two—and that's if you don't count the argument that I had with my captain over the weekend. Life is too short to spend it arguing, so...I quit."

"No!! You don't quit! You make it right! You make amends...put in a transfer...anything but just up and quit!" My voice rising in volume, I was shocked and did nothing to hide it; paying no attention at all to my thoughts as my mind reminded me that his choices were technically none of my business.

"There are other jobs, Amanda, in other cities...hell, even states. I have never been one to tie myself down to just one location. I do have options." Grabbing my hand as he spoke, he pulled me along and the dumbstruck feeling I had grew larger.

Looking up at him quickly as we started walking again, I said quietly, "You're planning on leaving aren't you??"

"Not yet."

"But...but...you liked your job...I was under the impression that you loved being a cop."

"I do." He said as he led me through another small crowd of people. "But there are some things that I love more."

Still flabbergasted, I continued my side of the argument as we reentered the building where I'm sure the second floor was now in a bit of disarray—having just lost a detective and all. "But what about your apartment? Your bills?? Ian, how are you going to pay for that stuff???"

Stopping suddenly, he leaned in close to me and said, "Amanda, I didn't do the job for the money. I did the job because I loved it. And when that feeling started to fade, I knew it there would be a time when I would just have to walk away. Today just happened to be that time."

"Oh", sensing that there was more to it than he was telling me; especially about his finances, I left it at that and followed him through the crowd toward the elevators that would take us down to the underground parking.

Minutes later, we were at his truck and as Ian unlocked it and opened the passenger side door for me, a thought occurred to me and I had to ask it. "Did you quit because of me?"

"No. Like I said, I knew that there would come a time for me to move on. I've made my decision and it had nothing to do with you." Staring back at me, I knew he was lying but decided to keep my opinion to myself as I climbed into the truck.

Making our way through traffic after leaving the garage took more time than it would have if I had just walked to the Circle K. Getting onto the Interstate after swinging into the convenience store to buy me a soda, Ian maneuvered the truck into the lane that would take us back out to Green Valley and we sat in silence along the way; my thoughts on the day's events and his seeming focused on getting us back to Brighton and the Yearling family in one piece.

Watching the overgrown cacti, flowering desert plants, and patches of dry, brown dirt pass by; I found myself thinking about Brighton, wondering what she was doing at this very moment. Knowing that I should really be heading into work tonight to make some money, I sighed heavily.

"What are you thinking about?" Ian asked as we closed in on the exit we needed.

"Brighton." I said, smiling to myself. "I should really go to work tonight, but I don't want to."

"So don't", he stated, giving me a quick look. "Whatever you two need, I can get for you."

Looking over at him I studied his profile for a second before saying, "Ian, you just quit your job...I think you're gonna need to hang on to your money."

"I told you that I didn't work because I needed the money. I am fine when it comes to that and I can afford to spend a little on you and Brighton if needed."

"What are you, some kind of trust fund baby or something??" I asked; laughter in my voice.

Hearing no reply, I stole another glance at him and recognized the tension in his jaw.

Oh, shit...he really is a trust fund baby!

"I'm sorry; it's none of my business." I muttered, looking back out my window as Ian reached the exit we needed and slowed the truck down considerably.

"Let's just say, that I don't have to work okay?? And neither do you."

Wanting to say, 'Oh, yes I do', I decided to just give him a quiet 'Okay' instead. Then, not knowing what else to do, I just clamped my mouth shut and focused on the road ahead of us. Seeing black smoke off in the distance as we headed in the direction of the house, I changed the subject. "Wow...looks like a fire out there."

Peering out through the windshield, Ian nodded in agreement.

As the minutes passed and we moved along in miles, I concentrated on the smoke ahead of us, wondering if some smoker had been careless enough to flick a lit cigarette out their window; starting a wild land fire in the process. Common in this area, wild land fires have come to find their own season...during the hottest and driest part of the year—July being in the middle of it.

Seeing the smoke more clearly now, my heart froze in my chest as I realized that the area it was thickest at was the same as where Sylvia and Alex lived. Stating my fears to Ian, I noticed the increase in speed as he stepped harder on the gas and by the time we reached the dirt road that would lead us to the house; black smoke was billowing around us.

"Ian?!" I exclaimed as he made a hasty left onto the road, the back tires on the truck skidding in protest as they left the pavement and failed to find traction in the dirt. "Oh...God..."

Passing each home to the left of us, I noticed that none of them were engulfed in flames, although residents were in their yards, peering down the road to see what was going on. As we grew closer to the house, the smoke made it nearly impossible to see and Ian had to slam on the brakes in order to avoid colliding with a sheriff's police cruiser. Throwing the truck into park, I was out of the truck in a second, beating him out of it as I took off running towards the house.

"BRIGHTON!!" I screamed and my lungs filled immediately with hot smoke as it drifted around my body.

"AMANDA!" Hearing Ian yell my name, I didn't bother looking behind me as I stopped to cough; tasting the blackness of the fire in my throat. Then, moving ahead as fast as I could, I barely registered the scene before me—too focused on finding my daughter.

Coming up on the back end of a fire truck, I ran into a fireman, pulling on him to get his attention. "WHERE IS MY DAUGHTER?!" I yelled; my voice already hoarse and cracking from the smoke.

"Lady, you need to get back!!" He yelled back at me and I pushed him off as his hands tried to grab a hold of my shoulders. Looking around frantically, I searched the men in their protective gear as they moved towards Sylvia and Alex's home and for the first time noticed just how bad the fire really was.

Engulfed in flames, the walls of the home were barely recognizable. Hearing a loud crash, the windows that looked over the porch suddenly blew and as my instinct took over, my knees bent and my arms covered my face, protecting it. Bringing my arms down again, tears stung my eyes and my lips felt as dry as the dirt I was standing on.

"BRIGHTON!!!!" I screamed again, knowing that there was no way she could hear me due to the volume of the flames as they lapped around the structure of the home. Then, suddenly and without warning my body was spun around so fast I almost fell. Pulling me back before I could even dig my heels into the ground to steady myself, Ian had a strong hold on my arms.

Trying to fight him off, I wanted to scream at him but could no longer speak as my throat continued to burn and my forehead dripped with sweat. Wrapping his muscled arms around my waist, he picked me up and as I balled up my fists to fight back, heavy tears swept down my cheeks.

Carrying me, Ian said nothing until he reached the front of the house that was closest to the Yearling home, where an ambulance was waiting. Finally dropping me on my feet, I looked up and cursed him, punching him in the chest as hard as I could.

"STOP!!" He yelled at me, catching my fists in his hands. "AMANDA!!! STOP!"

"IS SHE IN THERE??!!!" Trying to move around him, I wasn't fast enough as he grabbed a hold of me and pulled me to his chest. Sobbing, I was losing the will to fight, knowing in my heart that my daughter, my best friend, and the two people that I had ever really considered as my parents were dead and gone—eaten up by the burning flames as the danced their way through the house, leaving nothing behind but ash and smoke and the skeletal remains of anything that didn't burn completely.

"AMANDA!!!"

Hearing my name, I pushed Ian back and looked around frantically. Running from the direction of the burning inferno that was once her parents' home was Anna; her clothing, face and arms covered in black soot.

Seeing her, I cried out loud and ran to her. Grabbing her, I screamed, "WHERE'S BRIGHTON??!!"

Sobbing, she grabbed my shoulders and hugged me tight and I had to force her to look at me. "Anna, where is my daughter???" Forcing myself to calm down in order to get her to talk, I really wanted to shake her instead.

Then, Ian was pulling us both back to the ambulance and before Anna could say anything, she was being wrapped in a gray colored blanket and checked over medically by a man and a woman that I assumed came with the ambulance. Frustrated and still panicky, I turned away from her; the intention to run back to the house and search for Brighton myself feeding my adrenaline to new heights.

As if knowing my plan, Ian grabbed a hold of me again, refusing to let me go. "Stop, Amanda, you can't go near there right now!"

"I HAVE TO!!" I screamed at him, my voice rough and scratching and continuing to burn unforgivingly. "WHERE IS SHE???" Looking into his deep brown eyes, I briefly noted the tears that were building in his eyes as he pressed his lips together, having no answer to give me.

"They took her..."

Anna's own rough voice brought us both around and as she pushed aside one of the emergency workers, she tried to climb out of the ambulance but a fit of coughing stopped her immediately. Reaching her, I grabbed her and gave her a small shake as I demanded, "Who?? Who took her?!"

Trying to separate me from Anna, Ian put one arm around my shoulders and the other he used to try to get me to release her so that she could continue to be examined. Coughing violently, Anna was finally able to speak after drinking water from a paper cup; given to her by one of the medics. "I don't know. There were two of them." Then looking up at me, she added, "They shot Dad and they took Brighton. Mom and I tried to stop them, but one of them hit her and the other one..."

Pausing, I watched as Anna's face crumbled and her tears weaved their way through the black soot that covered her cheeks. My heart pounding violently in my chest, I whispered, "Did what, Anna???" suddenly not sure if I really wanted to know.

"He...dragged me to the kitchen...and..." looking up at me, I knew what she was going to say and I reached over and hugged her tightly, causing another coughing fit to sputter out of her mouth at that same time and I could feel the strength of it against my chest. Both of us crying now, Ian place one hand in the middle of my back, as if to try to steady me and asked, "What did they do with Brighton??"

As Anna and I separated, she looked up at Ian and said, "They took her. They said to tell you..." looking at me again she continued, "He said, 'tell that redheaded bitch that she should know by now what she needs to do to get her brat back'." Then, breaking down again, she sobbed as she added, "Oh God, she was screaming...SCREAMING...Amanda, I tried to stop them!! I tried!!!"

Clutching her against me, I looked back at Ian, not sure what to do now. His jaw rock hard, he said, "Stay her with her, I'll be right back."

Then, an image in my mind hit me like a freight train and I let go of Anna and took a step back, my body feeling weak and numb. "Ian..." I whispered, "It's him..."

Turning back immediately to me, I felt Ian's arms circle around me and hearing him demand, "Who??" I stumbled against him. Barely able to respond, my voice sounded far away and distant as I tried to explain, "The one...the one from the...sketch..." and then my eyes lost their focus and he became a blur an instant before my mind shut down and my body went limp in his arms.

Chapter Thirty

"AMANDA!!" Ian grabbed a hold of her body just before she hit the ground and yelled, "HELP! I need some help over here!!!"

Running over, a female medic grabbed a hold of Amanda's limp body, allowing Ian to readjust his arms underneath it. Picking her up, he hurried over to the back of the ambulance, just as Anna was trying to get out of it, a shocked look blanketing her face.

"No! Stay there, Anna!" Ian demanded, as he waited for the medic to position a mobile stretcher next to him. Laying Amanda down on top of it, he forced himself to step back in order to allow another medic to start examine her.

"Was she in the house??"

"No—but her family was."

Keeping an eye on Anna, Ian watched as the medic took Amanda's vitals and then proceeded to open up her shirt. Talking as he worked, he addressed Ian again, "And you are??"

"Detective Ian Sampson", reaching for his badge, it took a second for him to remember that as of two hours ago, he was longer attached to that title. Clearing his throat, he added, "Her boyfriend, her name is Amanda Pearson."

"What the hell is this??"

Looking over, Ian followed the medics stare and his eyes widened in alarm at the sight of Amanda's red, swollen shoulder. "She was shot over the weekend. *Jesus*...that looks infected." He said more to himself than the medic. Then, looking up at the man, he said, "I cleaned and dressed it this morning; the injury was a through-and-through and it did not look anything like this when I took a look at it. She's on an antibiotic, plus pain medication, but I don't think she's been taking them according to schedule." His heart pounding against his chest, if Amanda would have been awake at this point, he would have throttled her for not taking her meds regularly.

"Well, this wound is definitely infected. What I can't tell is if or how far it has spread through her body. Who worked on her??" Referring to the hospital where Amanda had been treated, Ian quickly gave him the information, adding the doctor's name as reference.

"Ok, we've got to get her moving." Then, looking past Ian, the medic yelled, "Gleason!! We got a serious one here!"

From the front of the ambulance, a woman dressed in scrubs and running shoes jogged over to them. Seeing the wound in Amanda's shoulder, she quickly started barking orders, starting with Anna first. "You need to be checked at the hospital. Step out while we load her in, please. Do you know this woman?"

Complying immediately, Anna stepped out of the ambulance and said, "She's my best friend."

"Okay, you get to ride along—we can get you both transported to the hospital together." Then, addressing Ian, she said "You can follow along, try to keep up. We're going to Mercy."

Before everyone could get moving, Ian suddenly thought of something and yelled, "Wait!! What about Anna's parents? They were in the house as well...and we've got a missing kid!"

"The older couple has already been transported; we were the second medical responders on the scene. I don't have any details on the either of them, but I do know that they were both coherent when pulled from the fire and they should have been taken to Mercy as well. I'm sorry, but I don't know anything about a missing kid." Then, moving the stretcher closer to the back of the ambulance, Ian watched as the two medics worked together; folding the frame to the bed down, then hoisted it up and slid it into the ambulance. Amanda's head rolled gently back and forth as they moved and positioned her and Ian felt his breath catch in his throat.

As Anna stepped back into the ambulance after Amanda was securely fastened down, Ian looked over at her and asked, "Were you able to tell anyone about Brighton??"

Nodding, the tears continued to fall down her face and Ian wanted to say something reassuring but was at a complete loss for words. Reaching over, he grabbed her hand and gave it a squeeze and said, "I will meet you there, okay?"

"Okay", Anna said, her voice cracking with emotion and obvious pain. "I'm not leaving Amanda until I know that she is going to be okay except to check on my parents."

"You need to let them check you out too, Anna. I'll be there soon." His promise made, he stepped back and jumped slightly as the male medic slammed the back doors to the ambulance closed after watching his female partner climb inside the back to continue monitoring both women.

Standing there until the ambulance had successfully left the scene; sirens blaring loudly, Ian turned and hurried back towards the house, now burning at a more calming rate as the firemen on scene had been able to finally get it under control. Reaching the police cruiser marked 'Pima County Sheriff' Ian found the man he was looking for discussing the event with one of the firefighters standing off to the side.

"Sheriff?" Catching his attention, Ian asked, "Can I have a word??"

Giving Ian a quick once-over, the sheriff offered his hand and introduced himself, "Sheriff McKinney."

"You know that there is a missing nine year old, correct??" Getting right to the point, Ian failed to introduce himself first and earned a questionable look from the sheriff.

"Yes and we are on top of that...Mr....???"

"Ian Sampson", leaving off the Detective portion of it, Ian added, "I know the victims."

"Oh! Well, in that case, can you give me some information?? I wasn't able to get much from any of them except that she is nine years old and has some type of disability."

"She suffers from traumatic brain injury; occurred after a car accident when she was little. She's got long red hair, straight, green eyes, stands about four feet six, thin frame..." Offering Sheriff McKinney what he knew, he received a look from the man as his details were direct and to the point.

"You say you're just a friend??"

"Once upon a time I was a detective." Ian said simply, adding, "I am dating Brighton's mother."

"Ah...got it. Do you know what she was wearing when last seen?"

Thinking back to breakfast, Ian nodded and said, "This morning she was wearing white shorts, a pink, sleeveless top with hearts and flowers designed on the front, her hair was pulled back into a ponytail, and she was wearing white ankle socks."

Eyeing Ian again, the sheriff muttered, "You sure you're not *still* a detective??" as he jotted Brighton's description down in his notebook. Then, after Ian added that Brighton also struggles when she talks, the officer raised his eyebrows at him for a second before adding the characteristic to the list. "I don't suppose you have any idea who we should be looking at as possible kidnappers, do you??"

"Actually, I do. Contact Detective Marie Gonzalez, Tucson Police Department. There is an ongoing case involving a shooting with the mother and additional threats on her life. Brighton may have been taken in retaliation to the unsuccessful attempts on her mother's life."

Gaining another look from the sheriff as he wrote vigorously in his notebook, Ian added before taking a few steps back, "I just quit the department today." Not waiting for a response, he then jogged back to his truck, jumped into the driver's seat and sped back down the dirt road; knowing exactly who he needed to contact at this point.

"Gonzalez!!" Heading towards the Interstate, Ian yelled into the cell phone when Detective Gonzalez finally answered. "Don't hang up!!"

Hearing nothing from the other end, Ian pulled his phone from his ear to see if he had been hung up on or just plain lost the call as he maneuvered the truck back towards Tucson. Seeing that the call was still connected, he immediately spoke into it again.

"It's Amanda's daughter! Brighton is missing...we think it's the guys who attacked Amanda Friday night!" Then, still hearing nothing, he said, "Gonzalez?? You there??"

"Yes, dammit!! Slow down, I'm writing!!" Then, "Where are you??"

"Heading back towards Tucson. We got to Green Valley—where Amanda and Brighton were staying for right now—and the house they were at was set on fire. Amanda's friend, Anna, was in the house with Brighton and her parents when two men broke in. From what I gather, they shot Alex Yearling, beat Sylvia Yearling, and...one of them raped Anna."

"Christ!!"

"Yea, according to Anna they grabbed Brighton and left a verbal warning for Amanda."

"That being....?"

"That by now she should know what she has to do to get Brighton back...something to that effect. The whole family has been taken to Mercy and from what I gathered Anna's parents were responsive when they were pulled from the fire. Amanda is on her way to the hospital as well", he added grimly, his voice quieting as he thought of her lifeless body on the stretcher.

"She staying put with Anna and her parents??" Gonzalez's question brought him out of his fog and he answered, "No, she's going in as a patient. She passed out in the middle of it all. We got there and the fire looked as though it had just flared up. When we found Anna and talked to her, Amanda said that the message that Anna had been told to give her had to be from the guy with the scar...the one she gave the details about to Doctor Eland this morning. I think she recognized something specific in the message, but she collapsed before I could be sure."

"*Shit!!!*"

"Yea...she passed out—cold. One of the medics looked her over and said she could have an infection from her bullet wound— her shoulder is a mess and...and..." Taking a deep breath, Ian forced himself to stop rambling as he bypassed a car moving along slowly in the fast lane.

"Okay—okay, Ian, calm down." Saying his first name got his attention and his throat tightened as he tried to talk, "Marie...Amanda's daughter is only nine. She doesn't talk—Marie, I need to know what else you found out about Amanda's case this morning."

"Ian—you know you can't ask me to do that—you quit *remember*??" The detective's voice dropped several octaves and Ian knew that she had lowered it in case anyone around her was listening. "Gonzalez—" he started to argue back immediately.

Cutting off Ian's pleas before they even got started, Gonzalez said, "*You* can't ask me to do that—but I *can* offer." Then giving him directions of a local safe house, which was currently unoccupied and not under any form of surveillance of any kind, Ian thanked her and hung up, gripping the steering wheel harder as his own tears silently fell from his eyes.

Veering off the Interstate thirty minutes later, Ian found himself up on the west side of town and, following the directions that Detective Gonzalez had given him; he located the house in question and passed it slowly, eyeing the front of it carefully.

Parking his truck down on the next block, Ian walked back to the safe house, watching the neighborhood around him as he moved. Seeing no one out on their lawns or porches, he reached the house and headed around to the back of it, avoiding the front area as much as possible just in case a peeping eye from the home across the street happened to glance at the empty house in the next few seconds.

The back, cut and cared for by a local gardening company and paid for discretely by the state, Ian stepped up to the back porch and approached the back door carefully. Not hearing a sound, he gently tried the doorknob and found it unlocked. Opening it slowly, he stood on the threshold, waiting for some sign that said Gonzalez had beat him there.

"Sampson?"

Hearing her lowered voice from inside the house, Ian stepped in quickly and closed the door behind him. Sitting at a small, round kitchen table, Detective Gonzalez had laid out the Pearson file so that it was easily accessible. Sitting down across from her, Ian gave her a small smile.

"Thanks for meeting me."

"Don't thank me yet...if I get caught, I'm comin' after your ass." She said with a brief smile and then got down to business. "Here's what I've got so far...

"The girl in the apartment, Samantha Green, has a long history of arrests and problems. Beginning in the late eighties, she was popped for shoplifting and drug possession. But as the years went by and she grew older, she became affiliated with both local and statewide drug runners. Her profession listed during a few of her arrests included dancing...all for a guy name Lucas Marvell, who owned a couple of clubs in the nineties in Los Angeles and Phoenix respectively.

"In 2002, Green was popped again under the name Felicia Buckley and this time in L.A. in connection to a prostitution ring. Apparently, Marvell had her propositioning girls—off the street, out of runaway shelters, that sort of thing—and turning them into working girls. When she got busted, she skipped bail, fled L.A. and hadn't been heard of since until Saturday night when we pulled her body out of Pearson's apartment."

Sitting back in his chair, Ian considered the information that Gonzalez had just covered. Then, thinking of something, he asked, "What happened to Marvell?" as he tried to find some connection in all this to Amanda.

"Closed down the bars in L.A. and registered two new ones in Phoenix and Glendale, under the same name. Some of the ex-dancers I was able to get a hold of said that Lucas Marvell was a short man with an indistinguishable laugh—" Looking up at Ian, Gonzalez raised her eyebrows at him as they both said in unison, "Lucky Serifino".

"Yea, that's what I'm thinking...and get this," Gonzalez continued, "the M.E. found a flash drive in one of Samantha Greens jacket pockets when he was going through personal effects on the body. The tech guys were able to get some information on it, but not much."

"What'd they find?" Sitting up in his chair, Ian wondered quickly if there was damming evidence on it that they could legally tie this whole mess together with.

"Something called 'Silent Auction'. From what they can tell, it was some kind of file, but it was too damaged to pull anything else. They also think it was the only thing on the drive."

"You think that Green was trying to warn Amanda about something??" Ian asked.

"It's a theory. If Lucky Serifino is really Lucas Marvell and Green was still working for him, who knows. Maybe Serifino is knee deep in this thing." Shrugging her shoulders, Gonzalez gave Ian a second to add his thoughts.

"And if whoever it was that attacked Amanda was really working for Serifino as well, that could explain how they knew that Amanda had survived the gun shot, where her apartment was located, and where she was hiding out in Green Valley..."

"How do you connect what happened at her friend's house with this??"

"Matt the Bouncer?" Continuing after Gonzalez nodded her head at him, indicating that she know who he was talking about, "he worked at Lucky's. He also took Amanda to the Yearling house on Sunday—according to Amanda, Lucky himself insisted on it."

Sitting back in her chair, Detective Gonzalez stared at Ian and admitted, "I could really use you on this, you know."

"I'm here..." Ian responded, ignoring the underlying message in her statement.

"You know what I mean. I'm willing to bet my salary that Captain Leary hasn't even mentioned your resignation to anyone yet." When he didn't say anything, she pressed on, "You seriously gonna let our little disagreement change the course of your career???"

Shaking his head at her, Ian took a minute before answering. "It's not just that—you were right, Gonzalez. I wasn't thinking or acting like a cop in that room today. I was more focused on Amanda and trying to protect her and I didn't realize it until you said something. If I can't be one hundred percent unbiased, how can I do my job effectively??"

"So what—you gonna just barge into Lucky's Girls as a civilian?? I know that's exactly where you're going when you leave here! You're gonna end up getting yourself arrested in the process and really screw your life up!!"

Not wanting to admit that she had a point, Ian said nothing. Then, watching her sift through a large black bag that she had carried all of the case files in that they had just examined, he gave her a surprised look when she pulled out his detective credentials.

"I knew that you were going to be stubborn about this, Sampson, and I do not want to have arrest your ass when you find yourself in trouble—which I know is exactly what will happen if you don't take these back."

"How the hell did you—??"

"Convince Captain Leary to hand them over??"

"She gave me a pretty convincing argument—something about how you had suffered a brief breakdown and didn't know what you were doing." Without warning, a third voice joined the conversation and, reacting to it immediately, Ian stood from his chair, heart racing in his chest.

Standing behind Ian, in the now opened doorway of the safe house, was Captain Leary, a small smile on his face. Entering the house, he closed the door behind him and commented, "But I'm not sure if you are past that little event yet, Sampson—you didn't even hear me coming!!"

Placing both hands on his hips, Ian dropped his head to the floor and tried to get the anxious feeling that had just swept through his body to back off a bit. Looking up at his captain, he shook his head and said, "Just feel lucky that I wasn't armed...I was ready to shoot you before even realizing it was you!"

"Well, if you don't mind, use your service weapon on someone else, please." Placing Ian's weapon on the table, the captain gave him an expectant look, wanting to know if he really was going to lose one of his best detectives or if the man had finally come to his senses.

Looking back to Gonzalez, Ian sighed. Leaning over he picked up his badge and opened it, looking at his identification listed inside. He really loved being a cop. But he honestly believed that he loved Amanda more. He was not going to choose between the two of them...job be damned, he would run to her if it came down to that.

"I crossed the line, Captain." He said as he raised his eyes to meet Captain Leary's.

"You really care about this woman, Sampson?? So much that you'd throw your career away???"

"Yes." Ian's response was adamant. "And I'm not going to end it."

Sighing heavily, he eyed Ian, as if considering his options, and finally asked, "And the only people that know about this...indiscretion...is standing in this room correct??" Looking at both of his detectives, he gave them each a hard look, wanting an honest answer from the both of them.

Affirming his question, Gonzalez looked up at Ian, who said, "Unless you count Amanda and her family, yes, it's just us. I didn't really advertise it."

"Good." Then, stepping back towards the back door, ready to leave, Captain Leary gave Ian one final set of instructions before walking out the door, "Then put that damn badge back in your pocket and holster your weapon, Detective. We've got a child to find!"

Chapter Thirty-One

"Shut that fucking kid up, Lenny, or else!!"

Driving down a patch of dirt road, David was losing it quickly. The kid would not stop whimpering and he was ready to forget his orders and take her out. In the backseat with her, Lenny tried talking to her softly.

"Shshsh...it's gonna be okay, really. But you've got to be quiet now." Feeling a bit sympathetic for the kid, Lenny placed one hand on her bare knee but pulled it back quickly when she flinched and pushed herself against the backseat door she was leaning on, trying to get as far away from him as she could.

"Let's just get her to the drop off point and get the hell out of here!" David said loudly, maneuvering the stolen SUV across two lanes of road as he drew closer to the turn off he needed.

The road coming up ahead quickly, David slammed on the brakes; not caring about the two people in the backseat as he did. Pushed forward, Lenny steadied himself against the back of the front seat and the girl screamed as her back quickly skid across the car door.

"LENNY!!" David shouted at his partner, swearing again at him to shut her up.

Looking at her, Lenny tried to explain the situation again but to no avail, the only response he was getting out of her was a loud whimper. Her bright green eyes wide with terror, she stared back at him and he knew that she was terrified. Wanting to touch her long red hair, Lenny held fast; knowing that if he did, she would cry out again and the next sound she made may just be her last if David couldn't get his temper under control.

Making a sharp right, David slammed his foot down onto the gas pedal, causing the car to swerve in protest as the tires tried to find traction on the dirt road. Gaining control over the vehicle again, David wiped the palm of his hand across his brow, cursing the desert heat as he did. The car had no air conditioning; all it could manage to spurt out was quick puffs of warm air. Deciding right then and there that he would never accept another job unless he picked out the wheels he was to travel in, he breathed a sigh of relief as their drop-off point came into view.

A two story stucco home, the property was protected by a cinder block wall, reaching at least eight feet tall by David's calculation. A heavy looking metal gate marked the entrance onto the property and seeing it closed, David had to bring the SUV to an abrupt halt.

Suddenly the cell phone next to him on the seat began ringing and he grabbed it and flipped it open and put it to his ear. Listening from the back seat, Lenny tore his eyes from the young girl to watch David and listen in on his side of the conversation.

"Yes, we're here, open the fucking gate!" David yelled into the phone and Lenny cringed without even realizing it.

After listening to the caller, David calmed himself considerably and said, "The package is ready."

Then, the gate ahead of them stirred to life, automatically moving outward and David flipped the phone closed, ending the call. Waiting until the gate gave him enough room to pass through, David then stepped on the gas, moving slowly now as he approached the home; whistling softly as he took it all in.

A wraparound porch greeted the front of the yard, which was covered with a dirt floor and landscaped with Arizona plant life. Two large balconies graced the long windows that looked over the front of the house on the second floor. A large picture window took up most of the first floor on this side of the house; giving it a rich, elegant look. Marking the doorway was an oversized oak door and as David pulled in front of the home, it opened wide and two men stepped out.

"Get the kid", David instructed Lenny as he stepped out of the vehicle.

Lenny, looking over at the girl once more, hesitated for a second before complying. Taking in her red hair and green eyes one more time, he slid across the seat to let himself out, then walked behind the vehicle to open the girl's door.

Immediately moving away from him, the girl cried out again, trying to keep as much distance away from Lenny as possible and scrambled to the other side of the back seat. Through the open door, Lenny peered in at her and said, "You've got to come out now", and reached in to offer her a hand.

The girl, eyes wild with fear, kicked at his hand and she immediately turned around to try to open the opposite door in an effort to crawl out of the vehicle and run. Grabbing her ankle, Lenny pulled her back, trying not to hurt her as she continued to kick her size four tennis shoes at him.

Growing angrier, David reacted immediately; wanting nothing more than to put a bullet in the kid right then and there. Pushing Lenny out of the way, he reached in and grabbed at the girl's legs, and finding purchase on both, pressed down hard on her thighs with his fingers. Screaming in pain, the girl balled up her fists and tried to punch him but was too weak to do anything to stop from being yanked out of the back seat.

"GET THE FUCK OUT OF THE CAR!!!" David screamed at her as he pulled unforgivingly on her small body. Finally, he succeeded, as he fisted one hand around her soft red hair and he pulled her from the confines of the back seat. Cursing at her again as he then wrapped his strong fingers around her thin arms, he pushed her forward, towards the two men who were now making their way to the car. "*Jesus*, you're as bad as your mother!!"

Losing her balance, the girl fell forward; landing on her knees and Lenny reacted quickly. Reaching her, he knelt down and tried to help her stand. "Always a sucker for the redheads..." David muttered in disgust; wanting nothing more than to focus his anger on his partner now.

Looking up at Lenny, the girl forced back a sob and pursed her lips together, willing herself not to scream or cry out anymore; as if understanding now that it would only get her into more trouble. Flinching slightly as Lenny gently helped her stand, she faced her kidnapper with wide eyes and sniffled as her silent tears continued to free fall down her thin face. Then, noticing the other two men approaching, her heart exploded against her chest as she wondered quickly what was going to happen to her now.

"Take the girl into the house", instructed the taller of the two. Heavyset and bald the man gave the girl a quick look over as his partner, a shorter, thinner man, placed one hand on the girl's shoulder and led her away.

Turning towards David, the large man said, "The original target???" wanting to know if the mother had been taken as well.

"She wasn't there. According to the instructions, I was to collect the collateral if needed. It was needed."

"And the others in the home??" Giving David a stern look, he knew that David had been ordered not to add to his already long line of human terminations.

"Alive and kicking that last I saw." Smiling to himself, the details of his assault on the household flashed through his mind. Taking the younger, black-haired woman in the kitchen had not been part of the deal, but he hadn't been able to contain himself upon laying eyes on her tall, thin body and the terrified look in her eyes. "They probably required some hospital care, but each had a heartbeat when I was done.

"Your payment then."

Taking David for his word, the man reached into his jacket pocket and David tensed immediately. Expecting the unexpected was part of David's forte. Reaching around his back, his fingers flirted with the weapon tucked into the back of his dirty jeans; a semi-automatic Beretta; then relaxed when seeing the man pull out a white envelope. Tossing David the envelope, the man turned from him and headed back towards the house; only to stop just before the porch and turn around again, as if waiting for David and Lenny to successfully exit the property.

Watching the exchange, Lenny was suddenly confused. "We done?" he asked David, believing that there had to be more the contract, or were they just supposed to walk away now?

"Looks that way." David said tightly, the feeling of leaving the business at hand unfinished building quickly. Thinking back to the redhead that got away, David turned from the house and stalked past Lenny towards their vehicle. Getting in, he started it and let it idle softly as he decided that walking away now was not going to satisfy him in the least. He was going to get the redhead. And if he played his cards right, he may just end up a bit richer than he was sitting right now.

"Lenny!!"

Hearing David holler at him from the SUV, Lenny hesitated before turning his back on the house, the contract, and the girl. Thinking of her wide green eyes and long red hair, a matching pair of goose bumps crept down his arms. Yes, he was a sucker for the redheads—no matter what age.

Wondering what was going to happen to the girl, he sighed heavily; knowing that there would be nothing he could do for her...if he stepped up and tried to take her for himself, would she spend her life staring back at him with terror with those beautiful green eyes??? And as he got into the vehicle, he was granted one last look at her long red hair as she was escorted across the yard towards the house and his eyes drank her little body up; as if knowing that if nothing else, he would at least have the memory of her to think back to whenever he needed.

Wanting to run, but not knowing in which direction, her emerald eyes frantically searched the area around her. Seeing nothing but desert, she knew that if she did try to get away, she would be more lost than she was now. Remembering what her mother had taught her about the desert, she knew better than to run off blindly.

Thinking of her mother, she closed her eyes tight for a second as her mind tried to work right and the events that had led her to this point drifted swiftly across her memory and she tried desperately to grab a hold of one.

Auntie Anna making pancakes...was that this morning???

Nana's roses...

Mommy's red hair...

Opening her eyes again, the girl wiped her fingers across them, frustrated that she couldn't put one single memory together right. She knew that she was different from other people; her mother had told her that was what made her so much more special than anyone else. But right now, as the grip on her shoulder tightened and she was pushed forward into the strange house, she wished that she was normal. That she could say something to make them let her go—make a full sentence without her thoughts and her voice breaking it all apart.

Then, she was in the house and the door shut tightly behind her and as she heard, "Hello, Brighton", coming from the man standing in the room before her, confusion set in as her mind slowly connected the man's face to his name. And in knowing him, a deeper feeling of terror squeezed her heart and she knew that something was terribly...terribly wrong.

Chapter Thirty-Two

As soon as Ian walked across the squad room floor, he knew that neither Captain Leary nor Detective Gonzalez had mentioned anything about him resigning from the job only a few hours before. No one stopped to question his appearance, give him a look of wonder as to why he was there, or said anything to him period. Instead, the floor was in a state of urgency, his fellow officer's frantically working together to find nine-year-old Brighton Pearson. Upon hearing the details of her kidnapping and the connections it may have to the case that two of their detectives were currently working on; volunteers to help find the girl were coming out of the woodwork.

Off-duty officers, part-timers, and even civilian volunteers were stepping up, asking what they could do to help and the feeling was overwhelming for Ian—especially considering the fact that he was more than just a little connected to the girl and her mother. Making his way to his desk, he looked up towards the back of the room and, in noticing the posted color photograph of Brighton attached to a whiteboard, swallowed hard against the lump already forming in his throat.

"Sampson!"

Hearing his name over the volume of voices in the room, he turned where he stood and caught Gonzalez' eye. Following her short wave, he weaved his way back towards the center of the room and nodded at their captain, who was at her side.

"We need to brief everyone—and now! We've got patrols ready to hit the streets and we need to get the word out to the media. Can you do the briefing??" Her voice stressed, he knew that she was worried and he was suddenly thankful to be working alongside her. When a cop ceases to care about the cases that they were working on, it was time for a career change. Taking a quick look around the room told him that along with him and Gonzalez, everyone here was here for the Pearson family and this spoke volumes.

"I can do it." He said quietly, not sure if he was positive about his answer; this being one of the reasons that he had decided to resign earlier. Becoming personally connected to the victims involved in a case causes issues; he'd seen it several times with other officers in the past. Of course there hadn't been a case that he knew of in which the officer began a *sexual* relationship with the victim; but he had seen cops that got too close to a case and it ate them up inside when things did not turn out the way that they had hoped. Nonetheless, he was here to do a job and getting Brighton back was more important than his feelings as this point.

"ATTENTION!!!"

Captain Leary's voice boomed across the room and everyone suddenly fell silent as they turned their attention to their head supervisor. "We need to brief everyone and instead of moving into our conference room, we are doing it right here, right now; so listen up people!!"

Turning where he stood, Ian made sure that all eyes were on him before speaking. In child abduction cases there was no room for mistakes or misunderstandings. Brighton had been missing for over four hours now; the clock was ticking and Ian wasn't going to spend extra time briefing someone who should have been listening in the first place.

"Sampson..." Gonzalez caught his attention quickly and he turned to face her. Pulling a chair to him, she silently suggested that he stand on it so that he could both be seen and heard as the room of officers, personnel, and volunteers seemed to almost double in size at the captain's announcement.

"Thanks, Gonzalez." Ian said as he stood up on the chair. Then, loudly, asked, "Can everyone see and hear me??" and took a second to make sure that everyone was paying attention.

"At approximately 2:45 this afternoon, nine year old Brighton Pearson was abducted from her friend's home in Green

Valley. Her picture is posted on the wall", pointing to it, all eyes focused on Brighton's most recent school picture and then returned to Ian, "She is approximately four-feet-six-inches, fifty-seven pounds, has long red hair, green eyes, and suffers from traumatic brain injury which affects her memory and speech patterns.

"We believe that Brighton was kidnapped as a result of several failed attempts made on her mother, Amanda Pearson; who, as some of you may know, was shot outside Lucky's Girls this past weekend. We believe that the men who attacked Ms. Pearson outside the bar are the same ones who took her daughter. As of right now, we have a composite of one of those men—the main feature being a long scar running from under his left eye and down the side of his face. He is also described as being approximately six feet tall, of muscular build, between 25 and 40 years of age, and having long brown hair and dark colored eyes.

"We also believe that there is a second man involved, only described as being of a thinner build, but there may be others involved in this as well. These men have to be traveling in a vehicle inconspicuous enough to pull this off without drawing too much attention, such a van or SUV. Keep on the look-out for stolen vehicles reported over the start of the weekend up until today.

"These two men may also be involved in the murders of four other women in and around our area; please note that these men are considered armed and extremely dangerous. While you are out there, be careful and make sure to call for back up before approaching either suspect if you happen upon them. Our main focus is finding Brighton safe and unharmed and not to lose anyone along the way."

Pausing for a moment as Ian noticed a raised hand near the back of the room, he motioned for the uniformed officer to ask his question. "Are we in line with the Sheriff's department since the abduction occurred in Green Valley?"

Answering for Ian, Captain Leary's voice rang loudly across the room, so that everyone could hear him. "We are. Amanda Pearson and her daughter reside here, in Tucson, however the Yearling family reside in Green Valley. As you may have heard, Alex and Sylvia Yearling, along with their daughter Anna, were also injured when the abduction occurred. Mr. Yearling suffered a gunshot, Mrs. Yearling was physically assaulted, and Ms. Yearling was sexually assaulted; we believe by the same man that we have the composite on."

"Sampson", getting his attention as quietly as possible was Gonzalez and looking down at her Ian noticed that she was holding a thick stack of papers. Seeing Brighton's face on the front, he addressed the crowd again. "Detective Gonzalez and I will be passing around a photo of Brighton, plus copies of the composite made of our main suspect. The information listed on both is also there—memorize her photo—at this point, she could be anywhere. Check in often and be safe out there!"

Waiting a few seconds to make sure that there were no other questions; Ian stepped down from the chair and took half of the stack of copies from Gonzalez. Handing them around, they made sure that everyone received a packet and then met up again in the center of the room where Captain Leary was keeping watch.

"Good job, Sampson. Gonzalez, you got a call from the tech department while you were meeting Sampson earlier; they've got something for you, check in with them." Turning from Gonzalez to Ian, the captain instructed, "Head over to Mercy, see if you can get any other details out of any of the victims; maybe one of them will remember hearing or seeing something that will give us a clue as to where the girl could have been taken."

"Got it, Captain." Ian replied, and then turning to Gonzalez said, "Call me on my cell if anything comes up. Let me know what the Tech guys say."

"Will do." Turning, the detective took a step and then called back to Ian again, "We'll get her back. Be sure to tell Ms. Pearson that." Nodding at her, Ian was suddenly at a loss for words and before his feelings betrayed him in front of everyone, he headed towards the stairs.

Nearly a half hour later, Ian pulled into the parking lot at Mercy. Finding a spot in the visitor's section, he hurried into the main part of the hospital; unsure of exactly which department Amanda and the Yearling family would be in now.

Finding out that they were on different floors, Ian headed to the third floor first to check on Amanda. Exiting the elevator, he followed the signs to find himself facing a petite blond who was busy reading a magazine on the up and comings of the entertainment world at a small desk marked for information.

Eyeing Ian quickly, the blond blushed and put her magazine aside and flashed him a bright smile. Offering her his badge, Ian requested the room that Amanda was in and ignored the interesting stare the girl at the desk gave him. Following her instructions, he found Amanda's room and entered it quietly.

Seeming to be sound asleep, Ian inhaled deeply as he noted the machines she was hooked up to. Similar to the ones that had monitored her vitals on the night she had been shot, he tried to ignore the steady beeping that went off every second or so; stating that her heart was still beating at a normal rate. Stepping close to her, he watched her chest slowly rise and fall and then reached over to softly touch her cheek.

"Can I help you??" A voice from behind made him jump slightly and he immediately pulled his hand back. Turning, he cleared his throat and addressed the nurse who had just entered the room, offering her his credentials as he explained his presence. "Detective Ian Sampson, Ma'am. I need an update on Amanda Pearson."

"Oh, of course. Let me call for the doctor, wait here a second."

Leaving him in the room, Ian once again turned his attention back to Amanda. Dressed in a light brown hospital gown, her arms lay at her sides; one of them housing a needle just below her wrist that was connected to an I.V. Her face sullen and dark, she looked as though she hadn't slept in days. Her thin frame distinguishable underneath the thin blanket that was tucked in around her, she also looked as though she hadn't eaten in days and Ian made a promise to himself that as soon as she was out of here, his main focus was going to be to get her to eat more.

"Detective?"

A male voice called quietly from behind and Ian turned to find himself staring at an older man with thin, graying hair and a wrinkled, clean shaven face. Shorter than Ian, the white coat that distinguished him from the other staff on hand hung long and loose; giving Ian the impression that it was much too big for the man.

Nodding at Amanda's doctor, the pair stepped out of the room so as to not disturb her. Cutting right to the chase the man quickly explained her condition and Ian swiftly wondered if her doctor had somewhere else to be right at that moment.

"Ms. Pearson suffered an infection stemming from a gunshot wound—from what I read in her file—that happened on Friday evening. The infection spread through the blood and that, combined with obvious exhaustion, caused her body to break down per say. We've got her hooked up intravenously to counter the infection, giving her fluids to help maintain her strength and health, and are now just letting it work through her body while she rests."

"So…she'll be okay??" Hoping he didn't sound any less professional than he was trying to be, Ian raised his eyebrows at the doctor, his spirits lifting considerably.

"Oh, yes! She will be fine. We've just got to get this infection under control."

Finally able to breathe and concentrate again, Ian notified the doctor of his patient's missing daughter and that fact that her life may still be in danger. Explaining that a uniformed officer will be assigned to her room until further notice, the doctor nodded understandably and shook Ian's hand, stepping backward as he did; obviously late for something.

Now alone outside Amanda's room, Ian pulled out his cell phone to call Gonzalez. Getting her voice mail, he left an update of Amanda's current condition in his message and ended the call. Then after making contact with Captain Leary, he requested for an assigned officer. Adding that one should be also assigned to the Yearling family—just in case—Ian hung up after being assured that two officers would be dispatched there shortly to start a rotation.

Standing in the doorway of her room, Ian took a moment to watch her sleep, assured himself that she would be alright and then headed back to the elevators to the second floor; where the patients listed as "critical" were cared for.

Heading down another corridor, Ian passed a small waiting area on his left and immediately stopped short; having seen Anna sitting in one of the chairs. Calling to her, she looked up and reacted quickly; running to him in hopes of hearing news about Brighton.

"We are still looking", he explained grimly before asking about her parents.

"Mom is okay; they've got her in a room on the same floor as Amanda and want to keep her overnight. She's got a lot of bruises but nothing is broken and they think she can come home tomorrow." Then pausing as if remembering that there is no home for them to go to, Anna put her hands over her face and began to cry into them.

Gently moving her hands, Ian asked softly, "What about your dad?"

Looking up at him, Anna's tear soaked eyes met his. "He's not too good. He was shot in the leg, but on the way here, they said he had a heart attack. Last I heard, they were still working on him, trying to get the bullet out of his leg and making sure his heart is okay." Then, the dam broke and Anna crumbled. Reacting immediately, Ian braced her against his body and guided her over to an empty seat and sat her down in it.

"Do you have any other family?? Anyone that can come and be with you?"

Nodding, Anna sniffled and said, "My aunt is on her way now from Phoenix. She should be here in an hour or so", her voice cracking as she spoke.

"Okay. There will be an officer stationed here—"

"What?! Do you think their coming back?!" Cutting him off, the panic in Anna's voice matched the terror he read in her wide eyes and he tried to calm her down quickly. "No—it's procedure.

There will be an officer outside Amanda's room as well. We are just taking every precaution right now."

Hearing Amanda's name caused Anna to sit up straight again in her chair, wincing slightly as she did; indicating the pain she must still be in after her attack. "Amanda! I haven't checked on her yet!!"

Trying to calm her down again, Ian placed both hands on her shoulders, trying to keep her sitting still as he said, "Anna, Amanda is okay. She's got an infection from the bullet wound and she's exhausted, but otherwise she is okay. She's on the third floor. I just checked on her and she is sleeping. Just like your dad, she is in good hands. Are *you* okay??"

Crying again, Anna nodded, putting her head down as she said, "I was examined when I got here and...the doctors took some...evidence..." Familiar with the processes involved in completing a rape kit, Ian knew exactly what Anna had been put through when she arrived with Amanda. Not needing to hear anymore, but thankful that she had been examined; Ian made a mental note to have someone from that station call about the kit when he returned.

Anna's eyes filled with tears again as she then said Brighton's name softly; as if trying to change the subject off of her and onto her best friend's daughter instead. Knowing that there was nothing he could tell her, other than that come hell or high water he would find Brighton, he knew better than to make false promises. Doing so for any victim can come back to haunt an officer and at this rate, Ian didn't need to see any ghosts any time in the near future.

At that moment, his cell phone rang and he left Anna to stand in the corridor to answer it. On the other end, Gonzalez's voice came through; animated and loud.

"Sampson! Where are you?? We've got something!"

Moving down from the waiting room automatically, Ian's heart began beating faster as he briefly explained his current location and then demanded, "Tell me you got good news, Gonzalez!"

"Silent Auction—the name of the file that was on the flash drive found on Samantha Green??" Not waiting for Ian to respond, Gonzalez went on without missing a beat. "It's not just a file...it was a web site!"

"A web site??" Ian's eyes narrowed as he tried to keep up with Gonzalez.

"The tech guys discovered an old link on the web and were trying to figure out if it was somehow connected to the file. As of fifteen minutes ago, they had nothing...but, Ian, the site just popped up! It's up and running and the guys are trying to hack into it!"

Confused, Ian interjected and said, "Hack it?? Can't they just click on it and open up the web page??" Familiar with some of the underlying workings of the World Wide Web, Ian had assumed that if the site was available, they should be able to access it.

"No, it's under some kind of protection—", her voice fell silent for a second and he heard her ask someone on her end for clarification. A second later she came back and corrected herself. "The site is password protected. All we can see is the title of the page, there's nothing else listed on it except a box asking for a username and password. They guys here are trying to hack it now."

"Any word on Brighton??" He asked, changing the subject for a second.

"We've got her picture and information out to the media and a tip line set up already. We've had a bunch of calls so far, but nothing concrete yet." Then, a bit more quieter, Gonzalez added, "Sampson, I really think the bar owner, Lucky—or whatever the hell the guy's name is—is involved in this somehow. There's too much pointing back at him."

"Yeah, I've been thinking the same thing ever since you went over your findings at the safe house. Want to go visit him??"

"Can't. Captain Leary says that he filed some kind of official complaint yesterday...with the mayor...we can't go near him without something concrete."

"Shit, you're kidding!!" Running a hand through his hair, Ian turned around to find Anna standing in the doorway of the waiting room, listening intently. "Gonzalez, I gotta go. I'm getting ready to leave here; I'll meet back up with you when I get back to the station. Tell the techies to keep on it."

"Will do!"

That said, Ian closed his phone and stuffed it into his jeans pocket. Walking back to Anna, he passed by her in the doorway; not wanting to give her any news out in the open corridor. Watching him expectantly, Anna returned to her seat and waited.

"We may have something—but it's nothing solid yet." Seeing Anna's face begin to light up, Ian clarified that they were still actively looking for Brighton before asking, "Anna, do you remember anything from the attack that may help us find her? Anything that was said between the two guys that took Brighton??"

Thinking hard, Anna took a minute but shook her head no, frustrated with the fact that she had nothing to give him that would help him find her Goddaughter. Trying to get her to let herself off the hook, Ian then said, "It's okay, Anna. None of this is your fault. There is nothing that you or your parents could have done to stop them from taking Brighton. We'll find her, okay??"

Pressing her lips together, Anna fought back her tears and nodded.

"I've got to get back to the station. You have my cell phone number??" After watching her nod at him again, he said, "Call me the minute you hear about your dad. I will get a hold of you once Brighton is found and if you go up to see Amanda, and she's awake, will you give her a message for me??"

Catching Ian's eye, Anna made a small attempt to smile and whispered, "Yes".

"Tell her that I love her...that we are working diligently to find Brighton...and, even though I know she won't...tell her to go back to sleep!"

Leaning over, Ian hugged Anna briefly and then left the room. Heading back down to the first floor, he exited the hospital and headed back towards downtown; praying along that way that by the time he got there, Gonzalez and the tech guys would have something to go on. Believing in his gut feelings, Ian knew that Lucky Serifino was involved in all of this and, in wanting nothing more than to put a bullet between the man's eyes, he unconsciously bent his trigger finger back and forth in anticipation.

Nearly a half hour later, he was running up the flight of stairs that led to the station floor. Bypassing it quickly he continued all the way up to the third floor, where the technical department was housed. Their main focus being Cybercrimes, Ian knew that if anyone could hack the Silent Auction website, it would be the fifteen people in that department that knew the functioning of the Internet inside and out. He just hoped that by the time he reached their large, computer-ridden office; they would have something that would help tie this whole case together and in the process, guide them to finding Brighton—praying that it was before anything tragic happened to her.

Slowing to a jog, Ian passed offices on both sides; each marking different employee services for the law enforcement men and women who were assigned to this station. The lateness in the day left most offices closed up tight; their owners having gone home already. Reaching the back end of the floor, Ian forced himself to stop and catch his breath before entering.

The double doors that opened up to the oversized room of computers, analysts, and techies; as Ian liked to call them; were wide open, as if assuming he would be entering at any second. Doing so, Ian scanned the room for Detective Gonzales. Finding her leaning over the shoulder of a mousy-haired girl that couldn't have been a day over eighteen; Ian crossed the room quickly to see what they were so heavily concentrating on.

"Gonzalez," he said as he approached, "what'd they find??"

Turning towards Ian, the detective answered grimly, "Not much yet, according to Sara", nodding towards the young girl staring at her computer monitor, Gonzalez paused for a second before explaining, "The website is highly secured. She's been trying to hack into it since I called you but no luck so far."

Looking over her shoulder, Sara tried to offer him more information concerning what she was doing. Cutting her off quickly, Ian admitted his ignorance when it came to technical talk and asked instead if there was any way she could figure out where the website was being controlled from.

Nodding, Sara said, "Yea, and it's usually pretty simple, just need the IP address and I can track the site."

"Can't you get if off the webpage?" Gonzalez asked, peering at the screen over the girls' shoulder again.

"I could if I could get onto the site. This page here is just a login screen. There's an address for it, but it's not leading me anywhere. If I had login information or an account recorded with the site, I could enter it and go from there." Then, admitting she needed a break, Sara suddenly stood up from her system.

"Wait a minute!" Growing angry quickly, Ian grabbed the girl by the arm, stopping her from moving past him. "We've got a missing nine-year-old out there! We don't have any time for breaks!"

"How 'bout the bathroom, Detective??? I've been on this for nearly two hours straight and I need to use the restroom!" Pulling her arm out of his grasp, Sara glared at Ian and walked towards the opened doors that would lead her to the third floor facilities.

"Calm down, Sampson—that girl's been working her butt off trying to help!" Giving him a stare of her own, Gonzalez sank into a nearby office chair and rubbed her temples.

"Well, is there anyone else working on this??" Frustrated, Ian ran a hand through his hair. "We're running out of time—I can feel it!"

"Hey!! I got something!!"

Turning towards the excited voice that came from the other side of the room, Ian's heart raced in his chest as he crossed the floor in long strides; Gonzalez on his heels. "What?! What do you got??"

"Okay—using a JavaScript formula to decrypt—"

"Save the geek speech, Techie! Speak English and do it quickly!!" Giving the scrawny looking, freckled-face man a hard look, Ian raised his eyebrows at him; silently challenging him to ignore his demand. Swallowing hard, the tech gave Ian a startled, yet nervous, look and turned slowly away from him and sat down at his computer as he said, "I got in…"

"Okay!!" Then, forcing himself to calm down, Ian asked, "What are we looking at??"

Reminiscent of an antique shopping catalog, the site boasted greatly aged merchandise for the collector at heart. Interactive and automated, Ian watched as the merchandise that was available for sale slowly moved across the screen; each with a small blurb pertaining to authenticity, era of creation, and opening bidding price sectioned neatly under each and typed in an Old English looking font. In the few seconds that the tech had hacked the site, Ian eyed Elizabethan-era dresses and corsets, Renaissance paintings and equipment, and Romanesque statues float across the screen; all claiming to be authentic and of extreme value.

"What the hell is this??" Ian muttered, more to himself than Gonzalez or the techie.

"Well…the site is called *"Silent Auction"*…maybe that's exactly what it is…an auction site…" The techie, looking over his shoulder at the two detectives but immediately returned his eyes back to his computer screen after receiving deep frowns from the both of them.

"This is what Samantha Green had on that flash drive in her pocket???" Gonzalez asked, not expecting an answer from anyone. "This can't be connected her death…"

"Unless the stuff isn't really authentic..." Ian offered, but felt like there had to be more to it than just a bunch of old crap that most people wouldn't spend two cents for, let alone thousands of dollars.

"Or...unless this really isn't what is offered on this site..." Interjecting his own opinion, the techie peered closer at the items as they continued their way across the screen and, in finding a nearly invisible triangular shape on the bottom left hand corner of the page, clicked on it and sat back as it opened up to another page.

Staring back at the three of them was a small disclaimer. Set against a black screen and typed in white lettering, it was the only message on the screen and it got their attention immediately. Sending goose bumps up his arms, Ian listened as the techie slowly read the notice aloud:

"IF YOU HAVE RECEIVED NOTICE OF THIS RARE OPPORTUNITY, REMEMBER THAT YOUR AUCTION PRICE IS NONNEGOTABLE. PAYMENT IS DUE UPON WINNING PRICE; MERCHANDISE WILL NOT BE SHIPPED UNTIL VERIFICATION OF FUNDS HAS BEEN COMPLETED. AS IN PAST OFFERS, THIS RARE PIECE OF REAL ESTATE WILL ONLY BE AVAILABLE FOR BIDDING OVER THE NEXT THREE HOURS. SILENT AUCTION IS NOT ACCOUNTABLE FOR UNSAVERABLE OUTCOMINGS ONCE THE MERCHANDISE HAS BEEN SHIPPED."

"Sampson...this doesn't sound like they are auctioning off antiques..." Gonzalez's remark reached Ian's ears just as the techie pointed the curser over the disclaimer and clicked twice on it.

Suddenly, the page changed again and they were looking at a live feed; one trained on the merchandise currently for sale by *"Silent Auction"*. And as Ian stared into the terrified emerald-green eyes of nine-year-old, Brighton Pearson, his heart stopped within his chest, the small hairs on the back of his neck stood at attention, and his mouth went completely dry.

"*Jesus....*" Gonzalez said, her voice strained.

"Wait—isn't she the missing girl??" Turning towards both detectives, the techie's face had a hint of green in it as he asked, "They're gonna *sell* her???"

Straightening his back, Ian's jaw tightened as he clenched his teeth together hard enough to feel a headache threaten his temples. Fighting the tears of anger that immediately built behind his brown eyes, along with the urge to yank the techie's computer monitor off of his desk and throw it out the nearest window, he answered, "That's exactly what they're gonna do—and we've got less than three hours to find her before she disappears for good."

Chapter Thirty-Three

'Mommy???'

Her little voice broke through the darkness that surrounded me. Staring into a black sea of nothing, I held my breath; wanting to be sure it was really her before answering.

'Mommy—where are you?!'

Hesitant, I answered nervously, 'I'm here...Brighton???"

'Mommy!!! I can't find you!!'

Heart pounding against my chest, the quick beats of it drummed loudly in my ears and I was afraid that if it got any louder, I wouldn't be able to hear her voice above it.

Her voice!

She can talk?!

This can't be real!!

Am I dreaming?? Yes—I've got to be! But her voice...it's so...REAL!

Unsure of myself, I held fast...afraid to move or reach out, not knowing what was in front of me.

'Brighton...' I whispered as hot tears suddenly fell from my eyes. 'Where are you?' Knowing that she couldn't possibly hear me over the fierce thumping of my heart, I struggled to keep it together; hoping against all hope that the darkness would somehow fade into light.

Then, suddenly, I couldn't breathe. Feeling something in front of my mouth, I immediately became frantic. Feeling myself begin to suffocate quickly, I raised my hands in retaliation and felt only my opened mouth. But still—I CAN'T BREATHE!!

Clawing at my throat, Brighton's scared little voice grew louder and I know that something terrible has found her and forcing air into my burning lungs, I—

Eyes flying open, my dream was suddenly cut off and the hand that had been covering my mouth tightened quickly. Terror rose up from my chest like a tidal wave and I knew that it wouldn't be long before I was dead. Brighton's beautifully small face swept across my mind only to be replaced immediately with a man's and in that second I knew I was facing a do-or-die situation and I was NOT ready to die—if he was going to kill me, I was going to take a piece of him with me...whatever piece I could grab a hold of.

Raising my hands to fight him off, my eyes grew wide as he leaned close and sneered. His hand now pinching my nostrils closed, I tried to draw a breath underneath his thick fingers but couldn't and I dug my heels into whatever it was I was lying on.

"Feel like seeing your bratty daughter again, *Bitch*???"

A whiff of alcohol swept from his breath as he tightened his grip and his black eyes pierced mine and I tried to shrink back from him. Smiling, his ugly scar crinkled along the side of his face and I stopped struggling immediately in wondering just what he knew about Brighton.

"Yea, I got your attention now don't I??" Looking down at me, he continued; his breath nearly intoxicating and I had to force myself to focus. "You want your daughter back?? You'd better listen up, real good, then."

"What's going on in here?!"

A female's voice called suddenly from across the room and the scarred man quickly removed his hand from my mouth and as he glared at me hard he replied stiffly, "Just updating Ms. Pearson here about her missing daughter", as if not worried in the slightest as to who the voice belonged to. For all the either of us knew it was a cop at the door; his body obstructing my view of anything in that direction at the moment.

Never leaving my face, his black eyes darkened; challenging me to make a sudden move or cry out for help. Feeling trapped, I froze, knowing that if I did call attention to what was really going on, I'd never see Brighton again.

Seeming satisfied that I was not going to be any trouble, the man stood up straight and it was then that I noticed the uniform he was wearing. Dressed as police officer, my mind scrambled, wondering quickly if he in fact, was a cop.

Looking over his shoulder at the woman who had just interrupted him, the long scar on the side of his face gleamed under the harsh light of the room and I was suddenly aware of two things; first: I was in the hospital—*again*—and second: the man standing over me was the same one who had tried to rape and kill me only days before.

Pausing for a moment, neither of them said anything and I wondered quickly if the lady in the doorway was silently questioning whether or not my intruder was telling the truth. Finally, she spoke up and requested that he hurry up with the update and leave me to get some more rest.

Giving me a hard smile, the scarred man looked over his shoulder at her again and replied, "Of course. Ms. Pearson needs all the rest she can get."

Completely obstructed from my view, I never saw the woman and in a way I was thankful. If she had been able to see my face, she would have known immediately that something was wrong and any information that this man had on my daughter would have never been given; he would have killed me and her first—I just knew it. Staring back at him, my body tensed under the thin, brown blanket that covered it as I waited for him to say something.

Turning from me, I watched him walk towards the doorway and I suddenly thought that he was just going to leave. Sitting up quickly, I opened my mouth to say something that would stop him but realized that I didn't need to as he reached out and closed the door to the room; locking it into place. Knowing that no one would be able to interrupt him again without having to knock first, he turned to face me again as his mouth turned into a wide smile.

"Here's how it's gonna go", he started, calling the shots immediately, "you're gonna get dressed and we are gonna walk outta here, all nice and peaceful. Any trouble out of you and I won't hesitate to cut your pretty little throat. Got it, *Hellcat*??"

Tears building behind my eyes, I nodded; remembering the events that had occurred the last time he called me 'Hellcat'. Then, taking a chance, I struggled to ask, "Where is my daughter?? What did you do to her???"

Smiling, he simply stared back at me and I debated quickly on whether or not I should demand answers before making any attempt to move. Taking a deep breath, I forced the question that was burning in my mind as a single tear escaped one of my eyes and traveled slowly down my cheek. "Is she...is she...still...alive???"

"No more fucking questions!!" His dark voice rising instantly in volume, he started towards me and I reacted immediately by swinging my legs around the side of the bed. Knowing that I had next to nothing on underneath the gown that I was dressed in, I tore my eyes away from his and searched the room for my clothes; assuming that they had to be stored somewhere close by.

"Put these on."

As he directed me, he tossed a white shopping bag in my direction and, opening it, I found a pair of jeans and a t-shirt with a pair of white tennis shoes underneath. Both the look and the smell of the clothing told me that they had not been purchased recently— but in fact had been worn by someone else at some point and probably never washed and I cringed inwardly at the thought of wearing some strange woman's clothing, but complied without making a sound.

Pulling the jeans on first, I wanted to get the bottom half of my body covered without giving him any sort of eyeful and in doing so, thought of Anna; just knowing that this was the same man who had assaulted her in her parents' kitchen.

The thought of this made my eyes water instantly but before my tears could further betray me, the man was demanding that I hurry it up. Getting the jeans on and buttoned, I turned away from him to remove the gown but felt a strong pull on my arm as the I.V. housed in my left hand restricted much movement.

"Pull it out."

Looking up, I immediately noticed his intent stare and a violent shiver ran down my spine. Tearing my eyes from his black ones, I looked down at the small needle that was continuously feeding my body with whatever medicine the doctors here had decided to administer while I was having nightmares about the whereabouts of my daughter.

Placing two fingers on either side of the small contraption, I tried to pull the I.V. needle out as gently as I could and felt my stomach turn. Closing my eyes, I steadied myself and took a deep breath and then pulled on the top of the contraption that housed the needle. Feeling it exit my skin, my stomach did another flip and I swallowed hard and closed my eyes even tighter.

Standing there for a few seconds, I finally opened them and looked down at the small puncture wound on the top of my hand. Knowing that I should cover it, I quickly glanced around the room for something to use but found nothing. Tearing off the hospital gown, I finished dressing as fast as I could; knowing that I had no choice but to do what he said.

"Let's go."

His demand filled the silence of the room and as I took one last look around, I turned towards him and wondered if we were going to be able to just walk freely out of here. Worried now that if someone stopped us and what his reaction to it would be; I said a small prayer, asking whoever was listening to watch over me and my daughter, hoping against all hope that I get to see her again.

Walking towards the door to the room, I waited while he opened it. Not seeming to care if anyone noticed us leaving, he took a step out and motioned for me to take the lead. As we headed down the wing to the nearest exit, I suddenly realized that I had no idea what floor we were on, where Anna was, or her parents for that matter. Hoping that we didn't run into any of them on the way out, the man directed me to a set of elevators at the end of a hallway that met the wing. As we passed hospital staff, a patient or two, and people that were obviously friends or family of someone housed here, no one took any notice of us—he is dressed as a *cop* after all—and I wondered briefly just how long it would be until someone entered the room I had been assigned to and found it empty.

Entering the elevator, we were the only two occupants and as the man reached over and pressed the button marked for the lobby I glanced quickly at the opening the doors offered. As they started to slowly close, I had the sudden urge to leap through them and run. Remembering immediately that if I did, I would be signing my daughter's death sentence; I forced myself to stand completely still as tears quickly built up behind my eyes.

As if hearing my thoughts, the man stood behind me and said, "Thinking of running?? Go ahead...you'll never see your daughter again..."

Hearing the smile in his voice, my heart raced and I tried to refocus my thoughts by watching the numbers light up as we passed each floor on our way down to the lobby. Seconds later, a loud 'ding!' rang through the small space and the doors opened. Ahead of us, people mulled about, heading off to different areas of the hospital; no one even looking at us as we headed straight for the large double doors that would lead us out into the hot Arizona sun; now starting its decline to the west of us.

Reaching the outside, the man suddenly grasped my forearm in his hand and tightened his grip, causing me to wince before I could stop myself. Pulling unforgivingly, he moved with a purpose and I was forced to either keep up or be dragged as the image of his initial attack on me back in the Lucky's Girls parking lot invaded my mind's eye and my terror grew to new heights.

Keeping up with him in shoes that were much too small for my feet, I was limping by the time he pulled me to a stop. Facing a dark colored sedan, the first thing I noticed was the driver and immediately wondered if this was the same man that had been there when I was attacked. If so, I was truly on my own—if this is the same man who refused to help me in any way that night, he was not one I was going to find any sympathy from today.

Opening the back door, the man pushed me forward as his partner sat in the driver's seat; watching us carefully through the side view mirror attached to his door. Taking a moment to question my sanity; I quickly wondered if these two men really knew where Brighton was—what if he had lied to me? Was this a trick?? Was I really being driven off to only become a murder victim???

Feeling as though I had no choice but to comply, I got into the back seat of the car and watched as the man in the officer's uniform headed towards the passenger side and got in. Speaking in a low tone, I couldn't make out what he said to the driver, but felt the car move forward immediately after the passenger door was slammed closed. Looking around the parking lot that graced the front of the hospital, I searched people's faces as we moved past, wondering if I was ever going to see Brighton, Anna, or Ian ever again.

My captures; sitting quietly in the front seat; never acknowledged me, instead acted as though I wasn't even there. Eyeing the passenger carefully, I knew that he was the more dangerous of the two. Sitting there, dressed as a cop, I briefly wondered if such a uniform could be purchased on the street— were there stores in the area that actually sold officer uniforms to anyone who walked in?? For the most part, I thought not. But then, that would bring up a whole slew of more questions.

Was he a real cop??? If he was, was there any one out there who suspected that he was not a good one??? If he wasn't really a cop, where'd he get the outfit??? Could it be that he really knew someone on the police force that would just hand over a uniform for him to use???

More confused than ever, I kept my concerns to myself; knowing that any questions that I would ask would either just go unanswered or just lead me to more violence before meeting my death. As a shaky sigh escaped my lips, I tried to focus how I was going to get out of this and if they really were taking me to Brighton, how would we escape? How would we make it out alive? I would fight—damn straight I would—but would it be enough to see us through this in one piece??

Not having any answers to the questions swarming around in my head, I looked out my window again and immediately recognized the area we were in. Referred to as the industrial side of Tucson, I knew that we were close to the south side area; just on the outskirts of it. Watching large warehouse-sized buildings pass by separated by massive areas of empty desert, the driver slowed down in speed and I tried to keep count of the buildings that looked to be still in use and those that looked empty and deserted.

Pulling off of the street we were traveling on, we passed by a brightly colored building; the garage doors that were obviously used to allow delivery trucks to back up to in order to unload merchandise colored in different bright colors—blue, red, yellow, green, and orange. Reminding me of a child's box of crayons, I wondered just what was manufactured there but had my thoughts interrupted as the man with the scar looked over his shoulder at me for a second before addressing the driver; the setting sun illuminating behind him, causing me to squint when looking at him.

"Drive to the south side of the building, I want to enter from the backside of it." He instructed, obviously familiar with it. Doing as he was told, the driver slowed down considerably and shifted the direction the vehicle. Pulling up in between two large, solid looking buildings, the outside of each was littered with trash and looked as though neither had been in use for years.

With no windows visible from either building, I wondered quickly what they had been used for as the driver pulled over to the side of one and came to an abrupt stop. The passenger stepped out quickly and moved around the vehicle to open my door.

"Get out." He demanded; coldness and hatred dripped in his voice.

Hesitating a second too long, he suddenly reached in and grabbed a hold of my arm, pulling unforgivingly. Biting my tongue in order to avoid crying out in pain, tears immediately stung my eyes as I quickly left the confines of the back seat.

Not letting go of me, the man looked down at the driver and said, "Stay here. Anyone shows up call the cell." Nodding at him, the driver glanced over at me and I could have sworn that his look had a hint of sympathy in it. But before I could be sure, I was being pulled away from the car, towards the rear of one of the buildings.

Reaching a heavy steel door, the man suddenly turned me around and pushed me up against the door; the heat of it searing the thin t-shirt that I was wearing and I could feel it start to burn my bare skin underneath. Cringing against it, I tried to push off of the door, but the man stepped in close, pressing his body against mine.

"Listen up, Hellcat!" His breath stinking with alcohol and the effects of un-cared for teeth, I stared into his black eyes and held my breath; the tears now flowing freely down my face. "I could kill you at any moment. Don't forget that. The only reason you are still alive right now, is because I think I can get more for you alive than dead."

Automatically giving him a questionable look, I opened my mouth to respond but shut it quickly as he gave me a challenging look. Pressing harder against me, he lowered his voice and threatened, "Give me a reason, Red...we can have some real fun if you want..."

Swallowing hard, I tore my eyes from his and looked away from him; my mind screaming as my heart began to pound violently against my chest. Fighting the urge to fight him off, I held fast and waited to see what he was going to do. Backing away from me suddenly, he held his hard grasp on my arm and gave me another look; as if wondering if he should act on his threat now.

Suddenly, he pulled me away from the wall, turning me again so that I was directly in front of him. Twisting my arm behind my back, I couldn't stop crying out in both surprise and pain as he used my bent arm to direct me to the side of the steel door. Looking down, I noticed a square box that housed a small keypad. Entering in a code, a loud '*thunk*' came from somewhere on the other side and the man reached around my body to pull on the thick handle centered on the side of the door. Pulling it open, it took some effort and I knew that it wasn't a door that I would be able to push through easily if Brighton and I tried to escape through it if we got the chance.

Met by darkness on the other side, I was suddenly pushed forward again and as the door swung closed us inside and clicked heavily back into place, I tried to get my eyes to adjust to the lack of light.

"Move!" His breath suddenly in my ear and I stepped forward to put some space in between us. Facing a large, empty room, the stale air engulfed my senses and I could find nothing familiar in the scent. With nothing blocking my way, I moved towards the center of the room when he instructed me again. "See that opening near the back?" Noticing the large square section that looked empty of flooring on the opposite of the room, I nodded as he said, "Good girl. Let's go."

As we neared it, I saw that it opened up to a set of stairs that would lead us to the floor above and as a soft light emanated from the area, I didn't have to hear the soft muttering of voices to know that we were not alone in the deserted warehouse. Someone was up there—and the change in tone immediately told me that there it was more than just one person. My heart speeding up again quickly as I reached the bottom of the stairs, I started up them but was pulled to a stop. My arm suddenly free from his grasp, I grabbed onto the railing in order to steady myself.

Then, hearing an audible click, I looked quickly over my shoulder and was suddenly face to face with the barrel of a gun. My breath catching in my throat, I turned to face the stairs again and prayed that he hadn't just decided to kill me anyways. Closing my eyes tightly, Brighton's face once again swept across my mind as hot tears continued down my cheeks.

"Here we go..." I heard the man mutter and knew that he was talking more to himself than to me. Opening my drenched eyes, I looked up and forced my feet to move. As we moved slowly up the stairs, the light coming from the top floor crept in around me. And as I reached the very top, I came into full view of who the soft voices belonged to and came to an abrupt halt—my mind reeling in confusion as one of them looked up, recognized me immediately, and gave me a laugh that was more than just a little familiar.

Chapter Thirty-Four

"Well, well, well...if it isn't my favorite employee...."

"*Lucky???*"

Giving him a blank stare, I was barely able to whisper his name as the man with the scar pushed me further into the softly lit room. Then, shaking my head in disbelief, I knew that I had to be in some twisted, demented nightmare and I closed my eyes; willing myself to wake up.

"Well, isn't this a nice surprise."

Opening my eyes again, I stared into the amused face of Lucky Serifino...the man who I'd been employed by for over seven years. This man...who not only knew so much about me, but my *daughter* as well...I had confided in, laughed with, hell, I'd even cried with when things in my life were not going as smoothly as I'd hoped. I couldn't believe that this man...my *friend*...was somehow involved in the kidnapping of my daughter.

No—it had be some kind of mistake!

Turning to the man who still held a tight grip on my forearm, my boss ignored the ludicrous look on my face and addressed him; his voice changing quickly from pleasant and sweet to angry and threatening in less than a second. "Just what do you think you are doing??"

Harding his grip on my arm once again, I winced and gave him a hard look; knowing that even if I had the opportunity to run, I wouldn't. My feet were glued to the floor—I wasn't going anywhere until I found out just what the hell was going on and I was NOT walking out of here without my daughter.

"I thought you'd be interested in a deal." My kidnapper said; his voice unwavering.

"A deal??" Lucky answered him and gave him a sideways glance. "And just what, pray tell, do you have to deal with?"

Pushing me forward, the man replied with conviction, "The brat's mother".

Smiling, Lucky looked down for a minute and then took a few steps towards us, looking at me the whole time as he said, "And what makes you think I want her now??"

Suddenly, the man loosened my grip and I stole a glance at him over my shoulder and barely recognized a look of confusion as it swept over his face. Replaced immediately with a tight smile, he said, "You're a business man. I figured you'd want to sell the whole package instead just one piece of it. Get a lot more money that way. Which means they're both worth a lot more money than what I've been paid."

Sell?? Sell what package???

My mind reeling, I narrowed my eyes at Lucky, already questioning what my mind was trying to wrap itself around.

Sell...as if sell *Brighton*??

Was Lucky trying to sell my daughter???

Wait—he said 'package'...does that mean selling Brighton and I together??? Whoa—!!!

Opening my mouth to say something, I quickly shut it as two men from the other side of the room suddenly came to life. Looking down as they smoothly crossed the room in our direction; I saw movement as the fingers on Lucky's left hand shifted slightly. Looking up at my boss quickly, his eyes were focused on my kidnapper's eyes and a sinking feeling settled into my stomach as if knowing that something bad was about to happen. I slowly moved my arm until it was completely out of his grasp; surprised that he either didn't notice it or didn't care.

Stepping slowly to the side, no one noticed my movement and I wondered briefly if I was actually going to be able to flee the confines of the large room. Then, remembering Brighton and the fact that I had no idea where she was right at that moment; I suddenly felt even more trapped. I was not about to do anything that would jeopardize finding my daughter...but if this single moment was going to be my only chance to escape, where would I go?? Which direction would lead me to her....and then, a way out of here???

Slowly, I scanned my surroundings as I did my best to tune out the argument that was quickly rising between the men in the room. Nearly empty—save a couple of worn looking desks, some broken down office chairs, and a couple of rusty-looking metal cabinets that had been pushed off to one side of the large room— there didn't seem to be anything major obstructing me if I chose to run. Knowing that the staircase behind me led to the bottom floor, I searched the opposite of the room for some indication that there were other floors or rooms that could possibly be where Brighton was being held captive.

Noticing another set of steel stairs in the corner farthest from me, I quickly wondered where it led and took a small step in that direction. Hearing the voices around me rise, I kept my eyes on the stairs opposite my position and said a little prayer that I wouldn't draw any attention to myself as I took yet another baby step.

Suddenly, a sonic boom flooded the room and as the vibration of it flowed under my feet and rose through my body, I automatically dropped to my knees as a scream escaped my mouth. Covering my head with my arms, my heart pounded violently within my chest as my ears suddenly throbbed to the point that tears filled my eyes.

Then, feeling hands pulling on my arms, I was forcefully raised to my feet and I turned only to find myself face-to-face with Lucky. Giving me a stare hard enough to freeze the blood in my veins, his grip tightened on my upper arm and I cried out in pain as he dragged me across the room. Forcing myself to look back, I barely registered the body of my original capture and the quickly spreading halo of red that was growing around his head as he lay motionless on the floor. Uttering a whimper at the sight, I had no time to concentrate on him or the two men that were now lifting his dead body to move it as Lucky pulled on my arm again and forced my attention to the direction I was being yanked in.

"He's got a partner—find him and take care of it!!" Lucky shouted his instructions over his shoulder as he continued to drag me across the floor.

Heading towards the staircase that had caught my attention only moments before, I suddenly decided that I didn't want to know what was up there. Trying to drag my feet and pull against Lucky's unbelievably strong grip, I felt my mind unravel as I started to scream at him.

"WHERE IS BRIGHTON?!" Feeling him pull even harder on my arm, I continued to fight, wanting nothing more than to scratch his dull gray eyes out of their sockets. "WHERE IS SHE?! WHAT HAVE YOU DONE WITH HER??!!"

"Shut the hell up, Amanda!!" Was his only reply and as we reached the bottom of the staircase, he pushed me towards it. Falling against the side of it, the metal banister violently met my stomach and the upper half of my body immediately lurched forward as pain spread through my body like a hot flame.

The wind knocked out of me, I couldn't speak and as Lucky grabbed the back of my red hair to pull me backwards, I did the only thing I could think of at that moment—I drove my elbow into his midsection as hard as I could. Hearing him grunt, his hold on my hair was suddenly released and I forced my feet to move. Willing myself to climb up them, I used my hands to climb as my body screamed at me to stop, if nothing else but to allow the pain running through every muscle in it to subside.

Hearing Lucky yell my name in anger, I knew that it wouldn't be long before he caught up to me, but I kept going. The soft soles of my thin shoes thumped hard against the cold metal of the stairs as I ran up them as fast as I could; now not caring what I found when I reached the top. I was more scared of what Lucky and his henchmen would do to me if he caught me.

Reaching the top, my legs took over and I ran as fast as I could towards the middle of the room as my eyes frantically searched for where to go next. Then, coming to an abrupt stop, it took my mind a second to realize what I was seeing as my mouth went dry and my pounding heart came to a sudden stop.

Standing near the back of the room, next to a row of expensive looking computer equipment was my daughter. Her wide, terrified eyes holding mine, she gasped as the man standing behind her pulled back on her head and placed the blade of a knife against her small throat.

"*Brighton...*" I managed to whisper as hot tears flowed down my face and terror squeezed my heart. Holding my hands out in a submissive manner, I tried to swallow but my mouth was too dry and my voice cracked as I tried to reason with the thick looking man, "Please...*please*...don't...hurt her..."

Eyeing me carefully, the man smiled for a second and a chill ran down my spine as he pressed the shiny blade against Brighton's throat, causing her to whimper. Her hands on either side of her small body, she looked as though she was trying to steady herself and I knew that if she flinched in any way, she would be cut.

Taking a jagged breath, I took a step backwards, hoping that the man would see that I was done running and remove the deadly weapon from my daughter's throat. Hearing movement behind me, I tore my eyes away from her face and faced my employer once again.

"Let her go, Lucky!" Trying to get myself under control so that I could think, I pleaded with him as best I could. "She's just a little girl...let her go..."

Looking past me, Lucky ignored my demands and addressed the man holding Brighton. "Kill the feed and take the girl to the holding room." Staring back at me, Lucky placed both hands on his hips and, getting his breathing back under control, asked, "You have no idea what a precarious situation you have found yourself in, do you, Amanda??"

Trying to swallow, I forced myself to look back at the man who still had a strong hold on my daughter. Meeting her green, tear-filled eyes, I had to fight the urge to run to and wrap my arms around her; wanting to protect her. Staring back at me, she looked lost and confused. Then, she was suddenly being pulled as the man did as he had been told. Pushing her towards one side of the room, I noticed a closed door. Assuming that it had to open up to some type of office or something, I watched in terror as he pushed the door inward and forced her to enter the room, following her inside before closing the door behind them; shutting them both off from view.

And as suddenly it had been that I had found her—she was gone again— with the man who had just seconds ago held a knife to her throat.

Suffocating the sobs that were quickly building, I turned back to Lucky and hatred filled my eyes and hardened my jaw. "You bastard! Whatever it is you're into, Lucky...it has nothing to do with Brighton. Let her go!!"

"You see, that's where your wrong, my dear."

Cringing at the sweet sound of his voice, I suddenly wondered how I could have missed this...how is it that I worked with this man for so long and not be able to tell that deep down, he was really a psychopath?? How could I have allowed him insight into my life—my *daughter's* life—and not know what he really was??? What the hell kind of mother am I to put us into this situation???

Trying hard to push past the self-loathing that I suddenly found myself drowning in, I glared at Lucky as he continued talking. "You see, Amanda, business is business and when something threatens your business—well, steps have to be taken to ensure that it survives."

Shaking my head at him, I opened my mouth to question him but he cut me off quickly with a wave of his hand as he continued pacing the space in between the two of us. "You stumbled upon something more than just two idiots trying to get rid of a mistake. And this, threatened my business. As such, I am now protecting my business."

Sounding like he was trying to convince himself of this more than me, I kept my mouth closed and eyed him carefully, wondering just what the hell was going to come out of his mouth next as his eyes left mine and he concentrated on the movement of his feet.

"I have always been an entrepreneur of sorts, Amanda. From the bars to the clubs, to overseeing imports and exports...I am a self-made man. And I will not allow anyone to threaten what I have taken such care in creating."

Suddenly stopping mid-step, Lucky regarded me with a hard stare and I took a step backwards; feeling the tension between us build uncontrollably. Allowing him to continue, I pressed my dry lips together as my mind tried to concoct some type of an escape plan.

"Your daughter is a beautiful child, Amanda, as I'm sure you are aware. And there are people in this world that will pay for something so beautiful."

A sickening feeling spreading through me quickly, I shook my head in disbelief at him as I finally spoke. "You're planning on selling my daughter? You're going to sell Brighton...Lucky, what kind of sick bastard are you?!"

Smiling briefly at me, neither my tone of voice nor my words had any effect on the man as he said, "One who enjoys the finer things in life...and that, my lovely Amanda, requires money. And there is a lot to be earned in this type of business. Your beautiful child will earn much more than what I've seen in the past."

With his final statement, my jaw automatically dropped as my mind began swiftly piecing parts of my memory together and, suddenly, everything began to make sense.

The bloodied, blond-haired female in the trunk...

The destruction of my apartment...

The death of Samantha; or whatever the hell her real name was...

Matt's murder...

And finally...the kidnapping of Brighton and the attack on Anna and her parents...

It was all connected and as I continued to stand there, my body went numb and I was glued to the floor beneath my feet. Searching the room around me for nothing in particular, my eyes finally came to rest on Lucky's face and he nodded; as if knowing that I had finally figured everything out for myself.

"You murdered Sam...and Matt. How many more, Lucky??? How many more murders have you committed???"

Holding his hands up in defense, Lucky gave me an awestruck look when he said, "I didn't kill anyone, Amanda! Oh no, my hands are clean!!"

Scoffing at him, I accused, "You had them killed, then!!" before asking, "Why??"

"Well, because they threatened my business!" Exclaiming this matter-of-factly, a shiver ran down my spine and I knew that Lucky was more than just a little dangerous as he explained, "Your dear, dear friend, Samantha, was in this up to her elbows!" Nodding, he resumed pacing as he continued, "Oh, yes! She was guilty of so much! But when it came to you, Amanda—well, she just couldn't keep her head on straight about that."

"She was trying to warn me, wasn't she??" Suddenly understanding why Samantha was in my apartment the night it had been set ablaze, I went on, "She came to my apartment to warn me about you, didn't she, Lucky?" And then, Matt's murder suddenly made sense and I narrowed my eyes at him. "And Matt...he tried to warn me too, but I didn't pay any attention to it."

Nodding again at me, Lucky took a step in my direction as he said, "You see, having good people is the foundation for any good business. And those two helped me build this business from the ground up. They were involved more than you will ever know. But good things do come to an end. At some point, your assets become liabilities. And if there is anything that I have learning about good business, it is that liabilities have to be flushed out."

Then, taking another step towards me, Lucky gave me a threatening smile as he added, "They have to be distinguished, Amanda, and I'm sorry to say that this is just what you've become...a liability."

Chapter Thirty-Five

"I lost the feed!!!"

"What?!" Practically running across the room, Ian reached the computer technician in a matter of seconds. "What do you mean, 'you lost the feed', what—you mean...you lost the site??"

Suddenly nervous, the computer technician swallowed hard as his thin fingers maneuvered around the website that was now blank; save a small blurb explaining that the site's URL was no longer accessible. "I...uhhh...I don't know, Sir. It must have been deactivated." His face white as pure snow, he glanced up at Ian as the detective peered at the computer screen from over his shoulder. Trying to remain calm, he added in a small voice, "If whoever is running the site shut it down, I can't access it."

"Shit!!!" Clearly frustrated, Ian ran a hand through his hair and stood up straight. "Is there anything you can tell me about where the site was being run from?? A location—or address???"

"Ummm..."

"Got a hit!!!"

From across the room, another technician—this one older and female—stood from her desk that faced a bare wall and turned around, searching the room for someone of authority. Leaving the nervous kid, Ian barely registered a sigh of relief coming from the technician as he immediately crossed the room again. "What'd ya got?!"

Unable to hide a smile full of pride, the short haired woman spoke proudly as she answered, "I've got a general location."

Flabbergasted, Ian exclaimed, "A 'general location'?? That's it???"

Scoffing at him, the woman was not intimated by Ian in the least, and she retorted, "Well, it's better than nothing, Detective! I can give you the general location of where the site was being operated from...within a five-mile radius, mind you. And you're lucky I got it—being that the site was just shut down and all."

"Give it to me", Ian demanded as he pulled a small notebook out of the back pocket of his blue jeans and grabbed a pen off of the woman's neatly laid out desk.

"Here." Holding a computer printout in her hand, she shoved it at him and turned to sit down again, irritated with the man for not offering a word of thanks. Sighing, Ian recognized her dismissal of him as she turned her focus back to her computer screen and tried to sound thankful. "Good work, really—I mean it, thank you."

Watching her shrug her shoulders, the woman refused to turn around and face him. Taking the hint, Ian crossed the room again and before heading out of the large room, stopped to thank the other young technician for his help as well, who flushed crimson without speaking at Ian's sudden change in attitude. Reminding himself that he wouldn't have any type of lead on Brighton's whereabouts if these two techies hadn't known what they were doing, he made a mental promise to be a bit kinder to the people working in this department in the future.

Heading back down to the squad room, Ian searched the mass of people moving quickly around the floor for Detective Gonzalez. Not seeing her anywhere, he headed towards Captain Leary's office and found it empty. Turning, he moved towards his desk to grab his keys and weapon but stopped when running into another fellow detective who used to work alongside Gonzalez.

"Hey—you seen Gonzalez??" Ian asked, trying to stow the rushed feeling that was building in his veins for a minute. Seeing the large man shake his head, he requested that he give her a message as he grabbed a blank sheet of paper from his notebook and wrote down the information he had received from the techie. "If you see her, give her this. We've got a lead..."

"What's the lead??" Suddenly anxious, the detective had been working alongside everyone else looking for Brighton Pearson. Reading the note for Gonzalez, he then offered, "I'll gather the troops; we can cover more ground that way."

"Thanks, man. I'm heading that way now; call my cell when you get a team together."

Alarm quickly spread across the man's face. "Wait—you going alone?? Don't you think you outta wait til—?"

Cutting him off, Ian replied in haste as he armed his person and grabbed the truck keys from the top drawer of his desk. "I'm not waiting. And seeing as how I am not assigned to a partner right now, I'm not waiting for Cap to find someone. We've got five miles to cover—and that's hoping that they haven't moved Brighton...the site shut down as of seven minutes ago."

Nodding as if knowing that arguing with him wasn't going to get him anywhere, the detective said, "The team will be about ten minutes behind you. We've got some people on standby", as Ian retreated from his desk and started towards the stairs.

"Just get there quick, try to find Gonzalez, and call me when you're close."

Hollering the request over his shoulder, Ian then sprinted down the stairs, confident that the detective will do as he said and be about ten minutes behind him. Putting his cell to his ear, he tried Detective Gonzalez's cell but got her voice mail. Leaving her a quick message, he rattled the information she would need to meet him and hung up just as he reached the first floor and jogged across it to exit the building and get to his truck; parked out on the street instead of the underground garage. Moments later, he was heading south on the Interstate, praying that the area he was heading towards proved to be more than just a dead end.

Approaching the south side of Tucson, Ian's cell phone rang and he immediately put it to his ear; assuming it was Gonzalez returning his call. "Hey, Gonzalez, where the hell are you??"

The voice on the other end, clearly shaken, hesitated a second before asking, "Detective Sampson?? Ian???"

Preparing to exit the busy freeway, Ian quickly pulled the phone away from his ear to look at the caller ID; then, returning it immediately to his hear and said, "Anna?? Sorry—was expecting another call—what's wrong??"

Fearing that she was about to tell him that her father had passed away or something, Ian mentally prepared himself to talk her through it, as quickly as he could; not wanting to prolong the search for Brighton any longer than needed.

"It's Amanda, Ian...she's not here..."

Anna's voice came over the line in broken sobs and Ian pulled the truck into a small convenience store parking lot as soon as he cleared the three lanes of traffic that were heading down the frontage road alongside him. He ignored the blare of a horn coming from an angry driver that he had cut off in the process and said, "What do you mean? Amanda's not in her room? She get moved or something??"

"No! She's gone!! Her room is empty and no one seems to know where she is!"

"Ok, ok, calm down, Anna. She's got to be there somewhere."

His instincts kicking in, Ian knew full well that something was wrong. According to the doctor he had spoken with earlier, Amanda wasn't scheduled for any further testing or to be moved to any other room or floor of the hospital. Trying to push past the growing sense of dread building in the pit of his stomach, Ian opted to offer some suggestions of just where she could be. "Did you check her bathroom? Or the cafeteria? She may have woken up and decided to get something to eat or something. The hospital looked pretty busy when I was there earlier."

"Yeah, but Ian, she was hooked up to an IV...when I went to look in on her, it was lying on the floor near the bed. And the cop that is here—he said that the room was empty when he got here!

But one of the nurses—I don't know who—she said that there was another cop here earlier who was in the room, talking to Amanda…"

"Slow down, Anna, slow down!" Taking a breath, Ian tried to sort out everything that Anna was frantically saying over the phone. "There was a cop in the room, talking to Amanda?? When was this???" Noting the protocol, Ian knew that anyone stationed outside a medical room was not to engage whomever it was they were there to offer protection for. Their job was to remain outside the room; watching and waiting for anything out of the ordinary.

Getting no response, Ian's voice rose an octave as he demanded, "Anna! When was this?!"

"I…I don't know…" Hearing her confusion mix in with the obvious fear she was dealing with, Anna finally broke down; unable to say anything more.

"Anna, go back down to where your mom and dad are. Stay there. I'll be there as soon as I can. Put the officer that's with you on the line."

"Detective Sampson?" A young man's voice came over the line and he introduced himself quickly as if knowing that time was of the essence. "Officer Dakota here."

"Escort Ms. Yearling back down to the second floor. Her parents are both there—as patients. Do not leave the three of them until further notice. And close of the room that Ms. Pearson was in; it may be a crime scene. Call it in and get someone down there to check it out. Understand??"

"Yessir."

Hearing the phone being passed back to Anna, Ian tried to keep his voice calm as he spoke to her one more time. "I will find Amanda. You stay there, with your parents. The officer is going to stay with the three of you and under no circumstances are you to leave. If you hear anything from Amanda, call me immediately. I am working on something here that can't wait and I'll meet you there as soon as I can."

"They came and got her, didn't they?? Those men who...took Brighton...they came for her...didn't they??" Anna sobbed into the phone, causing Ian to grip the phone even tighter as his fear and anger mixed together and boiled though his veins.

Unwilling to admit that Anna's suspicions were probably right; Ian forced himself to ignore her questions and he reiterated his instructions instead. Hanging up seconds later, he gripped the steering wheel until his knuckles burned white and clenched his teeth.

Refusing to entertain any thoughts that included the death of either Amanda or Brighton, Ian instead focused on the five-mile radius that marked the possible points of where the website, *Silent Auction*, could have been run from. Yanking open the glove box, Ian grabbed a map of the city out of it and unfolded it; using the steering wheel to lay it on top of. Searching the area on the map gave him more of a sense of direction as the coordinates discovered by the Techies on the third floor sectioned out a small industrial area famous for large warehouse type buildings—some still in use, others he knew to be empty and vacant.

Narrowing it down, his prior experience as a beat cop reminded him which buildings were likely to still be in use, either by local grocery outlets or some of the big box stores around town. Closing his eyes, he pictured the area; noting the fact that there used to be at least a few empty buildings centered near the rear of the area; the majority of them famous for squatters, drug deals, and the occasional prostitution ring.

Assuming that an operation such as Silent Auction would be held in one of the buildings that caused no one to take a second look at, he swiftly recalled one or two structures that over the years was known to be free from criminal activity...probably due to the look of the them; instead of run down and falling apart, they were cared for; probably on the chance that they could be either sold or put to use at some point. Deciding to start there, Ian crudely folded the map back up, tossed it in the passenger's seat and pulled out of the parking lot.

Minutes later, he found himself driving in circles, from one occupied building to another. Then, coming to the end of one of them, he discovered another two-lane road that led him in the opposite direction. Frustrated, he hesitated for a second and then headed down it; hoping it would lead him in the right direction.

Not more than a half mile down this new path, Ian came face-to-face with two large buildings; neither looking occupied as the large parking areas that surrounded the both of them were completely empty, save some trash that was being gently tossed around by the warm breeze that moved in between the buildings. Looking around for some sign that he was in the right place, he slowed the truck down to a crawl and cautiously drew closer to the one to the left of his position.

Suddenly, a feeling of dread spread through Ian's body and he quickly turned the truck around to head back to where he'd come from. Considering the facts that both buildings were only surrounded by desert, not clearly visible from any of the other structures in the local area, and the fact that neither *felt* as deserted as they looked to be; he needed a plan of action before he got any closer.

Passing a few overgrown desert trees, Ian pulled off of the paved road, bounced over the curb that ran along the paved road, and headed for a group of them that would help hide the truck. Without any backup yet, he wasn't about to announce his presence to anyone that may be lurking around either building. Coming to a stop, he killed the engine, got out and began arming himself as if heading off to battle. Holstering his assigned weapon, he added a small, sheathed blade to the inside of his right hiking boot, tucked a smaller pistol into the back of his jeans and pulled his t-shirt over it, and hung his badge on a sturdy chain and placed it around his neck. If his instincts were right on about the location, he was not going to waste time digging his credentials out of his jeans to prove his status. Wearing them out, in front of his person, cut that procedure out of the equation and often saved a lot of time.

Moving as quietly as he could as the Arizona sun slowly dipped towards the west, Ian crossed the desert floor and reached the building on the left in record time. Pressed up against the west corner of the building, Ian searched the connecting walls that met the roof; looking for cameras or any other type of digital recording system that would be relaying his current location to anyone inside watching—if there was anyone inside, that is.

Seeing none, he quickly questioned if he was in the right place. Believing that if Silent Auction was being run out of this building, there would be some kind of surveillance set up to warn the people involved of possible intruders or the authorities; Ian decided to case the other building instead but stopped short when hearing the familiar sound of rubber on pavement.

Another vehicle was approaching and Ian's heart sped up in anticipation.

Peering around the corner that was offering him coverage, he listened as the squeal of tires marked the location of the incoming vehicle. Hearing it close in, Ian stepped back a bit; glancing around the corner every second or so.

Then, the car came into view and Ian's heart stopped; recognizing it immediately. As confusion set in, he pushed himself away from his hiding spot and stepped around the corner of the building, not thinking that being this out in the open placed a target on his forehead.

Watching the driver quickly step out of his dirt brown colored sedan, Ian wasn't noticed until he had nearly reached the front end of it and when the driver finally looked up and realized that he was no longer alone; he met Ian's icy stare and froze in his place.

And as Ian opened his mouth to question the man's sudden presence here, he never saw Captain Leary's nervous fingers wrap themselves around the handle of the pistol that was hidden from view under the large, expensively-tailored, suit jacket he was wearing.

Chapter Thirty-Six

"*Shit*, Sampson! You startled me!!" Captain Leary's dark eyes quickly flickered between Ian and the building to the side of them and Ian could have sworn he saw a wave of nervousness flutter beneath the man's thin eyelashes. "You the only one on scene??"

Thinking, Ian slowly returned his weapon to its holster and gritted his teeth. Eyeing his supervisor for a second, he finally answered, "Yea. I've been trying to reach Detective Gonzalez", then asked, "What're you doing here, Cap?"

"Well, I got the message that someone in the tech department narrowed down the possible location of where the website that has Brighton Pearson's picture advertised...and us being short on men...figured I'd come out and help with the search..."

Nodding, Ian chose his words carefully, unwilling to fully admit that his Captain was involved in this in any way, but also unwilling to forgo any possibilities at this point. "Task unit on its way?" he asked, trying to fish out as much information about Captain Leary's presence without calling question to it.

Age showing in his face, the Captain stared back at Ian before nodding. "Yes...I'm surprised I beat them out here." Then, moving out from behind the driver's side door, he closed it shut as quietly as possible and said, "You take a look around yet?"

"No, just found this place myself."

"Well, then, let's find a way in."

"Sure." Still uncertain of his Captain, Ian allowed the man to lead, watching his every move carefully. And when he suggested that they start with the building closest to them, Ian said nothing.

Coming to the only door on the side facing them, the Captain noted the keypad fixed to the metal door and whistled softly.

"Think this place is vacant, Detective?"

"Looks to be, Sir." Then, explaining as little as possible, Ian added, "I came from the south side of the building, there doesn't seem to be any other entrances save this one. But there's fresh tire marks...there", pointing to one the side of the structure, Ian brought the Captain's attention around as he moved towards the tracks and knelt down to examine the impressions closely and continued, "someone's been here recently."

"Hmmm...well, let's have a look around the other side—"

Suddenly, the key pad on the door came to life and both Ian and the Captain moved quickly and aligned themselves directly behind the huge steel door as a loud buzzing sound went off and it was slowly pushed forward from the inside. In doing so, Ian became the lead man as Captain Leary stood behind him; gun at the ready.

His own weapon set for action, Ian eyed the door carefully, waiting for the right moment to strike. The door pushed open wide, a thick clicking sound came from near the bottom of the door and Ian knew that whoever was coming through it had just pushed down on a door stop that had to be attached on the inner, bottom corner of it. Counting the seconds as they swiftly passed, Ian's heart thumped heavily in his chest and his body tensed.

A tall, burly-looking man came suddenly into view; the right side of his body first, followed by the rest of him as he moved away from the opened door. Then, obviously seeing Captain Leary's car, the man froze, his heavy boots softly coming to a dead stop on the concrete that graced the front of the building and met the parking lot.

Watching the man's head turn slowly to the right, Ian reacted immediately; grabbing a strong hold on his arm using his right hand and pulled him around forcefully until the front of his body cracked against the concrete wall of the building. Hearing a sickening thud as the man's forehead forcefully met the hard wall, Ian watched his body crumble to the ground. Never knowing what hit him, the man's eyes fluttered for a brief second, then closed all together and Ian immediately turned the man onto his stomach, cuffing his hands behind his back. If they were in the right place, Ian wasn't about to leave the unconscious man unrestricted.

Then, searching the guy, Ian discovered a concealed Beretta hidden beneath the man's coat jacket and handed it over to Captain Leary, who swiftly stowed it behind the waist band of his pants. Continuing his search for a few more seconds, Ian was satisfied that there were no other weapons on the guy and stood up again. Glaring down at the man, he fought the urge to give him a good kick in the ribs but stopped when hearing the Captain's loud whisper.

"Sampson!"

As if knowing what his detective was considering, Captain Leary pulled on Ian's forearm as he moved around to the opened door. Gun held out in front of his person, the Captain took over the lead again and Ian forced himself to follow; leaving the unconscious man to himself for the time being; praying he'd be back the moment the man came to so he could finish him off.

Entering the building, Ian took a swift moment to allow the heavy steel door to close almost completely. Using the door stop, he adjusted it so that it was opened just a fraction of a hair; that way Gonzalez and the rest of the team would be able to access the building upon arrival. In doing so, the fading Arizona sun was cut off and both men found themselves in near darkness. Allowing time for their eyes to adjust, the pair stood still and tried to take in what they could of their new surroundings.

"There...stairs..." Captain Leary's voice dropped to a whisper as he pointed out a metal looking staircase that led to the upper floor and Ian nodded in response after seeing that no one else appeared to be on this floor. Moving swiftly through the dark, Ian followed the Captain, carefully avoiding the scattered debris of broken office furniture, pieces of metal, and anything else he could see that would alert anyone else in the building if it were kicked aside or stepped on.

Reaching the bottom of the stairs, the Captain stopped and peered up them, noting a dim light coming from somewhere above.

Motioning to Ian, he allowed the detective to take the lead and as Ian moved around him with his finger on the trigger of his pistol; any suspicions that his Captain was somehow involved in this had left his mind.

Voices being heard from up above, Ian's blood pulsed quickly through his veins as he heard one coming from a female. Unsure if it was Amanda's voice or not; the tone was much too low to know for sure; he started up the stairs, forcing himself to move as quietly as possible.

Then, for some reason, Ian suddenly stopped halfway up the staircase and turned to look behind him and found himself utterly alone. Heart beating even faster, his eyes searched for Captain Leary through the darkness that surrounded the bottom of the stairs.

"Cap!?"

Barely audible, his whisper swept through the air and was gone without any response from his captain in return. His arms automatically bent at the elbows as he held his weapon close to the side of his face; its muzzle pointed upward, towards the ceiling. Not wanting to risk being heard by whoever was still talking in muffled tones on the floor above him, he clamped his mouth shut and headed back down the stairs as quietly as he could.

Reaching the bottom, he squinted in order to see back through the blackness that covered the room ahead of him. Sensing that someone was there, his heart sped up and he held his breath, standing as still as possible and the seconds clicked past.

Suddenly hearing movement, Ian placed his finger over the trigger, ready for anything, but removed it quickly as Captain Leary finally came into view. Breathing on the heavy side, he approached Ian and whispered, "Thought I heard something back there, but it was nothing. You ready??"

Eyeing the man carefully, Ian simply nodded and took a step to the side; motioning for the captain to take the lead this time. Feeling that he'd rather have him up in front of him, Ian's gut kicked in, telling him something about the man was off. But with no real time to address it, the detective chose to keep him in his sights from here on out and hoped that his instincts were having an off day.

Following Captain Leary up the stairs, the two moved silently and as the dim light from the room above slowly draped itself around them; Ian's mind automatically began a mental inventory of what he saw as it came into view.

Opening up into a large room, Ian silently categorized everything from the concrete flooring to the multitude of electrical sockets sporadically positioned on each wall. Running along the ceiling were long, tubular light fixtures; some offering a hazy, dim light while others were burnt out; their only coloring being the black scorch marks that ran the length of their glass casings.

Reaching the very top of the stairs, Captain Leary stopped as both men focused on the source of the muffled voices—three men; located at the opposite side of the room, near a makeshift desk and worn-looking office chair. Searching the room for the female voice he knew he had heard, Ian found no one else and immediately questioned whether or not he had imagined it or if the woman belonging to the voice had been stashed somewhere during the time he had spent looking for Captain Leary on the bottom floor.

An expensive looking computer system sat upon the desk and Ian's mind flicked back to the image of Brighton that the tech had discovered back at the station. Anger building, it was only further fueled as his eyes settled on a tripod and camera setup just sectioned off to one side of the desk.

"Police! Nobody move!!!"

Taking full lead, Captain Leary's voice boomed through the nearly empty room and Ian took his stance to the right side of his mentor and friend as the small group of men before them turned casually to face their visitors.

It was then that Ian saw that his first impressions of Lucky Serifino were right on, as the man himself stepped out into the open. Smiling, as if greeting old friends, Lucky stepped around the two taller men that he had been conversing with and held out his hands in welcome.

"Well, if it isn't my favorite detective", eyeing Ian carefully, Lucky's eyes then shifted to the captain as he added, "oh...and you've brought a friend."

"Cut the shit, Serifino, where's Brighton Pearson?" Ian's voice rose in anger as he targeted the bar owner's face with his weapon, ready to blow a hole in it at a moment's notice.

"Who??" Taking a steady step forward, Lucky's smile did not falter, but instead grew in size. "Brighton...who??"

"You know exactly who I'm talking about. Amanda Pearson's nine year old daughter, Brighton. We tracked the Internet link you set up to this location. Where is she?!" Demanding answers, Ian held a tight grip on his service weapon at the same time he mentally tried to calm his nerves. Taking Serifino's life would be more than just a little satisfying, but if he did...Brighton would be lost, and that wasn't something Ian was willing to risk.

Nodding as if suddenly coming to an understanding, Lucky casually looked down and said, "Ahhhh...Amanda....my favorite dancer." Then, peering up to steal a glance at the detective, he knew that he was getting the reaction he wanted as he continued, "You say her daughter is missing?? How terrible...absolutely terrible..."

Saying nothing in return, Ian's blood pressure rose as his jaw clenched shut. Waiting for an answer, Ian's eyes moved from man to man; watching for some sign of acknowledgement. Neither man moving, Ian knew that both were likely armed and ready to defend themselves and their boss and realized that, technically, he and the captain were outnumbered.

"Well...I know nothing about this missing girl, Detective...*Sampson*, is it??" Cocking his head at Ian, Lucky's smile reappeared on his face. "I am simply here out of interest. This building is in great shape, wouldn't you say?? I am always on the lookout for new business opportunities and this building has great potential. Can't you see it, Detective??"

"What I see in front of me is a perverted little prick who deserves nothing more than a bullet to the brain...and I'd be more than happy to oblige..." Breathing hard, Ian steadied his weapon, wanting nothing more than for Lucky to make a sudden move that would justify shooting him.

"Sampson!"

Hearing his Captain's voice, Ian steeled himself, knowing that if he crossed any type of line here...and Lucky survived...the man would never see the inside of a prison. Ignoring the urge to look over at him, Ian refused to take his eyes off of Lucky and his men and took a step forward.

"Captain Leary...you need to control your man..." Lucky's warning came without a hint of a smile as he took a small step backwards as he locked eyes with Ian. "As you can see, I am unarmed and unless you have proof of some criminal activity, I believe it is time that you left my building."

"Your building?? I thought you were here on the pretense of possibly buying this building." Trying to catch Lucky up in a lie that would lead to the whereabouts of Brighton and Amanda—Ian just knew that the bar owner was in this up to his elbows and that Amanda was here somewhere as well—his voice steadied as his anger finally settled in his stomach.

Running his tongue over his teeth, Lucky stole a glance at Captain Leary before stating, "Alright, gentlemen, I've had about enough of this."

And at that second, the urge to turn and look at his captain overpowered him and Ian tore his focus from the three men in front of him to the one man he trusted; who had at some unknown point left Ian's left side.

"Lower your weapon, Detective." Pointing his service revolver at Ian, Captain Leary knew he could no longer hide the truth from the man. "Drop it and kick it over", he instructed, unwavering or feeling guilty for anything that he had done.

Turning to face the man whom he had trusted for years with not only his advice and judgment, but with his *life* on more than one occasion, Ian gave the man a look that could kill as the questions surrounding this case suddenly all made sense—Captain Leary was the piece of the puzzle that Detective Gonzalez and he had wondered about when it came to the possibility that there was someone on the inside, feeding information to whomever was behind the murders and attempted murder of Amanda Pearson...not to mention the kidnapping of Brighton Pearson.

"It was you all along, wasn't it??" Turning to face the man, Ian reluctantly aimed his weapon at his Captain. "We thought that there had to be someone on the inside, helping whoever it was that shot Amanda to find her. You were the one offering information to Serifino...how long, Captain?? How long have you been working for *him*???" Saying nothing in return, Captain Leary glanced quickly at Lucky before staring back at Ian as his accusations continued.

"Gonzalez and I couldn't figure out how anyone could have known that Amanda had survived her attack in such a small amount of time. Being Captain, you had all the details on her, her daughter, and where we were in our investigation. And *you* gave it to *them*." Pausing in order to let it all sink in even further, Ian clenched his jaw tightly, feeling the pain reach his temples as he then asked, "How much did you get, Captain?? How much did Serifino pay you to turn on your own??"

"Enough to retire." Stating this without hesitation, Captain Leary gave his detective a hard stare. "Now drop your *fucking* weapon, Sampson...I don't want to have to shoot you."

Knowing he was outnumbered...and probably outgunned, even though the three men behind him had yet to draw any type of weapon...Ian pushed the thoughts aside and made the decision to act in a matter of seconds.

Taking full aim at Captain Leary, Ian's body moved as his trigger finger came alive. The vibration from it running through his fingers and up from his hand, he was so bent on killing the man that his mind never registered the return fire, coming from the Captain's own weapon... not until his body hit the floor underneath him and a hot flash of pain seared through his chest, that is.

The sound of it all threatening to make his head explode, Ian's ears rang as his mind's next few conscious seconds flew by. His brown eyes faltering behind fluttering lashes, the coldness of the floor swept through his body and he was suddenly aware of his own death approaching. Thinking lastly of Amanda and Brighton, Ian's breath labored as he heard one final statement from Lucky Serifino.

"Get the girl and the kid...let's be done with it—"

And then, as Captain Leary stepped over the man he'd once proclaimed as his top detective and friend, Ian heard her voice fill the room with a loud, but muffled scream that rattled his final moments of consciousness. Wanting to move, he couldn't, and pain quickly danced across both shoulders until he could no longer force his eyes to remain open and darkness wrapped a cold blanket over his still body.

Chapter Thirty-Seven

The gun pressed against the back of my head, my screams for Ian were cut off in an instant as my mind began to unravel. We were not going to get out of this—I knew that now. But if I was going to die, I was not going to do so without my daughter; Lucky was not going to get his hands on her...make a profit off of my nine-year-old...no way in Hell was that going to happen....just as I knew there was no way in Hell he was going to let her walk out of here safe and unharmed...

And as my tears streamed down my face, I took one final look at Ian's crumbled body and then turned to face the man holding me captive in one of the tiny rooms that probably served as an office at some point; unwavering at the sight of his weapon now pointed at my face.

"Give me my daughter." Trying to sound demanding, I tried to stop my lips from quivering and wasn't surprised to hear him laugh at me as I allowed my ever-building anger to further fuel my strength. Yes, I was scared—terrified, really—but I had to bite down on the terror I was feeling; if I showed it, I had a feeling that I would be in for far more than just the ending of my life.

"And what are you going to do if I don't??"

Full of arrogance, he used his free hand to grab a tight hold on the back of my head and pull me closer to him. Eyeing me, his dark eyes traveled down my front and I resisted the urge to spit in his face, knowing full well that if I did, he would probably kill me before I had the chance to tell Brighton one last time that I loved her.

Recognizing the lusty look he was giving me, I forced myself to take advantage of it. Shifting gears, I took a step towards him and I felt his grip tighten on the back of my head. "I can make it worth your while..."

Glancing at the closed door behind me, I watched as he actually contemplated my sudden offer and ignored my churning stomach as I ran my hands over his thick chest. His mouth turning up in a crooked smile, his light blue eyes met mine and I knew in an instant that I had him and I played the part even further as a new plan began to form in my mind. If I could get him to let his guard down, maybe—just maybe—I could get my hands on his gun. Having never shot one before, I was positive that I could figure it out quickly enough to put a bullet between his eyes. All I needed was the chance...

But that chance never came.

Just as his mouth reached mine, the door to our tiny enclosure opened and my plan came to a screeching halt. Suddenly free from his grasp, my heath throbbed immediately in pain as my heart sank. My proposal interrupted, I knew that my chance at survival had just dwindled down to nothing.

"Bring her out."

Turning to face the intruder, I couldn't help but gasp as recognition hit me like a ton of bricks. Ian's boss—I think he referred to him as his "Captain"—stepped to the side of the threshold to allow me and my captor passage. Being pushed through, I reentered the large room and couldn't help but glance over at Ian's body; his back being the only thing I could really see in this poor lighting.

Searching the room, I caught sight of Brighton as she was being pulled from another small room opposite me and I reacted immediately, my tears falling freely again down my face. Ignoring the men in the room, I ran to her as she pulled free from her own captor and sprinted to my now open arms. Gathering her small body, I held her tightly against me, knowing full well that this was the last time I was going to be able to hold her and felt her shudder against my chest as if she knew the same.

"Shshsh....it's okay, Brighton. Everything's going to be okay..."

Then, as if knowing that I was lying, she pushed away from me to look me in the eye. Unable to voice her thoughts, I read her face clearly and tried to wipe the tears from her green eyes and at the same time tried to take in the full site of her...her, thin, beautiful face...her vibrant, wavy red hair...her tiny frame...

"I love you so much, Brighton...you know that??" Pushing her hair from her face, I gently moved my trembling fingers gently down the sides of her cheeks, remembering instantly the day she was born as her short life flashed before my eyes. Her first smile. Her first birthday. Her first day of school...and all the days in between...I remembered it all as the seconds clicked past. "You are the best thing that ever happened to me..." Choking on my words, I grabbed her again and hugged her tightly again.

"Eeeoonn...?"

The whisper of his name caused me pull back from her slightly; remembering that the location of his body behind me was in clear view of her eyes. "Don't look, baby..." I tried to explain why but cut myself off. How do you explain death to a child—let alone, a *disabled* child?? I didn't know, but I knew that I wasn't going to have the time to figure it out as the understandable clicking sound of a gun being readied to fire broke the remaining silence of the room. Quickly, I stood and used my body to shield Brighton as best I could. Eyeing Lucky with hatred, I took one last chance to save my daughter.

"Let her go, Lucky. You have me...I'm the one you want....she doesn't have anything to do with this..."

"Oh...but she does...she has seen almost as much as you have." Taking a step towards us, he gave me a small, sick smile and my stomach churned, threatening to upheave any contents that may still be swarming around in there from my last meal. "She is a liability—just as you are, Amanda, and as much as I regret doing this, you now know what must be done to those that become a liability."

Anger building before I could stop it, I screamed at him, "BUT SHE'S A CHILD, LUCKY!!! A *CHILD*—!!" Suddenly, and without warning, the man I had recognized as the Captain of the police department sprang into action, as if wanting to get his job done and over with. Crossing the floor in two long, angry strides, he reached around me and grabbed a hold of Brighton's right arm. Screaming at him, Brighton tried to fight him off as I pushed with all my might against him, trying desperately to get him to let go of her.

"LET HER GO!!!" My throat on fire, my voice sounded hoarse and broken as Brighton's own terrified screams vibrated through the building.

Grasping the Captain's arm, I scratched at him as I desperately wedged myself between him and Brighton and heard him cry out in frustration. Coming to his aid, another one of Lucky's men came around the three of us; grabbing Brighton from around her waist as he lifted her into the air. Screaming even louder now, my mind reeled in knowing that if I didn't get her away from him— she was dead—and I would be next.

Balling my fist, I swung as hard as I could and as I connected with the side of the captain's face and his hands flew upward, trying to ward me off. In that second, I was pushed backward and collided with the man who still had Brighton in a bear hug. Out of the corner of my eye, I watched as he fell; landing on his back with her in his arms. Standing as quickly as I could, my next move was aimed at grabbing Brighton but before I could act, I was facing the barrel of a gun—and my world stopped in an instant.

Unable to move, my breath caught in my throat and my eyes flew shut so fast they hurt. The sound of violence shuttered through my body as I heard the gun go off and I jumped backward, unable to stop myself even though I knew there was nothing to save me. I was dead—*wasn't I*???

Still standing, I dared to open my eyes as the room around me flew into chaos. Seeing nobody in front of me, my ears burned from the sound of the gun having been fired and for a second, my body wavered as it threatened to collapse. Confused and unable to hear anything or think, I blinked a few times and took a hesitant breath.

Looking at the empty space in front of me, it took a few seconds for my mind to catch up with what my eyes were seeing.

The man—the *captain*—that had only moments ago aimed his deadly weapon just inches from my nose was gone—and it only took a flash of a second for me to automatically look down to discover why.

Blood pooling around his thick body, realization hit me like a ton a bricks. His gun just an inch from his fingers, I scanned the rest of his body as if in slow motion. Lying on his side, I could only see the side of his face. His left eye and mouth wide open, he looked as though his was in shock. The rest of his body motionless, a circular moon of red spread out from under his upper body and soaking through the expensive looking suit he was wearing. The strong smell of burning sulfur gave way to the realization that he had been shot.

But by who??

Then, my hearing returned and my eyes scanned to the room around me as my head threatened to explode from the noise. Turning slowly, I could see Lucky running towards the room that I had been held in; his remaining men running close on his heels.

"AMANDA!!!"

The sound of my name turning me around again, I gasped in shock at the site of Ian trying to stand; a gun in his right hand. Starting towards him, his angry brown eyes met my confused face and he raised one arm; waving at me as he demanded me to move as the room was suddenly invaded by the cavalry—all dressed in standard police uniforms.

Tearing my focus from Ian, I looked to my right and saw Brighton; standing alone with her hands over her ears. Bent over slightly she was still screaming and my breath caught in my throat as I took off as fast as I could in her direction. Reaching her, I grabbed her up and tucked her head into my shoulder as a wisp of air pulsed past my left ear.

A bullet!

My mind reeling, the gunfight was on before I realized it and, running with her in my arms, I reached one side of the room free of deserted offices. Using the wall to brace myself against, I quickly sank to my knees and sheltered Brighton with my body as the bullets continued firing behind us.

Daringly, I looked over my shoulder and watched as Ian's coworkers swarmed the floor; only to scatter as Lucky and his men fired upon them. Glancing back at Ian, I couldn't believe he was alive and bit down on my lower lip hard; as if trying to wake myself up from a dream. Then, he was being pulled backward on his backside; the female detective that I had met with at the station trying to get his injured body out of the line of fire.

Feeling caught with no place to hide, I returned my focus to Brighton, who had stopped screaming but still had her hands over her small ears; trying to cut out the deafening sounds as they rattled both of our bodies.

Looking back again, I could see that we were winning. Two of Lucky's men lay motionless near the office room that they had been trying to reach. The smell of death and gunpowder filled the room and as the shouts continued from the cops that had come to the rescue; I closed my eyes to them as I focused on trying to keep Brighton calm and used my body to block out the violence.

Suddenly, the back of my head was being pulled backwards and with a startled scream I was forced to let go of Brighton as I was dragged unforgivingly away from her. Then, pulled to my feet, I was turned around roughly and came face-to-face with Lucky, who had somehow managed to escape the gunfire only to reach my hiding spot.

Shrinking back from him, my heart raced against my chest as he turned me around to use me as a shield. Moving towards the center of the room, he positioned his weapon so that the barrel pressed against my right temple.

"FREEZE!!!"

"DROP YOUR WEAPON—"

"SERIFINO!!! DON'T—"

The entourage of uniformed men forming a half circle before us, I choked on my spit as Lucky yanked harder on the back of my head and the pain from my head and neck screamed in protest as it met the sudden heat from my throbbing shoulder.

"Lucky—"

Trying to get his attention, I was cut off quickly as he responded by hissing in my ear before turning his attention to the force in front of him.

"BACK UP!!" He demanded, to which no one moved. "Unless you want me to put a bullet in her head—BACK THE FUCK UP!!!"

Taking a small step forward, I was forced to move my feet. With my hands flailing at my sides, I quickly weighed my options.

I could do nothing—let Lucky try to get out of here using me as a way out...

Or...or I could fight back—and end up dead—either by one of the cops or by Lucky himself...

Not sure which seemed more right; I didn't want Lucky to get out of here and I definitely didn't want to end up dead, especially with my daughter as witness; I bit my lower lip hard as I eyed the men in front of me. Trying to make his way to the front of the group, Ian held one bloodied hand over the wound above his chest as his weak, shallow eyes met mine.

Whimpering at the sight of him, I heard Brighton crying from somewhere behind me and I closed my eyes; thinking of all the things that had happened to us up until this one moment. I had escaped death and even though I had known it before, I didn't realize the power of that knowledge until this very moment. I had been given a second chance—a second chance to do something good with my life; something to not only make my daughter proud of me, but to make me proud of myself as well.

And I'll be DAMNED if I was going to let Lucky kill that chance now!!

Making my decision, I sprang into action as I opened my eyes and gave Ian a hard look. Fisting both hands, I wrapped one around the other and with as much force as I could muster, drove my elbow into Lucky's side. Grunting more in surprise than in pain, Lucky automatically released the back of my hair and bent slightly forward and I took the advantage—wanting nothing more than to kill the man myself.

Raising my hands, I grabbed the back of his head and pushed down on it at the same time I raised my right knee, driving his head down onto it. Feeling his nose crumble immediately, his scream of pain filled the room and as soon as his head came back up, I struck at him as hard as I could; feeling the side of my wrist meet the softest part of his neck. Falling backward, he hit the concrete floor with a sickening thud and I fell to my knees; sobbing uncontrollably now.

Not realizing that Lucky had somehow managed to keep a hold of his gun, the man sat up suddenly, aimed it at my head...and was gifted with a single, explosive shot to the middle of his forehead. Immediately, his lifeless body crumbled backward as pieces of his skull, blood, and brain matter covered the side of my face and I screamed; unable to fathom what had just happed.

Sobbing into my hands, my body shook and as I rocked back and forth in my place, I felt my world finally come apart. Being pulled to the side quickly by unseen hands, I managed to catch a brief slight of Lucky as the blood from the hole in his forehead haloed around what was left of his head.

Then, Brighton was in my arms again—her soaked eyes searching mine for the sign that everyone was going to be okay. Looking at her, I wrapped my arms around her and hugged her tightly as Detective Gonzalez approached us carefully.

"Ms. Pearson??" Gingerly, she touched my shoulder and I looked up at her big brown eyes. "It's over. C'mon, lets' get you two outta here."

Nodding, I slowly stood; unsure if my shaky legs would hold me. Unwilling to let Brighton go, I held onto her as I tried to stand while the detective braced me as gently as she could. Giving Brighton a small smile, I finally stood with the detective's help and leaned against her for support. My head, neck, shoulder, and legs were all screaming at me to stop moving, but I trudged on, wanting nothing more to be out of this building for good.

"Wait—Ian??"

"He is being looked after, Ms. Pearson." Assuring me, I nodded again at her but scanned the massive group of cops for him. Not seeing him, I tried to stop but the detective was relentless. "We need to get you out to the ambulance, Ms. Pearson. Detective Sampson will be transported right along with you and your daughter."

"But—is he—"

Stopping suddenly, the detective met my scared eyes and judging from the grim look on her face, I knew that Ian was more hurt that it seemed. Thinking back to the way he had been holding his hand over his gunshot wound, it had looked to be in the chest area—which I assumed wasn't a good sign. Knowing that he had somehow managed to get up enough strength to shoot his Captain and save my life, I wondered now if that was going to be his final act.

Tearing up again at the thought of living through all of this just to lose him—I tried to push the thoughts out of my head as Brighton and I made our way down the metal staircase; where the bottom floor of the once vacant building was now lit up like a Christmas tree with lights of red and blue fluttering through the now opened doorway that marked the path to my salvation—not knowing anymore if it was going to lead to a life with or without the man I loved.

Chapter Thirty-Eight

Its funny how a person's life can change in an instant, isn't it??

If I hadn't danced for that stupid redneck, I never would have left work early that night. I wouldn't have witnessed the terrible murder of that poor woman, would have never been shot. My family would have also never been threatened, either, and to top it all off...I would have never met Ian...one good thing out of all that bad and at times it doesn't seem enough...

Thinking about this, my heart ached despite my view of the ocean below. The breeze warm, its salty heaviness whispered through the opened terrace and engulfed me, causing me to shudder as I closed my eyes. The smell of seaweed drifted in and I opened my eyes as the sound of a child's innocent laughter was carried into my hotel room. Shifting so that I had a better view of the white sand below, I smiled at the sight of a young boy trying to jump over the waves as they softly rolled in over his bare feet.

Despite this sight, I couldn't help but refocus on the events that led us here and as I sat back from the view, the images of the warehouse swept through my mind and I had to fight back the tears again. The healing stages not near complete; I knew that it would be a long time before Brighton would sleep soundly through the night—myself as well for that matter...

"Hey, Daydreamer...whatcha thinkin' about??"

The velvet thickness of his voice pulling me out of my thoughts, I turned in the overstuffed recliner that I was sitting in and faced him; the overwhelming feeling of love warming my insides immediately as our eyes met.

"Ma!!!"

Before I could say anything, Brighton bounced into the room, her smile brighter than I'd seen in a long time. Jumping onto my lap, she felt a little heavier and I smiled at the thought of how much better she was looking compared to four months ago. Lifting a heavy bag gracing the extravagant hotel's logo on the front, I peered inside to look over the treasures that had been bought for her. Eying a package of fragile-looking seashells painted in soft colors, a dolphin necklace with matching bracelet, and several bottles of nail polish, I couldn't help but grin back at Brighton's lit up face.

Sliding off my lap, Brighton headed into the bathroom with the bag, looking to try on her new jewelry and paint her nails. Looking up at Ian, I shook my head and tried to hide my smile as I said, "You're such a sucker!"

Crossing the room, Ian approached the side of the chair and bent down, careful of his still painful wound. Whispering in my ear, he replied, "Yea....I'm a strawberry flavored Dum Dum...wanna taste???"

Unable to stop myself, I elbowed him gently and laughed. Meeting his eyes, I bit my lower lip just before he pressed his mouth against mine. Lasting no longer than a few seconds, I felt his kiss all the way down to my toes and wondered briefly if he would always be able to make me feel this way.

"It's a beautiful day out there; want to go for a walk with me??"

Eyeing him, I hesitated before answering and returned my focus to the opened balcony and felt the soft breeze wrap itself gently around my face. Unable to stop myself, I quickly considered the last few months again, amazed again at how things had changed for Brighton and me so fast.

The moments immediately following our rescue from Lucky and his warehouse full of goons were scary...for all of us. When Ian's Captain took his shot at him, the bullet had entered his body just above the chest area; not too far from his heart. Bouncing around a bit before it ejected out of his back, the damage had been close to deadly and it was touch and go due to that and the significant amount of blood loss he had suffered. Admitting that there was no way Ian should have been able to stand, let alone shoot and kill his captain; I truly felt that someone above had been watching out for us that day.

My own wound, reopened during that final fight with Lucky, was pretty much healed now. Not having to bandage it up anymore, the only time I am reminded of it is whenever the weather turns cold; something that both Ian and the doctors at Mercy had informed me would probably never go away completely and I am learning to deal with it.

The investigation into Lucky and his 'business' turned up a slew of corruption—from the bar owner himself to a retired state senator and the leader of some tiny nation overseas. Using his powers of money and greed, Lucky had been turning out innocent young girls for years; hooking them on whatever drug he could find at a cheap rate and then turning around and selling them to the highest bidder under the site "Silent Auction". The man with the scar and his partner were used as a disposal team for the girls he considered as being 'unsellable'.

And despite the fact that in the last few months, over fifteen arrests had been made connected to Lucky's business; the scarred man's partner has yet to be found, and that I think is what keeps me up at night the most—that there are people involved in this who are still out there, free to continue on with what Lucky had so proudly started.

One good thing about all of this however, is that ten cold cases between Arizona and California involving murdered young girls have been reinvestigated so far; each one linked to Lucky in some way and considered solved. Giving families some closure, I can't help but consider just how close Brighton and I came to being added to Lucky's list of business transactions; or so he liked to refer to them as.

"Hey—you okay??"

Lost in my thoughts again, I hadn't realized that Ian had left my side. Standing on the other side of the room, he leaned up against the wall and gave me a worried look. Smiling to assure him, I went to stand but stopped as a swift knock came from the other side of the closed hotel room door. Without waiting for an answer, the door swung inward suddenly and Anna popped into the room.

"Jeeze...Anna, you've got to stop doing that!!"

My heart pounding, I silently cursed her for spooking me and gave her a grim look.

Frowning at me, she crossed the floor and grabbed both of my hands, pulling me to a standing position. "See, you've got to get out of this room. You need to get out, go play in the ocean—have some fun! You've been hiding out in this room too long!"

"I'm not hiding out!" I said, defensively. "I just—I just like the view from here."

"Huh...really??"

Eyeing me carefully, I knew Anna could see right through me and try as I may, I could never hide anything from her. The events of the last few months leaving me a lot more wary of my surroundings, I had to admit that I am much more cautious than I was before. In the two days that we had been here, I'd only been out of the hotel once; that being to witness to Brighton's face the first time she saw the ocean and put her feet in the blue water, to which she squealed with laughter. Other than eating in the dining area on the first floor of the hotel, I've been in here, viewing the outside world from the safe confines of our plush accommodations.

But, maybe she was right, maybe it was time that I got out and had some fun...

"Ok...ok...I'm up...what are we going to do?" I asked, giving in with a small smile.

"Well...", she started, glancing over her shoulder at Ian, "Brighton and I are going to meet Mom and Dad downstairs to do some exploring...and you and that gorgeous man of yours are going to hit the beach and soak up some Florida sun!"

Hesitant, I started to argue. Still trying to recover themselves, the last thing I was sure that Anna's parents wanted to do was to gallivant around a strange town with Anna and Brighton jumping around with excitement. Their home still in the rebuilding process has forced them to live out of their suitcases for the time being, while Brighton and I moved in with Ian—temporarily, of course.

Sensing my thoughts, Anna put up a hand to shut me up before I could even get started. "Nope, no arguments! You are going. And you're not going to worry about a thing! Mom and Dad planned this...you try to weasel your way out of it and Dad will have your hide!!"

Looking over her shoulder, Ian suppressed a smile and I shook my head at the both of them just as Brighton left the bathroom, blowing softly on her newly painted soft-pink nails. Turning to her, Anna asked, "You ready, Pumpkin??"

"Yes!!" Excited, Brighton gave me a quick hug then ran to give Ian one. Grabbing Anna's hand, the pair joyously bounded from the room and I couldn't help but laugh. Looking over at Ian, I watched as he approached me carefully, offering me his hand. "Ready?"

"Okay", I replied softly and let him lead me from the room. Heading towards the elevators, Ian placed one hand on the small of my back and I could feel the heat from his touch through the thin satin material that made up the sundress I was wearing; causing me to want to drag him back to the hotel room with me.

"Where are we going?" I asked, trying to clear my head.

"For a walk." His simple response caused me to look up at him as he added, "I love you—do you know that??"

"Yes..." my response filled with a questionable tone, I wondered just what was really going on. "I love you too, Ian. What is going on??"

Giving me an innocent look, Ian cocked his head at me. "What do you mean?"

Shaking my head, I looked down for a moment before answering, "You and Anna acted like you're up to something."

"Nope."

Looking up at him again, I caught a hint of a smile as it crossed his lips and as the elevator reached the bottom floor and the doors opened up, I called him a liar before stepping out quickly in order to hide my own smile. Grabbing for my hand again, Ian weaved his fingers through my own and made no reply; but instead led me past the hotel visitors and staff that were swarming around; each trying to get somewhere in a hurry.

Reaching the outside, the air greeted me warmly and I breathed it in deeply; suddenly thankful for it. Facing a cobblestoned walkway that wrapped around the hotel and paved the way to the beach, Ian switched from holding my hand to draping his arm across my shoulders as we made our way towards the sandy shoreline.

Stopping to take off my sandals, my toes sank into the soft sand and the heat of it sent goose bumps down my arms. The water, bluer than I've ever seen on any television show, crashed softly against the sand, inviting anyone interested to walk along the path it created along the shoreline. Closing in on it, I smiled as the water ran over my feet and turned to watch as Ian removed his shoes as well.

Walking slowly along the water, I took a moment to look out into it; momentarily swallowed up by the grand openness that it offered. Meeting the skyline, the ocean seemed endless and in certain areas looked blue-green while in others was baby-blue in color. Looking up, the sky was clear and picturesque; draped in blue from one end to the other.

"Thank you", I said softly.

"For what??" Ian asked, sounding surprised.

"For bringing us here." Then stopping, I made eye contact with him and added, "For wanting to be here... for saving our lives...for *everything*..."

Dropping his head, he gave me a soft kiss before whispering, "There is absolutely no place that I would rather be, than right here, right now, with you and Brighton and your family. You don't have to thank me for anything. I'm here because I want to be here."

Nodding as I bit my lip, I then asked, "What do you think you'll do when we get home?"

"About the offer?"

"Yea." The department was still searching for a new captain and Ian was offered the promotion before whisking us all away to paradise. Apparently, there were other offers as well...a department in California, a small town in Seattle, even the FBI threw their hand into the mix; each expressing interest in him. As for me, I had yet to return to dancing, or any other line of work for that matter. Encouraging me to focus on Brighton and myself, Ian continues to insist that I don't work; even though he returned to work three weeks after the whole ordeal went down.

"Well, that depends..."

"On what—?"

"What is that??" Cutting me off, I followed Ian's curious gaze over my shoulder to something shiny, buried halfway in the sand before us. "Oh!" I exclaimed, turning fully around, "it looks like a huge shell! Brighton would *love* it!!"

Wading through the sand, I leaned over to look at it and marveled at the mix of colors it displayed. Large in form, the shell looked like some type of conch and was decorated with bright colors and a glossy finish and looked as though it should have been on a gift shop's shelf for purchase, not something carried in by the sea.

"I wonder if someone bought it and lost it", I muttered and ran a finger over the top of it, feeling that the ripples and crevasses that twisted around the top of it were soft to the touch.

"Check to see if it's got a price tag or something on it. Maybe someone bought it from the gift shop and lost it out here by mistake." Ian's suggestion made sense, the shell looking out of place here in the sand.

The bed of sand that it had sunk in thick and moist, I knelt down to get a better angle on it. Lifting it, I knew that this had to be a store-bought shell and I tipped it over in my hand to allow the sand inside escape from the wide hole located on the side of it. As it emptied, something mixed in with the sand came out and before it hit the sandy floor underneath my feet, I caught it.

"Wait—there's something in here—" I said, my curiosity building intensely.

Sifting the mound of sand around in my hand in order to find out what was hiding in the conch, I gasped as a large, bright diamond ring suddenly came into view. "Ian...??"

As Ian took a hold of my wrists, I looked up at him, confused as my mind started to scramble a bit. Taking the ring out of my hand, he looked down at me and suddenly, it all made sense and my sand-covered hands went directly over my mouth—shocked as to what he getting set to do.

Stepping in close, Ian wrapped one arm around my waist and making eye contact said, "Amanda, I love you—more than I have ever loved anyone in my life. You walked away from me once, and that is something that I don't ever want to go through again. I want to take care of you and Brighton, to grow old with you, to be by your side always. Amanda...will you do me the honor?? Will you marry me???"

"Oh, God", I whispered, unable to say anything else as tears sprang from my eyes.

"YES!!!"

So caught up in the moment, I hadn't noticed that Ian and I were no longer alone. Brighton's loud affirmation as to what my answer should be turning the two of us around; I couldn't help but laugh as Anna knelt down behind her and hugged her to her chest as her parents stood off to the side, each of them smiling widely in anticipation.

Looking up at Ian, we locked eyes and I said, "I think you have your answer."

Cocking his head at me, he asked, "So...that's a yes??" Then, nodding at him, he shouted, "She said yes!!" as he wrapped both arms around me and lifted me into the air as cheers from our small audience were sounded off. Bringing me back down, he gently placed the oversized diamond on my finger and said, "I love you."

"And I love you", I replied, meaning every word of it.

And then, just before we were bombarded by everyone else that I loved, I pulled him to me. Running my fingers through his thick brown hair, I tugged teasingly and brought his mouth to mine, hesitating only to whisper, "You know what you're in for don't you???"

"Hell, yes", he whispered back. "And if I died tonight, I would be an extremely happy man!"

Made in the USA
San Bernardino, CA
18 June 2013